ARCHANGEL FALLEN

A SPECTRE THRILLER

C.W. LEMOINE

This book is a work of fiction. Names, characters, places, and incidents are either products of the author's imagination or used fictitiously. Any resemblance to actual events or locales or persons living or dead is entirely coincidental. The views in this book do not represent those of the United States Air Force Reserve or United States Navy Reserve. All units, descriptions, and details related to the military are used solely to enhance the realism and credibility of the story.

2016 Edition

Cover artwork by Liz Bemis-Hittinger of Bemis Promotions.
www.postscript-media.com

Copyright © 2015 C.W. LEMOINE
All rights reserved.
ISBN-10: 1514294834
ISBN-13: 978-1514294833

This book is dedicated to the men and women of law enforcement.

Blue Lives Matter.

THE *SPECTRE* SERIES:

SPECTRE RISING (BOOK 1)

AVOID. NEGOTIATE. KILL. (BOOK 2)

ARCHANGEL FALLEN (BOOK 3)

EXECUTIVE REACTION (BOOK 4)

BRICK BY BRICK (BOOK 5)

SPECTRE: ORIGINS (PREQUEL SHORT STORIES)

Visit www.cwlemoine.com and subscribe to C.W. Lemoine's Newsletter for exclusive offers, updates, and event announcements.

"Courage is not having the strength to go on; it is going on when you don't have the strength."

— *Theodore Roosevelt*

PROLOGUE

Tampa, FL
1845 Local Time

"**I** should be home by midnight, sweetie. Kiss the girls for me and tell them I love them. Love you," he said before hanging up as he pulled into the crowded parking lot.

It was a weeknight, but The Silver Fox Gentleman's Club was always busy, pulling in crowds from the base just a few miles away. Transient aircrew flying into MacDill for the night loved blowing their hard-earned per diem on the girls working their way through college. It was easy to get lost among the close-cropped GI haircuts filing in and out of the place at all hours of the night.

Blending in was exactly why Charles "Ironman" Steele had chosen this meeting location. As the director of a highly classified covert unit, he spent a lot of time trying to blend in.

Although for the 5'9" 200 lb. Steele, blending in wasn't always easy. His bald head and general lack of neck seemingly made him stand out in even the most military looking of establishments.

Ironman checked his watch as he flashed his retired military ID at the burly bouncer. He was fifteen minutes early. The bouncer pretended to study the ID for a moment and then waved him through the mirrored glass door. The relative silence of the lobby gave way to a blaring rock song as a girl made her best effort at flailing around the pole on stage. The banner above her proudly announced "Amateur Night" as the younger airmen waved singles at her and cat called from the base of the stage.

Ironman chuckled to himself as the girl struggled with her top. He found a table in the corner of the dark room away from the stage and sat down. His white t-shirt and faded jeans glowed under the neon lights. He had changed out of his Desert ACUs that he usually wore just before driving out of the secure facility nestled in the center of MacDill Air Force Base near United States Central Command Headquarters. As his wife would tell anyone, Ironman was not known for his fashion sense.

As a former F/A-18 pilot and Joint Terminal Attack Controller that had been embedded with Navy SEALS in Afghanistan, Ironman preferred a uniform to anything else. The only variation he had ever needed was the change from summer whites to dress blues for which the Navy was famous. Otherwise, he preferred a flight suit or fatigues.

A scantily clad waitress shuffled up in her high heels to Ironman's table. He ordered an ale and asked for the $5.99 steak special – the rarer the better. As the petite young blonde finished taking his order, he slipped her a twenty and sent her on her way.

Ironman scanned the room as he leaned back into the plush booth. He hadn't chosen the location by accident. He had a complete scan of the entire room and its rowdy occupants, including the most important part — the door. As he continued the scan, he found the man he was looking for. The tall, slender Asian stood out in the homogenous crowd of military aviators, but given what Ironman knew about the man, he wondered if the guy even cared. *Ruthless* was the only word he could come up with to describe him.

Ironman checked his watch again as the pretty little waitress delivered his beer. It was 1900. His Breitling was still set to GMT from his recent trip to the sandbox. He never bothered changing it to local. It was always easier to just do the quick math to remind him where he was. As the Director of Project Archangel, he almost always lived out of his go-bag in some third world country. The world was full of hotspots, and although the current administration was nearing the end of its second term, the business of covert war had never been better.

Covert war. He had always thought it was a cute saying, but that was his job. He had been hand-picked by the previous administration to develop a team of special operators and aviators that could be deployed anywhere in the world at a moment's notice with a minimal footprint while being self-sustaining. With its fleet of advanced Close Air Support fixed wing aircraft and helicopters, they could fight their way into any hot spot in the world and fight their way out without the US Government getting their hands dirty.

It had been the perfect retirement job for Ironman. He still got to see his wife and two girls most of the time while making money hand over fist as a high-level contractor and still being at the tip of the spear. It was a spear that, for the most part, even the highest level Pentagon officials didn't know had been thrown until they read about it on the Internet days — and sometimes even weeks — later.

But despite the nice scenery as another sorority girl clumsily tried her luck on stage, his presence in the booth represented a part of the job he hated. His group was full of high-level operators and fighter pilots. They were all Type A personalities that worked hard and played hard. Most of the people he recruited had been screened extensively, but every now and then one guy would slip through the cracks. And then he would have to do damage control.

Sometimes it was simple — the former SEAL who just couldn't turn it off after spending three months being shot at and ended up putting five people in the hospital during a bar fight. Or one of his pilots who wound up in jail after leading police on a high-speed chase at speeds over 170 mph in a Corvette ZR1 while wearing Night Vision Goggles at three AM. Those were easy, and often pretty funny. But Cal "Spectre" Martin was different.

Spectre had been a problem child from the start. Ironman had been reluctant to even hire him. It had been his boss, then Secretary of Defense (SECDEF) and current Vice Presidential Candidate Kerry Johnson who had pushed the issue.

Ironman unwrapped his silverware from the paper napkin as the petite blonde returned with his steak. She walked off, and he checked his watch one more time. 1915. *Spectre was late.* He looked back over at the Asian man he had picked out earlier. They made eye contact briefly as Ironman shrugged it off and returned to his steak.

It didn't surprise him. Nothing in the file that Johnson's aide had dropped on his desk screamed reliability. In fact, other than graduating at the top of his pilot training class, Spectre's flying career had been less than impressive. Spectre hadn't even upgraded to Instructor Pilot before being grounded after a deployment in Iraq.

In doing his due diligence, Ironman had pulled the mission report from Spectre's last flight. Spectre had shown a reckless disregard for the current rules of engagement by employing ordnance while his flight lead was refueling at the tanker. He had even continued to prosecute the attack after the only qualified controller on the scene had been disabled. Although Ironman admitted that Spectre had probably saved more than a few lives that night, the action was evidence of a general lack of flight discipline.

Ironman had warned the SECDEF that Spectre wasn't a good fit for the team. Spectre just didn't meet the standard that had been set for Project Archangel's pilots. On top of that, Spectre hadn't flown in over five years. He had been working at a gun supply store in South Florida. Ironman initially resisted based on Spectre's resume alone. When SECDEF effectively directed him to shut up and color, Ironman saluted smartly, said "Aye, Aye," and drove down to Homestead, Florida to recruit Spectre. His first opportunity had been at the funeral of Spectre's fiancée.

Ironman had never read the official report on the mishap involving Chloe Moss, but he knew there was more to her death than he had access to. The initial reports and eventual Air Force Accident Investigation Board investigation all said that Chloe Moss had fallen victim to spatial disorientation. Controlled flight into terrain, the reports said. But in his circle, the rumor mill had been running wild. The possible theories ran the gauntlet from defecting to Cuba to a covert counterintelligence mission against the Chinese. Despite his high-level clearance, he didn't have a need to know for a lot of programs, but Ironman knew that the truth was somewhere in the middle while still being very far from the official cover story.

Spectre had seemed pretty shaken up at the funeral, and Ironman wasn't even sure Spectre would return his phone call. He was hoping Spectre would just throw the card away and go on about his life. As he finished the last few bites of his steak and checked his watch again, he wished Spectre had. He would have much preferred to be spending his evening with his two daughters.

At first, it appeared that Spectre was just as high level as any of the other members of the team. When Spectre made it through every level of the intense physical training, as well as the flight training, Ironman thought his initial assessments had been proven wrong. Spectre performed as well as any pilot he had put through the course, and almost as well as some of the Special Operators through the hand-to-hand combat and weapons phases. Ironman had been cautiously hopeful that Spectre had become the one-in-a-million undrafted free agent that football teams salivate for.

But a tiger can't change his stripes, and when Ironman received the phone call that Spectre's aircraft had been downed in Iraq, he kicked himself for letting his guard down. Spectre had failed to abort a mission when a pair of Syrian fighters scrambled to intercept his team. And when he finally did make the abort call, he managed to get himself shot down in the process. They were lucky Spectre's aircraft had been the only one lost, but the team lost nearly three days trying to recover Spectre from bad guy land — time that could've been spent keeping chemical weapons out of the hands of terrorists in Syria.

Even more surprising to Ironman was the SECDEF's reaction to the initial news. Although Ironman was not a huge fan of the man's politics, he'd always thought Johnson to be a fair and compassionate person. He had been taken aback when the SECDEF outright refused to authorize an immediate Combat Search and Rescue Operation to find and retrieve Spectre. It was one of the very few times Ironman had clashed with his boss. Johnson's concern for creating an even bigger international incident had become more important than not leaving a man behind. Despite his reservations about Spectre, he was still a member of the team and deserved to go home to whatever family he had. It was simply unacceptable to Ironman.

Making matters worse, Spectre's tag along had been very vocal in launching a rescue mission. To Ironman, Joe Carpenter was perhaps the closest thing to the magical free agent in the deal. Carpenter had been an Army Ranger and Air Force TAC/P. He was squared away and highly motivated. His record spoke for itself, and when Spectre asked to bring Carpenter along as part of the deal, it was a no brainer. Ironman wished he had stayed on the team after Spectre had been let go.

Let go. It was a polite way of saying fired. After being shot down in Syria, there was simply no way to justify Spectre's presence on the team. As with his hiring, the SECDEF led the charge with his firing. There was no valid argument against it. Spectre had saved the other aircraft he had been escorting, but the entire incident could have been avoided if he had stuck to protocols and aborted. *He was just too much of a wild card.* Ironman had been disappointed that Carpenter quit in protest, but given their long-standing history together, he wasn't surprised. It was a shame Carpenter had been killed a few days later.

Ironman checked his watch one more time as the Asian man stood from his table and approached. It was almost eight PM and it had become quite apparent that Spectre was a no show. *At least he had gotten a cheap steak and free entertainment out of the deal.*

The man walked up to Ironman's booth and took his place across from Ironman. He was wearing a dark button down shirt and slacks. His dark goatee gave way to a sinister smile as he watched Ironman push aside his plate.

"Are you enjoying yourself, Mr. Steele?" he asked.

"I can think of better ways to spend my evening," Ironman replied. "But not many."

"I'm sure your two daughters would much rather have you home," the man said flatly.

Ironman's brow furrowed. He never discussed his family outside of the people he trusted on his team, and the man across from him was neither on his team nor particularly trusted. He tried to hide his anger.

"Did I hit a nerve?" the man said. He spoke with a slight Chinese accent, but his English was flawless.

"What do you want?" Ironman asked impatiently.

"You said he would be here. He is not. Why?" The man's voice was almost robotic to Ironman. Beyond the forced grin, he seemed to exude no emotion whatsoever.

"I don't know. I guess he had a change of heart," Ironman replied with a shrug. "He wasn't exactly thrilled with me at the funeral." Ironman had attended Carpenter's funeral, but despite Ironman's offer to get to the bottom of Carpenter's mysterious death, Spectre had been nothing but flippant during their brief encounter after the service.

"Do you know where he went?"

"Look, Xin, or Jiang, or whatever it is you go by," Ironman said as he slid out of the booth and put another twenty on the table. "I did what I was told to do. He didn't show up. There's nothing else I can do at this point."

Xin stood to meet Ironman. He was nearly the same height, but much smaller in stature than the much bulkier man.

"You are right," Xin replied calmly.

Ironman waited for him to say something else as he stood within feet of the man. Ironman was used to dealing with angry special operations operators all the time, but Xin was downright scary. There was just something about him that creeped Ironman out.

"Let me know if I can do anything else for you," Ironman finally said, breaking the awkward silence.

"I will," Xin replied.

Ironman nodded and then turned to walk out, passing the stage as a wet t-shirt contest was just beginning. He shrugged off the feeling of terror he felt deep within his gut. He had landed on aircraft carriers at night in rough seas and bad weather, but nothing compared to the pit that had formed in his stomach.

"What have I gotten myself into?" he mumbled to himself as he stepped out into the humid night air in the parking lot.

CHAPTER ONE

NAS JRB New Orleans
0335 Local Time

Major Jeff "Foxworthy" Vaughan cycled his flight controls and checked his engine instruments one last time as he took the runway in his F-15C. He looked over into his canopy mirror to see the taxi light of his wingman three hundred feet behind him as Major Jake "Buzz" Bronson followed him onto the runway.

It was dark out. The airfield was still closed, and other than the ambient lighting of the city of New Orleans a few miles away, the relatively clear skies were pitch black. The runway edges were barely illuminated from the pilot controlled lighting that stayed on after field hours.

With the tower closed, Foxworthy had contacted New Orleans Approach for takeoff clearance and coordination for their scramble. It had barely been fifteen minutes since the klaxon had gone off, waking him from his nap. He and his wingman had been scrambled to intercept an unknown aircraft crossing the Air Defense Identification Zone out over the Gulf of Mexico without talking to anyone.

After making the short taxi out of the alert hangars at the end of the runway, Foxworthy lined his aircraft up on the Runway 22 centerline and lit the afterburners. He watched his engine instruments, confirming the nozzle indicators showed "two good swings" as the afterburners lit and rocketed his F-15 down the ten thousand foot runway. Seconds later, Foxworthy's wingman took the runway and followed suit as the two climbed out to the southeast toward the target.

"WatchDog, Bayou Zero One airborne, passing one-five-thousand," Foxworthy said as he checked in with the military controller that would be directing the intercept. He pulled out his Night Vision Goggles from their case, clipped them to the bracket on his visor, and flipped them down over his eyes. The green image changed the abyss of darkness in front of him to a green monochrome presentation. The moonlight illumination was low, and even with the goggles, there wasn't much of a discernible horizon or clear delineation between the dark, calm waters and the sky.

Foxworthy had flown the F-15 as an Air National Guard pilot for nearly fifteen years. He had seen the unit transition from the F-15A to the basic F-15C and finally to the upgraded F-15Cs with AESA radars. He had been scrambled more times than he cared to count on varying targets ranging from crop dusters to helicopters and even airliners.

Airliners scared Foxworthy. Since 9/11, the mission of the alert pilot had changed significantly. Gone were the romantic musings of being scrambled up against the hoard of MiG-29s invading the U.S. Mainland and fighting to save the day. It had long since been replaced with the idea of terrorists using passenger jets as weapons against critical infrastructure targets.

The harsh reality was that he might have to use one of the eight radar-guided air to air missiles on his wing to shoot one down to prevent an even bigger catastrophe. It was not a very palatable thought for the crusty Major.

But as Foxworthy looked over to see Buzz rejoin in a combat spread formation a mile and a half off his left wing, he was confident that tonight's mission would be relatively benign. The initial Intel they had received when they checked in with their Command Post for the tasking was that it was a slow-moving aircraft located seventy miles southeast of New Orleans. The aircraft was not responding to WatchDog's repeated identification calls and required a visual identification.

"Bayou Zero One, bogey BRAA one-zero-zero, fifty-nine, five thousand, cold, maneuver," the WatchDog controller responded, giving Foxworthy the Bearing, Range, Altitude, and Aspect of the unknown aircraft. As they cruised along at seventeen thousand feet and four hundred knots, the aircraft was just under sixty nautical miles away from their current position.

"Sounds like he's in WHODAT," Buzz said over the auxiliary radio. The WHODAT airspace was the name for the military working airspace they used during training to practice their air-to-air tactics.

Foxworthy checked his radar. Seconds later, the Active Electronically Scanned Array Radar had picked up the target, and the track file indicated the radar was tracking the aircraft. He moved his cursors over it and took a radar lock. The unknown aircraft was moving at just under ninety knots and had appeared to be orbiting at five thousand feet.

"Bayou Zero One, radar contact," Foxworthy said to alert the controller that he was now tracking the unknown aircraft and required no further point outs.

"WatchDog copies," the controller responded. "No traffic between you and the bogey, cleared to elevator at your discretion."

"Bayou Zero One," Foxworthy replied sharply. At almost four in the morning, it was not surprising that the controller had given them unrestricted ability to descend to the target's altitude. Except for the cargo air carriers, there were few aircraft out flying, which was the only thing that bothered him about the aircraft they were intercepting. It was rare to get scrambled so early in the morning on an "Unknown Rider" call.

"Two cleared wedge," Foxworthy directed as he started his descent down toward the aircraft. His wingman said nothing and collapsed from his perfect line abreast formation to a fluid formation behind Foxworthy's aircraft.

Foxworthy watched the radar indication as the unknown aircraft continued to orbit. He pulled up the Sniper Pod display above his right knee and tried to get an infrared look at the target as they closed inside of twenty miles.

Leveling off at ten thousand feet, the clear summer night's sky became even more difficult to discern from the calm waters below. They were flying in an area peppered with oil rigs that stayed lit up twenty four hours a day, making it easy to momentarily confuse up for down. Foxworthy remained cautious as they sped toward the orbiting aircraft. He knew it might be easy to get spatially disoriented if they weren't careful.

"Two's eyeball bogey," Buzz said on their auxiliary radio, indicating he had picked up a visual on the aircraft through his Sniper Advanced Targeting Pod. "Looks like a multi-engine prop of some sort," he added.

"One copies," Foxworthy replied. Seconds later, the white-hot infrared image of his targeting pod showed the same thing. It appeared to be a four engine propeller-driven aircraft with a twin boom tail configuration. Although they were still too far out to get sufficient detail, the initial image was confusing to Foxworthy. He couldn't quite identify it.

Foxworthy checked his radar display again. They were nearing fifteen miles. As he started his descent down to intercept the aircraft, the radar suddenly broke lock and filled with chevrons, indicating it was receiving electronic jamming.

As if on cue, Buzz piped up on the auxiliary radio, "Two's clean, strobes east."

Foxworthy acknowledged and went back to his radar display, trying to make sense of it. He had fought against jammers before in training, but had never seen or heard of it happening on a real world alert scramble. *It just didn't make sense.* He turned his attention back to his targeting pod image. The aircraft had rolled out of its orbit and appeared to be descending straight ahead. Foxworthy opted to continue the intercept visually.

"One same," Foxworthy finally responded on the radio. "Have you ever seen anything like this, Buzz?" Although Buzz had spent time in the Active Duty Air Force unlike Foxworthy, the two had been in the same squadron together for nearly a decade.

"I was hoping it was just my radar," Buzz admitted as Foxworthy looked out and saw the surprisingly large aircraft flying slowly over the water.

"Let's set up an orbit here at seven thousand, I don't know what this guy is doing," Foxworthy said as he leveled off. He could see the aircraft through his NVGs, but the targeting pod image was fairly clear as they leveled off and set up an orbit just outside of five miles. It was a large cargo aircraft of some sort. Foxworthy wasn't sure, but it looked Russian.

He looked back at his radar screen. *Still jammed.* As he looked back out at the aircraft through his goggles, he noticed it getting lower and slower. It appeared to be completely blacked out with no lights on at all. He tried picking it up using his naked eyes, but all he could see were the lights from nearby oil rigs.

Foxworthy zoomed in using the targeting pod infrared image. The aircraft's flaps appeared to be down, but its gear was up. Seconds later, the aircraft touched down on the calm waters. *It landed! A float plane?* Foxworthy's mind was racing.

"Dude, did you just see that?" Foxworthy yelled excitedly on the auxiliary frequency.

"What's a floatplane doing out here?" Buzz responded after a pregnant pause.

"WatchDog, Bayou Zero One, the target aircraft appears to have landed," Foxworthy said to the controlling agency.

"Say again, Bayou," the controller queried. It was obviously not the response he had been expecting.

Foxworthy double-checked what he was seeing in his pod by zooming in and out. The seaplane slowed to a crawl as it approached one of the oil rigs.

"Bayou Zero One, I say again, the target aircraft has landed and appears to be approaching one of the oil rigs out here," Foxworthy repeated.

"WatchDog copies," the controller responded. The confusion was evident in his voice as well.

As Foxworthy continued watching the seaplane taxi up to the oil rig, a low-pitched beeping caught his attention in his headset. He looked up at his Radar Warning Receiver. The green circular display had just lit up as the beeping intensified. *He was being targeted by a surface to air missile. Nothing made sense.*

"Bayou Zero One, spiked," Foxworthy announced over the interflight frequency. His heart started racing. *Is it real? Or related to the jamming?* The adrenaline began surging as the indication grew stronger. He had never seen anything like it.

"Two same!" Buzz responded.

His Radar Warning Receiver was lit up like a Christmas tree, indicating that a SAM's target acquisition radar was locked to him.

"Bayou Zero One, WatchDog, I checked with the Director. The aircraft is in international waters. You're cleared to disengage and RTB at this time," the controller directed.

"Bayou Zero One is defensive!" Foxworthy responded as the indication changed pitch and his RWR indicated that a target tracking radar was engaging his aircraft. He knew he was just seconds away from a potential missile launch.

"Bayou Zero One, you are directed to disengage, do you copy?" the controller said firmly. "Vector two-seven-zero and RTB at this time."

Ignoring the call, Foxworthy lit the afterburners and executed a break turn while expending chaff to attempt to break the lock of the radar. His wingman followed suit in the opposite direction, using their in-flight data link to keep track of each other.

"Bayou Zero One, WatchDog," the controller attempted again.

"Standby," Foxworthy replied as he strained under the G-forces.

He continued maneuvering his aircraft away from the target aircraft's last known position. As they cleared ten miles, the Radar Warning Receiver suddenly fell silent.

"One's naked," Foxworthy said on the auxiliary radio.

"Two same, I'm at your five o'clock and seven miles," Buzz replied.

"Cleared rejoin," Foxworthy replied, trying to stay calm as he turned back toward New Orleans. "What the hell was that?"

"I have no idea," Buzz replied, still breathing heavily.

* * *

"That's bullshit!" Foxworthy barked as the young female Intel airmen finished trying to explain her theory on why they thought they were locked up by a surface to air missile system. Foxworthy and Buzz were standing in the vault in the main squadron building on the other side of the field. They had taken their HUD and targeting pod footage to the Intel section to debrief the mission as soon as they landed. The five-foot-tall Staff Sergeant Laney Crowe cowered as the tall, lanky Foxworthy leaned over her desk.

"So you're telling me that the SAM indications were just in our heads?" Foxworthy asked before she could get a word in.

"No, sir," SSgt Crowe said timidly. "But based on the electronic interference you both received during the intercept and the location, it's likely that the SAM indications were erroneous caused by the communications equipment on one of the nearby oil rigs."

"I know about erroneous indications," Foxworthy said. "But it never resolves from an acquisition indication to a tracking indication."

"And if it were erroneous, I wouldn't have gotten it too," the much stockier Buzz added.

"Yes, sir, but the SAM system that would've had to lock you both up has not been retrofitted to mobile or sea applications. We have no intelligence to suggest that any country had any ships capable of carrying a similar system in the Gulf of Mexico at that time," SSgt Crowe said as she pulled up the Naval Warfare Intelligence Assessment on her computer.

"What about an oil rig?" Foxworthy asked.

"Anything is possible, sir, but the oil rigs in that particular region are all U.S. based companies. I will certainly file it in the report."

"And the aircraft? What was that?" Buzz said, picking up the printout of their targeting pod footage showing the four engine aircraft.

SSgt Crowe spun around in her chair and pulled up the file marked SECRET on her computer. A color image of an aircraft similar to the one they watched land appeared on the screen.

"This is the closest thing I could come up with," SSgt Crowe said. "It's a Chinese Harbin SH-5 used mainly for maritime patrol and cargo."

The wheels started spinning in Foxworthy's head, trying to piece it all together. He was a part time Guardsmen, but his full time job was doing safety surveys and motivational speaking on oil rigs for a group he created called Mach Two Consulting. He knew there were Chinese oil rigs out in the Gulf, but he had never heard of an amphibious aircraft landing near one.

"So could that plane have been going to a Chinese oil rig?" Foxworthy asked.

"I pulled up all the registries in that area, and there are no Chinese based companies there," SSgt Crowe responded. "It's also important to note that there were only six of these aircraft ever made, and one crashed in 2013, so I'm not completely sure that's what we're looking at."

Buzz rubbed his forehead with his beefy hand. "So what do we actually know from all of this?"

"We know that a seaplane landed in international waters, sir," SSgt Crowe responded with a shrug. "I will forward this mission report up to the Eastern Air Defense Sector and see what they say."

"Thanks, Laney," Foxworthy said with a resigned sigh.

CHAPTER TWO

FBI Miami Field Office
Miami, FL
0715 Local Time

"What are you doing here, Michelle?" Special Agent Waters said, peering into her cubicle. "The boss said he sent you home for the week after what happened yesterday."

Special Agent Michelle Decker looked up from the report she had been reviewing. The typically attractive blonde, in her t-shirt and jeans, looked tired and run down. She had been operating on caffeine and adrenaline for days. The last seventy-two hours had been the most trying of her career, and perhaps her entire life.

Since Cal Martin had suddenly popped back up after an abrupt disappearance a year ago, she had been burning the candle at both ends. She hadn't slept more than three hours in days. She had nearly been killed on the roof of a luxury hotel. She had watched her friend die in a horrific explosion. And the man at the center of it all had gone from the hero to the victim to the villain in a matter of weeks. It was almost too much for her to handle.

"Oh hey, Dan," Decker replied weakly. "I'm just reviewing the initial report Simms wrote about yesterday. Have you seen him?"

"He's about to brief the boss in the conference room in fifteen minutes," Waters replied. "I think he might have a new lead on your boy."

Decker glared at Waters through her bright blue eyes, causing him to submissively look away and throw up his hands. "Sorry, poor choice of words," Waters added.

"It's ok," Decker replied hoarsely as she closed the file and stood up. "Thanks for the heads up."

"You're not thinking about going in there, are you?" Waters asked as Decker took a swig from her coffee mug and stepped past him. "The boss is going to be pissed if he knows you're here."

"I'll deal with it," Decker announced as she continued past him toward the conference room. She could feel the eyes of various agents staring at her as she made her way through the sea of cubicles toward the large conference room in the corner of the office. Word traveled fast. She knew everyone was aware of what she had been through and Special Agent in Charge Rick Fields's subsequent order to go home and get some rest or find a new line of work. Her services were no longer needed in the case as she had gotten too emotionally attached to the suspect in the eyes of the new lead investigator, Special Agent Simms.

Decker had never really had a strong opinion either way of Simms until he had been assigned to track down Martin. She had heard rumors about him— the former accountant with a knack for building nearly foolproof theories about cases early on, but refusing to be flexible if proven wrong. Decker believed he was doing just that with Martin.

After the disappearance from protective custody that left two dead agents in its wake, Simms had immediately concluded that Martin was the prime suspect. He refused to listen to any theories that her recently deceased friend, Agent Baxter, offered. Instead, his theory persisted as the evidence mounted against Martin. Deep down, she knew Martin was innocent, but she had no way of convincing Simms.

Decker stopped at the closed conference room door and took a deep breath. She knew she was walking into the lion's den, but deep down she knew it was the right thing to do. She had already committed herself too much to the case to just let it go and walk away. She had the scars and bruises to prove it.

She slowly pushed open the door, revealing the tall, lanky Simms at the podium in the front of the room. He was preparing to brief the grouping of senior Special Agents and representatives from other agencies seated around the oval conference table. The room fell silent as she stood awkwardly in the doorway.

"Michelle, I'm surprised to see you here," Special Agent in Charge Rick Fields said, breaking the silence. His tone did not hide his disapproval. "You're supposed to be on leave," he added.

"Yes, sir," Decker replied timidly. "But as this is my case, I was hoping to sit in to answer any questions you may have, sir."

"Was your case," Simms corrected smugly. "I can answer any questions from here."

Fields frowned as he brushed his bushy mustache and considered her request. Decker's face reddened slightly as she stared down the lanky accountant slouching over the podium. She wanted to reach out and snap his feeble looking neck. Same team or not, she hated him.

"You've been on this case longer than anyone, Michelle," Fields said after a short deliberation. "You can sit in, but when this is over, you and I are going to have a talk."

Embarrassed by the confrontation, Decker was still blushing as she scrambled to take a seat near the back of the conference room. Simms laughed arrogantly as he watched her panicked movements.

"I think we have everyone here," Fields said as he looked around the room. "Whenever you're ready, Agent Simms."

Decker took an inventory of the badges surrounding the table. She recognized most of the dozen or so people in the conference room. Half were agents from her own office, but there were also representatives from the ATF, Florida Highway Patrol, and Air Force Office of Special Investigations. She didn't quite recognize the AFOSI agent, but she guessed that his interest related to the death of Special Agent Baxter.

"Thank you, sir," Agent Simms began as he clicked to the title slide. "As most of you know, I am Special Agent Simms, the lead agent in the Cal Martin investigation." He stopped as he smirked briefly at Decker in the back of the room before adjusting his tie and advancing to the next slide that showed a photo of Cal Martin.

"This is Cal Martin. His only known alias is 'Spectre'. He was originally brought into FBI protective custody last week after an attempt was allegedly made on his life in the hospital," Simms continued.

Decker rolled her eyes as she folded her arms and crossed her legs. *Alleged attempt on his life.* Spectre had been attacked while on a houseboat in Key Largo by a small micro-UAV with a warhead on it. The attack killed his best friend and nearly killed Spectre as well. She had taken up Spectre's protective detail while he was still recovering in the hospital, thwarting a second attempt on Spectre's life by a Russian female assassin. *The attempts on Spectre's life were anything but "alleged."*

"Two days ago, Martin disappeared from the motel where he was in protective custody. Two agents were found dead on the scene and the hard drives of the surveillance footage had been destroyed. At that time, I issued a BOLO for Mr. Martin." Simms clicked to the next slide, showing the crime scene photos of the bodies of the two agents. He paused for effect as the audience took in the images of their dead brothers.

Simms advanced to the next slide, showing the bodies of Victor Alvarez and three of his men hanging in a dimly lit barn. He paused for effect, and then clicked forward to a second slide showing a closeup picture of the bodies. They each had dime-sized bullet holes in their foreheads. Their bodies were suspended from the rafters like cuts of meat hanging from hooks in a butcher shop. "This is Cuban Intelligence Agent Victor Alvarez. Our investigation led us to an isolated farmhouse in the Redlands of Homestead. Upon arriving at the scene, we found Alvarez and his men tied up in this fashion. One of the SWAT members on the scene took this picture shortly before the barn exploded, killing eight Miami-Dade SWAT Officers and an AFOSI Special Agent."

"I'm sorry for your agency's loss, Special Agent Riley," Simms said, feigning a look of concern as he gestured to the lone AFOSI agent in the room. The man nodded as he stared at the mahogany table. Unlike Simms's fake compassion, it was obvious to Decker that Riley's pain over the death of Baxter was real. Decker tried holding back tears as well. She had grown fond of Baxter while working with him over the last year.

Simms advanced to a slide showing the charred remains of a burned down barn as he continued, "Before he was killed, Special Agent Baxter uncovered a fifth body. It had been booby-trapped with explosives. The ATF has taken the lead on that aspect of the investigation, but this morning, we were able to get a positive ID on the body."

"His name was Marcus Anderson," Simms said before advancing to a picture of the former Marine. Decker gasped as the tears began flowing. It was the first she had heard of the identification of the body. She had always been afraid it might be that of Cal Martin and was slightly relieved that it wasn't, but hearing that Marcus had been killed was devastating to Decker. Marcus had been under the FBI's protective custody as well. He had been in critical condition in the hospital the last time she had seen him. Her world was spinning. *They had gotten him too.*

The Florida Highway Patrolman seated near Decker turned and asked her if she were ok. She tried to wave him off as the room turned to stare at her. She felt overwhelmed. The exhaustion and stress of the last three days had crushed her. "I'm fine," she finally managed. "Please continue."

"Mr. Anderson had been in FBI protective custody as well," Simms continued. "He was a known associate of Martin. Martin worked for Anderson in a gun supply store until it closed about a year ago."

"Once the farmhouse scene was secured, I obtained a warrant for the arrest of Cal Martin," Simms said as he minimized the slide and pulled up a video. "Several hours later, a Florida Highway Patrol Trooper pulled over a vehicle matching Martin's truck. Special thanks to Captain Dixon for joining us and providing the video. It certainly speaks for itself."

Simms nodded at the Trooper seated next to Decker and clicked play on the video. Decker watched as the Trooper ordered Spectre out of the vehicle and told him to put his hands on the tailgate. Spectre offered to identify himself as the Trooper approached and asked if he had any weapons on him. The Trooper then attempted to arrest Spectre. Decker watched in horror as the scene unfolded. Within seconds, Spectre had taken the Trooper to the ground and handcuffed the Trooper with his own cuffs. He took the Trooper's radio and handgun from him and sped off in his truck, leaving the Trooper handcuffed in front of his cruiser. As the video concluded, Simms closed the video player and reopened his presentation.

"As you can see, we're dealing with someone extremely dangerous," Simms said, trying to make eye contact with Decker. "These are certainly not the actions of an innocent victim."

Simms then pulled up a map of Florida and said, "We believe Martin used mostly back roads to avoid further detection as he traveled north. He then continued on a route approximately parallel to I-10 Westbound before entering Louisiana."

Simms clicked to the next slide, showing a picture of a license plate on a white pickup truck and the plate number written in a clear font on the bottom of the picture. "Early this morning, we received our first hit via the Automatic License Plate Recognition Camera system in St. Tammany Parish, Louisiana, near the Louisiana-Mississippi border."

He advanced to another map, this time of Southeast Louisiana. There were highlighted circles trending westward toward Baton Rouge. "These circles represent additional hits. The last hit was outside of Baton Rouge on I-10 Westbound. We believe he is within a fifty square mile area of that region."

Simms clicked forward, ending the slide show before walking out from behind the podium. "My team and I will fly to Baton Rouge to coordinate with the field office there to continue the investigation. It is my goal to find this man before he can hurt or kill anyone else. Are there any questions?"

Decker sat in stunned silence. Her confidence in Spectre's innocence was dwindling. She had convinced herself that there was no way he could have turned like that. *He was too passionate – too determined to do the right thing no matter what.* She had seen it first hand when he mounted a mission to rescue his fiancée from Cuba. She had seen his resolve and intensity. *He was a good guy.*

But the death of his best friend, Joe Carpenter, had broken him. She watched him spiral into depression in that motel room. She had seen a man that had become a shell of his former self. *But had he jumped that far over the edge? Was he really the monster Simms had made him out to be?* Decker was no longer certain of anything.

"Do what you need to do to find this guy," Fields chimed in. "We may need to get HRT involved. This guy has already proven extremely dangerous, and if he's holed up somewhere, it could get ugly. I do not want another Ruby Ridge on our hands." The FBI Hostage Rescue Team was their elite Counter Terrorist Unit, serving as a tactical option for extraordinary hostage situations or other law enforcement activities.

"Yes, sir," Simms said with a look of satisfaction. As a former lawyer, Decker recognized the look. It was the look of a man who had just wowed the jury and slam-dunked his case. Simms knew everyone in that room was on board with hanging Cal Martin. Decker's confidence had even been shaken. His case was solid.

"Keep me updated, anyone else have anything?" Fields added.

"Sean Baxter was a good agent and an even better man," Special Agent Riley said, clenching his teeth. "Make this son of a bitch pay."

Simms smiled. He lived for moments like these. He had rallied the troops and his bosses. "It will be my pleasure, sir," he said, trying to contain himself.

As they all filed out of the conference room, Fields motioned for Decker to follow. He led her down to his large executive office and motioned for her to have a seat as he closed the door behind her.

"You look like shit, Michelle," he said as he sat down behind his large wooden desk. Decker's face was still covered in bruises from the fight two days prior. She had bags under her eyes. She hadn't even bothered to try to cover it up with makeup.

"Thanks, sir, I try," Decker replied sarcastically.

"What are you even doing here? I told you to take a week and you're back, what, sixteen hours later?"

"This is my case," Decker shot back. "I can't just walk away and pretend like it never happened."

"To what end, Michelle? Are you going to see it through even if it kills you?" Fields asked.

"You know I can see this through, sir," Decker said, leaning forward.

"Cut the 'sir' crap, Michelle. And I know you're more than capable. You're one of the best agents in this office. We both know it," Fields said as he leaned forward onto his forearms to meet her glare. "But you're no good to me dead. And right now, you're a danger to everyone around you. You need to disengage and get some rest."

"C'mon, Rick," Michelle said incredulously as she leaned back and crossed her arms. "You don't believe that, do you?"

"Yes, I do," Fields snapped. "Look at you. Your eyes are bloodshot from crying. You haven't slept in days. You were almost killed by a crazy bitch on a roof. No one can keep that kind of pace up. *Not even you.*"

Decker stared at him without saying anything.

"You have gotten too close to this case," Fields continued. "I want you to go home and get some rest."

"But—"

"But nothing," Fields interrupted her, holding up a finger. "All of your cases have been reassigned. I want you to go home, find a nice place, and go on vacation. I don't want to see you again for the next two weeks. Think of it as my gift to you."

Before Decker could get another word in, Fields added, "And if I see you anywhere near FBI property in that time frame, I'm going to refer you directly to counseling until the Bureau is convinced every little demon in that pretty little head of yours is exorcised. And you know how methodical they can be with that. Got it?"

"Ok," Decker mumbled.

"Now get out of here," Fields said dismissively as he turned to the monitor to his right. "I mean it, Michelle. I'd better not see you."

"Got it," Decker replied as she got up and walked out.

Decker walked straight to her cubicle on her way out to pick up her coffee mug. She had been defeated by the system. The thought of supervisor-mandated counseling was enough to make her heed Fields's warnings. She could just imagine what the psychologists would come up with, leaving her manning a desk for the rest of her career. She conceded that there was nothing more she could do.

As she reached her desk, Analyst Samantha Hayes approached her cubicle. The portly analyst smiled as she held up a disc between her chubby fingers. "Did you want me to give you this or should I give it to Agent Simms?"

"What is it?" Decker replied without looking up as she packed up her things to head out the door.

"It's the ATM footage on the Martin case. I wasn't sure if you were still in charge of it or if he had taken over, so I thought I'd ask you first," Hayes replied. "He kind of creeps me out," she added in a soft whisper.

"What ATM footage?" Decker asked. She couldn't remember a request for any ATM camera footage.

"From the ATM across the street from the motel," Hayes replied. "I just got it this morning and finally finished filtering it. You guys are probably going to want to see it."

Decker hesitated for a moment. She looked back at the hallway leading to Fields's office and then back at Hayes.

"I'll take it," she said as she grabbed the CD from the analyst and walked out.

CHAPTER THREE

Glynn, LA
0630 Local Time

His lungs burned as the sweat poured down his face. Although the sun had barely risen, it was already over eighty degrees, and the humidity made it feel even hotter. Even in the relative shade of the woods, the air felt thick and saturated. There was just no good time to go for a run during a Louisiana summer.

He was on his third mile. With his dog, Zeus alongside, he had run out of the woods and onto the levee of the nearby Mississippi River before turning around and heading back home. His shorts and t-shirt did little but soak up the sweat pouring out of his body as he tried to keep pace with the former military working dog.

His body was sore. He had been beaten, cut, and bruised. His arms were stiff and his joints ached from the hours spent hanging from the rafters of an old barn two days prior. His muscles were sore from the two fights he had been in. He still couldn't believe what had happened.

As Cal "Spectre" Martin made his way along the footpath between the towering pine trees, he tried to clear his mind. He had arrived at his childhood mentor's house the day prior, and after eating and telling "Bear" all that had happened to him in the last two years, he had slept nearly fourteen hours. His body had reached its limit.

The last month had been a complete nightmare. He had been shot down in Syria. His best friend had been killed in an attempt on Spectre's life. He had been kidnapped, interrogated, and left to die before finally building up the resolve to fight his way out. He had found the man who had changed his life forever over the last year - the man who stole his fiancée and what little semblance of a life he had left after leaving the Air Force.

But Spectre had found little comfort in leaving the man to die. Instead, he found that the situation was much worse than he had ever imagined. The Chinese had been behind it all, and they would stop at nothing to kill him. According to Victor Alvarez, they were in every level of government. There was nowhere to hide.

Spectre pushed himself harder as he neared the last mile of his run. His body screamed for him to stop and walk, but he ignored it and pushed through. The running cleared his mind. He needed to stay in peak shape for what lay ahead.

Spectre still couldn't believe he had become a wanted man. He had been the victim. The FBI vowed to protect him. They had seen the lengths to which his potential assassins were willing to go, and put him in protective custody in a dumpy South

Florida motel as Agents Baxter and Decker hunted down his assassins.

Decker. He still hadn't sorted out his feelings for her on a personal level. Theirs had been a unique relationship. He had never really given it much thought after the death of his fiancée. She seemed interested, but he was too distracted. It wasn't until Victor Alvarez threatened her that he realized there might be something more there. Alvarez had managed to push a button Spectre didn't know existed. He wanted to protect her — to save her. Spectre had realized he cared for her.

Spectre couldn't wrap his head around how she had allowed them to make him a villain. *Did she even have a say in the matter? Did she even know? Or was it part of the Chinese infiltration of the government?* The questions swirled violently in Spectre's head.

He had been shocked to learn that a warrant had been issued for his apprehension. When a Florida Highway Patrol Trooper pulled him over on his way to Tampa, Spectre thought it had to be a mistake. But when the trooper tried to arrest him and said there was a warrant out for the murder of a federal agent, Spectre just couldn't understand it. *What federal agent? Who had been killed?*

Spectre stopped suddenly as the realization hit him. His confused running partner stopped a few yards later. Victor Alvarez had threatened to hurt Michelle Decker. Spectre's mind raced and his stomach turned as he considered the possibilities. *Was she the federal agent that had been killed? Was he being framed for her death?*

Spectre felt sick as he tried to catch his breath from the run. The idea that another woman in his life had been taken from him was at the forefront of his mind. He felt utterly helpless.

Zeus returned to his position at Spectre's side as they walked the half mile back to the secluded cabin. After realizing that he could trust no one, Spectre had made the trip from Florida to Glynn, Louisiana near Baton Rouge. He had driven through the night, avoiding major roads and highways until he hit Baton Rouge and had no other choice. He had taken the Trooper's radio and used it to avoid roadblocks and their attempts at finding him after they realized he had disabled the Trooper that attempted to arrest him.

Spectre froze as he neared the end of the footpath leading to the cabin. He saw a white Tahoe with SHERIFF markings on the back parked behind his three-quarter-ton pickup truck. Spectre squatted down as he grabbed Zeus's collar and tried to conceal himself and the dog in the foliage. He reached into his waistband and grabbed the butt of his concealed Glock x 36 chambered in .45 ACP.

He surveyed the area around the large cabin. There were no other patrol cars or deputies, other than the one parked behind Spectre's truck. Spectre considered his options. *Avoid. Negotiate. Kill.* They were the priorities he had learned from his Sensei in his Krav Maga training over the years. It was always better to try to avoid a fight first. If that weren't possible, talking his way out of it would be the next best option. Finally, once all other options were exhausted, he would kill.

With his truck blocked in by the police SUV, Spectre had no method of flight other than on foot. If they were there to apprehend him, they would easily track him down in a matter of days. Spectre cursed himself for being so careless as to let down his guard and go for a run with no means of escape. His hit-and-run bag and all the resources he needed to disappear were in that truck.

Spectre drew his Glock 36 from its holster and carefully made his way through the brush. Zeus followed suit behind, also being slow and deliberate after Spectre gave him the "down" command.

Clearing the open area around the house, Spectre methodically made his way around the tree line. As he neared the side of the house, he could see into the kitchen area through one of the windows. He saw his small stature friend sitting at the kitchen table next to a much taller and burlier man. They appeared to be drinking coffee and laughing about something.

Spectre sat and watched the two men. Bear traditionally hated all forms of government. He had always assumed that included the local government as well. *Had Bear notified the authorities? Was the Sheriff there to arrest him?*

Bear had been a father figure to Spectre since his parents had been killed in a car accident when he was a teenager. He refused to believe that the man that had been there for him through some of the worst times in his life would turn him in to the authorities. But with all Spectre had been through in the last year, nothing really surprised him anymore.

Spectre and Zeus made their way around to the back of the cabin while still staying concealed in the woods. There were no other deputies or officers that he could see. If the man sitting next to Bear had come to arrest Spectre, he hadn't brought any back up with him.

Satisfied that the perimeter was clear, Spectre snuck his way back to the brush where he had a view into the kitchen. As he looked back into the window, he saw Bear picking up the empty coffee cups and the larger man standing. He was wearing a polo shirt with a badge embroidered on it and cargo pants. His handgun was holstered on his left side, but he didn't appear to be wearing a traditional duty belt.

Spectre watched as the two men walked out to the front porch and shook hands. The large deputy lingered for a moment and then headed to his SUV. Moments later, he started the engine and backed out before turning around and heading out the gate and onto the narrow path out of the woods toward civilization.

Spectre waited until the Tahoe was completely clear and Bear walked back into the cabin. He holstered his weapon and tapped his thigh for Zeus to follow along. As he walked into the cabin, he found Bear sitting at his computer, reading through the latest headlines.

"Have a nice run?" Bear asked without looking up.

"Who was that?" Spectre asked as he stopped a few feet from Bear's desk.

"That was Sheriff Thibodaux," Bear replied, still scrolling through the headlines. "You should've come in to say hi instead of hiding in the woods like a creepy pedophile."

Spectre blushed at the realization that he hadn't been as stealthy as he hoped. "You saw me?"

Bear spun around in his chair and pushed his reading glasses to the top of his sandy white hair. "Son, I'm almost seventy, but I still have twenty-fifteen vision," he replied with a sly grin. "Besides, Rambo, that white t-shirt does stand out a bit."

"So what about the Sheriff?" Spectre asked, ignoring Bear's jab.

"Did he see you? Probably not. Does he know about your warrant? Absolutely."

Spectre frowned. He didn't know what to say, but he realized he had to come up with a game plan for a new place to stay very quickly.

"Don't worry, Fred is a good guy. He knew your dad too. I don't think it's him that you should be worried about."

"What was he doing here anyway?" Spectre asked.

"Fred and I have coffee on Thursdays. Today is Thursday," Bear replied, pointing at the calendar.

Spectre looked up at the calendar. The days had all started to run together since he and Joe Carpenter had left Tampa en route to Marcus Anderson's houseboat. It all felt like one long day.

"So what did he say?"

"The Feds have started a manhunt for you. They're setting up shop in the Baton Rouge office and they know you're in the area," Bear replied.

"What's the warrant for?"

Bear laughed. He pulled his reading glasses back down to his nose and spun around to face the computer. Seconds later, he had the warrant pulled up on the screen.

"Terrorism, seven counts of first-degree murder, arson—"

"Wait!" Spectre interrupted. "Does it say who they think I murdered?"

Bear clicked through a few more screens and then said, "Special Agent Sean Baxter, Deputy Brian Hernandez, Sergeant Jay Derrick—"

"Ok," Spectre said, cutting him off. *Sean Baxter.* A flood of feelings rushed Spectre. It was a mix of relief and sadness. Spectre liked Baxter. He had helped Spectre in their mission to Cuba and in finding where Chloe Moss had taken the stolen F-16. They weren't close, but Spectre had always liked Baxter. He was saddened by his death, but deep down, he was greatly relieved that it wasn't Decker.

As Spectre stood there deep in thought, Bear continued reading through the report. "Oh, and here's another new victim... Marcus Anderson, didn't you say you worked for him?"

The news hit Spectre like a 2,000-pound JDAM. He stumbled back, leaning against the back of a nearby couch for support.

"Marcus is dead?" Spectre mumbled.

Bear strained to read the report. "Says here they ID'd the body this morning and added the charge to the warrant."

Spectre slid down the back of the couch onto the floor. He stared out into oblivion as he tried to process the news. He had lost his best friend to the houseboat explosion. Marcus had been on the ropes, but had been expected to pull through. He had just lost his two closest friends.

"Marcus is dead," Spectre repeated as he held his head in his hands.

CHAPTER FOUR

Decker's Townhouse
North Miami Beach, FL
0825 Local Time

Decker walked in the front door of her modest townhouse and reset the beeping alarm. She threw her backpack down and did a quick sweep of the downstairs area. The alarm had done little to prevent her house from becoming a crime scene two nights prior.

The man had startled her in the dead of night as she tried to sleep after the trail to find Cal Martin had gone cold. He had entered her townhouse through a window with the intent to rape and kidnap her. Upon questioning, she realized he was one of Victor Alvarez's men, and his confession under gunpoint led to the discovery of the farmhouse where Baxter and the six SWAT officers had been killed.

Decker went into the kitchen and pulled out a protein bar from one of the cabinets. She could still see the bloodstains on the cabinets and floor where she had stabbed and shot the man. After staring at it for a moment, she realized she was too tired to care about cleaning it up and decided to leave it for another day. *Plenty of time to catch up on housework in the next two weeks,* she thought.

Unwrapping the protein bar, Decker grabbed a bottle of water out of the fridge and walked around to the living area before collapsing onto her leather couch. She picked up the remote from the coffee table and turned on the TV. It was still on one of the 24-hour news channels. She was rarely home when working a case, and she only really watched TV for the news anymore.

She turned up the volume as one of the political commentators discussed the latest headline. Senator Madeline Clifton of Massachusetts had chosen Secretary of Defense Kerry Johnson as her running mate for the November Presidential elections. The commentator was discussing the impact it would have on the campaign's foreign and economic policy platforms. The panel discussed the conflict between Johnson's attempt to downsize the United States military footprint in the Pacific and Southeast Asia versus Clifton's campaign promise to continue to support Japan and Taiwan against the continued encroachment of the growing Chinese Military Complex.

Decker zoned out as she finished the last few bites of her protein bar. Politics had never been of much interest to her. In her world, it didn't matter what letter they had behind their names. They were all essentially the same once in office, with each President carrying on the same or similar policies as the one before, even if under a different name. The political arena involved too much pandering and showmanship to ever appeal to her.

As the panel completed its analysis of Johnson's career as a billionaire businessman, the news anchor transitioned to the current story about the manhunt for Cal Martin. A female reporter on the scene at the farmhouse relayed the information almost word for word from Agent Simms's brief she had just left. Decker wondered why the FBI was being so loose-lipped about the entire situation during the continuing investigation.

"One government official I spoke to on the condition of anonymity told me that Martin was discharged from the Air Force after a so called 'traumatic incident' in Iraq in 2009. The FBI considers him armed, mentally unstable, and very dangerous," the reporter said as Martin's service picture popped up on screen. "Authorities are urging anyone that may spot him to contact the FBI hotline at the number on the screen. I will continue to keep you updated as the story unfolds. Back to you, Ron."

Decker turned off the TV and spiked the remote into the couch, causing it to bounce onto the floor. She wanted to send it through the TV. She was certain the "anonymous source" had been Simms. *That weasel was using the media to build his case.* She knew the real story behind the "traumatic incident." Cal had saved a convoy under heavy fire. His commander had grounded him for not following the overly restrictive rules of engagement. It was the same commander that she had arrested for selling secrets to Cuban Intelligence Agent Victor Alvarez. Cal Martin was a not the monster Simms was making him out to be. Decker was sure of it. *But why did he run?*

Decker turned over the possibilities in her head. She tried to look at the case objectively, muting her friendship with Martin. There was no doubt that he had been targeted by Victor Alvarez. The houseboat Martin and his friends were on had been hit by a micro-UAV with a small warhead. Decker had found the backpack and manuals for the UAV in Alvarez's hotel room in the Biltmore. He had also been targeted by a female Russian assassin. She had seen that part first hand.

Decker and Baxter had placed Martin into protective custody at the Flamingo Paradise Motel in Miami. She had only seen him once between dropping him off and his disappearance. It was after he and a young agent found themselves in the middle of an armed robbery in progress. Martin had left the scene and gone back to his room, trying to drink the pain of his friend's death away.

He had been in a terrible state. She had found him in his t-shirt and underwear, sitting in the chair beside the bed with the TV on mute.

"You're better than this, Cal," she told him.

"Nothing matters anymore," he slurred. He had been drinking straight from the bottle of Jack Daniels. His thousand-yard stare was still etched in her memory. He had checked out long ago.

"I should've just let the kid kill me," Martin slurred. "Would've done everyone a favor."

"Please, Cal," she pleaded. "Pour out the bottle. Don't do this to yourself."

"Go find your boyfriend Baxter and leave me alone!" Martin yelled, waving the half-empty bottle at her.

Despite the knowledge that his condition was depression and alcohol-induced, his words had stung. She hated seeing him like that. He was a broken man, beaten by life. But he was no murderer. And even playing devil's advocate, there was no way he sobered up enough to murder two agents and escaped.

Decker knew that her mind would never settle down enough to rest, forced vacation or not, until she found Cal and figured out what happened. She didn't trust Simms to approach the matter impartially, and it appeared the Bureau had jumped fully on board with his handling of the case.

She walked over to her backpack and carried it to the small office near the staircase of her two-story townhome. She booted up her laptop as she pulled out the CD Samantha Hayes had given her before leaving. It had been a heat of the moment decision to take it from her, but she doubted Simms would even attempt to look at it. He had made up his mind about Martin, and as far as he was concerned, his case was solidified at the farmhouse. In his mind, nothing before that even mattered anymore.

Decker pulled the CD out of its case and inserted it into the computer as it completed its boot cycle. The drive whirred to life as it read the data. Moments later, a video player appeared on the screen with a black and white fishbowl image from the ATM camera at the gas station across the street.

Decker noted the time at the bottom of the screen. She pulled out her notebook that she had been using to take notes on the case. She found the time of the suspected disappearance and moved the time slider at the bottom of the video to a few minutes prior. She leaned back in the chair and hit play.

The image was grainy and pixelated, but it was enough to make out a man exiting a sedan. It looked like he was wearing a hat and carrying a pizza box, but she couldn't tell. The man left the view of the camera before reappearing on the second-floor breezeway where Martin and his protective detail were staying.

Decker leaned forward to the edge of her chair as the man stopped in front of the protective detail's room. Just as the man started to knock, a man approached the ATM to withdraw money.

"Are you fucking kidding me?" Decker growled.

She hit fast forward on the video player as the man fumbled with his wallet and made several attempts to enter his PIN before withdrawing his cash. Decker paused the video as the man finally exited the field of view.

Decker frantically searched the video for clues. The doors to both rooms were open. She could see the sedan that the pizza guy had exited earlier in the video. Its trunk was open. Decker hit play on the video. Within seconds, the trunk closed, revealing the pizza man. She paused the video, trying to get a better look. It was grainy. She could not make out facial features or anything identifying other than his dark hair and tan skin. She hit play again. The man appeared to look around as he wiped his hands on his pants. Apparently satisfied that no one had seen him, he got back in his car and sped off.

Decker leaned back in her chair and let out a frustrated sigh as she rubbed her temples. She was exhausted from the lack of sleep and events of the last few days. Her thoughts felt sluggish and labored. She knew she needed to get some rest if she was to be able to figure out anything in this case, but she didn't have the patience. She wanted answers.

The video was eating at her. It seemed obvious, but she just couldn't put it all together. Was the pizza guy Alvarez? She pulled out the notes she had taken from Agent Baxter's description of the crime scene.

One body near the doorway. One body further in. Blunt force trauma to the near body with two bullet wounds. Single bullet to the forehead in the far body. No sign of struggle or markings of any kind in Martin's room.

Decker returned to the last footage before the ATM customer blocked the field of view. The pizza man stood in front of the protective detail's suite. She imagined him pushing the door in, shooting twice, and then killing the other agent in the corner of the room. It made sense to start with the protective detail first. *But why hadn't Cal put up any fight at all?*

She moved the slider of the video player back to the last images of the man behind the trunk and hit play. The distance and the quality of the video made it hard to tell for sure, but he didn't appear to be rushed or injured as if he had been in a fight. He was somewhat casual in his closing of the trunk and getting back in the car. She watched the car leave the parking lot again. This time she noticed the rear end sag slightly. *Something was in there.*

Decker thought back to her conversation with Cal in the room earlier in the day. *He had given up.* It was the only answer that made sense. Cal Martin had come face to face with the man trying to kill him, and he had given up. That was why the man had closed the trunk. *Cal was in the trunk!*

As video finished playing a second time, Decker tried to think of where to start. The farmhouse was an active crime scene, and given her status with the Bureau, they would never let her anywhere near it. Anything she did moving forward was on her own time and at her own risk. She didn't care. She wanted to see it through. *She needed to see it through.*

She flipped through her case notes, looking for something to stand out. As she flipped through the pages, she found their conversation with Rick Fields in the conference room. Cal had been sure that his former boss Charles Steele had been behind the houseboat attack. They had even run into him at Carpenter's funeral.

Was he involved in this? Decker asked herself. *There's only one way to find out.*

CHAPTER FIVE

Glynn, LA
0812 Local Time

After the initial shock of Marcus Anderson's death had worn off, Spectre did his best to compartmentalize it. He tucked away the sadness he felt for the loss of his last remaining best friend and tried to push forward. *Marcus wouldn't have wanted him to dwell on it. He would have wanted him to kill.*

Although he was able to overcome his sadness, the feeling of rage was much more powerful. The people behind Victor Alvarez had taken everything from him. They had managed to take from him the woman he had once thought he would spend the rest of his life with. They had killed his two best friends. They had tried to kill him, and when that failed, they tried to take his freedom by framing him for the murder of Marcus and the Federal Agent.

On the drive from Florida to Louisiana, Spectre had struggled with the why. It was clear to Spectre that the attempts on his life were related to his mission to Cuba to save his ex-fiancée. Victor Alvarez had told him as much. But beyond that, he couldn't understand it. His mostly unknown enemies had waited over a year to strike. *Were they that patient? Why now?*

But the news of Marcus's death had muted the *why*. Spectre no longer cared *why*. *Why* was a plea from victims. He had played that card already in mourning the loss of Joe Carpenter. It had nearly cost Spectre his life. *He refused to go down that road again.*

The *why* had been replaced with *who*. *Attack your attacker*, his Sensei had told him in the waiting room as they looked on at the struggling Marcus in ICU. It was a mantra of Krav Maga he'd learned as a Black Belt. The only way to truly stop an attack was to kill. *Kill their will to fight. Kill their ability to fight. And if all else fails, kill them.*

But Spectre only knew what Victor Alvarez had told him. The Chinese had been behind the operation to steal an American F-16 using his ex-fiancée. Jun Zhang was the man that had hired Alvarez to execute it. In a nation of over one billion people, that left Spectre with few leads.

After pushing through the nausea and forcing himself to eat the bacon and eggs Bear cooked, Spectre retrieved the black bag he had taken from the farmhouse in Homestead. He brought it out to the small living room of the wooden cabin and opened it, revealing the laptop and money he had taken from the office in the house Alvarez had taken him to.

Spectre pulled out the laptop and set it down beside him as he rummaged through the duffel bag. It was filled with neatly wrapped hundred dollar bills that Alvarez had been using to fund his operation. After a few seconds of trying to find anything beyond the money, Spectre dumped the contents of the bag out onto the cloth couch.

"I see you've decided to pay the boarding fee," Bear said as he walked over from the kitchen.

Spectre responded with a forced chuckle as he pushed aside the pile of money, looking for something to tie Zhang to Alvarez and give him a location to start his search.

"That will probably cover at least one or two nights here at Hotel De Bear," Bear said, staring at the pile of money.

"This is at least a quarter million dollars," Spectre said dryly as he continued his search.

"Ok, three nights then," Bear offered.

Still ignoring Bear's deadpan humor, Spectre continued digging through the pile until he found a folded manila envelope buried in the miniature mountain of money. He unfolded it and opened the clasp, pulling out papers and receipts.

"What'd you find?" Bear asked as he slowly made his way to the couch. He had a barely noticeable limp. Throughout Spectre's childhood, Bear had always told him that it was from one leg being shorter than the other, but as Spectre grew older, he realized that the scars were indicative of a much more engaging story. He guessed that it was most likely an injury Bear received in Vietnam.

"Looks like hotel receipts," Spectre said as he pulled open the first piece of paper. As he opened the folded paper, the Biltmore logo stood out at the top of the letterhead, with room charges for the Everglades Suite listed beneath it.

"Biltmore huh?" Bear said as he looked over Spectre's shoulder at the receipt. "You see that? My rate is a good deal compared to what this David Hernandez was paying."

"He was paying a lot less than eighty grand per night," Spectre said as he studied the receipt. It was made out to David Hernandez and paid for by a corporate account for a company called Hua Xia Holdings. He had never heard of Hernandez, but the company funding the suite was apparently related to the Chinese operation.

"Did he get bacon and eggs for breakfast though?" Bear quipped.

"I don't know," Spectre said as he turned his attention to the laptop. He pulled it onto his lap and pressed the power button, waiting as it entered its boot cycle and flashed the Windows logo on the screen.

Seconds later, the laptop finished its boot cycle, displaying a request for a password.

"I don't know what I expected," Spectre said, throwing his hands up in exasperation. He knew it was probably foolish to think that an intelligence operative left an unsecured laptop lying around, but he figured it was worth a shot. "Well, this is a dead end for now."

"Hold on, I think I have something for that," Bear said as he shuffled off to his makeshift home office.

"You can hack laptops now?" Spectre asked incredulously. "You're seventy years old!"

"Sixty-nine, thank you very much," Bear replied as he continued opening and closing drawers at his computer desk. "And just what in the hell is that supposed to mean anyway?"

"I don't know," Spectre replied. "I just didn't picture you as the hacker type. You don't even own a cell phone."

"Ah ha! Found it!" Bear said, holding up a CD proudly. "This should do it."

Bear walked over and sat on the recliner next to Spectre. He motioned for Spectre to hand him the laptop, and Spectre complied, still confused by the world's oldest hacker sitting next to him.

"So you live in a cabin in the woods, but you go around hacking computers for the hell of it?" Spectre asked as Bear, pulled his eyeglasses down and inserted the CD into the laptop's tray.

"Who said anything about hacking?" Bear said as the computer made a beeping noise.

Spectre gave Bear a confused look as Bear typed away on the laptop. Moments later, Bear pushed his eyeglasses to the top of his head and looked up.

"I'm in," he said with a smile as the Windows logon theme music played on the laptop.

"Seriously?"

"I told you, I'm sixty-nine years old," Bear said as he handed the laptop back to Spectre.

"So?"

"So, sometimes I forget my passwords," Bear replied with a wink.

CHAPTER SIX

Lake Pontchartrain Causeway Bridge
Metairie, LA
0935 Local Time

After completing the debrief and alert shift changeover with the incoming pilots, Foxworthy spent a few minutes in the operations building of the squadron before heading home. Although most of the pilots were out flying their morning sorties, most that were hanging around had never seen or heard of anything like what he and his wingman had experienced on their alert scramble.

Like Foxworthy, several pilots had been scrambled on unknown aircraft crossing the U.S. Air Defense Identification Zone without talking to anyone. It was something that happened with some regularity. Sometimes it was a private business jet that mixed a frequency change while having transponder issues.

Sometimes they would encounter drug smugglers that required intercept by U.S. Customs and Border Protection aircraft out of Hammond. And sometimes it was just a transport helicopter pilot flying to or from one of the many oil platforms in the gulf with his head up his ass and not following appropriate procedures. But no one had ever heard of a cargo seaplane landing at one, much less getting spiked by a surface to air threat.

As Foxworthy entered the twenty-four mile bridge connecting the North Shore of Lake Pontchartrain to New Orleans in his Jeep Cherokee, the intercept was stuck in his mind. His experience as a fighter pilot told him that something didn't add up, but his experience as a small business owner specializing in the oil industry told him that what happened was just plain wrong.

Two years prior, Foxworthy started Mach Two Consulting with two other fighter pilots. After having lunch with friends in the oil and gas industry, he realized he could apply the concepts he'd learned as a fighter pilot in Operational Risk Management and cultural safety to the oil industry. Using scientific behavioral models developed by a psychologist on his staff, he and his business partners went to various refineries, oil platforms, and oil rigs to train the oil field workers on the concepts of ORM.

The idea had been hugely successful. Management and field workers alike loved the real world experience and stories the pilots brought from the cockpit and how they related their experiences to even the lowest level worker. In turn, the companies were able to show their commitment to risk mitigation, further reducing their liability in various areas. In two years, Foxworthy had grown the company from a small operation in his home office with no budget to a medium sized organization generating high six figure profits.

He had spent weeks at a time on oil rigs out in the Gulf of Mexico, observing, training, and debriefing the workers on their safety practices. Having seen the day to day operation of an oil platform out in the gulf firsthand, he was certain that the night time seaplane landing was unusual for all of them, even the Chinese platforms.

Although the Chinese lived by their own rules in international waters, they still played by essentially the same rules as the United States. Most were operated by American companies under leasing agreements with Chinese oil companies. Some were wholly owned and operated by Chinese companies, but as far as Foxworthy knew, those were mostly in the eastern Gulf of Mexico and near Cuba. In the area they scrambled to, he had not heard of any at all, and the Intel analyst that took their debrief confirmed as much. *It just didn't add up.*

Traffic was relatively light as Foxworthy finished the thirty-minute drive across the two lane bridge. The bulk of the traffic was still heading southbound as the North Shore commuters made their way into the city. It was a commute he was glad he only had to do a few times per month as a Traditional Guardsman at NAS JRB New Orleans in Belle Chasse.

After exiting the Causeway on the East Causeway Approach, Foxworthy made a left onto Highway 190 and then pulled into his office complex off Lonesome Road a mile later. He was exhausted from the flight and sitting alert, but he had work to do. The five or so hours of sleep he had managed before being scrambled combined with copious amounts of coffee would have to be enough to keep him running.

Foxworthy pulled into his marked space in front of their unmarked offices and walked in. His secretary was busy typing as he walked past the reception area and through the single doorway. The office had once served as a doctor's office before Foxworthy picked up the lease for his consulting company and he thought the waiting area would be a nice touch for potential clients visiting.

"Good morning, Mr. Vaughan," the young brunette said as Foxworthy walked by her desk. "I've put all your messages on your desk and Mary has a pot of coffee brewing in the break room."

Meghan "Mary" Jane was an F/A-18 pilot with the Navy Reserve unit at NAS JRB New Orleans. She and Tom "Crash" Packard, a fellow F-15 pilot in Foxworthy's squadron, were Foxworthy's business partners.

"Thanks, Jeanine," Foxworthy said as he continued down the narrow hallway to his corner office. Once inside, he pulled out a polo shirt with his company's logo and khaki pants and changed out of the green flight suit he had been wearing. As he sat down and logged onto his computer, there was a knock at his door.

"Come in," he said, leaning back in his executive leather chair.

"Hey boss," Mary said as she walked in the door. She was a modestly attractive redhead in her mid-thirties. As a pilot for the F/A-18 squadron down the ramp, she and Foxworthy had flown against each other many times before going into business together. The daughter of a wealthy oil tycoon from Lafayette, Mary had been one of the driving forces in Mach Two getting its initial contracts and growing as quickly as it did. She served as the company's director of operations when not flying F/A-18s on the side.

"Hey Mary," Foxworthy said with a smile. As attractive as she was, Foxworthy had never seen her as more than a kid sister. Despite his reputation as a womanizer, he had never crossed that line with her or anyone on his staff. The money was too good to risk.

"I thought you were taking off today? Didn't you sit alert?" Mary asked as she made herself comfortable in the chair across Foxworthy's desk. She was also wearing a white polo with their company's logo and khaki pants – the standard uniform for office days and the time they spent in the field.

"I did," Foxworthy responded as he scrolled through his inbox full of e-mails. "But I figured I'd get some work done before going home. Besides, last night was just *weird.*"

Looking up from his monitor, Foxworthy noticed the quizzical look on Mary's lightly freckled face. He told her the story of their alert scramble in detail from beginning to end as she listened intently.

"First time anyone that I talked to has ever heard of that," Foxworthy added as he finished the story.

"I have," Mary replied nonchalantly.

"Standing by for a sea story," Foxworthy said with a chuckle. Mary was notorious for telling stories from her deployments at sea, and she especially loved pointing out that she had seen more combat than the land-loving F-15 pilot. It was a source of daily ribbing the two enjoyed.

"My last cruise on the George Washington before I became a quitter," Mary began, referring to her time on the U.S.S. George Washington prior to leaving active duty to become a reservist.

"We were out in the South China Sea supporting the Japanese Maritime Defense Force doing Maritime Interdiction. A couple of Chinese ships had rammed Japanese cargo vessels that had gotten too close to a Chinese oil platform they had planted right in the middle of a shipping lane," Mary continued as Foxworthy listened intently.

"My wingman and I were out doing standard maritime patrols," Mary said, pausing as she saw the confused look on the Air Force pilot's face. "You know, looking for the assholes ramming boats and getting their side numbers."

"Ah," Foxworthy replied, gesturing for her to continue.

"Anyway, we passed one of the boats at low altitude and ended up flying near the oil platform. We were both spiked by a surface to air missile acquisition radar, but we managed to bug out before they tracked us."

"Holy shit," Foxworthy replied. "What'd you do?"

"Reported it to our Intel. A few days later, they sent out a dedicated flight to orbit the platform to confirm it, and they launched on the flight lead. He got pretty lucky because the thing guided on his aircraft but fused late. They were using old Russian missiles," Mary said dismissively.

Foxworthy was leaning forward on the edge of his seat, captivated by her sea story. "And then what happened?"

"The problem went away," Mary said with a satisfied laugh.

"Went away?"

"You don't remember the news about the oil platform in the South China Sea in 2010 that had an explosion due to," Mary paused for effect as she threw up her hands to make quotation signs, "'unknown reasons'?"

Foxworthy thought about it for a minute. He vaguely remembered hearing something in the news about it. But it had been on the heels of the Deepwater Horizon's oil spill in the Gulf of Mexico in April of that year, and the massive cleanup efforts and continuing news coverage had eclipsed it.

"Vaguely," Foxworthy responded.

"Well, those reasons weren't all that 'unknown' to some of us," Mary said with a grin as she lowered her voice to a whisper and leaned it.

"You mean you guys?"

"Yup! High Speed Anti-Radiation Missiles can cause a few explosions of their own, especially when they hit a cache of surface to air missiles on an oil platform," Mary said. Her green eyes sparkled with satisfaction.

"Why wasn't that in the news? That's an international incident!" Foxworthy replied.

Mary rolled her eyes and laughed. "Do you think the government would announce something like that when we were still entrenched in Iraq and Afghanistan?"

"Yeah, but the Chinese would have seen it as an act of aggression," Foxworthy shot back.

"Only if they weren't shooting surface to air missiles at American aircraft," Mary responded. "It was handled diplomatically and that was the end of it."

"So you think that's what happened to me this morning?" Foxworthy asked, thinking back to the surface to air missile indications he had received on his alert scramble mission.

"Maybe," Mary responded as she considered the question. "But we get erroneous surface to air missile indications in that airspace in the Hornet all the time, and no one has ever shot at us. Could just be your equipment."

"That wasn't a spurious spike," Foxworthy said dismissively. "We both were no shit being targeted."

"Do you know which platform you were flying over?"

"No," Foxworthy replied. "But I still have the coordinates for it, and it can't be too hard to find the only Chinese operated platform in that area."

Mary frowned. "If there is one," she said, shaking her head.

"You know, Laney Crowe said that same thing," Foxworthy responded with a grin. Although Mary wasn't on his radar, SSgt Crowe had definitely crossed his mind as a woman he wouldn't mind seeing naked. She was a tight-bodied twenty-five year old that often flaunted it with tight yoga pants while working out at the base gym.

"Knock it off, you perv!" Mary barked, tapping the desk as she realized what he was thinking. "You'll get kicked out of the Air Guard and then no one will hire us."

"Totally worth it," Foxworthy said with a chuckle.

"You need a wife, dude," Mary replied as she folded her arms. "And Jesus."

"Too expensive," Foxworthy replied, still laughing. "But seriously, what about the platform? You really think it's nothing?"

"Look, I'm having dinner with Papa Bear tonight in Baton Rouge," Mary replied, trying to humor him. "I'll ask him what he knows."

"Ohhh, dinner with dad," Foxworthy with a surprised look. "Is your boyfriend finally meeting him tonight? The murse?"

"One, he's a nurse anesthetist," she said, holding up a finger.

"Sugar daddy!" Foxworthy yelped.

"And two, this is his second time meeting Papa Bear," Mary replied as she raised a second finger.

"Second time, huh? I hear wedding bells."

Mary dropped a finger, leaving just her middle finger up as she tried to suppress a laugh.

"With all due respect," she said as she got up to walk out, "you're an idiot."

"That's sir to you!" Foxworthy said, still laughing as the feisty redhead walked out.

"I said with all due respect!" Mary said over her shoulder, smiling as she closed Foxworthy's door behind her.

CHAPTER SEVEN

MacDill Air Force Base
Tampa, FL
1335 Local Time

Decker flashed her FBI credentials at the sentry working the front gate. He studied her ID for a moment before waving her through. She realized she probably looked nothing like the picture. Her hair was up, in a ponytail. She wasn't wearing makeup, but her mirrored aviator sunglasses mostly masked the bruises on her face and bags under her eyes. She barely even recognized the chipper woman represented by her official FBI picture.

She drove down the main drag of the sprawling Air Force base to the United States Central Command building. From her quick research before heading out the door, the building she was looking for was just behind the massive complex responsible for the United States operations in the Middle East, Central Asia, and North Africa.

She found the small building wedged between the CENTCOM headquarters and the flight line where several helicopters and small turbine aircraft lined the ramp. She pulled her government Chevy Malibu into a parking spot near the front of the large u-shaped building close to what she thought should be the main entrance. The building was mostly unmarked except for a small placard that said "Dynamic Aviation Consulting Group" next to the mirrored glass doors.

Decker gathered herself as she downed the last of her coffee, exited the car, and headed for the door. A red sign on the door warned that she was entering a controlled area in which unauthorized access was prohibited. Decker tried the door but realized it was locked. She found a call button on the side and pressed it. She couldn't see through the mirrored glass, but seconds later, a larger woman opened the door.

"Can I help you?" the woman asked. Her demeanor was cold and aloof, as if she had grown tired of people wandering up to the wrong door over the years. She wore a plain polo shirt and 5.11 tactical cargo pants.

"I'm here to see Mr. Steele," Decker said as she held out her credentials and tried to look beyond the much larger woman. Decker was easily a half foot shorter and hundred and fifty pounds lighter than the burlier woman.

"Is he expecting you?" the woman asked, still opening the door only enough to determine Decker's intentions.

"No," Decker said as she retrieved her credentials. "But I'd like to speak to him."

"Remove your glasses, please," the woman, ordered as she studied the ID. She grimaced as Decker pushed them to the top of her head, revealing the bruises and fatigue from the last few days.

"Please, come in," the woman said as she opened the door for Decker.

Decker walked into the small reception area. There were several pictures of men fast-roping from helicopters and combat aircraft in action lining the walls. The woman returned to her seat behind the small desk. Decker noted the 9MM Glock on her right hip as she turned to pull out a large green book from the table lined with security camera monitors behind her desk.

"Sign in, please," the woman said as she pushed the book forward toward Decker.

Decker took the pen the woman had placed on top of the open book and filled in her name along with the date and time. The woman picked up a nearby phone and dialed a few numbers. Decker overheard her tell the person on the other line that an "FBI lady" was there to see him.

"What is your name again?" the woman asked, holding the phone away from her ear.

"Special Agent Michelle Decker," Decker replied as she finished filling out the logbook. "Here to see Charles Steele."

The woman relayed the information to the person on the other end of the phone. Seconds later, a stocky man with a bald head emerged from a narrow hallway to Decker's right.

"Special Agent Decker, it's good to see you again," Steele said with a smile as he extended his beefy hand. He was wearing a black polo shirt with the initials D. A. C. embroidered on the right side of his chest. "Although I wasn't expecting you today."

Decker accepted the handshake as she tried to think back to her brief encounter with Steele at Carpenter's funeral. She didn't remember talking to him at all when Spectre confronted him at the cemetery. It didn't sit well with her that he seemed so familiar with her.

"We haven't technically met," Decker replied as she watched the smile vanished from his face.

"Now that you mention it, you're right," Steele said, brushing off the jab. "I'm Charles Steele, President of Dynamic Consulting Group. How can I help you today?"

"May we speak somewhere privately?" Decker asked, looking over at the woman at the reception desk still intently listening to their conversation.

"How rude of me! Right this way," Steele replied, gesturing for her to follow. He led her down the long, narrow hallway from which he had recently emerged. The walls to her right were lined with more action posters as they passed several vault doors to her left. Decker followed Steele to the end of the hall, where he opened the door to his office on the right. It was a large suite, complete with a large LCD TV and windows behind his desk that overlooked the busy flight line. There were pictures of what Decker assumed to be his daughters and wife in frames around the office.

"What can I do for you?" Steele asked with a warm smile as he took his seat at his desk.

"Cal Martin," Decker said abruptly. She studied his face as he shifted uneasily in his chair. The warm smile transitioned to a mild grimace.

"What about him?" Steele shot back. His warm persona had been replaced by a gruff state of agitation.

"When did you last speak with him?" Decker asked flatly.

"At the funeral," Steele responded as he rubbed his nose and momentarily looked away. Decker caught the clue of deception shortly before Steele realized it himself and quickly withdrew his hand and tried to regain eye contact.

"I understand," Decker replied. "He was pretty mad at you, wasn't he?"

Steele shifted in his chair again. "Yeah, I think Carpenter's death really rattled him. Joe was a good man."

"What do you know about Carpenter's death?" Decker asked. After returning from Carpenter's funeral, it had been

Spectre's initial theory that Steele was behind the assassination attempt. Although she later found evidence that Victor Alvarez had been behind it, Decker knew that there was some connection, but she couldn't quite put her finger on it.

"Explosion of some kind on a boat," Steele responded, this time without breaking eye contact.

"Why do you think Cal Martin was so angry with you?" Decker asked, trying to test whether Steele would help her make that connection.

"I fired him," Steele said dismissively. "He lost his job and best friend in a few short weeks. Hell, I'd be mad too."

"That's it?" Decker asked skeptically.

Steele laughed nervously. "So that's what this is about? Martin thought I killed Carpenter?"

"I didn't say that," Decker replied. She let the implied accusation hang in the air, waiting for Steele to talk.

"I can promise you, I wasn't even in the country when that happened," Steele said. "I can show you my passport. In fact, I was in Qatar when we got the news, and flew straight to New Orleans for the funeral."

"Why did Cal lose his job here?" Decker asked, trying to get Steele back on track.

"He ran out of fuel on a mission. Lost a pretty expensive aircraft and got himself captured in the process," Steele said. He sat back in his chair and nodded toward one of the camouflage gray A-29 Super Tucano light attack aircraft taxiing in.

"What kind of mission?" Decker prodded.

"I don't know if you noticed all the vaults as you walked in here, but the missions we do are classified. You'll have to make a request with DOD for access."

"That's ok," Decker replied. Decker thought back to Martin's meeting with the Special Agent in Charge of the FBI Miami field office. He had been convinced that Steele was the man behind the death of his friend Joe Carpenter, but his reasoning had been mostly circumstantial. The link just didn't seem to be there.

"Anything else?" Steele asked impatiently.

"What about drones?" Decker asked.

"Excuse me?"

"You told Cal that he would be better off flying drones," Decker responded. "Why?"

"Because you can't get shot down in a drone," Steele replied with a hearty chuckled.

Decker's eyebrow perked. "But you just said he ran out of fuel."

Steele's eyes widened as he realized what he'd said. "You can't eject and get captured," Steele said with a stutter. "That's what I meant."

"So you told Cal that he would be better off flying drones because you thought that would be a better fit?" Decker said with a nod of approval.

"Exactly!" Steele replied, still recovering from the realization that he had almost accidentally divulged a classified detail of their mission. "I even tried to refer him to another company that specializes in that."

"Is that why he contacted you yesterday?" Decker asked. She was bluffing. She had no idea whether Spectre had contacted him at all since the day of Carpenter's funeral, but she had come this far, and Steele had already gotten caught in his own lie. It was the only play she had left in her playbook.

There was a pregnant pause as Steele sized up the petite woman across from him. Decker watched Steele's eyes. In interrogations, the eyes were the gatekeepers of the truth. It was a science of body language Decker had learned both as a prosecutor and as a seasoned FBI agent.

"No," Steele replied, apparently looking at the bookcase over Decker's left shoulder.

"Then why did he contact you?" Decker asked, pushing the bluff further.

"I said I haven't talked to him since the funeral," Steele said as he rubbed the back of his neck. "And as I am a fairly busy man, I think it's time for you to leave and end this fishing expedition."

Decker knew she had him. He was stressed and lying about not having talked to Martin since the funeral. She had struck a nerve with him, and she wasn't going to back down.

"Where is he?" Decker asked, ignoring Steele's attempt to end the interview.

"I have no idea," Steele said, standing to escort Decker out. Decker kept her seat as the stocky man towered over her.

"Where is Cal Martin?" Decker repeated.

"You need to leave," Steele said as he closed to within a foot of Decker. "I will call you if I have any further details."

Decker stood, going toe to toe with the much larger man in front of her. "Mr. Steele, you're lying to me," she said, unfazed by his threatening posture. "And if you don't start cooperating, I will flood this place with federal agents. We will go through every record, every phone call, and every computer in this place until I find what I'm looking for." The bluff had just gone beyond the point of no return. She was so far off the reservation that if Fields found out, she would likely not only lose her job, but find herself spending time in prison.

"Is that so?" Steele said, smiling as he took a step back.

"You don't want to test me," Decker snarled.

Steele laughed as he held up his hands. "Lady, you have no idea what you're dealing with here. Don't bite off more than you can chew."

"Try me," Decker snapped.

Steele backed away and headed for the metal filing cabinet behind his desk. He pulled out a set of keys from his pocket and unlocked the middle drawer. After thumbing through it, he pulled out an inch-thick brown folder and tossed it on his desk toward Decker.

"This is obviously personal for you," Steele said as he watched Decker eyeing the file. "That's Martin's personnel record. It's not a lot, but it contains his emergency contact information, psych evals, training records, and the information we used to hire him. That should get you pointed in the right direction."

Decker was shocked by the sudden reversal in Steele's cooperation. She could tell he was still hiding something, but she had not expected him to suddenly throw her a bone.

"Why are you giving me this?" she asked skeptically.

"You're a determined young lady," Steele replied, picking up a fatherly tone. "You would have gotten it one way or another."

Decker slowly picked up the file from Steele's desk and briefly thumbed through it. "You're hiding something," Decker said, tucking the folder underneath her left arm.

"Maybe," Steele said with a grin. "But so are you."

"Excuse me?" Decker asked. The accusation caught her off guard.

"You're not here on official business. In fact, I would wager no one from the Bureau even knows you're here. This is all Michelle Decker," Steele said, sitting back in the leather chair behind his desk. "Am I right?"

Decker blushed. He had called her bluff and the interview was starting to spiral out of control. His smugness was unsettling. He had been playing her the entire time.

"Keep lying to me and you'll find out," Decker said, regaining her composure as she tried to shake off Steele's jab.

"Well, ok then," Steele said as he leaned back in his chair with a hearty chuckle. "Take one of my cards and call me if you have any questions. Feel free to show yourself out."

Decker grabbed one of Steele's business cards from the dispenser at the edge of his desk and turned to walk out. "Thank you for your time. I'll be in touch," she said as she headed toward the door.

"Oh, and Michelle," Steele called as she reached the door. He leaned forward on his elbows.

Decker stopped, waiting for him to say something as she stared at the door.

"Be careful out there," Steele said in a fatherly tone. "Lots of dangerous people out there. Including Cal Martin."

Decker opened the door and walked out, ignoring Steele's thinly veiled threat. As she walked out, a bearded man with a lean, muscular physique wearing 5.11 tactical pants, a baseball hat, and a black polo shirt walked into Steele's office. He lingered in the doorway, staring at her ass in her tight jeans until she was out of sight.

"Hey Ironman, who's the angry battered housewife?" the man said through his red-tinted beard. It was former SEAL Team Six member James Redman, one of the tactical team leaders of Project Archangel.

"Special Agent Michelle Decker," Steele replied. "FBI."

"Whoa, a Fed?" Redman asked. Ironman motioned for him to enter and close the door behind him.

"Are you working on anything important right now?" Ironman asked.

"Just finishing up a debrief," Redman replied. "So, no."

"Clear your schedule and grab your go bag," Ironman directed.

"Is this about the hot blonde?"

"Follow her," Ironman said. "And take Tanning with you."

CHAPTER EIGHT

US Attorney's Office
Baton Rouge, LA
1315 Local Time

Special Agent Simms had spent most of the two-hour flight in the FBI's Cessna Citation from Miami to Baton Rouge studying the forensics report from the farmhouse crime scene in the Redlands.

The ATF and Crime Lab teams were still working diligently to sort through the relatively large crime scene and help put the pieces together. They had already been able to find traces of military grade Semtex near the bodies of Baxter and Anderson. It was assessed that Martin had rigged Anderson's body with the Semtex, knowing that investigators would happen upon it during their initial investigation. What sent chills up Simms's spine was that it could have been him instead of Baxter. He had never been the type to get his hands dirty, and this time it had saved his life.

Carl Simms graduated from the University of Ohio with a Masters in Accounting and Finance. His obsessive compulsive nature made him a natural in the field of accounting. He loved the structure and order of it all. He excelled in the tax code where others thought it monotonous and tedious. His professors lauded him as a shining star.

Although the IRS would have been a natural first choice, Simms returned to his hometown of Terrytown, Ohio to work with his uncle in private practice. The money was decent, even for a brand new CPA, but the challenge just wasn't there. And after two years, Simms started looking for something more to challenge himself.

Simms was twenty-four at the time, and although he loved tax code, the IRS just wasn't hiring. His search landed him with the FBI. They were heavily recruiting accountants to go into the field of forensic accounting.

Although academically superior in every way, Simms struggled with the entry requirements to the FBI. The Physical Fitness Assessment was most troubling. He could run and sprint as well as anyone, but his scrawny physique and general lack of upper body strength made it hard to pass the rigorous push-up requirement. It wasn't until a few days before his twenty-fifth birthday that he finally passed the pre-academy screening and was able to continue on to the FBI Academy at Quantico.

After passing the Academy, Simms was sent to the Boston field office to work organized crime. It was there that he first met Michelle Decker. At the time, she was fresh out of law school and working for the federal prosecutor's office. The young, ridiculously attractive attorney was always a thrill to work with. They were nearly the same age, but he had never been able to work up the courage to ask her out. *Hard to believe that was almost ten years ago*, he thought.

Since building an impressive record of convictions in organized crime, Simms had dabbled in counterterrorism and other major crimes. He had only been with the Miami Field Office for three months, and Cal Martin represented only his second attempt at tracking down a fugitive. He welcomed the challenge.

Simms studied Martin's file after settling into his temporary office at the FBI's satellite office, located in the US Attorney's Office in downtown Baton Rouge. What the FBI had on Martin showed him to be every bit as dangerous as the initial assessment Simms had made at the Flamingo Paradise Motel crime scene.

Martin had just turned thirteen-years old when his parents were killed by a drunk driver in Southeast Louisiana. A man named Charles Jennings had fostered him in his home until Martin left to pursue his degree at Louisiana State University in Baton Rouge. After graduating, Martin joined the Air Force Reserve where he flew F-16s until his service record abruptly ended shortly after a deployment to Iraq.

Martin worked for a small gun store for years before he was hired by a Private Military Contractor out of Tampa. Less than a year later, his employment from that group ended as well, and Martin was allegedly attacked while on a houseboat. He was taken into FBI protective custody, where reports showed he became heavily intoxicated before he killed two agents and fled to the farmhouse.

To Simms, the pieces all fit together perfectly. He was the orphaned Iraqi war veteran suffering from PTSD. He was highly trained through his time in the military, working at a gun store, and his year with a military contractor out of Tampa. His file simply screamed domestic terrorist, and it both thrilled and terrified Simms that he was chasing someone so dangerous. *Cal Martin would be his ticket to a supervisory position.*

A knock on the door startled Simms out of his fantasy. "Come in," he said as he closed Martin's file and pushed it off to the side of the small desk. A younger agent carefully opened the door, barely peeking his head in. His dark, thinning hair contrasted with his ultra-tan complexion.

"Hey, sir, there's someone here I think you need to talk to," he said. It was Special Agent Brett Venable, the liaison Simms had been given for their time in the area.

"Who is it?" Simms asked.

"Some local Sheriff," Venable replied as he opened the door further.

Simms immediately got up and walked out with Venable. He had only been settled in his temporary office for thirty minutes, but he was ready to start pursuing leads. *Every second that ticked by only gave Martin more of an advantage.*

"He said he knows where our suspect is, so I thought you might want to talk to him yourself," Venable said as the two walked down the narrow hallway. Venable was significantly more muscular than the tall, slender Simms, who was wearing a blue long sleeve button down shirt and black slacks.

"Who is he?" Simms asked, increasing the pace.

Venable pulled out a piece of paper and struggled trying to read his own handwriting. "Sheriff Thibodaux of Point... Co... Coup... Coupee Parish," he replied.

Simms pushed the younger agent aside and opened the door to the conference room, where the old Sheriff was sitting with his arms folded. He was wearing a polo shirt and khaki pants and his handgun was holstered at his side.

"Sheriff," Simms said, holding out his slender hand. Thibodaux grabbed his hand, nearly crushing every frail bone with his gorilla grip. "Thank you for coming out," Simms said, trying not to show the pain.

"It's not a problem, Agent..." Thibodaux said, trailing off. He had an accent that was hard for Simms to place. It was a mix of a southern drawl with what sounded slightly French to Simms. He had never spent any time in Louisiana, so he guessed that it was a local accent.

"Special Agent Carl Simms and I'm the lead agent on this case," Simms said as the two sat down with Thibodaux at the head of the conference table. Venable took his place across from Simms and prepared to take notes.

"Ok, Carl," Thibodaux responded.

"So you've seen this man?" Venable asked, pulling out a file photo of Martin from his time in custody.

"No," Thibodaux responded.

"Then why are you here?" Simms asked impatiently as he shot Venable a look of contempt. He did not have time to be wasting with local Podunk sheriffs while Martin was at large.

"Well, Carl," Thibodaux replied, ignoring Simms's rudeness. "I'm here because I know where your suspect is."

Thibodaux pulled out a piece of paper and pushed it to Simms. On it, an address was written. "He's staying here," Thibodaux added.

"Charles Jennings?" Simms asked as he picked up the paper.

"Very good, Carl. How did you know?"

"I read Martin's file," Simms responded smugly. "So, tell me, Sheriff, how do you know he's here?"

Thibodaux sat back in the chair and folded his arms. "I have coffee with Mr. Jennings every Thursday at his house. He and I have been friends for many years. This morning, I observed a vehicle matching the description on the BOLO put out to local law enforcement. The plates were missing, but I wrote down the VIN and ran it through NCIC."

"And you're just now telling us this information?" Simms asked as he did his best to mask his building anger with the slow-talking Sheriff. "Why didn't you arrest Jennings?"

"Our jail is full right now," Thibodaux responded casually. "And I don't think Charlie knows anything about what's going on. He's kind of, off the grid, I guess you could say."

"So why didn't you go back with your deputies and arrest him?" Simms asked through his clenched teeth.

"Carl, I have four road deputies at any given time on patrol in my parish covering over five-hundred-fifty square miles," Thibodaux said, laughing off Simms's mounting frustration. "I don't have the manpower to try to take down a man that you listed as armed and extremely dangerous in your warrant."

Simms could feel the vein in his forehead throbbing as he considered the possibility that Martin had been within their reach and was back on the run.

"Besides, I figured you Fed boys would want to take the credit anyway," Thibodaux said with a wink.

"Thank you for your time, Sheriff," Simms said as he quickly exited the room. Venable shot out of his chair and hurried to try to catch up as Simms stormed out of the small conference room.

"Let's get a fixed wing asset up to do covert surveillance on that address," Simms ordered as his long, lanky legs propelled him down the hallway toward their makeshift operations center. "And tell HART to expect a no-knock warrant tonight if we can verify he's still there."

"Copy that, sir," Venable responded as he struggled to keep pace.

CHAPTER NINE

South Tampa, FL
1437 Local Time

Decker cleared the exit to MacDill Air Force Base and headed north on South Dale Mabry Highway. She was still rattled from her exchange with Steele. He had gotten the best of her, and she hated him for it. It was unacceptable for an experienced agent, much less a former lawyer.

She drove north through light traffic, eyeing the thick brown file on the passenger seat as if it were at risk of getting up and walking off. She was still surprised that Steele had given it up so easily, but for now, it was the best lead she had. She thought that looking into Martin's past and figuring out why this was all happening was the best way to understand where he might go next and how she could save him. Simms and his entourage could worry about chasing their tails while she did the real police work.

Decker couldn't take the suspense anymore as she pulled into the nearby parking lot of a chain hardware store. She backed into a remote spot in the mostly empty lot and picked up the file.

Decker pulled out her legal pad and pen to take notes as she opened the first section of the folder. It contained basic information for Cal — emergency contact information, military service history, and resume. The service history and resume were as she had expected. She knew everything about Cal's record from her previous investigation. There were two contacts in the emergency contact information section. One was Marcus Anderson and the other Charles Jennings. She wrote his name, phone number, and address down on her legal pad before continuing to flip through the pages.

The second section was the questionnaire he had filled out to gain his security clearance. The thick document contained all of the addresses, friends, family, jobs, and foreign travel Martin had done over the last ten years. Decker felt sad for Cal as she thumbed through the next of kin. Both parents were listed as deceased, as well as a younger brother. She could see why he had become so attached to Marcus and Carpenter. They were the closest to family he had in his young age.

She flipped to the next tab with an abbreviated medical history. From what she could gather, he was a perfectly healthy 6'1", 193 pound, brown haired, blue-eyed thirty-four year old male. She thumbed past the medical history to the psych evaluation. As part of his pre-employment screening, the company had done a comprehensive assessment of Cal Martin's psychological well-being and fitness for duty.

To: Charles Steele
From: Dr. Doug D. Bennett, Ph. D.
Re: Pilot Applicant Calvin Martin
Classification: U/FOUO

    Profile is based on standard psychodiagnostic tests and face-to-face interview in accordance with company mandates.
    Subject Calvin Martin presents as a healthy 34yo white male. Physically unremarkable, typical outward fitness level for a military fighter pilot. Appropriately alert and engaged, bordering on high-strung. Analysis follows:
    Martin can be broadly characterized as intelligent, driven, and moderately authoritarian, with an internal locus of control and powerful but partially conflicted just-world beliefs. He is aggressive and impulsive; characteristics appropriate to his vocation, but honed to an especially fine and perhaps brittle edge by the circumstances of his adolescence. As is often true of fighter pilots, while generally impulsive and independent, his level of compulsiveness for what he considers important details is at the very high end of the normal range.
    Martin is a somewhat guarded individual. His attitude throughout the examination was cooperative, but it was clear that he considered the process as a necessary, but not desirable element of the checklist toward continuing to do something he loves. His "buy-in" to the validity of the process and its goals was clearly not strong.
    The early and unexpected death of his parents when he was thirteen years old is a clear and unsurprising landmark in Martin's personality development. As a result, he was raised from puberty through adolescence by an adult male who fits a military/survivalist archetype.
    Martin believes in his own ability to plan and control many aspects of his life, and has a

need to associate such planning and control with positive outcomes. However, he is conflicted on this dimension. His parents' deaths and the recent death of his fiancé' have forced him to the unsettling-for-him recognition that bad things can happen to good people.

Martin believes that success and respect can and should be earned. He strives toward both, and holds a very high standard for those who earn his respect. This set of characteristics plays into his attitude toward authority and relationship with authority figures (see below). Martin's sense of personal achievement on various dimensions is somewhat inhibited by the fact that Charles Jennings was ultimately only a stand-in for Martin's biological parents, whose approval he can never gain as an adult – indeed he has an idealized concept of his parents' qualities and their plans for him before they died.

It is my opinion that his aggression and impulsiveness stem from a related need to constantly prove himself, in line with this idealized concept of his parents' vision of him as an adult, and Charles Jennings's bigger-than-life archetype. The positive result of this is Martin's likely very powerful reaction to adversity. He will not be easily defeated by circumstance, and will remain driven, and mission oriented in dire situations. The negative result is that he may escalate threatening situations unnecessarily, and in some circumstances may over-estimate his own ability to respond to same.

Given the above elements, it is expected that Martin will be highly loyal to individual causes or agencies that meet his standards. This loyalty will extend to strong leaders or agents of authority who earn his respect. However – and this is a substantial caveat, he can be expected to react very poorly to those who have not in his mind earned their authority. Authorities who do not meet his standard may be at best covertly ridiculed by Martin, and their command of him will be negatively affected. Overt rebellion is not unlikely under worst-case circumstances. His reaction to authority should also be considered in the context of his internal locus of control, aggression and impulsiveness. Martin will often think he can solve problems better than those whose command he is under.

In my opinion, Martin is fit for duty based on this evaluation. He should be monitored closely, however, and his command staff should be aware of relevant aspects of his profile and past.

A copy of this report will be filed in Martin's training jacket.

Nothing further.

Decker nodded and smirked as she finished reading the psychiatric evaluation. It was exactly what she had figured out herself in working with him. She had seen him disregard his own personal safety and freedom to try to save the woman he loved. She had seen him as hard headed and determined while refusing to yield in principle. It was a quality that she found highly attractive.

Decker flipped to the next tab. There was an envelope attached to the inside flap with an address on it. She opened the envelope, revealing a metal key and a piece of paper with a series of four numbers followed by the pound sign. She plugged the address into her phone and realized it was a self-storage location just a mile north of her on the highway she had been on earlier.

Decker flipped to the final tab of the brown folder. It listed all of the training Martin had undergone with Dynamic Aviation Consulting Group along with the grades he received. Decker was not surprised that he scored high marks in hand-to-hand combat and marksmanship. She knew he was a black belt in the Israeli Survival Krav Maga system, and he had also worked in a gun store with its own shoot house and simunitions for years.

All of Martin's scores seemed to indicate that he was doing well in his new career. Instructors at every level praised his attention to detail, positive attitude, and how quickly he learned new concepts. It didn't make sense to Decker that he would have made the mistake of running out of fuel in an aircraft, given the grade sheets she saw.

But Decker realized that probably wasn't what actually happened. Steele had let it slip in their conversation. *Shot down.* That was why he said Martin should fly drones instead. *Had he been shot down?* Decker decided it really didn't matter at this point. Someone had been behind the assassination attempts in South Florida, and she was determined to find out who. She wasn't sure if Steele was behind it all as Cal had once suggested, but it was quite clear he was hiding something.

Decker put her Chevy Malibu in gear and pulled out onto the highway toward the self-storage location. As she pulled out, the glimmer of another car caught her attention in her rear view mirror. As she continued northbound, she realized it was a white SUV. She remembered seeing a similar vehicle in the parking lot of the Dynamic Consulting Group building.

Reaching back into her training, Decker decided to attempt a Surveillance Detection Route to prove to herself whether her newfound paranoia was justified. She had spent plenty of time in her career following other vehicles, but she hadn't executed a true SDR since training. In the field, usually only the undercover agents had to worry about being followed.

Decker turned off the main highway onto a side street, watching the SUV behind her several car lengths back. Without waiting for her pursuers, she made her first right and ducked into a subdivision and stopped at a stop sign before turning left. As she continued eastbound, she saw the white SUV roll through the stop sign and take a left behind her several hundred feet back. *That son of a bitch sent them to follow me,* Decker thought.

Decker continued eastbound until she reached South MacDill Avenue. She took a left and accelerated, leaving the SUV behind as she attempted to lose them. She continued north, putting distance between herself and the SUV until reaching Gandy Boulevard, where she made another left and floored it once again.

She could see the onramp to the expressway a quarter mile ahead. She kept her speed up, looking back to check the status of the SUV trying to follow her.

Decker felt the impact before she heard it. The crushing blow came from her right side, knocking her head into the window next to her before the airbags deployed and knocked the wind out of her. The world seemed to stand still as she heard the glass breaking and screeching as the four door sedan skidded into the opposite direction curb.

The world had gone dark for Decker, but she could still hear voices. She couldn't quite make out what they were saying, but it sounded like men yelling. She heard gunshots as she drifted in and out of consciousness.

Moments later, she felt the door being pulled open, causing her to hang limply against the seatbelt. She tried to move, but her dreamlike state wouldn't allow her. She tried to force her eyes open, looking up to see a bearded man standing over her.

"You're coming with me," the man said.

And then Decker faded into unconsciousness.

CHAPTER TEN

Glynn, LA
0355 Local Time

Special0355L

Special Agent Simms stared intently at the screen of the Toughbook laptop as he sat in the back of the unmarked Tahoe. He was watching the video downlink feed from the sensors of the Pilatus PC-12 surveillance aircraft orbiting high above.

The black and white infrared image showed the small cabin surrounded by thick vegetation and trees. A large pickup truck was parked in front of the cabin as it had been since the first aircraft had picked up surveillance the day prior. There was only one road in or out of the cabin, and as far as they could tell, no one had traveled it in the last twelve hours. If Cal Martin were ever there, he was still there.

The team had briefed the mission just after 2 a.m. Simms had been able to go back to his hotel room after dinner to get just four hours of sleep before heading back in to prepare for the takedown and arrest of Cal Martin. He had changed out of his typical suit and tie in favor of tactical pants and polo shirt.

Simms watched as the sensor operator in the aircraft slewed the pod around the house. He could make out the white hotspots and IR strobes of the three man teams that had surrounded the cabin under the cover of the woods. The teams already on the ground were all FBI Hostage Rescue Team operators. Simms had called in the heavy artillery to ensure another Redlands disaster didn't occur. His SUV was parked behind two Bearcat armored vehicles, each with six man teams from various SWAT and EOD members from local and federal agencies. Behind his vehicle, another Tahoe with bomb sniffing K-9s was parked waiting for their convoy to roll out. All teams appeared to be in position and ready to move.

"You guys ready?" Simms asked, looking up from the screen. Agent Venable was driving with a detective from the Louisiana State Police riding shotgun. The two looked back at Simms and each gave him a thumbs up.

"All players, Leroy Jenkins," Simms said, using the code word he had come up with to indicate the start of the mission. As an avid online gamer in his younger years, Simms had been especially proud of himself in his creation of the code words for the night's mission.

The two Bearcats in front of the convoy lumbered forward toward the entry to the house. They were simply support for the other three teams. The timing was designed to work out that the support vehicles would arrive just as the teams on foot cleared the house. The PC-12 would use its FLIR pod to scan for any attempts by Martin to escape into the woods.

"Charlie Three, lights out," one of the HRT members announced over the tactical frequency, indicating that power had been cut to the cabin.

As the convoy sped down the long gravel and dirt road, Simms watched the three teams close in on the cabin. He knew they were all wearing Night Vision Goggles, giving them a total advantage as they approached stealthily.

They passed the open gate and cattle guard as they neared the last quarter mile of the dirt road. Their initial surveillance imagery had shown it to be closed, and Simms had briefed that the Bearcat would just ram through earlier that evening. He wondered to himself if he had missed it or if the gate had intentionally been left open.

The tactical frequency was quiet as the convoy continued to lumber down the dark road. The drivers of the convoy were all wearing Night Vision Goggles as their vehicles remained blacked out. Simms tried to focus on keeping up with the tactical situation from the airborne feed as he bounced around the inside of the Tahoe. The lack of visual cues and claustrophobia from not being able to see outside made motion sickness a real threat for Simms. He tried to concentrate.

The teams split up to surround the large cabin. Simms could see two IR strobes blinking at each corner of the cabin's four corners as the remaining five operators stacked up on the front door. Simms watched as they kicked the door in and the IR strobes disappeared into the large cabin. The two Bearcat vehicles in front of the convoy reached the opening near Martin's truck and peeled off in opposite directions as the heavily armed SWAT and EOD members dismounted to set up a perimeter. Simms felt the SUV he was in skid to a stop as he held his breath waiting for word from the HRT teams.

"Alpha One has one in custody, but the princess is in another castle," the HRT leader said over the radio.

"Say again?" Simms snapped as he slammed the Toughbook shut and exited the Tahoe. *How could they already know Martin was gone?*

"One in custody, one only," the team leader repeated.

"Send in the dog," Simms ordered.

One cue, the Bearcats and SUVs shined their floodlights on the cabin, creating near daylight conditions in the dark forest. A K-9 with his handler emerged from the SUV behind Simms and headed toward the building as the HRT team emerged from the cabin nearly carrying a much smaller man out by his arms.

They walked him to the back of the Bearcat to the left of Simms and searched him. Satisfied he had no weapons, they left him sitting under heavy guard.

"What's your name?" Simms demanded as he walked up to the man sitting Indian-style on the ground.

"These fucking things are too tight," the man responded.

"Charles Jennings?" Simms asked, shifting under the weight of his body armor. "Are you Charles Jennings?"

"Who's asking?" Bear responded. "You'd better have a warrant."

Simms pulled a warrant from his vest and held it up in the air. "We have a warrant, and you are currently harboring a fugitive from justice, Mr. Jennings," Simms said as he squatted down over the defiant older man.

"Who?" Bear asked. "I just got up to take a piss and y'all sent in a SWAT team."

"Mr. Jennings—"

"This is a police state!" Bear interrupted. "Look at all this equipment! Why do you need tanks and bazookas? Whatever happened to the Fourth Amendment?"

"Mr. Jennings, if you don't cooperate, I will arrest you for harboring a fugitive from justice, do you understand what that means?" Simms asked.

"Yeah, you'll violate more of my rights," Bear shot back. "If I'm not under arrest, can you take these fucking torture bracelets off me?"

Simms stood and turned to Venable, who was standing a few feet behind him. "Uncuff him," Simms ordered.

"Sir?" Venable asked.

"Stand him up and get him out of those cuffs," Simms said in a low voice. "He won't cooperate if we don't."

Venable nodded and helped the small-statured man stand before removing the handcuffs. Bear rubbed his wrists where the cuffs had dug into his skin.

"Now will you talk to us, Mr. Jennings?" Simms asked with a forced smile.

"About what? Why you feel the need to abuse an old man with a bad prostate?"

"Cal Martin," Simms replied. "We know he was here."

"Do you know what it's like to have a man point a gun at you while you're trying to keep a steady flow in the middle of the night?" Bear asked, blowing off the questioning. "Let's just say I shouldn't have trusted that fart."

An EOD technician walked out as Simms contemplated putting Jennings back in handcuffs. "All clear, sir," she said as she approached with the K-9.

"Search every inch of that house," Simms said to Venable. Venable nodded and took off at a jog toward the house as Simms turned his attention back to Jennings.

"Y'all better not break anything!" Bear yelled at the departing agent. "I know this government is too broke to pay me back."

"Mr. Jennings, do you think this is a game?" Simms asked. "Do you have any idea what Cal Martin did?"

"Well, the way you guys are acting, did *he* kill Jimmy Hoffa?" Bear asked with a feigned look of shock.

"He killed three federal agents and six SWAT officers," Simms said. "Good men who served their country. Men with families."

"I'm sorry for their loss," Bear replied solemnly.

"Cal Martin is a dangerous man, Mr. Jennings, and every minute of our time you waste increases the potential that someone else won't be able to go home to their family," said Simms.

"Cal is not a criminal," Bear said.

"That is for the court system to figure out," Simms replied. "Not you."

"I haven't seen him," Bear said defiantly.

"His truck is here, Mr. Jennings. We have a witness that places him here earlier this morning," Simms said. His patience was beginning to wear thin with the old man.

Simms waited as the old man stood staring at him. "Last chance, Mr. Jennings."

"I haven't seen him," Bear replied flatly.

"Turn around and put your hands behind your back," Simms said, pulling his handcuffs from the pouch on his belt. "You're under arrest."

"Just don't taze me, bro," Bear replied as he turned around holding his wrists together behind his back.

CHAPTER ELEVEN

Red Stick Motel
Baker, LA
0755 Local Time

Walking out from his motel room into the empty parking lot, he had to laugh as he hit the unlock button on the key fob. For a man on the run, he couldn't imagine a more conspicuous car than a 2002 35th Anniversary Edition Camaro SS with bright white stripes and a candy apple red paint job.

But that had been Bear's argument. "Hiding in plain sight," he called it. No one would expect Spectre to be cruising around in a brightly colored sports car. The authorities would be looking for Spectre's truck, and if he had to get away, the twelve-second-quarter-mile-capable hot rod would give his pursuers a serious run for their money.

After he and Bear had stripped as much data as possible from the laptop and done all the follow up research they cared to do, Spectre and Zeus had made the four mile hike to Bear's cousin's house. They were the nearest neighbors to the isolated cabin, and Spectre bought their prized hot rod off them with a handful of cash from the bag he carried. He had packed only the essentials – cash, weapons, and ammo. Everything else, he could buy along the way. With another couple of hundreds thrown in for good measure, the aging couple even agreed to watch Zeus for him.

Spectre could tell they knew something nefarious was afoot, but Bear assured him that the couple were equally downtrodden by the man and could be trusted as the family that they were. Spectre felt like he was putting a lot of trust in people he didn't know lately, and he didn't like it.

But surprisingly, Sheriff Thibodaux had also come through for them. Spectre hated the idea of putting Bear at risk, but Thibodaux had warned Bear that the FBI was hot on Spectre's trail. He didn't have long to make his escape. It had been Bear's idea to have Sheriff Thibodaux throw out the tip to the feds to give Spectre enough time to get away and find the people behind this nightmare.

Settling into the cockpit of his new ride, Spectre pulled out a piece of paper from his blue jean pockets. On it, he had scribbled the address and turn-by-turn directions for his first stop. He took a minute to memorize the instructions and then fired up the Camaro's V8 engine. Spectre pulled out of the narrow parking lot of the run down motel and headed south toward Highway 61. From there, he headed south toward downtown Baton Rouge.

Once off the freeway, Spectre took the side streets to his first destination. Spectre thought traffic seemed relatively light for a Friday morning, but it had been years since he had roamed the streets of Baton Rouge as a college student. He navigated around the various pedestrians and busses and found the downtown address he was looking for off Main Street.

After confirming the address, Spectre found a parking spot a block away and inventoried his gear. He pulled out his Glock 17 and tucked it away in his In-Waistband-Holster near the small of his back and covered it with the t-shirt he was wearing. He pulled a black baseball cap out of his bag and pulled it down low over his face. He studied the information he had written one more time and took off toward the downtown office building.

Approaching the two-story rectangular building, Spectre's head was on a swivel. The sidewalks were busy with people in suits leaving and entering the nearby bakery and coffee shops. Spectre continuously scanned each person's hands and eyes, alert for any potential threats as he made his way to the building.

Spectre pushed open the glass door marked "CAJUN OIL AND GAS" and walked in. The building's modest exterior belied its lavish interior. The locally owned and operated oil and natural gas exploration company had spared no expense in furnishing their corporate headquarters.

The attractive young brunette smiled as Spectre walked up to the large marble reception desk in the center of the lobby. "How may I help you today?" she asked.

"I'm here to see Mr. Tom Jane," Spectre replied, returning her smile.

"Do you have an appointment, sir?" the receptionist asked as she picked up the phone.

"I'm sorry," Spectre said. "I don't."

"What's your name, please?"

"David Hernandez," Spectre said using the alias he had found in the laptop. After a tedious search and translation of the files on Victor's laptop, Bear and Spectre determined that David Hernandez was one of the many aliases Victor used as a spy.

"One moment, please," she replied as she spoke to Tom Jane's secretary. He was the president and CEO of the growing oil and gas exploration company. In researching the Hua Xia Holding Company, Spectre and Bear had found that the company owned a significant interest in Cajun Oil and Gas, LLC. Spectre had also found contracts signed by Tom Jane on Victor's laptop for oil platforms off the coast of Cuba. Although the Hua Xia Holdings Company appeared to be a ghost entity, Cajun Oil and Gas seemed to be a natural starting place for Spectre.

"His secretary said to send you up," the receptionist said as she hung up the phone. "His office is upstairs."

"Upstairs and then which direction?" Spectre asked.

The receptionist chuckled softly. "It's the entire second floor."

"Ok then," Spectre replied. "Thanks for your help."

Spectre walked up the wooden staircase behind the reception desk. He checked his shirt as he ascended the creaking stairs, careful to ensure that his gun was not printing or showing. When he rounded the second flight, he found a door with Tom Jane's name prominently displayed.

"Mr. Jane asked that you have a seat in his office," the older woman said as Spectre walked in. "He should be back any minute now."

Spectre nodded graciously as he continued past the woman into the expansive office. The lavish accommodations Spectre had seen downstairs were eclipsed by the office. It was obvious to Spectre that the oil business had done well by Mr. Jane, providing him with the funds to have his own minibar, putting green, and oversized LED televisions. The huge office could have easily been a nice bachelor pad. Spectre guessed it was at least two thousand square feet.

Spectre wandered around the huge office, taking it all in. The glass windows overlooked the street he had entered from on one side, and the Mississippi River on the other. The large executive desk was made of a rich mahogany with a leather couch on one wall and leather chairs on either side of the desk. Spectre took a seat.

As he waited for Jane, he noticed the engineering degree from LSU and MBA from Tulane University on the walls. There were pictures of a younger woman in a flight suit along the cherry bookcases. Spectre leaned in, noticing that she was an F/A-18 pilot standing next to a Hornet on the deck of an aircraft carrier in the picture. Spectre was impressed.

"You're not David Hernandez," a gruff voice from behind Spectre said, startling him from his daydreaming. Spectre shot up from the chair as he spun around. A man in a dark blazer and gray slacks stood a few feet from him. He appeared to be in his early forties – too young to be Jane.

"And you're not Tom Jane," Spectre replied, keeping his right hand near his back.

"Jack Robertson, head of security," the man replied. He appeared to be in good shape to Spectre – probably former military. His haircut was high and tight. He scowled at Spectre. "Now who are you?"

"I'm here to see Mr. Jane," Spectre said. "Will he be here soon?"

"I won't ask again," Robertson growled. "Who are you and what are you doing here?"

"I'm here to see Mr. Jane," Spectre said, holding up both hands. He was too close to the security chief to be able to draw and shoot in time. As he sized up the situation, he realized that he'd have to meet any attacks with hand to hand techniques. "I don't want any trouble."

"Using that name you do," the man said. Spectre watched as his right arm pulled out a collapsible baton and flicked it open. He held it low and to his side.

"You don't want to do that," Spectre warned.

"Last chance to walk out of here under your own power," Robertson said.

"That's not very nice," Spectre said. "Do you treat all your guests this way?"

The man wound up with the 24-inch baton in his hand and lunged at Spectre. Having anticipated the movement, Spectre stepped in, crossing both arms above his head to intercept the blow at the man's wrist. Using the man's momentum, Spectre turned while redirecting Robertson. He grabbed the man's right wrist with his right arm and hyper extended it across his body while using his left to create a choke hold. After hearing the audible pop of Robertson's right elbow dislocating and the thud of the baton falling to the floor, he kicked out the man's right knee while still choking him with Robertson's head twisted to the left.

"I asked you nicely," Spectre said as the man choked and gasped. Spectre pulled a handgun from the belt holster hidden by the man's jacket and tossed it on a nearby couch.

"Fuck you!" he wheezed.

"Not today," Spectre said before slamming Robertson's head into the mahogany desk.

As Robertson went limp, Spectre picked up the baton on the ground and collapsed it against his thigh. He stuffed it in his back pocket and hurried to the door to lock it. Robertson groaned on the floor as Spectre dragged him to the nearby leather chair. He pulled the rope from the nearby curtains to secure his arms to the arms of the chair.

"You weren't on my radar, but now that we're here, let's chat," Spectre said as Robertson groaned.

"Come on, it's not that bad," Spectre said, slapping Robertson's face. "You should see what the Syrians do to their guests."

"Fuck off," Robertson said.

Spectre reached into his back pocket and flicked open the baton. "I believe you said something about a permanent limp earlier. If I were you, I'd take your own advice."

"Who the fuck are you?" Robertson asked as his head bobbed from side to side.

"I ask the questions," Spectre said as he sent the baton crashing into Robertson's kneecap. Spectre put his hand over the man's mouth to muffle the scream as he thrashed.

"Can we please have an adult conversation now?" Spectre asked as the man stopped moving and Spectre slowly removed his hand.

"What do you want?" Robertson asked as he tried to catch his breath.

"Where is Mr. Jane?" Spectre asked.

"He plays golf on Friday mornings," Robertson replied. "He won't be in until noon."

"How do you know David Hernandez?" Spectre asked as he squatted down in front of the bleeding man.

"Fuck you," Robertson shot back.

Spectre pulled out the Glock 17 from its holster as he set the baton down on the desk behind him. "You look like a pretty tough guy, Jack. Iraq? Afghanistan?"

"I used to be a State Trooper," Robertson said proudly.

"Ah, one of those," Spectre smiled as he held up the Glock. "Well, let me ask you, Trooper, have you ever dealt with someone who has nothing to lose?"

Robertson's eyes widened with fear as he recognized the look in Spectre's eyes. As Spectre leveled the Glock at Robertson's forehead, he realized he was less than a five and a half pound trigger pull away from losing everything.

"Ok!" Robertson relented. "He was a business associate of Mr. Jane."

"Go on," Spectre said as he leaned back against the desk and held the gun against his lap.

"He was our point of contact to set up exploratory drilling off Northern Cuba," Robertson said. "He helped us work the deal to make sure we used less than ten percent American parts to avoid sanctions."

"This company? Cajun Oil and Gas?" Spectre asked impatiently.

Robertson shook his head no. "Chinese National Oil," he replied.

"How?"

"We set them up with all the equipment and some of the hands," Robertson replied. "I just handled security. I swear!"

"Where did the money go?"

Robertson shook his head as the sweat poured from his forehead.

"Where did it go?" Spectre barked as he held up the Glock again.

"Hua Xia Holdings! My God! I have a family!" Robertson cried.

"And they funnel the money back into this company as investors?" Spectre asked, lowering the weapon.

Robertson nodded slowly.

"Is that who Jun Zhang works for?" Spectre asked. Although the illegal workings of an American oil company were fascinating and decidedly newsworthy, none of it really mattered to Spectre. He wanted to find the people responsible for tearing his life apart and killing his friends, not uncover another international conspiracy.

"Who?" Robertson asked. He started to tremble as he realized that the response would not work with Spectre. "I swear I don't know who you're talking about! We always worked with a guy named Chang! Liu Chang!"

"So you've never heard of Jun Zhang?" Spectre asked.

"No, please," Robertson pleaded, "please don't kill me."

"Who does Chang work for?"

"Hua Xia," Robertson mumbled.

"Where can I find him?" Spectre asked.

"He has an office in New Orleans," Robertson said. His voice was shaking as he looked away.

"Where?" Spectre barked.

"He'll kill me if he finds out," Robertson said. His voice wavered as he started to cry. "He'll kill my family."

"Tell me," Spectre demanded. "You don't need to worry about him right now."

"It's off Poydras Street, I'll give you the address," Robertson reluctantly replied.

CHAPTER TWELVE

Freedom Star Deepwater Oil and Gas Platform
Gulf of Mexico
1015 Local Time

Foxworthy stared listlessly out the cockpit of the Bell 406 LongRanger helicopter as it raced across the calm, glass-like ocean. Foxworthy hated flying helicopters ever since his training in the "helo dunker" water survival course. The helicopter's natural tendency to flip onto its back after splashdown required specialized training in underwater egress and Foxworthy was not a fan. If available, he had always chosen to sit up front with the pilot where he knew he could get out quickly without having to follow a reference point. He refused to relive the nightmare of nearly getting lost while trying to get out during training.

As the Freedom Star, a large semi-submersible, self-propelled oil drilling platform, came into view, Foxworthy wondered if Mary had made it on board yet. She had called in late the night prior after dinner with her father saying she would be hitching a ride on one of his helicopters. Although it looked better for his team of three to arrive at the same time, Foxworthy couldn't argue with her methods. The Freedom Star was operated by her father's company and she had been instrumental in getting them the lucrative contract to give Crew Resource Management and Leadership training for all of his company's platforms.

The pilot slowed the helicopter and entered a hover as it reached the landing platform on the southeast corner of the rig. With no wind, the pilot effortlessly set the helicopter down as the Helicopter Landing Officer wearing a red hard hat jogged up and opened the side door. Foxworthy and Tom "Crash" Packard exited the helicopter each carrying a backpack, ducking their heads until they cleared the spinning rotor blades.

The Helicopter Landing Officer offered them each a white hard hat and motioned for them to follow him down a set of stairs and into a small briefing room.

"I'll take your life vests," he said, pointing at the horse-collar style life preservers the two were wearing. The two men handed them to the crusty Helicopter Landing Officer, who disappeared, closing the door behind him.

"Where's Mary Jane?" Crash asked. He was in his late forties with salt and pepper hair and at least a head shorter than Foxworthy.

"She said she'd meet us here," Foxworthy said as he leaned against the chair.

"Must be nice to have connections," Crash replied with a crooked grin.

"Start getting us work and you can show up whenever you want as well," Foxworthy replied.

They were interrupted by a younger man walking in. He walked in and put the binder he was carrying on the podium in the corner of the room. Finding the remote to the projector, he hit the power button and logged onto the computer to start his presentation.

"I'm Richard Sharpe, and I'm the Safety Tech for Cajun Oil and Gas here on the Freedom Star," he said. He appeared to be in his mid-twenties to Foxworthy – young for a man in this line of work.

"You guys are from Mach Two Consulting, right?" he asked as Foxworthy and Crash took seats at the front of the small room.

"I'm Jeff Vaughan and this is Tom Packard," Foxworthy replied. "Thank you for having us."

"Mr. Jane's daughter is with you as well, is that correct?" Sharpe asked.

"Yes," Foxworthy replied. "And do you know where she is?"

"She's already settled into her room," Sharpe replied as he pulled open his presentation. "She'll meet you in the main briefing room on the third deck when we finish with your safety briefing and walk around."

"Ok, let's get started," Sharpe said as he pulled up a picture of the Freedom Star. "Welcome to West Delta 121 G, also known as the Freedom Star. As you know, the Freedom Star is operated by Cajun Oil and Gas out of Baton Rouge under lease by Standard Petroleum and Trust. This is currently the third largest semi-submersible drilling platform in the Gulf of Mexico, producing nearly one hundred thousand barrels of crude oil per day."

Foxworthy and Crash listened intently as Sharpe continued the briefing, going over the layout of the platform and its various safety procedures. It was the standard safety run-down they had heard on every platform they had been on – a requirement for every first-time visitor to the platforms.

"Gentlemen, if there are no questions, I'll take you on the tour and you can meet with the Operations Team Leader," Sharpe said as he logged off the computer.

Foxworthy and Crash looked at each other and then shook their heads. "Let's begin the tour," Sharpe said as the two men grabbed their bags and stood to follow.

Sharpe led them out of the small briefing room and down the narrow passageway. The tall Foxworthy had to duck as they made their way back out onto the outer perimeter walkway. A light sea breeze had picked up, making it somewhat pleasant for midday in the middle of August.

Sharpe showed them the various locations that they would be working and familiarized them with the safety protocols at each area. As Crew Resource Management consultants, they would be spending the next three days doing both classroom and hands on instruction with the crew of the Freedom Star. Being able to navigate safely and efficiently around the platform was essential to their success.

After completing the tour, he showed them to their shared room with two sets of bunk beds. They dropped off their bags on their bunks and followed Sharpe to the Operations Team Leader's office. The OTL was responsible for the daily operations and decision making for the Freedom Star.

Sharpe knocked on the door softly and pushed it open. "Hey boss, the other two from Mach Two Consulting are here," he said. Foxworthy noticed the redhead sitting in the chair across from the OTL as the graybeard stood to greet them.

"Mark Miller, nice to meet you," the Team Leader said, extending his hand to Foxworthy. The three men exchanged pleasantries and Miller returned to his seat.

"Hey boss," Mary said, turning to Foxworthy and Crash. "Did y'all make it here ok?"

"So far, so good," Foxworthy replied as he and Crash took seats in the cramped office.

"I have your proposed schedule from Miss Jane," Miller said as he put on his eyeglasses. "Everything looks good to me. Mr. Sharpe will get you guys whatever you need while you're here, and please let me know if there's anything I can do for you."

"Thank you, Mr. Miller," Foxworthy said. "We're looking forward to working with your crew."

"If you'll excuse me," Miller said as he got up to walk out. "I have a production meeting in fifteen minutes. Please use my office as much as you need. Lunch should be starting in the galley in fifteen minutes if you're interested."

"Thank you, sir," Foxworthy said with a gracious smile. Miller left the small office and closed the door behind him. Mary pulled a laptop out of her bag on the floor to get started.

"What's his story?" Foxworthy asked after confirming the door was closed.

"Longtime friend of Papa Bear," Mary said. "He's been with the company since the early nineties."

"Anything I should know?" Foxworthy asked, pointing with his thumb toward the door.

"He likes me," Mary replied with an impish smile.

"And?" Crash interjected.

"And that's it. He's tough on his crew, but fair. Really nice guy," Mary said with a shrug.

"How does he feel about us being here?" Crash asked. It was always a delicate balance in their line of work. Some Team Leaders loved the idea of fighter pilots coming in to help minimize their risk and give their crew pointers on objective-oriented action. Others hated it and thought that it was just another ploy by the company's safety geek to cover their asses against lawsuits. Lack of cooperation could easily make the three-day stay extremely painful for their team.

"Like I said; he likes me," Mary replied. "I think we'll be fine."

"Ok," Foxworthy said, waving his hand. "But more importantly, what's up with that cryptic text message last night? How'd dinner with dad go?" Mary had sent him a text message just after midnight saying nothing more than, "I'll meet you there." Foxworthy's attempts to follow up had been met with silence.

Mary blushed. "Well," she said as she shifted uneasily in the chair. "We might've pushed it up a little too much last night."

"So?" Crash asked impatiently.

"So we decided to stay at Papa Bear's house instead of trying to drive home to New Orleans and Daddy said he'd fly me out on his chopper," Mary said.

"So it went well with your dad and the murse, I take it?" Foxworthy asked.

Mary punched Foxworthy in the shoulder, causing him to withdraw in pain. "How many times do I have to tell you to stop calling him that?"

"Guess we know who wears the pants in the family," Crash said from a safe distance. Mary shot him an angry redhead look that made him recoil slightly.

"Don't make me come over there," she warned.

"So did it?" Foxworthy asked, rubbing his shoulder.

"It went fine," Mary replied. "They like each other."

"Did you ask him about the Chinese oil rig?" Foxworthy asked.

"Jesus, Fox, are you still on that?" Crash asked, shaking his head. They had talked about it for the entire four hours from the time Foxworthy picked Crash up in New Orleans until they strapped into a helicopter in Houma. "I thought we decided it's best just to let it go?"

"No, you decided that," Foxworthy said. "I'm just curious. So what did he say?"

Mary frowned. "He was kind of weird about it."

"What do you mean?" Foxworthy asked.

"I don't know," Mary said, shaking her head. "I can't put my finger on it, but he just seemed to be avoiding the question. He, usually, tells me everything."

"What did he say?" Foxworthy pushed.

"He just kind of cut me off and said, 'I don't know anything about the Chinese.'"

"Ok, but isn't that what SSgt Crowe said during your debrief, Fox?" Crash asked. "What's the problem?"

"It's just the way he said it so abruptly," Mary replied." It bothered me."

"Did you ask him what he meant?"

"No," Mary said. "Before I could, he and Ryan started talking about golf and ordering shots."

"It went downhill from there," Mary added.

CHAPTER THIRTEEN

Tampa, FL

Decker's blue eyes fluttered open as the pain hit her. Her senses seemed to reboot slowly like an old computer. She was startled as she saw the large bearded man standing over her. She tried to retreat, only to realize that she was lying in her bed and her right arm had been immobilized in a sling wrapped around her body. She felt a tug on her left arm as she pulled against an IV.

"It's ok, relax," the man said as he gently pushed her back down. "You're ok."

"Who are you?" Decker shrieked. Her voice was hoarse. It hurt to talk. Her entire body was sore. The last thing she remembered was the impact and seeing a bearded man walking up to the car as she lay in a daze. She wondered if it was the same man.

"They call me Redman," the man said with a disarming smile. He was tall – at least six foot two. He was wearing and tan dry wick t-shirt that showed off his muscular physique. Decker felt his presence calming, although she was still in a panic trying to figure out where she was. "Your name is Michelle Decker, right?"

"Where am I?" Decker asked as she tried to piece it all together. "What am I doing here?"

"You're safe now," Redman replied. "Your shoulder was dislocated in the crash. We reset it, but it's probably going to hurt for a while. You took a pretty nasty hit in that little car of yours. We've had you on pain killers and sedatives to make you comfortable."

Decker took a pain inventory. Her shoulder was throbbing. Her entire chest was sore from the seatbelt. Her head felt bruised and swollen, and she felt like she was in a dreamlike trance. She couldn't tell if it were from the pain killers or from the impact.

"I'm going to let you get some rest," Redman said. "We can talk more when you feel better."

Without waiting for a response, the large man walked out of the tiny room and closed the door behind him. She heard what sounded like the twist of a lock as the door shut. Decker looked around the small room. It appeared to be a bedroom with bland walls. There was a night stand to her right and an IV pole with a bag of saline and a drip of some sort to her left. The only door was just past the foot of the bed.

Decker leaned over to look behind her. She groaned as the pain hit her. She wondered if she had also broken or bruised a few ribs in the car crash. There was a small window behind the night stand. It appeared that they were on the upper floor of a building, maybe second or third floor, Decker guessed.

She rolled onto her back to catch her breath as the pain intensified. She was already sore from the lack of sleep and fights in the days prior, but this was much worse. This was worse than anything she had felt before. She wondered how long she had been out.

Decker tried to place the man that had just left her bedside. She vaguely recognized him from the moments after the wreck, but she was almost sure she had seen him before. *But where?* Her mind drew a blank.

Yelling voices interrupted Decker's contemplative moments. She could hear men shouting beyond the doorway. *And running.* It sounded like someone had run down stairs. Moments later, there was a loud crash followed by gunfire. *Gunfire!* Decker's heart raced as she heard the steady pop of muffled gun shots. She rolled lazily and sat upright on the side of the bed as the IV tugged against her left arm. She winced as she held her left arm up high enough to grab with her immobile right hand. After a few unsuccessful tries, she grabbed the IV with her right hand and pulled, sending blood everywhere.

Decker pushed past the pain and stood. She rushed to a nearby window. As the sound of gunfire increased, she assessed her escape options. There was no fire escape. The closest method of escape was to jump from the window to the roof of a nearby townhome. With a fear of heights that had been made worse by a fight on the roof of the Biltmore Hotel, Decker hated that option.

The gunfire seemed to stop momentarily as Decker unlatched the window and tried to push up. *Stuck.* The only way out would be to break through it with her good hand.

Decker heard the door unlock as it flung open. Redman stumbled in with a gun in each hand. Startled, Decker turned and backed into the window. Redman approached her. He was bleeding from his head and left arm. He appeared to have been shot at least once, perhaps more.

"Here, take this," Redman said as he spun the handgun in his right hand around to Decker. "One in the chamber, seventeen in the mag."

Decker reluctantly took the gun with her left hand. She was predominantly right handed, but had some training from the Academy in shooting with her left as well.

"What's going on?" Decker asked as she looked over the bloody man.

"Can you shoot left handed?" Redman asked, ignoring her question.

Decker nodded as her adrenaline spiked.

"Good. Shoot anyone that comes through that door," Redman said as he turned and limped back toward the door. "Try to get out of here if you can."

"What about you?"

Redman smiled as the blood trickled from his forehead. "I live for this shit," he said as he exited the small room and closed the door behind him.

Decker went back to the closed window. She used the butt of the Glock to shatter it, giving her a path of escape. She assessed her options as the gunfire continued downstairs. It looked to be about a ten foot drop from where she was. *No way.* Just a few days prior, Decker had done the rooftop escape with two healthy arms and legs. She knew there would be no way she could stop herself from sliding off the second roof if she made the jump.

Decker went to the corner of the room where her IV was and tried to create a cover position. The gunfire stopped once again as she aimed the gun at the door. Seconds later, the door was kicked open, sending pieces of the wooden door frame in all directions.

Decker took aim and fire two shots, missing on the first, but hitting center of mass on the second as the first man wielding what appeared to be an MP-5 entered. Decker fired two more rounds at the falling man, hitting him once more as he fell forward.

Bullets peppered the bed and zipped over Decker's head as she ducked back down for cover. Another attacker was preparing entry through the same doorway. Decker waited patiently, hoping for the man to enter the doorway's "fatal funnel" so she could launch her counter attack. For now, it just seemed as though the man was blindly firing from outside the doorway.

When the gunshots stopped, Decker popped back up to return fire, ignoring the excruciating pain from the movement. She sent two rounds into the doorframe as the man peaked around the corner. A third bullet hit the man in the throat, causing him to drop his submachine gun as he stumbled past the doorway.

Decker waited for other attackers as she held her position. For the time being, she had a decent tactical advantage. She knew that she couldn't keep it up forever, though. Eventually, she would have to move forward.

Seconds felt like hours as she waited for another attempt to storm the bedroom. When none came, she stood gingerly. She struggled to hold the full-sized Glock up and ready with her left hand, but willed herself to do it anyway. *Hurt later,* she thought.

Decker stepped over the body of the first attacker as she made her way to the doorway. She cleared left and right, finding the body of the other attacker on the ground as she made her way to the stairs. The scene below was horrific. Bullets peppered the walls with broken glass and blood everywhere.

As Decker descended the stairs, she found Redman at lying at the base of the stairs. He had multiple gunshot wounds and was barely breathing. Decker continued down into the room lined with computers and desks. There were bodies everywhere. The men looked Asian to Decker, but there was another man that was dressed similar to Redman lying next to the door.

Decker moved as quickly as she could to him, but he had no pulse.

Decker frantically searched the downstairs area for a phone. When she found it, she dialed 911 and requested assistance. Not knowing her location, she asked the operator to trace it before leaving the line open and returning to Redman to render first aid.

"You have to get out of here," Redman gasped as he struggled to breathe.

"Help is on the way," Decker said, holding Redman's head up.

"They…" Redman said as he choked. "They'll kill you."

CHAPTER FOURTEEN

The ambulance had beaten the police to the scene by at least five minutes. Wasting no time, and taking Decker's word as an FBI Agent that the scene was secure and safe, they assessed the situation and called for additional units.

By the time the police arrived, it was just a crime scene. James Redman died shortly after warning Decker to flee. She had seriously considered heeding his advice, but as a law enforcement officer, she knew the right thing to do was to stay and help investigators as a witness. The case would require a significant investigation.

Decker surveyed the scene as the medics tended to her injuries and the police began to cordon off the crime scene. There were at least a dozen bodies in addition to the two bearded men. They were all wearing civilian clothes and appeared to be Asian with close-cropped haircuts. They appeared to be military of some sort. The submachine guns had been strewn about reinforced her theory. This had been a targeted operation. *But against whom?*

Decker still had no information about the men that had presumably come to her aid. They also appeared to be military types – Special Forces, probably. They had apparently made an attempt to save her life and protect her, at least Redman had. Even as he lay dying, he had tried to get her to save herself. *But why? What was he so afraid of?*

"Ma'am," the medic said, interrupting her train of thought. "We're going to need to transport you to the hospital now."

"Ok," Decker said meekly.

They moved the straps on the gurney and lowered it for her to sit on. "I can walk," Decker said, waving it off.

"Department policy," the medic responded. Decker reluctantly complied. Once on the gurney, the secured the straps and shoulder harness and extended the legs to wheel her out. They were stopped by a pair of men in suits just as they cleared the doorway. Decker realized they had been in a small townhome in a residential area as they made it out into the sidewalk in the front yard.

"Special Agent Decker?" one of the men said as he held up his credentials. "I'm Special Agent Kemp and this is Special Agent Cooper from the Tampa field office."

Decker was startled by the man's immediate knowledge of her identity. It was not unusual for the FBI to be called in on a scene of this magnitude, but it was usually after the local detectives went through it. And more disturbingly, she hadn't told anyone her name except the paramedics. She studied the man's credentials as he held them up in front of her.

"Michelle Decker, right?" the man asked again. "Miami Field Office?"

"I'm Michelle," Decker responded cautiously. The hair on the back of her neck was standing up. She wanted to flee, and the straps on the gurney and her general lack of mobility due to her injuries were making her claustrophobic.

"We've been looking for you since yesterday," Cooper responded. "Tampa PD called us when they found your Malibu and blood and bodies, but not you."

"Bodies?" Decker asked as she struggled to remember the accident.

"Two bodies, both males," the other agent responded. He was an attractive black man with a shaved head. His voice was almost soothing to Decker. "Like the ones in there," Kemp added.

Time was still distorted for Decker. She had no idea how long it had been since she had been on her way to the storage building. As the agents explained their presence, it started to make sense. Her claustrophobia and urge to run began to subside as she realized they were there with a legitimate purpose.

"Do you mind if I ride with you to the hospital?" Kemp asked with a disarming smile. "Agent Cooper will follow."

"Ok," Decker said.

The medics loaded her into the back of the yellow ambulance. Once she was secure and they hooked her up to the EKG, the paramedic started an IV.

"This vein is gone," the paramedic said, pointing at the dried blood where Decker had ripped out her IV. After a few seconds of searching, the paramedic found a new vein and inserted the needle with the IV line.

"This will help with the pain," he said as he inserted the needle into the line.

As the ambulance cleared the scene, Decker relaxed under the effects of the painkillers. The steady drone of the ambulance's diesel engine was almost soothing as she drifted in and out of sleep. She could barely make out the unmarked car following closely behind with Agent Cooper.

"We can talk more when you're feeling better," Agent Kemp said, sitting across from the paramedic.

Decker felt at ease as the ambulance continued on. Her body was relaxed, almost numb. Her mind was still racing one hundred miles per hour though. She desperately wanted to find out who the two men in the house were, and who they were fighting.

She felt a jolt as the ambulance seemed to turn down a rough road. She could hear gravel being kicked up in the wheel wells, but it didn't register. Her body was still numb, and her mind was focused on the men in the townhouse.

Decker felt the ambulance make a sharp turn and then come to a stop. Moments later, the cab of the ambulance was flooded with light as the doors flung open. She tried to open her eyes, but the bright lighting only made it harder. The world was a blur as they wheeled her out. Nothing registered.

"Michelle Decker," a male voice said as they wheeled her to a stop. Her eyelids were so heavy. She tried to force them open.

"Wake up, Michelle," the man repeated.

Decker tried to register what her eyes were seeing. A male figure was standing over her. Her vision was blurry. She tried to move, but couldn't. She felt paralyzed. As her eyes focused, she could barely make out a man with dark hair and a dark goatee. She couldn't place his accent. *Chinese maybe?*

He leaned over the gurney to within a few inches of her face. She felt terrified. She couldn't move. His brown eyes were sinister. *Pure evil.*

"Don't worry, it will wear off soon," the man said.

Decker's eyes darted around the room in search of answers. As if answering the question posed by her racing eyes, the man said, "My name is Jiang Xin. Don't worry; you will know me very well soon."

CHAPTER FIFTEEN

Interview Room A
U.S. Attorney's Office
Baton Rouge, LA
1300 Local Time

Despite his refusal to cooperate, the federal agents that had been handling Bear had treated him well. The Agents initially took him to the Point Coupee Parish Jail, where he was processed and given breakfast. Sheriff Thibodaux had made sure that Bear was given his own cell and treated with the utmost respect by the Corrections Officers.

After a few hours napping in his cell, the Agents returned and took him to Baton Rouge in their unmarked Crown Victoria. With traffic, they arrived at the U.S. Attorney's office just after 11:30. They gave him a ham and cheese sandwich with iced tea for lunch. It wasn't bad treatment for a criminal, Bear thought.

As he sipped on his coffee in the windowless interrogation room, he looked up at the surveillance camera in the corner of the room. He knew they were watching him. It was a waiting game. They treated him well, but he knew they were trying to soften him for the next line of questioning. He had already waived his right to an attorney. Bear knew they didn't have anything worthwhile to charge him with anyway. It was all about finding Cal Martin.

Leaning back in the metal chair, Bear wondered how much progress Cal had made in finding the people responsible for his personal nightmare. He had seen Cal grow from a teenager into a good man. And with every story Cal told Bear during his short stay, Bear became more convinced that he had done well in helping to raise Cal. *The boy was a hero.*

The door creaked open as the tall, slender Simms walked in carrying a file jacket. Bear hated the lanky bureaucrat. The man represented everything that was wrong with the system. He seemed slimy, selfish, and narcissistic to Bear. Just in their short interview, Bear could see that his interest in Cal had little to do with justice and everything to do with opportunistic career progression. Bear enjoyed pushing the man's buttons, but he knew Simms could be downright dangerous for Cal.

"Can I get you another cup of coffee, Mr. Jennings?" Simms asked as he sat down at the table across from Bear and placed the file in front of him. "Water maybe?"

"I'm fine, thanks," Bear replied. "The service here is pretty good."

Simms forced a crooked smile. "I know we may have started on the wrong foot this morning, Mr. Jennings, but I think you and I both want what's best for Cal Martin."

Bear laughed at the appeal to Bear's relationship with Cal. *Clever.*

"And what do you think that is, Agent Simms?" Bear asked with a raised eyebrow.

"For Mr. Martin to be safe," Simms replied.

"Safe? You mean like sending a small army to arrest him? You think that is *safe*?"

The fake smile vanished from Simms's face as he pulled four 8 x 10 photos from the folder and spread them across the table. They were pictures the investigators had taken of the barn after the explosion. Bear could barely make out charred human remains. He winced.

"This is what we are dealing with, Mr. Jennings. As I told you this morning, the bodies you see in the pictures are of law enforcement officers. Officers that had families," Simms said. "Do you think I would risk having that happen again?"

"Cal didn't do this," Bear replied as he pushed away one of the pictures and folded his arms. "Cal wouldn't do that."

Without acknowledging Bear's statement, Simms replaced the four pictures with four more. Bear watched as Simms presented more crime scene photos. They appeared to be of a motel room. There were close-ups of two bodies that had visible gunshot wounds.

"These two men had families as well," Simms said, shaking his head solemnly. "They were trying to protect Martin and this is what happened to them."

"Cal didn't do that either," Bear dismissed with a wave of his right hand as he looked away. "He didn't do any of this."

"Mr. Jennings, you told us you haven't seen him, so how could you be so sure?" Simms asked.

Bear leaned forward onto his elbows, looking Simms directly in the eyes. Simms looked away momentarily, intimidated by the man's directness.

"My sister had a son with Cerebral Palsy that's a few years younger than Cal. His name was Carl," Bear said, still staring down Simms. "When Cal was a teenager, he used to visit Carl every day after school and tell him about his day. Now, Carl couldn't talk, but Cal knew Carl could understand, and every day, Cal would stop by on his way home and spend an hour with him."

Simms rolled his eyes at the stall tactic. "So?"

"Carl had a dancing Santa Claus statue that he loved. It was life-sized. And one day, some kids down the road broke in and stole it. Nobody locked their doors back then, they just walked in and took it, you see," Bear continued.

"Ok," Simms replied.

"Well, the day Cal came home, Carl was sad that he lost his dancing Santa. So after spending his standard hour, he went looking for it," Bear said. "He had a pretty good idea who did it. These Fontenot boys were known for little pranks like that, and they were twice Cal's size. He used to be scrawny like you."

"So anyway, he found the dancing Santa. They had strung it up in a tree with a noose and scattered the rest of its parts everywhere in their yard, so you know what he did?"

"Called the police?" Simms asked.

Bear laughed. "Of course you'd say that. No, he confronted the Fontenot boys. Ended up getting a bloody nose and some bruised ribs out of the deal, but he made those boys regret it. And then he saved up his money from working at the grocery store and bought Carl a new Santa. It was the happiest I've ever seen Carl. Poor Carl died two months later, bless his soul."

"So Martin has a history of violence? Is that your point?" Simms asked impatiently. "You're not exactly making his case, Mr. Jennings."

"I've known Cal Martin since he was a little kid," Bear replied. "I know how his father raised him. I know how I helped to raise him. I have never known Cal to back down from a fight, no matter what the odds are. You may think he's running from you, but in reality, he's running to something. Maybe you should be more worried about helping him than arresting him."

"That's what the courts are for, Mr. Jennings," Simms replied dismissively. "Now, let's talk about what we found in your house."

As Simms started to pull his notes from the file jacket, he was interrupted by a knock on the door. "Excuse me for one minute," he said as he stepped out to meet Venable in the hallway.

"What is it?" Simms snapped.

"Sorry to bother you, sir, but I was asked to pass a message to you from SAC Fields in Miami," Venable said.

"Get on with it," Simms said impatiently. "I'm in the middle of this interrogation."

Venable handed him a paper with a handwritten message. "He wanted me to tell you that Special Agent Michelle Decker's car was found a last night by Tampa PD. They've been unable to find her. I've tried to pull the report for you, but so far it's not coming up in the system."

Simms read the note Venable had transcribed from Fields. "He thinks Martin may have been involved with it? That's impossible!" Simms scoffed.

"He said the Tampa office has taken the lead, but he thinks it might be related to the Martin case and wants you to track it down from this end," Venable said.

"Ok," Simms said as he walked back in with the note and sat down across from Bear.

"I have to pee," Bear said as he studied Simms. "Coffee just goes right through me."

Simms studied the note, ignoring the grinning old man across from him.

"Michelle Decker," Simms said, looking up from the paper. He watched the old man's reaction, catching the tell he had been looking for. There was immediate recognition.

"Huh?"

"Huh?" Simms shot back, catching him off guard.

"What does she have to do with anything?" Bear asked. He remembered her from Cal's retelling of the events of the last year. He could tell Cal had feelings for her, despite the complicated nature of their relationship.

"How do you know her?" Simms asked.

"I didn't say I did," Bear replied.

"You're lying, Mr. Jennings," Simms said. "The list of federal obstruction charges is growing."

"I am cooperating," Bear replied. "I've never met her."

"Maybe not, but Martin has told you about her," Simms said. "Mr. Jennings, I know you think this is a game, but her life may be at risk."

Bear rubbed his eyes. He enjoyed pissing off the lanky bureaucrat, but when someone's life was at risk, he couldn't keep the charade up – especially not when it involved someone Cal seemed to have feelings for.

"What happened?" Bear asked.

"Her car was found totaled yesterday in the middle of Tampa. She has been missing ever since," Simms said.

Bear frowned at the news.

"Please, Mr. Jennings," Simms pleaded. "If you have any information that could help us find her, now is the time to tell us. Her life may be in grave danger."

Bear considered his options. He didn't want to give Cal up, but Cal had also been very clear in his departing instructions. All of his friends were in danger. If anything seemed out of place, Bear was to use their emergency contact procedures. Bear was sure that Cal would want to know about Decker going missing, but the skeptic in him didn't trust Simms. *Was he part of the conspiracy? Was this a ploy to get Bear to give Cal up?*

"I can get with the U.S. Attorney and work on immunity for you, Mr. Jennings," Simms offered.

"Do you really think she's in trouble?" Bear asked. "Is this a no shitter?"

"Think about the story you just told me, Mr. Jennings," Simms said. "If what you said is true, then you know that Cal would want you to do the right thing. Especially if it can save a life."

Bear let out a labored sigh as Simms waited with bated breath.

"No one else needs to die over this," Simms said, breaking the silence.

"Ok," Bear relented. "I can contact him."

"You're making the right decision, Mr. Jennings," Simms said with a look of smug satisfaction. "Good choice."

CHAPTER SIXTEEN

Project Archangel Operations Facility
MacDill AFB
Tampa, FL
1415 Local Time

"Mr. Secretary, I understand your concerns, but if you don't meet this threat head on, it will continue to grow until it's no longer manageable," Ironman said as he stared at the large projector screen on the wall. He was in a secure video teleconference with Secretary of Defense Johnson and his Deputy Secretary, Chaz Hunt on a separate screen.

"ISIS has spread more quickly than even we could have imagined, but this is exactly what you created this unit for. We can go in, cut the head off, and neutralize this threat without anyone knowing it's us," Ironman continued. The Islamic State of Iraqi and Levant (ISIL) was a growing threat in the U.S.

political arena. Key parts of Iraq had fallen as the group pushed east out of Syria in hopes of creating an Islamic Caliphate.

"I understand that Charles," Johnson said he pulled his reading glasses down over his aristocratic nose. He held up the report that Ironman had sent just a few hours earlier. It detailed an Operations Plan to deploy Project Archangel to find and kill the group's principal leaders. "But as you know, it's an election year, and we can't risk getting into another prolonged engagement in this region."

Ironman let out an exasperated sigh as he sat back at his desk. Ever since Johnson had been picked as a potential Vice Presidential running mate, he had lost the initiative in assigning missions. And in Ironman's eyes, since being officially announced as the Vice Presidential Candidate a few days prior, he had become downright useless. Even the covert nature and plausible deniability afforded by Project Archangel's charter wasn't enough to convince him to take the necessary action as the world burned around him. It was maddening to Ironman.

"But sir, I just think that-" a knock on the door interrupted Ironman. He was in a secure facility with very limited access. Everyone in the building knew not to interrupt him during his planning meetings with the boss. *Something had to be wrong.*

"Is everything ok?" Johnson asked over the video link.

"I don't know, sir, let me find out, can I get back with you later?" Ironman asked.

"Secretary Johnson will be unavailable for the next few hours," his Chief of Staff interjected. "We will reconvene tomorrow."

"Thanks, sir," Ironman said as he disconnected the feed and opened the door.

"This better be good," Ironman growled, opening the door to see an exasperated operator standing before him. It was former Delta Sniper Freddie "Kruger" Mack, Project

Archangel's lead interrogator and one of four tactical team leaders.

"We've got issues," Kruger said as he looked over to make sure the video teleconferencing equipment was off. He was wearing 5.11 tactical pants with a black polo shirt and hat. His reddish tinted beard made him look much older than he was. "Is that thing off?"

"Yeah, we're disconnected. What's going on?" Ironman asked. His level of concern was elevated. Kruger never ventured to this part of the vault, especially not during strategic meetings with the politicians.

Kruger leaned in to Ironman and lowered his voice. "Safe house is compromised. Redman and Tanning are dead," Kruger whispered.

"What the fuck!" Ironman bellowed. "When did this happen?"

"Cooper called me about twenty minutes ago. They've been trying to keep the locals from sniffing around too much. He said there are bodies everywhere," Kruger replied. Special Agent Cooper was one of their liaisons with the FBI. Project Archangel had four others within various agencies whose job was to help ensure Project Archangel remained an unknown program.

"What about the girl?" Ironman asked as he pushed past Kruger in the narrow hallway between vault doors.

"Gone," Kruger said, shaking his head. "No sign of her."

"Goddammit! How am I just finding out about this now?" Ironman snapped.

"We're just finding out," Kruger said. "They must have gotten blindsided because neither Tanning nor Redman hit the panic button. I didn't want to interrupt you until I was sure."

"Tell Cooper to meet us there," Ironman ordered. "Let's go."

* * *

Project Archangel Safe House
Tampa, FL
1430 Local Time

An unmarked Ford Fusion was waiting in front of the townhouse as the two blacked out Tahoes sped around the corner. The two SUVs made an abrupt stop behind a marked Tampa Police car that had been ordered to ensure crime scene security as the FBI took over the case.

A tall man in a suit exited the unmarked Fusion and approached the lead Tahoe. Ironman exited the passenger seat as Kruger and the other operatives spread out over the scene. Their job was to collect as much evidence as possible and then sanitize the scene of any trace of their presence.

"Agent Cooper," Ironman said, acknowledging the approaching FBI Agent. He had been assigned and read in to Project Archangel for the last three months. The position was handpicked by the Secretary of Defense and appointed by the President. Even the Director of the FBI was kept in the dark on the agent's real purpose, knowing only that he was a liaison for a highly classified counterterrorism mission with the Department of Defense.

"Mr. Steele," Cooper said, shaking Ironman's hand. "I'm sorry the locals got here first. I've tried to mitigate it as much as possible. This guy is here just to watch the perimeter."

"What happened?" Ironman asked as the two headed toward the front door with Kruger in trail.

"Haven't nailed down the exact timing yet, but approximately two hours ago, at least a dozen men assaulted your safe house," Cooper said, pointing to the first of the bodies at the doorway. "A gun battle ensued shortly thereafter. So far, we've found a dozen bodies, not including Tanning and Redman. Have not ID'd a getaway vehicle."

Kruger shook his head in disgust as he listened to Cooper's clinical accounting of the scene at large. Tanning and Redman weren't just bodies. They were good soldiers who had fought bravely for their country.

"Are these Chinese?" Kruger asked as he squatted down over the first body, noticing the Chinese tattoo on the man's arm.

"As far as we can tell," Cooper replied. "No ID on any of them."

The three walked into the house, careful not to disturb the scene. A body with a sheet over it lay just inside the entryway. Ironman bent over and peeled back the sheet, revealing the bloody face of former Navy SEAL Brian Tanning. Ironman shook his head as he looked at the hero's lifeless face. Death was part of their job, but he never thought he'd be looking at such a horrific scene just minutes from their own base of operations.

"A woman called 911 and reported at least one person requiring medical assistance," Cooper said, pointing to the covered body at the base of the nearby stairs. "I think that was Redman."

"Fuck me," Kruger said as he walked past the shot up communications equipment and approached Redman's body. Redman was Kruger's best friend in Project Archangel. The two had served closely in Afghanistan in their time in the military prior to being recruited, and had been part of the same recruiting class. Kruger pulled back the sheet. Redman's lifeless eyes seemed to stare back at him. He closed Redman's eyelids and replaced the sheet.

"Who in the fuck did all of this?" Kruger yelled. "Goddammit!"

"Where is the girl now?" Ironman asked as he watched Kruger pace around the crime scene.

"Unknown," Cooper said with a shrug. "She wasn't here when the Paramedics showed up. Probably fled the scene. I arrived just as Tampa PD finished securing the scene and sent the Ambulance home. No one left to save."

"Oh bullshit!" Kruger exclaimed.

"Agent Cooper, can you give us a second?" Ironman asked as he tried to intercept the pacing Kruger.

"No problem, sir," Cooper replied as he turned to walk out the door.

Ironman closed the distance between Kruger and himself as he waited for Cooper to clear the area. "What's going on?"

"This is horseshit," Kruger said, staring Ironman down. "He's lying."

"You think so?" Ironman asked.

"You don't think I can tell when someone is lying to me?" Kruger growled. "That little pencil dick is lying."

"What do you mean?"

"You told Redman to follow the girl, right?" Kruger asked.

"Yes," Ironman replied. "I told them to follow her and report back in case we needed to do damage control."

"No, I get that," Kruger said, waving his hand dismissively. "And when the shit hit the fan, they did what they had to do. I don't think any one of us would fault them for stepping in like that. I can't think of anyone on the team that wouldn't have done the same damned thing in their shoes."

"Ok..." Ironman said, still trying to figure out where Kruger was going with his rant.

"So they took her here," Kruger said, turning as he held his hands up. "This place is off the grid. Not a swinging dick knows about it except the people read in. Address doesn't exist on Google Maps. All of the neighboring townhomes are empty and monitored. It even gets swept for listening devices every other day."

Ironman folded his arms and nodded.

"They checked in at the appropriate times per the communications plan using those secure phones," Kruger said, pointing to the shattered electronics across from Redman's body. "And then this morning, they get completely blindsided by this group of assholes? Less than twenty-four hours later?"

"Sometimes even the best let their guard down," Ironman offered.

"Bullshit," Kruger snapped. "You know as well as I do that these two didn't get blindsided. I don't even have to wait for the techs to finish looking at this scene. I'll bet you the motion detectors were disabled, the video feed was cut, and these two did their best against the worst possible odds."

"These do look like professionals," Ironman said as he surveyed the room.

"Professionals who knew the layout of the security system," Kruger said. "And as for the girl, well, look up." Kruger pointed at the blood trail going down the stairs to Redman's body and then the two bodies lying outside the bedroom door.

"I'm listening," Ironman responded.

"Look at the blood trail and those two bodies," Kruger replied. "Redman was bleeding up there and died down here. Cooper just said Redman was alive when the girl called 911. Those two didn't get past Redman if he still was able to fight. So that leaves only one person left, and she's not here."

"So where is she?" Ironman prodded.

"Taken," Kruger stated flatly.

"Taken?"

"Little Miss FBI didn't just walk off. Redman's SUV is still in the garage and these guys didn't leave a vehicle either. Someone took her," Kruger said. "I'm guessing they came back to get her."

"And you want to find her?" Ironman asked.

"Find her and you'll find the little fucks that did this," Kruger said, gritting his teeth.

Ironman nodded as Kruger continued pacing around the crime scene, taking in every bullet hole and blood splatter. Cooper was chatting with the Tampa Police Officer as Ironman exited into the humid midday air.

He pulled out his personal smartphone, found the contact he was looking for and typed, "Need to meet. 911" before stuffing the phone back into his pocket and heading to the marked unit to talk to Cooper.

CHAPTER SEVENTEEN

One Shell Square
Poydras Street
New Orleans, LA
1650 Local Time

Liu Chang frowned as he looked out the window of his sixteenth story corner office. The streets below on Poydras Street were packed with thousands wearing black and gold flowing toward the Mercedes-Benz Superdome just a few blocks away. The Saints were playing their first preseason game and the streets would be crowded with drunk fans on his walk home.

Chang couldn't complain though. He liked America and New Orleans in particular. He had grown accustomed to the lifestyle he had made for himself over the last five years. By American standards, it wasn't extravagant by any means, but compared to where he grew up in Xinxiang just three decades earlier, it was the life of royalty.

He pulled his dark coat on over his silk button-down shirt. Five o'clock was early by Chang's usual standards, but it was Friday and he had already sent most of his staff home. If he hurried, he could make it back to his apartment in time to Skype with his sister in Beijing before she went to work at a textile factory in the Fengtai District. It was rare that he caught her before her shift, but on Saturdays, the plant didn't open until nine AM.

Chang shut down his computer and stepped out of his office. The mid-size corporate office of Hua Xia Holdings of America consisted mostly of open air cubicles. He and his Operations Manager were the only two with full-size offices. He walked past the empty cubicles and past the receptionist's desk before turning off the lights and locking the main door. Another perk of working in America was the hours. Although he typically worked sixty hours per week, weekends were, usually, not included. Business stopped after everyone went home on Friday.

Walking down the wide hallway, Chang noticed that the neighboring offices were also empty. The accounting firm across from their office had likely been gone for hours to tailgate for the Saints game. The CPA in charge had offered Chang seats in their suite numerous times, but he always politely declined. There were some parts of American culture he just couldn't buy into, and football was one of them.

Chang took the elevator to the lobby. As he walked out on the marble-floored open area, he noticed that the mini-bank and coffee shop were still open. A man wearing a baseball hat pulled low over his face caught his eyes. He was wearing a t-shirt and jeans, and he looked like he hadn't shaved in several days. *Rugged.* That's the word Chang thought of. It seemed out of place in the state's tallest building which was, usually, filled with clean cut corporate professionals.

He avoided eye contact as he passed the man sipping on what appeared to be a coffee at a small table. There was something about the man that was just unsettling – an energy about him that just made Chang uneasy.

Chang saw himself as a bureaucrat and middle man. He ran the day to day operations in Hua Xia Holdings, financing business ventures of many varieties. In New Orleans, his focus was mostly on oil and gas ventures, but as a state-funded organization, he also funneled money into other activities of great interest to the People's Republic of China.

But Chang was proud of the fact that he never got his hands dirty. That was left to men much rougher than he would ever be. To the Americans and the City of New Orleans, his company was a welcomed presence representing international business cooperation. To his superiors in Beijing, he was a skilled tradesman in the art of financial misdirection and deception.

Walking out onto the concrete steps, Chang briskly made his way down to Poydras Street and took a right toward his apartment. He merged with the crowd of rowdy fans as they chanted "WHO DAT" en route to the game. They walked shoulder to shoulder, ignoring the first side street and crossing without stopping.

The mob continued for two more blocks. Chang stopped at the intersection of Poydras and Baronne Streets and waited for the pedestrian signal to clear him across. As he looked back toward his office, he thought he caught a glimpse of the man he had seen in the café. A chill shot down his spine.

Without waiting for the red signal to change to white, Chang looked both ways and hurried across the four lane intersection, dodging the cars creeping along in bumper to bumper traffic. Once clear, he briskly walked to the surface street access door of his apartment complex and leapt up the stairs.

Looking over his shoulder as he rounded the first flight, Chang nervously watched for the man from the café. As he reached the third floor, he stopped and waited. *Nothing.* He breathed a sigh of relief as he realized he had overreacted.

Chang opened the third-floor door and turned right down the hallway to his apartment. Reaching his door, he pulled out his key and turned the lock. His heart was still racing from the adrenaline and sprint up the stairs. He hated that he had allowed the stranger to rattle him so. He hadn't been so shaken up since his first days in New Orleans when he thought a street gang was following him.

Taking a deep breath to calm himself, Chang slowly opened his apartment door. As he stepped into the foyer, he was suddenly shoved forward. He stumbled and tripped, falling face first into the carpeted living area as he vainly tried to arrest his fall.

He heard the door slam shut as he struggled to make sense of the situation and rushed to turn over and face his attacker. He rolled his small body onto his back and tried to crawl backwards. To his horror, the man from the café was towering over him with a gun aimed at Chang's head. The man said nothing as he slowly approached the retreating Chang.

"Get away!" Chang yelped in heavily accented English. "What do you want?"

"Stay where you are, Mr. Chang," the man said, still calmly pointing the gun at Chang. He looked like a giant to Chang – like a character out of an old American Western.

"What do you want?" Chang said, freezing in place. The man stopped just a few feet from Chang. He had received minimal weapons and hand to hand combat training before leaving for America, but he dared not try it. Even if he had been proficient and the man unarmed, Chang was sure that fighting the American Cowboy would end poorly for him.

"I just want to talk to you," the man said, lowering his weapon. Chang caught a glimpse of his eyes beneath the baseball hat pulled low over his face. His blue eyes were intense. It was the same energy Chang had perceived earlier. "If you answer my questions, I will not hurt you."

The man tucked the handgun into holster at the small of his back. "But if you lie to me or stall or even think about wasting my time, you will regret it. Do you understand?"

Chang nodded slowly as he sat looking up at the angry American.

"Who is Jun Zhang?" the man asked. Chang's eyes widened. Zhang was a high-level figure in the Chinese Ministry of State Security. The man was treading very dangerous waters.

Chang hesitated.

"I won't ask again," the man warned.

Chang's mind raced. The man before him seemed more than capable of killing him, but Zhang had a reputation of extreme brutality. The MSS was not an organization he wanted to cross. His job involved daily interaction with them. They would certainly know he had talked.

"I don't know him," Chang lied, looking away as he said it.

The man turned his hat around so Chang could see his scruffy face. The back of the hat had MOLON LABE written across it in white letters. Chang found himself wondering what it meant as the man stared menacingly at him.

"I want you to look me in the eyes and say that again," he said calmly. "I don't think you are a threat to me, but if you don't start telling me the truth, you will leave me no choice."

"I'll help you, he's Chinese intelligence, now start talking," he added.

"Ministry of State Security," Chang corrected the man. "He's the head of Sector Six Military Intelligence."

"Sector six?" the man asked as he squatted down next to Chang.

"Southeast United States," Chang responded. *I'm already dead*, he thought.

"Where can I find him?" the man asked.

As Chang stared at the man, the realization suddenly hit him. There was only one man that could be asking those questions, and that man was just as marked as Chang would soon be. He had heard stories of his bravery, but in person, he seemed even larger than his reputation.

"You're Cal Martin," Chang blurted out. "Spectre!"

The man shot up and took a step back. "How do you know that name?"

"The man who stole an F-16 from Zhang. The man who shot down MiGs and escaped a Syrian warlord. The man who can't be killed. You're the one everyone is looking for!" Chang said. He had heard the rumors of Martin as if he were a real life version of an American action hero.

"Who is looking for me?" Spectre asked. "Zhang?"

Chang shook his head. "Zhang is too high up. He doesn't do any of the… how you say… grunt work."

"Then who?"

Chang thought about it for a minute. "Jiang Xin."

"Jiang?" Spectre asked, struggling through the pronunciation of the name.

"Jiang Xin," Chang repeated. "He's Zhang's top Lieutenant. Very dangerous."

"I'm not worried about dangerous," Spectre said. "Where do I find him?"

Chang shrugged. "I don't get involved in their operations."

"What do you do?" Spectre asked. "You run the holding company, right?"

Chang nodded. "Hua Xia Holdings of America invests in hundreds of companies in many different areas. I manage the day to day operation in this region, including funding for Zhang's operations."

"Then you know you should know how to find them," Spectre said.

"I know where the money goes," Chang said. "But they are never in the same place for very long."

Spectre carefully considered his next question as Chang sat staring at him." But I can help you find him!" Chang blurted, breaking the silence.

"Why would you do that?"

Chang looked down for a moment and then said, "Because Zhang had my cousin executed."

Spectre stood and helped Chang to his feet. Chang was much shorter and flabbier than the more muscular Spectre.

"And I hate him," Chang added.

CHAPTER EIGHTEEN

Spectre entered the One Shell Square building through the service entrance on Perdido Street. He used the access code Chang had given him. Spectre still didn't entirely trust Chang, despite his cooperation.

Chang seemed to be nothing more than a mid-level bureaucrat. He was vaguely aware of all of the operations he had helped facilitate, but he had no direct knowledge. It was hard for Spectre to separate him from the rest of the Zhang's men. Spectre saw them as all equally guilty.

But Chang made it clear that he held a passionate hatred of Zhang. His cousin, Kung Lao, had been arrested and tortured by Zhang. At the time, Zhang had been a much younger operative in the Chinese Ministry of State Security. Lao had been working for a Chinese software firm that did business with several U.S. and Taiwanese companies. Zhang took him from his home one night on suspicion of treason. Chang was sure Lao had no way of knowing that the American CIA had been involved in the business meetings with the Americans.

Zhang's team raided Lao's home and questioned him in front of his wife and young son. He even threatened to kill Lao's infant son when Lao claimed innocence. At the end of the night, Lao was taken to a detainment facility where he died of unknown causes three months later. His family wasn't even allowed to give him a proper burial.

If nothing else, Spectre could see that Chang was telling the truth about Lao and his feelings for Zhang. The passionate hatred was definitely there. Chang had done well in hiding it in the five years he had been in America.

Spectre entered the service door and took the stairs up to Chang's office, bounding four steps at a time as he ascended to the sixteenth floor. The black backpack he carried added little weight to his workout. Chang had given him very precise instructions on how to minimize his exposure to cameras and roving security patrols in infiltrating the New Orleans skyscraper.

Exiting the stairwell into the office corridor, Spectre quickly made his way to the offices adjacent to Chang's office. Spectre verified he was at the right suite and set down the bag. The FOR LEASE sign confirmed that it was empty. . Spectre took the hammer Chang had given him out of the bag, covered his face as he turned away, and used it to shatter the glass. After clearing the shards of remaining broken glass from the frame, Spectre stuffed the hammer back in his bag and stepped through.

Once inside, Spectre made his way to the corner office nearest the window. He pulled out the hammer and began chipping at the Sheetrock until he made a hole big enough to slide through. Once his entrance was created, he shimmied his way through the hole and found himself standing in front of Chang's computer.

Spectre pulled out a piece of paper Chang had given him with the appropriate usernames and passwords. Once logged in, Spectre found the ledger spreadsheet with all of the entries for Zhang's operations for the past year. There was an incredible amount of data to sort through. He hit print, sending ten pages of spreadsheets to the nearby printer. Once printed, he grabbed the ten sheets and stuffed them into his backpack.

Satisfied he had the data he needed, Spectre pulled out the hammer and went to work, destroying Chang's computer and desktop. He found the hidden wall safe Chang had talked about and opened it with the combo he had been given. After taking the stacks of crisp hundred dollar bills, Spectre used the hammer and screwdriver to remove the hinge pin and take the door off to make it look more like a burglary.

He checked his watch, timing his next move for when Chang had told him the guards usually made their rounds on that floor. Spectre continued his path of carnage through the main offices, rummaging through desk drawers and destroying computers and monitors as he made his way to the exit. Once he was in the main lobby, the motion detectors activated, setting off a high pitched audible alarm.

He threw the backpack over both shoulders and raced for the door. Using a hammer, Spectre shattered the glass door and stepped through. He sprinted back toward the stairwell. As he rounded the corner, he froze as he came face to face with a security guard wearing a black sport coat and gray pants. He hadn't expected to see a guard there.

"Stop right there!" the man ordered.

After a moment of hesitation, Spectre continued forward, striking the man in the side of the neck with the palm of his hand. The brachial stun almost instantly dropped the man to the ground. Spectre grabbed the man's radio and sprinted toward the door. He listened for indications that more guards or police would be following.

Reaching the tenth floor, Spectre exited into the corridor and headed toward the stairs on the opposite end of the building. He was unmolested as he hit the stairs and continued down to the ground level where he exited out on Poydras Street.

Spectre merged into the crowd of rowdy Saints fans still funneling to the game. He heard the sirens of the New Orleans Police Department as they tried to make it past the gridlocked traffic on the surface street.

Spectre continued with the crowd toward the Super Dome until he was sure no one was following him. He found the Internet café he was looking for three blocks over and ducked in, finding an open computer in the relatively empty café.

He placed his backpack down next to him and opened the web browser on the computer. Spectre had not brought along any cell phones, laptops, or tablets from Bear's house. His only method of communication was a gun forum message board of which Bear was a member.

Spectre logged in using Bear's credentials and looked into the draft folder of the private messages of BearWarrior69. Spectre hoped he would find nothing. No news was good news in this case. Their contract was that Spectre would check it daily and it would only be used in case of emergency. As the Draft folder loaded, Spectre's stomach turned as he found a message waiting for him.

Come back as soon as possible. Go to the nearest police station. Or go back to my house. These guys just want to help you. Otherwise, you might get hurt. Michelle is missing. Cal, this is for the best. Face it son, you can't run forever.

-Charlie

Spectre rummaged through his bag and found a pen and one of the papers he had used to print the ledger. Bear signing his name as "Charlie" was part of their agreed on code that an embedded message was contained within the draft. Spectre scribbled the first letter of every sentence. C-G-O-T-O-M-C-F.

Spectre stared at the letters on the paper. The C was for "Cal." The words became clear. "GO TO MCF." Spectre instantly recognized what Bear was trying to tell him. Michelle Decker was missing, and Bear knew Spectre would want to find her. MCF was the ICAO code for the MacDill Air Force Base Identifier.

"Clever old man," Spectre said with a chuckle as he deleted the message and started typing his own response.

Spectre typed "WILCO. IP INBOUND" and clicked "SAVE DRAFT" before logging off and putting his papers back in his bag. He had a long drive ahead of him to get to Tampa.

CHAPTER NINETEEN

Ballast Point Park
Tampa, FL
1930 Local Time

Overlooking Hillsborough Bay, Ballast Point Park was abuzz with locals and tourists enjoying the summer Friday afternoon. Skaters, joggers, and dog walkers filled the park's sidewalks, and the nearby boat launch was packed with people securing their boats for the evening.

Ironman sat patiently on a metal park bench with a scenic view of the bay as a family picnicked nearby. He had been waiting for the last five minutes, taking in the mild evening as he thought about what he would say to Xin.

Although Ironman was accustomed to dealing with testosterone-fueled operators, Xin was different. He was quiet — too quiet. The man had a reputation of being deadly and ruthless, but his demeanor demonstrated a knowing calmness.

While he would never admit it to anyone but himself, deep down Ironman was terrified of what Xin was capable of doing.

"Your bald head is very easy to spot," a voice from behind him said. Ironman looked at his watch as Xin approached and sat down next to him. It was precisely 19:30. It was par for the course in his dealings with Xin. He always managed to arrive exactly when he said he would. He was never later nor early.

"Good evening," Ironman replied, looking over at Xin. Like Ironman, Xin was still wearing sunglasses despite the setting sun behind them. "Thank you for coming on such short notice."

"What can I do for you?" Xin asked as he stared straight ahead at the boaters on the water.

Ironman turned to face Xin as he leaned in and lowered his voice. "Your men killed two of my best operators," he said.

Xin smiled as he pulled off his sunglasses. His eyes were dark, almost dead-looking. "And your men killed twelve of mine," Xin replied. "So?"

Ironman struggled to hold back his rage. "So," Ironman said, trying to calm himself. "You said you weren't going to hurt her."

"I'm not going to hurt her, but your men need to be kept on a shorter leash," Xin said.

"My men did what I told them to do," Ironman snapped. "That's no reason to attempt a snatch and grab in broad daylight. What were your men thinking?"

"Are you questioning my methods?" Xin asked as the smile vanished from his face.

Ironman hesitated for a moment and then said, "No, but I don't think the boss is going to be thrilled when he finds out we lost a safe house, two men, and nearly compromised everything."

Xin held his hand up. "The objectives have changed," he said.

"And just what is that supposed to mean?" Ironman asked.

"It means you should do what you're told and stop asking so many questions," Xin said forebodingly as he stood. "You know what the stakes are."

Ironman stared at Xin through his dark sunglasses as Xin nodded and turned to walk away. Once Xin was clear, Ironman pulled out his phone and dialed the first number in his contact list.

"Hey honey," Ironman said as the woman picked up. "Are you and the girls ok?"

* * *

Project Archangel Operations Building
MacDill AFB, FL
1955 Local Time

"Hey boss, where've you been?" Kruger asked as Ironman walked into their Emergency Operations Center. It was a room in the center of the vault with monitors displaying newsfeeds, satellite images, and secret message traffic regarding hotspots all over the world. The EOC served as their initial planning area for all of the team's deployments.

"Checked on Lydia and the girls," Ironman said as he approached Kruger. He and another operative were huddled around Julio Meeks, one of Archangel's best computer specialist. Meeks had been instrumental in locating Cal Martin after his aircraft had been shot down in Syria.

"Copy that," Kruger replied. "Coolio here has a lead on the van they used to escape our safe house during the attack."

Meeks looked up from behind his hipster glasses and laughed. "Coolio" was the name the late Joe Carpenter had given him after pressuring him to find Martin. Even after Carpenter and Martin left Project Archangel, the name seemed to stick.

"I cross referenced the license plate of the van that struck Agent Decker's car with any other known vehicles," Meeks said as he spun around in his chair to face Ironman. "Obviously the plate on the van turned up nothing. Registered to a non-existent company out of Tampa, but when I pulled their records, there was another vehicle registered to the same fake address."

"Fake address?" Ironman asked.

"Well, it's real," Meeks submitted, "but there's nothing there. They're just using it for mail forwarding."

"Ok, go on," Ironman said. Since pulling him out of trouble with the authorities and offering him a job with Project Archangel, he had always been impressed by the kid's work ethic and intelligence.

"So I looked for an ALPRS hit on the second plate, and wouldn't you know it, a camera near our safe house picked it up right before the approximate time of the event," Meeks said. He turned to his monitor and showed Ironman a picture of the bumper of the white fifteen passenger van that the Automatic License Plate Reader System camera had taken as it drove by.

"I found about forty more hits on that plate after the event as well," Meeks said, pulling up a map of the Tampa area that traced the approximate route of the van. "The last hit was outside of Peter O'Knight Airport."

"We think they're staging out of a hangar somewhere on the field," Kruger interjected.

"Do you think that's where Decker is?" Ironman asked as he studied the satellite view of the airport.

"Maybe," Kruger replied. "Could be a different van or another team that grabbed her, but I know that if we find these assholes, we'll get a lead on the girl."

"Alright, Kruger, you have point on this one, let me know what you need," Ironman said.

Kruger flashed a smile through his red beard. "Two, three man teams and the Pilatus should do just fine."

"What? No Close Air Support?" Ironman asked with a grin.

"Don't think I haven't thought about it," Kruger laughed.

CHAPTER TWENTY

Interview Room A
U.S. Attorney's Office
Baton Rouge, LA
2000 Local Time

Bear let out an exaggerated yawn as Simms entered the room. As part of their agreement, they had been keeping him in a nearby hotel under protective custody. After showering and preparing for bed, the agents of his protective detail told him to get dressed again, cuffed him, and took him back to the interview room. Bear wondered how much longer he could keep stiff-arming them before they would finally catch on and end his game.

Simms sat down across from Bear at the small interview table. His suit was still neatly pressed, but Bear could tell he was starting to get sloppy. His patience was wearing thin, and his anxiety was clearly evident in his slender face.

"You made me miss Wheel of Fortune," Bear said, breaking the awkward silence. "It's my bedtime."

"Where is Martin?" Simms asked impatiently.

"You saw the same message I did," Bear replied. "He said he's on his way."

"On his way *where*, Mr. Jennings? Where is Cal Martin going?"

Bear shrugged. He hoped Spectre was well on his way to Tampa to try to find and rescue Decker. At least Spectre's response had indicated as much.

"Here? There?" Bear responded. "I'm not a psychic, Agent Simms. You read the same message I did. I told him to come home and he said ok."

"He said, 'Wilco, Mr. Jennings.' What does that mean?"

"Will comply," Bear scoffed.

"And IP Inbound?" Simms asked.

"Initial Point," Bear explained. "It means he was leaving wherever he was and is on his way." Bear lied. He knew Spectre was acknowledging Bear's message and indicating that he was leaving his current location en route to try to find Decker.

"What was he doing in New Orleans?" Simms asked, pulling out a sheet of paper with an Internet Protocol Address trace.

"Saints are playing tonight," Bear offered with a wry smile.

Simms shook his head in disgust. "You still don't get it, do you Mr. Jennings?"

"I'm just saying, the man is a big Drew Brees fan," Bear said, ignoring Simms.

"Maybe he wanted to see a game one last time before he turns himself in," Bear added. He watched Simms rub the back of his neck. He could see he had reached a boiling point with Simms. The game would soon be over.

"Mr. Jennings, you agreed to cooperate with us and yet here you are, stalling for time," Simms said. "You stand to go to prison for the rest of your life. Is that really what you want?"

"Mr. Simms," Bear said, losing his jovial tone. "I've lived sixty-nine years on this earth. My wife has been dead for many years. I have no family. I just have dogs. Besides, I probably only have a few more years left anyway. Cal Martin is the closest thing to a son I've ever had. And you are not the first pencil-necked stiff that I've come across. Do you think I would ever choose you, a two-faced bureaucrat, over a man that I know will do the right thing no matter what?"

"Mr. Jennings—"

"No," Bear snapped, cutting him off. "I'm not done yet. I know your kind. You'll lie to me and tell me what you think it is I want to hear. As if you're doing this for Cal's safety, and it's the only way to save the girl. But we both know that's a lie. You're only here to get another notch on your belt. You don't give a shit about him or the girl. . But don't worry, if there's anyone that will find her, it's Cal."

Bear realized his mistake as he saw the recognition in the face of the slimy agent across from him. Simms flashed a big smile as he collected his papers and stood.

"Thank you, Mr. Jennings," Simms said, still grinning from ear to ear. "You've been a big help."

"Wait! Cal should be on his way soon," Bear said, trying to backtrack. He knew it was too late. He had let his disgust for the system and its representative get the best of him.

"I'm sure he will be," Simms laughed as he went to open the door. "And, by the way, the deal's off."

"Enjoy your night in the parish jail. Maybe they'll have Wheel of Fortune on the communal TV," Simms added as he left wearing a smug grin of satisfaction.

Agent Venable was standing outside the interview room as Simms exited. "I have something you might want to see," Venable said.

"What is it?" Simms asked. "We need to call for the jet and get the team ready to move."

"It's a police report from Baton Rouge Metro from earlier today," Venable said as he handed Simms the report. "White male fitting Martin's description battered the head of security of a local oil and gas company."

Simms grabbed the report from Venable's hand and read it quickly as they continued walking down the hallway toward his makeshift corner office. The report said that a white male had entered the offices of Cajun Oil and Gas around midday. When the chief of security tried to make contact with the man, he threatened the man with a weapon before blindsiding him. The chief of security reported that the unknown man attempted to gain entry to the safe, but when he was told that only the owner had the combo, he fled. The victim also reported that the suspect asked questions about another company in New Orleans.

"Well, this explains the New Orleans connection," Simms said as they reached his office. "But it doesn't matter anymore."

"Do you want me to follow up on it?" Venable asked as Simms entered his office and began packing up his laptop and other personal items.

Simms stopped and looked at the young agent. "That's a good idea," Simms said. "Follow-up with the victim here in town and see if you can figure out what he was doing in New Orleans. We can add those charges when this goes to trial."

"Where are you going?" Venable asked.

"Tampa," Simms said with a big smile.

CHAPTER TWENTY ONE

Tampa, FL
0335 Local Time

The single 1200shp PT-6A-67 Allison turboprop droned along effortlessly as the Pilatus PC-12 orbited high above Tampa. The pilot, "Jenny" Craig, had the blacked out Pilatus in a thirty degree bank turn at fifteen thousand feet above the sleepy city. It was high enough to be well above Tampa International's Class Bravo controlled airspace, but low enough that the aircraft's tail mounted Electro-Optical/Infrared/Thermal Imaging sensor had a high quality view of the objective below.

Kruger leaned over sensor operator "JAX" Jackson's shoulder as he slewed the pod over the hangars below. He and his team of six were dressed in Kryptek Camouflage with parachutes, helmets, and Night Vision Goggles, as well as MP-7 machine guns, chambered in 4.6 x 30MM.

"This is the most likely target," JAX said as he zoomed in the thermal image on the handheld display. The reconfigurable PC-12 cockpit could host an array of sensors as well as electronic jammers and other sensors. For the night's mission, they had removed the sensor operator stations to make room for Kruger and his team, leaving only JAX to operate the remaining pod and Jenny to pilot the aircraft. She sat alone in the cockpit, wearing a pair of Night Vision Goggles.

"Most likely?" Kruger asked, studying the image. It was a large hangar on the south side of Peter O'Knight Airport across Hillsborough Bay from MacDill AFB where they had launched quietly from the closed airfield just thirty minutes earlier.

"That looks like your van," JAX said, pointing to the square hotspot in the corner of the hangar. "And those four blobs are your targets." There were what appeared to be four men on cots behind a large aircraft.

"Any patrols?" Kruger asked.

"One guy," JAX said, slewing the pod over to the blob next to the hangar. He switched the camera to Infrared, showing the outline of a man smoking a cigarette. "Should be a pretty clean insertion."

"Well, let's go wake'em up," Kruger said as he turned and gave his team the thumbs up. They began checking each other's gear. Each man was equipped with a HALO suit, gear bag, Night Vision Goggles, and black Mechanix Gloves. Their body armor contained MOLLE pouches with spare magazines for their MP-7s.

Kruger quickly briefed the team on the infil and exfil plan, using JAX's screen as a reference. Once he finished and everyone was up to speed on the plan, Kruger crouched down in the small cabin and walked to the cockpit, tapping Jenny on the shoulder to let her know of the impending jump. She connected the MBU-5 oxygen mask to her helmet and JAX followed suit. Once all players were ready and their oxygen masks were on, Jenny depressurized the cockpit and JAX opened the jump door on the left rear of the aircraft.

Jenny piloted the aircraft into position and illuminated the jump lights. In sequence, Kruger and his men exited through the jump door.

Kruger had done hundreds of High Altitude, Low Opening Jumps in his career, but he considered this to be one of the easier ones. Although the runway lights were off, the green and white rotating beacon made it easy to quickly find the airport, and the Night Vision Goggles under the full moon made it easy to spot the hangar cluster at the south end of the field.

From fifteen thousand feet, the freefall was relatively short. Kruger and the five other men were in near perfect formation as they descended through the dark sky. Kruger checked his wrist altimeter. Despite the relatively low threat of being spotted, he still didn't want to take any chances. They had already seen what these men were capable of at the safe house.

The HALO jump had been former MARSOC member Logan Greene's idea. In their brainstorming session before the mission, the unique location of the airport presented several challenges. At that hour, helicopter insertion would be too risky. The airfield was closed and even the quiet Little Bird OH-6s would wake everyone up.

They considered driving onto the field, but the Tampa PD patrol made that an unpalatable option. They would never be able to justify a civilian casualty. The lone patrol also ruled out a waterborne insertion from the bay and cutting into the fence. Operating in friendly territory was much more challenging than Iraq or Afghanistan.

So Greene pitched the HALO jump idea. They could fly high above the airspace under the cover of darkness, unheard by the enemy below. The lower opening carried with it some risk,

Greene admitted, but that's why they were part of Project Archangel in the first place – they were the best at what they did. Besides, Greene argued, the PC-12 would need to be airborne anyway to help them find the correct hangar.

Kruger loved the plan, and with Ironman's concurrence, they briefed the mission. It was the first time Project Archangel had ever planned a mission on American soil. Despite technically being contractors and immune to the Posse Comitatus Act forbidding military involvement on U.S. soil, it was an exception that everyone on the team acknowledged as being a one-time event. They did not want to get into the business of operating amongst American civilians.

Kruger watched the altitude click down as the monochrome green image of the ground rushed toward him. At seventeen hundred feet above the ground, Kruger grabbed the ripcord, pulling it precisely at fifteen hundred feet. The opening shock jarred Kruger, a feeling he always hated as he steered the fully opened canopy toward the northern edge of the hangar clusters.

A minute later, Kruger touched down as Greene followed behind him. They quickly collected their chutes and gathered their gear, storing all of it discreetly near the northernmost hangar as the other four operatives landed and regrouped with them.

"Punisher One, Pepsi," Kruger advised over his throat mic, using the code word to let everyone know the team had successfully rendezvoused. Ironman was sitting back in the Emergency Operations Center, watching the datalinked sensor feed from the PC-12 and listening to the radio network.

"Copy, one tango, southwest corner," JAX responded, letting them know that the lone guard was still in the same location.

"Roger," Kruger said as the rest of the men gathered up their gear. The team was a mix of former Special Operations Forces from all branches. Kruger led team one, callsign

"Punisher One" consisting of former Navy SEAL Mike Roland and former Army Ranger Ty "Tuna" Turner. "Punisher Two," led by Greene, consisted of former Green Beret Dave "Axe" Axelrod and former Air Force PJ John Wilson. Kruger felt Wilson was especially important to the team. Air Force PJs were best combat medics in the world. Wilson was one of three assigned to Project Archangel, and Kruger never planned a mission without at least one of the three on board.

The two teams of three split up, with Kruger's team taking the west end of the rows of hangars and Greene's team taking the east end. They moved quietly and quickly, clearing left and right as they passed the three long rows of community hangars before reaching the lone large hangar at the south end of the field.

Greene's team stopped at the northeast corner, finding the power box to the hangar. He went to work, cutting the padlock with the extendable pair of bolt cutters he had in his combat pack.

Kruger peered around the corner, finding the guard smoking and staring out into the distance. As the power was cut and the light above him went out, the guard turned away from Kruger, distracted by the sudden darkness. Kruger slung his MP-7 around his back, drew his combat knife, and slowly approached the distracted man as Roland and Tuna covered from the corner.

In one smooth motion, Kruger grabbed the man's mouth with his left hand and twisted his head away as he drove the blade down into the man's neck, through his jugular vein and windpipe. Kruger yanked the man firmly back as he tried to struggle, causing him to fall backwards as Kruger dragged him toward the corner of the hangar. By the time Kruger reached Tuna and Roland, the man was dead.

"Still clear, no movement inside," JAX announced over the tactical frequency having watched Kruger take out the lone guard.

"Punisher One copies," Kruger responded as his team stacked up against the southern door on the main hangar door.

"Punisher Two ready," Greene said. His team was preparing to enter through the eastern side access door.

"All players, Coke," Kruger said, using the code word for green lighting the operation.

The two teams entered simultaneously. Through his Night Vision Goggles, Kruger could see the infrared pointers of each man's rifle as they searched the hangar. The dots were invisible to the naked eye in the pitch-black hangar.

Kruger's team found the van and cleared it. There was no one anyone around it. Greene's team cleared the eastern end of the hangar. The two teams regrouped and continued, in a V-formation, toward the far corner where the men lay sleeping on cots.

They moved with lightning speed, descending upon the four sleeping men. Greene and Kruger covered as the other four operators grabbed the sleeping men and put them in flex cuffs.

"Millertime," Kruger called as they quickly escorted the four men out of the hangar. Before leaving, Axe pulled out his digital camera and snapped two pictures of the aircraft inside the hangar. He had never seen one quite like it and thought it might be good for later intel.

Jenny began a spiraling approach from fifteen thousand feet in the blacked out Pilatus. The flat pitch of the four-blade prop helped to act as a speed brake as she entered the tight spiral for the runway. With the expertise of a seasoned pilot, Jenny bled off sufficient airspeed, dropped the landing gear, and made a tight turn from base to final on Runway 18 as JAX held on for dear life.

Kruger and his men continued to the edge of the taxiway that joined the large hangar with the runway. At the last instant, the PC-12's landing light appeared just as the aircraft crossed the runway threshold. It landed and slowed aggressively, turning around in front of the ten men.

JAX opened the cargo door as the men waited at the taxiway. As he stuck his head out into the night air, he realized they had missed a critical step in their planning.

"There's too many of them," he said, shaking his head as he pointed to the kneeling prisoners.

"What?" Kruger yelled over the engine noise of the turboprop.

"That makes eleven passengers. You have to leave two or we'll never get airborne!" JAX yelled.

Greene raised his suppressed MP-7 to the back of the head of the nearest prisoner." I can fix it," he said as he took aim.

Kruger lunged at Greene, pushing him out of the way before he was able to fire off a round at the defenseless prisoner.

"Are you fucking stupid?" Kruger asked." That's not how we operate."

Greene was angered by Kruger's reaction and stood up to him as Tuna started to pull him back." Come at me, bro!"

"Guys, we don't have time for this shit!" JAX yelled, pointing to the approaching headlights a quarter of a mile away on the main ramp.

"What's the call, boss?" Roland asked.

Kruger considered his options as the seconds ticked by. He knew he would have to deal with Greene later, but for now, he had to decide what to do with the extra prisoners. He looked up to see a pair of red and blue strobes illuminate above approaching headlights.

"Cut these two loose," Kruger directed, pointing at the younger of the two men.

"Are you kidding me?" Greene yelled, still being held back by Tuna.

"Load the other two and let's go," Kruger said, gesturing for Axe and Wilson to load up their prisoners. Roland assisted as the two complied, leaving Greene, Kruger, and Tuna with the two remaining prisoners.

"Leave them cuffed, but let them go," Kruger directed. Tuna pulled the two men up to their feet and pointed back toward the large hangar with his hand. Needing no further encouragement, the two men took off running, nearly falling over themselves as they headed back to the hangar.

"Give us a moment," Kruger said to Tuna. Tuna nodded and entered the running PC-12. The police car's siren soon became audible in the distance.

"C'mon, Kruger, we gotta go!" JAX yelled as the police car raced toward them. Kruger ignored him, staring down the younger Marine in front of him.

Kruger leaned in close to Greene, grabbing his vest. "Look bub, I know you're new here," he said calmly. "But if you ever try to pull a chickenshit stunt like that again, I will destroy you in place. Do you understand?"

Greene nodded slowly as he realized the seriousness in Kruger's tone. Kruger had a reputation within the team of being one of the deadliest of operators in both his current and former lives. The realization that he had crossed the line slowly set in.

"Now lock it up and get on the plane, we've got work to do," Kruger said. Greene followed Kruger into the side door as the police car approached.

Jenny firewalled the engine, launching the Pilatus down the runway past the speeding police cruiser. As the aircraft became airborne, the team held on as Jenny entered an aggressive left-hand turn toward MacDill. She left the gear down, setting up for a straight in approach at the nearby MacDill.

Kruger watched on JAX's FLIR screen as the police car peeled off from the runway in pursuit of the two released prisoners on the taxiway.

"That's why it was better to let them go," Kruger said with a smile to Greene. "Lesson learned."

CHAPTER TWENTY TWO

Project Archangel Detention Facility
MacDill AFB, FL
0430 Local Time

Tucked away on the south end of MacDill Air Force Base, the ammo and weapons storage facility housed Project Archangel's secure detention and interrogation facility. Hidden amongst the real bomb dump that previously served as a storage facility for live bombs and missiles for the F-16 schoolhouse that once operated out of MacDill, the facility was completely hidden from satellite view.

According to the government, the facility did not exist. But for the unacknowledged organization, it served as a temporary detention and interrogation facility for prisoners brought back from conflicts overseas, notably the Middle East. The facility allowed interrogators like Kruger to go to work before handing prisoners over to official channels where they would end up in cushier facilities like Gitmo.

Kruger swiped his access badge and entered his six-digit PIN. The metallic lock whirred open. He held up his credentials to the guard standing watch who opened the metal gate for him to enter. He had changed into his 5.11 Khaki Pants and Polo shirt as Julio pulled the data on their two guests.

Liu Kang was a pilot for the Chinese People's Liberation Army Air Force. According to his service record, he had mostly flown cargo aircraft before his service record suddenly stopped at the rank of Major. Based on their assessments, it was believed that Kang had transitioned to the Chinese Ministry of State Security sometime shortly after the record ended.

Quan Chi had no military service record that Meeks could locate. He was much older than the forty-year-old Kang. Chi's file ended with earning an engineering degree from Tsinghua University. He had seemingly been off the grid ever since – a clear sign that he had been involved in espionage with the Ministry of State Security.

Kang was still sitting in his boxers and white t-shirt as Kruger walked in, placed a folder on the table, and then released Kang's restraints. He decided to work on the pilot first, seeing him as a much easier mark than the seasoned operative. He needed quick Intel on the location of Decker and the men behind the attack on the safe house. The State Department could worry about breaking them for their state secrets later when they were formally turned over.

Kang rubbed his wrists as Kruger sat down across from him. "That is a gesture of good will," Kruger said with a smile. "Abuse my gesture of goodwill by spitting, clawing, hitting, or otherwise attempting to harm me, and you will immediately regret it. Do you understand?"

Kang stared blankly at Kruger. Kruger made an exaggerated head nod in response. "I know you speak English Mr. Kang, so at least nod your head if you understand."

Kang nodded slowly.

"Good," Kruger said. "Now let's get down to business."

"I wish to speak to the Chinese Ambassador," Kang said in a thick Chinese accent.

"The nearest consulate is in Houston, Mr. Kang," Kruger said with a smile. "I don't think you want to wait that long in here."

"I will wait," Kang said defiantly as he held his head high.

Kruger leaned back in the chair and crossed his legs in a relaxed posture. The silence created tension as Kang's eyes started darting around the room.

"You must treat me humanely," Kang said. "It is in the Geneva Convention."

Kruger laughed as he watched Kang dig deep for his resistance training. His laugh made Kang even more uncomfortable, causing him to fidget nervously in his chair and shift his hands around on the table.

"I don't know anything and I won't talk," Kang said, his confidence slowly waning.

Kruger smiled at Kang through his bushy red beard, holding eye contact with the man until the smile suddenly vanished from his face.

"You seem like a pretty smart fellow, Mr. Kang," Kruger said. "So I won't play any games with you."

"Thank you," Kang replied nervously.

"I know who you are and who you work for," Kruger said, tapping the manila folder. "I know everything about you, Major."

Kang said nothing as he watched Kruger's finger linger on top of the file.

"But do you know who I am?" Kruger asked.

"No," Kang said, shaking his head slowly as he continued to watch Kruger's hands.

"Up here, look at me," Kruger said, pointing up to his eyes. "You're going to want to pay attention to this."

Once Kang made eye contact again, Kruger continued, "I am no one."

"No one?" Kang asked nervously.

"Well, of course, my name is Kruger," Kruger responded. "But you see, like you, I don't exist."

Kruger let the words hang in the air as he watched Kang's facial expression change. The look of recognition was unmistakable. That was the beauty of dealing with covert operatives. They understood the inner workings of the business more than anyone.

"None of this truly exists," Kruger said, holding his hands up. "No one will ever know we were here. Isn't that interesting?"

Kruger noticed Kang's leg start to bounce up and down nervously.

"So, of course, the Geneva Convention might apply, but only if we actually existed," Kruger said.

"I told you I don't know anything," Kang said, his voice shaking.

"Oh, sure you do," Kruger said as he uncrossed his legs and leaned in toward Kang. "And I'm sure you believe that I have the ability to extract the information from you. Everyone breaks eventually, you know."

Kang nodded as he watched Kruger stand and pace around the room.

"I'm sure you've heard of my methods," Kruger said. His voice deepened ominously as he slowly made his way around the table behind Kang. "Some are obviously less humane than others, but I'm sure you've seen much worse from your own people. The Chinese are pretty efficient. I'll give you that much."

"But so am I," he added.

Kruger let the tension build as he continued pacing around the room. He could see the perspiration building on Kang's head and neck. He was slow and deliberate in his movements. *Sometimes the fear of torture is worse than torture itself.*

"But we don't have to go down that rabbit hole," Kruger said, returning to his chair to face the growingly anxious Kang.

"I'm just a pilot," Kang said meekly.

"Of course, you are," Kruger said, flashing his smile again. "And that's why I think we can bypass the formalities."

"I don't know anything," Kang said. The tapping of his foot grew more intense as he continued fidgeting with his hands.

"Sure you do," Kruger said in a reassuring tone. "You don't even know the question yet."

"The question does not matter Mr. Kruger. If I talk to you, I am a dead man when I go back," Kang replied.

Kruger opened the manila folder, reviewed the paper on top, and then spun the folder around to face Kang. "Here you go," he said as he pushed the file toward Kang.

"What is this?" Kang asked as he studied the papers in front of him.

"Your new identity, Mister," Kruger paused to look at the paper. "Jun Lee of San Jose, California. You're really going to love it there."

"I hear it's lovely year round," Kruger said as he watched Kang examine the paperwork in front of him. "All you have to do is answer my questions."

Kang looked up at Kruger with a confused expression. "You can do this?"

"I can," Kruger said, closing the file and pulling it back to him. "But I only have one to offer between you and Mr. Chi next door. So whoever gives me the best information will get it."

"And if neither of us tells you anything?" Kang asked, showing a flash of confidence.

Kruger laughed as he sat back in the chair holding the file. "Of course you'll both talk. The question is what method you'll choose."

"A choice?" Kang asked.

"Life is about choices, Mr. Kang. Are you familiar with the hammer and the carrot?"

Kang shook his head.

"Let's call this the carrot," Kruger said, holding up the file. "One of you will get a new life in sunny San Jose, where no one will ever find you."

"On the other hand, I'm sure you're intimately familiar with the hammer, both literally and figuratively. Do you really want that option? Everyone talks eventually," Kruger said ominously.

Kang stared at the folder in Kruger's hand.

"What do you want to know?" he asked finally.

"Excellent choice, *Mr. Lee*," Kruger said with a grin. . "Let's start with you, what do you do?"

"I fly the King Air in the hangar," Kang replied eagerly.

"And who is your boss?" Kruger asked.

"I work for the Ministry of State Security, Mr. Kruger, I have many bosses," Kang replied. "You will have to be more specific."

"Who runs your operation here in Tampa?" Kruger asked impatiently.

"Kato Ling," Kang replied.

"And is that who ordered the operation this morning?"

"No," Kang responded, shaking his head. "I flew Ling in this morning, it couldn't have been him."

"Then who?"

"I don't know of any operations this morning," Kang replied reluctantly.

Kruger frowned. "So you didn't see the van full of bullet holes in your hangar, or notice that you had twelve fewer men this evening? Have you grown tired of the carrot already?"

"No!" Kang yelped.

"Then I suggest you tell me the truth," Kruger warned.

"I don't know anything about the operation," Kang said, holding up his hands. "But I know Jiang Xin has been in town the last couple of days and he has brought his own men in. They have been searching for someone."

"A girl?" Kruger asked.

Kang shook his head. "I do not know this man's name, but I know he must be very dangerous for Xin to be looking for him."

"Why?" Kruger asked. "Who is Xin?"

Kang's brow furrowed. "He is very deadly, Mr. Kruger."

"Who is he?" Kruger pushed.

"He comes straight from Beijing. He is an expert," Kang said, looking away.

"An expert in what?" Kruger asked.

"Death, Mr. Kruger," Kang replied uneasily.

"Where do I find him?" Kruger asked, unaffected by Kang's dramatic description.

"I don't know," Kang said. As he watched Kruger's expression change, he quickly added, "But I have heard that they are operating on a ship docked in the East Bay."

"Do you know the name?" Kruger pressed.

Kang nervously shook his head. "Beijing... Beijing Star?"

"Ok," Kruger said as he stood and walked over to Kang. He reattached the arm and leg restraints as Kang watched him with a confused look.

"I thought we had a deal," Kang pleaded.

"We do," Kruger responded as he picked up the file and started for the door. "Now it depends on what your friend next door says."

CHAPTER TWENTY THREE

Freedom Star Deepwater Oil and Gas Platform
Gulf of Mexico
0445 Local Time

"**I**t's too way early for this shit," Crash groaned as he stared listlessly at his plate of eggs and bacon. He was seated across from Foxworthy and Mary at a table in the small cafeteria on the second deck of the Freedom Star. He could barely hear Mary laugh at him over the noise of the roughnecks and roustabouts milling about and carrying on conversations as the day crew of the massive oil platform in the Gulf of Mexico started their day.

"For twelve hundred bucks per day, you'd better get used to it," Foxworthy said from across the table. "You've got two more days of this."

Crash downed the Styrofoam cup of lukewarm coffee he had been nursing as he tried to shake off the sleep. "I know, but damn," Crash replied.

"Don't be such a pussy," Mary said, still laughing at him. "I know you Zamboni Drivers have never been to real war, but on the ship—"

"Oh great, now look what you've done," Foxworthy interrupted. "Another 'war story' from the Warrior Princess over here."

"Wait, who are you calling a Zamboni Driver?" Crash asked with a feigned look of shock.

"You Eagle guys," Mary replied, grinning ear to ear. "All you guys do is clean up the air picture—the 'ice'— so that the real players can go in and take care of business."

"Ouch," Foxworthy said. A crooked grin flashed across Foxworthy's face. "But tell me, oh wise one, how many jets was your squadron flying the day before we left?"

"One," Mary said solemnly as she hung her head in shame. With its aging fleet of early A-model F/A-18s, her squadron had been having issues in recent times with jets being down for maintenance or out for depot-level inspections. "But that's different! We're a reserve squadron and the jets are old!"

"Crash, how many Zambonis did we put up?" Foxworthy asked, gesturing to Crash, who had finally perked up.

"Well, Mr. Foxworthy, I do believe we flew a four V four, so I think that's…" Crash made an exaggerated attempt to count it out on his fingers in front of Mary. "Eight!"

"How about that? Not bad for a Guard unit full of Zamboni drivers," Foxworthy said as the table erupted in laughter.

With his team fully awake and engaged, Foxworthy brought out the itinerary for the day and began briefing his troops. Their morning would begin with splitting up and observing various areas of the platform as part of their Safety Survey. In the afternoon, they would meet with the supervisors of each area and give them detailed debriefs on how to manage risk and work together as a team. Foxworthy loved spending time on the oil rigs. While it was lucrative, he also felt that he was making a difference and connecting with the people on a more personal level. It was very rewarding to see the crews implement their training as Foxworthy's team observed on day three.

As Foxworthy finished covering the itinerary and the three stacked their trays, a short, stocky man with a beard walked up to their table. The rest of the cafeteria had mostly cleared out as the crews went to their work centers.

"Mr. Vaughan?" the man asked as the three collectively turned to look at the man. "I'm Josh Zweeben, do you remember me?"

"You guys did a presentation for us on the Big Cajun 17 off the Mississippi coast a few months ago," Zweeben added as he recognized the look of confusion in Foxworthy's face.

"Oh hey, Josh," Foxworthy replied. "It's good to see you again. Please, join us."

Zweeben wasted no time in accepting Foxworthy's invitation and took a seat next to Crash. "Your story about intercepting that MiG in Iraq was awesome," Zweeben said as he crowded into Crash's personal space. "It must be such a huge adrenaline rush flying those F-15s every day."

Foxworthy nodded with a gracious smile. He always made a point of trying to relate his war stories to the work the men and women did on the oil rigs. People were constantly approaching him telling him how great they thought the stories were and how it helped them realize that they could apply it to their daily jobs.

"I'm glad you enjoyed it," Foxworthy replied.

"Oh, I did," Zweeben replied excitedly. "And ma'am, your story about landing at night on an aircraft carrier in bad weather – that gave me goose bumps!"

"So what do you do on the Freedom Star, Josh?" Mary asked.

"I'm the geologist," Zweeben replied. "It's not as exciting as you guys flying fighter jets, but I really like it."

"Do you work for Cajun Oil and Gas?" Foxworthy asked. It was always a crap shoot on the oil platforms as to which company the person they were talking to actually worked for. There were so many contractors and subcontractors on each rig that it was hard for Foxworthy to keep them all straight.

Zweeben nodded. "Most of the time," he replied. "But not always. Sometimes I subcontract out to other companies."

"I'll bet you've been on a lot of these rigs then," Crash said.

"Boy, you're telling me!" Zweeben replied. "I've been all over the Gulf, it seems like."

"Let me ask you something," Foxworthy said, seeing an opportunity to put to rest an issue that had been bothering him for days.

"Go ahead, sir," Zweeben responded cheerfully.

Foxworthy lowered his voice and leaned in. "Do you know of any Chinese oil rigs in the Gulf?"

"Oh, here we go again," Crash groaned as he rolled his eyes. "Let it go, Captain Ahab."

Foxworthy gestured for Crash to stop as he watched Zweeben's eyes dart nervously around the room. The small cafeteria was empty except for them.

"Promise you won't say anything," Zweeben said nervously. "You guys are good at keeping secrets, right?"

"Part of the job," Foxworthy replied reassuringly. "So I guess the answer is yes?"

"Yes, there is one," Zweeben replied softly. "But it's not run by the Chinese."

"Then how do you know it's Chinese?" Crash asked skeptically.

"Because I was a geologist on it," Zweeben replied. "It's a semi-submersible called the Jupiter Rising."

"And Cajun runs it?" Foxworthy asked.

"Sort of," Zweeben replied. "I was assigned to it directly by Mr. Jane, but my checks were all from a company called Chinati Oil."

Foxworthy looked at Mary, who was also leaning in to hear Zweeben's story. She was frowning at the implication that her father might be involved.

"Chinati?" Foxworthy asked.

Zweeben shrugged. "I never really asked because it was good money and Mr. Jane is a good man. He asked me to keep it quiet and I never really thought much of it because everyone was American on the crew."

"So what makes you think it was Chinese?" Crash asked impatiently.

Zweeben hesitated for a minute, looking around nervously again to ensure no one was eavesdropping. "Because an entire half of the platform was completely off limits and I was up one night and saw one of the crew boats show up with nothing but Chinese men."

CHAPTER TWENTY FOUR

Tampa, FL

The sound of the lock clunking open startled Decker out her daze. She had been sitting in the corner of the hot shipping container drifting in an out of sleep – at least she thought it was a shipping container.

After meeting Xin, a burlap hood had been placed over her head and she was wheeled through a warehouse and offloaded. The hood had been worn through enough that she could barely make out the metal walls and a door as they propped her against the back wall and locked the doors behind them. Whatever drug they had given her had finally worn off hours later as she slowly regained control of her arms and legs. The paralysis had been the most terrifying aspect of the entire event.

Not that Decker wasn't still scared. Her options for escape were nonexistent. Her arms were flex cuffed behind her back and her right shoulder was in terrible pain. She wasn't sure if she had broken ribs from the crash or if maybe the effects of the drugs still hadn't worn off, but her breathing was labored and painful in the hot, humid air of the metal shipping container.

The door opened, sending a rush of much cooler air in as she watched the silhouette of a man approach through her burlap hood. His boots clicked against the metal floor as he walked up to her and abruptly pulled the hood off her face.

The overhead light was blinding as her eyes struggled to adjust, but the cool air hitting her face was a welcome relief. Although she was bordering on dehydration, she was still sweating profusely in the stuffy shipping container. She struggled to focus as the man stood over her and blocked the single overhead light.

"Hello, Agent Decker," the man said with a hint of a Chinese accent. As Decker's eyes adjusted, she recognized the dark-haired man standing over her. It was Xin. His presence sent chills down her spine. There was something about him that was just... *sinister*.

"What do you want from me?" Decker said hoarsely. Her eyes darted around the room, assessing her situation for the first time. Her initial guess that she was in a shipping container had been dead on. She could see the chalk writing and an outline of where a manifest had been near the door. As her eyes adjusted further, she could see the walls of the warehouse beyond the door.

Xin smiled through his dark goatee. Decker continued to assess her situation. She thought back to what the dying man had told her on the stairs of the house. The man had apparently known that her life was in danger. *Escape was the only path to survival.*

But an escape attempt wouldn't come easily. Even if she could manage to unbind her hands, the pain in her shoulder made her right arm nearly useless. There was no way to fight her way out. The lack of options scared her even more than the man standing over her.

"I want to know what you know, Agent Decker," Xin said ominously. "Starting with Cal Martin."

"Cal Martin?" Decker asked.

Without saying a word, Xin backhanded Decker, causing her to spit blood as she coughed and recovered from the blow.

"Do not play dumb with me, Agent Decker," Xin barked. "I know all about your relationship with Martin."

Relationship? Decker thought. *That's a new one.* Decker's mind raced as she tried to figure out Xin's interest with Cal. The assassination attempts on Cal Martin had been orchestrated by Victor Alvarez and a Russian girl. To her knowledge, there had never been a Chinese link.

"I don't know what you're talking about," Decker replied defiantly. "I haven't seen him in days."

Xin smiled. "But you're looking for him," he replied. "And I think you know where he is."

Decker laughed. "If I did, do you think I would be in here?" she asked as she spat more blood from her bloodied lip.

Xin bent over and grabbed Decker by the throat, raising her to her feet. He was deceptively strong for his size, standing only a few inches taller than the five foot five inch Decker. She choked and gasped for air as he eased his grip while still pushing her against the metal wall of the container.

"You are going to tell me what I want to know," Xin said calmly as he stared menacingly into Decker's blue eyes. His eyes were dark, almost black. His stare was unsettling to Decker.

"I don't know where Cal Martin is," Decker said weakly before turning her head away from Xin and coughing. "Why do you want him so badly?"

"Yours is not to question why, Agent Decker," Xin said. "But I do not believe you. I think you know where he is."

Decker shifted under the weight of the man's hand against her throat. If Simms were correct, Cal Martin was likely somewhere in Louisiana. She had only been in Tampa to find out what happened to cause him to flee and help prove his innocence. As she stared into the eyes of the man before her, she was pretty sure she had found the biggest clue yet.

"I don't know," Decker lied.

Xin calmly withdrew his right hand from her throat. As she relaxed against the wall, he suddenly and violently punched her in the stomach, causing her to double over onto the ground as the blow knocked the wind out of her.

"This is your last chance, Agent Decker," Xin said as he watched her roll on the ground while wheezing and gasping for air. "I am going to give you more time to consider your cooperation. Know that you will tell me what I want to know. That much is given. The choice you face is how much pain you are willing to endure."

Xin let the words hang in the air for a moment and then turned to walk out, slamming and locking the door behind him. Decker slowly rolled onto her back and leaned against the metal wall. She grimaced under the pain as she tried to regain control of her breathing.

As she finally calmed herself, Decker thought back to her investigation, desperately trying to remember anything that might place Xin in the puzzle. There was no doubt in her mind that he was Chinese. *Was it Chinese mafia? Or from the Chinese Government?* Neither option made sense to her.

Her prevailing theory had always been that the assassination attempts on Cal and his friends had been based on their involvement in recovering Cal's fiancée and a stolen F-16. The same man that had orchestrated the theft of the F-16 had been behind the assassination attempts. *Or so she thought.*

Victor Alvarez had been found dead in the barn of a farmhouse in the Redlands of Homestead. Simms was convinced that Cal Martin had been working with Victor, but from what she knew of Cal, that theory was ludicrous. Cal hated Victor, and although she wasn't sure what Cal's involvement was at the farmhouse, she was sure the two had not been working together. She had proven as much to herself by watching the ATM camera at the motel.

The Chinese angle was completely new to her. And then it hit her. *The micro-UAV!* In searching Victor Alvarez's hotel room at the Biltmore, she found the backpack and tablet used to control the micro-UAV that had killed Carpenter and injured Martin and Marcus Anderson. It had been identified as a Chinese ASN-15 and the instructions had been in Chinese with English translations. *That's it!* Decker thought.

But the realization that the two were related only brought up more questions for Decker. She tried to put the questions aside as she focused on the more pressing issue. Xin would be back, and his warning had been clear. He would not stop until she told him everything. *She needed an escape plan.*

CHAPTER TWENTY FIVE

South Harbor Industrial Complex
Tampa, FL
0915 Local Time

The red Camaro SS slowed to a crawl and then stopped along the tree line as it reached the end of the white gravel road. Spectre exited the car and made his way through the nearby thick brush to the other side of the tree line. He was carrying a pair of binoculars he had purchased at a sporting goods store during the ten hour drive from New Orleans to Tampa.

Using the thick brush as concealment, Spectre turned his baseball cap backwards and pulled the high-powered binoculars out of their case while focusing them on the harbor. Beyond the tree line was a fence and staging area of thousands of red, blue, and green shipping containers.

The shipping yard was quiet. To the north of the compound, another shipping yard appeared to be busy with activity, but as Spectre scanned the shipping containers in this yard, he could find no activity or people.

Spectre pulled out a crumpled up paper from his cargo pants pocket as he tried to shake off the sleep. He had driven through the night, stopping only to take a four-hour nap in an empty parking lot once he reached Tampa. He stared at the page of the ledger he had identified as most likely serving as a base of operations for Decker's kidnapping.

At least Spectre hoped it was a kidnapping. Bear's message had been purposefully cryptic. Decker was missing. Through their pre-coordinated code, Spectre determined that Bear wanted him to go to Tampa. How Bear knew Tampa was the place to go wasn't clear to Spectre, but he assumed it had something to do with his interactions with the FBI.

Spectre's confidence in Bear's direction grew upon studying the ledger. Out of the ten pages he had printed, there were only five references to Florida. Most of the entries were in Miami, including the Biltmore Hotel and the farmhouse in the Redlands that Victor Alvarez had used to torture and question Spectre before he escaped.

The only entry for Tampa was the shipping yard in the South Harbor Industrial Complex. The particular entry was listed as Warehouse 118 on South Harbor Boulevard. Hua Xia Holdings apparently had funneled money into the construction of a new warehouse and shipping yard on the southern side of the industrial complex.

It was so new, in fact, that when Spectre attempted to research it at an Internet café using Google Earth on one of his stops, the only things he could see were the shipping containers and construction equipment. According to Google, Warehouse 118 did not yet exist, but as Spectre confirmed the number and went back to his binoculars, he found the newly constructed building behind the sea of shipping containers.

Spectre continued his scan around the warehouse with his binoculars. He found an armed guard at each corner of the building. They were dressed in black and looked to be Chinese. They also had what appeared to be black AK-74s slung over their chests.

As he continued his surveillance, Spectre found two more guards that he had previously missed on foot patrols in the shipping yard. They were similarly dressed and carrying the same black AK-74 rifles. Spectre cursed himself for missing them on his first scan. His fatigue was starting to affect his attention to detail. He knew it would get him killed if he weren't careful.

Returning his attention to the warehouse, Spectre watched as a side door opened and a man emerged. As Spectre zoomed in, he noticed the man had thick dark hair and a dark goatee. He was dressed differently than the guards. Spectre also caught the glimmer of a nickel-plated handgun in the man's shoulder holster as he moved north along the building.

Spectre thought back to his conversation with Chang. *Could that be Xin?* The description was close, at least from what Spectre could see with the binoculars. He watched the man stop and chat with the northern guard for a few minutes. He had an air of importance about him. He was apparently running the show as the guard nodded and took off at a jog toward the door from which the man had recently emerged.

As the guard entered the building, the man pulled out what appeared to be a secure satellite phone and placed a phone call. Spectre crouched lower as the man seemed to look right at him. Spectre knew there was no way the man could see him, but it still caused a surge of adrenaline through Spectre's body.

The man hung up the phone and lit a cigarette. Moments later, the previous guard emerged from the building. He and another guard were on each side, dragging someone out toward the smoking man. The person's hands were bound and head was covered with what appeared to be a burlap sack. *Decker!*

He watched as the two men dragged her toward the man in charge. The man motioned for them to follow, and the four disappeared behind the building. Spectre's heart was racing.

Taking off in a near sprint, Spectre quickly made his way through the brush until he reached the fourth generation Camaro. He opened the door and popped the hatchback, revealing several large bags, backpacks and hardened cases.

Spectre took a deep breath and exhaled slowly, trying to calm himself as he formulated a plan. He had no doubt that he had just witnessed Decker being moved. There was no one left to help him. *No one left to trust.* His only option was to go it alone. Spectre knew he was the reason her life was in danger. He would save her or die trying.

Unzipping the large green bag, Spectre pulled out the black, lightweight plate carrier. He had taken all of the gear he had from working at Project Archangel and for Marcus and transferred it from his truck to the Camaro before leaving Bear to delay the FBI for him. He took off his hat and put the plate carrier on over his head, tightening the Velcro straps as he checked it over. He had installed light weight ceramic Level IV front and side trauma plates, as well as three loaded rifle magazines in pouches on the front and a chest rig holster next to his combat knife on his left shoulder.

Spectre pulled an FN 5.7 handgun out of its hardened case, loaded it with a fresh twenty round magazine, and chambered a round before inserting it into the chest rig. The FN's 5.7 x 28mm SS198 round was capable of penetrating soft body armor. With its low recoil and high magazine capacity, it was Spectre's favorite sidearm.

With his armor set, Spectre unlocked the hardened case, revealing his H&K 416 chambered in 5.56 NATO. He pulled the single point sling over his shoulder, clipped it to the rifle, and inserted the loaded PMAG thirty round magazine before releasing the bolt to chamber a round. Spectre checked the EOTech Holographic Hybrid Sight and magnifier and then put two spare rifle magazines in his cargo pants pockets. He grabbed a pair of wire cutters out of his tool bag before putting his hat back on and closing the hatch.

Keeping his rifle up and ready, Spectre made his way through the tree line. Using the 3.25x magnifier on his EOTech sight, Spectre located the two roving foot patrols. Confident that he could make it to the fence line undetected, Spectre slowly made his way to the chain link fence while holding his rifle high and ready.

At the fence, Spectre pulled the wire cutters out and cut a small hole to squeeze through as he entered the shipping yard. Sweeping left and right with his rifle as he made his way across the rows of red containers, Spectre approached the southernmost guard.

Using the containers as cover, Spectre followed the guard who was mindlessly walking away from Spectre. Seeing no one in the area, Spectre shifted his rifle to his back and grabbed the guard in a chokehold while kicking his right leg out and pulling the man off balance. Spectre tightened his grip until the man stopped struggling then dragged the man's limp body out of sight.

With the first guard down, Spectre held up his rifle and started toward the far, northernmost guard. Spectre's adrenaline was pumping, but he focused on his breathing. He quickly and quietly made his way through the rows of shipping containers, stopping at the intersection of each aisle to ensure that there were no unseen guards.

Spectre stopped as he drew within fifty yards of the second guard. The man appeared to be much more alert than the first. He was diligently checking each container as he made his way from row to row.

As Spectre stalked his next victim, he was suddenly stopped dead in his tracks as he rounded the corner of one of the containers to see the barrels of two rifles pointed as his face.

"Drop it and don't move," the man growled. Spectre wasn't even given a chance to respond before he felt the hit from behind and his world went black.

* * *

"Sandman, Pegasus Three One," the female voice said over the secure radio. It was the voice of Jenny flying the U-28 surveillance aircraft over the harbor that Kang had told them about.

Kruger turned from his seat in the operations center of Project Archangel and picked up a portable radio. "Go for Sandman," he said.

"Sandman, you might want to see this," Jenny replied. "I've got a mover at the perimeter. JAX is sending video now."

"Copy, good handshake," Kruger said as he opened the Toughbook Laptop and confirmed that he was receiving the video feed from the aircraft. Kruger watched as the black and white video feed from the U-28 showed a sports car heading south on the hardball road. The car stopped at the end and an occupant exited into the tree line. As if on cue, JAX switched the pod to infrared, showing the white-hot image of a man hiding in the tree line.

"Who the fuck is that?" Kruger asked to himself as he watched the man sitting in the tree line. Kruger picked up the radio and keyed the mic, "Banzai Zero One, Sandman." Banzai was the ground surveillance team they had staged on the north end of the harbor as they tried to get a tactical plan together to mount a potential rescue mission for the hostage.

"Banzai Zero One," former Army Ranger Ty "Tuna" Turner responded.

"Do you have eyes on the vehicle south of your position?" Kruger asked.

"Affirm," Tuna responded. "Red Camaro."

The video feed caught Kruger's eye as he watched the white blob exit the trees toward the Camaro. JAX switched the video link back to the Electro Optical TV mode, showing a clear picture of a man standing at the back of the Camaro hatch. "Standby," Kruger said as he watched the man pull gear out of the hatchback.

"Banzai is contact, single, appears to be doing something near the rear of the vehicle," Tuna advised over the radio.

"Sandman sees same," Kruger responded. "Coolio, do we have anyone else in the field right now?" Kruger asked as he turned to the young cyber analyst.

"Not that I know of, sir, just the four-man surveillance team," Julio Meeks responded.

"Banzai, standby to intercept," Kruger said over the radio.

"Banzai Zero One," Tuna responded.

Kruger watched as the man pulled a rifle and then closed the hatch before heading back toward the tree line.

"Go get that guy, Tuna," Kruger said as he watched the unknown man move through the tree line. He was dumbfounded that someone appeared to be assaulting the warehouse in broad daylight.

"Banzai, be advised, subject is armed," JAX interjected over the radio.

"Banzai shows same," Tuna replied.

"Nonlethal," Kruger instructed. "I want to talk to this guy."

"Banzai is inbound," Tuna said. Kruger watched as the team of four headed from their northwestern position of concealment. JAX continued to call out movements of the man as he cut through the fence line and made his way through the rows of shipping containers.

"He's engaging the southern patrol," JAX said.

Kruger watched in stunned silence as the man effortlessly took down the inattentive southern guard.

"He's heading northwest for the other patrol, recommend you set up between the rows, I'll talk you on," JAX said.

As Kruger watched the man move toward the second guard, he studied the man's movements. "We trained this guy," he said to himself as Ironman entered behind him.

"What's going on?" Ironman asked as he watched the video feed over Kruger's shoulder.

"This has to be one of our guys," Kruger said as he watched the team carry the man's limp body away after knocking him out and disarming him. "This dude just tried to assault the warehouse in broad daylight as a singleton. Who the fuck is he?"

Ironman studied the pixelated digital feed as the men carried the man back out to safety.

"You're right, we did train him," Ironman said unemotionally. "That's Spectre Martin."

CHAPTER TWENTY SIX

"**G**et up," the man said in heavily accented English as he and his associate stormed into the shipping container. Decker noticed the rifles slung on their backs as they jerked her to her feet and each grabbed an arm.

"Jesus," Decker groaned as the grunt to her right pulled on her injured shoulder. "You guys don't have to be so rough," she added.

"No talk," the apparent leader said as they started walking her out of the container. The pace picked up as they cleared the container out onto the concrete warehouse floor. Decker's feet barely made contact with the floor as the two men forced her toward the nearest exit.

Decker's vision was obscured by the worn burlap sack over her head, but she could make out the warehouse and several vehicles and boxes as they dragged her the twenty-five feet to the door. She tried to make as many mental notes of her surroundings as she could. It was a habit from investigations, but she also knew it could be beneficial to her eventual escape attempt.

The thick, warm air hit her as they forced her through the narrow doorway. She had no idea what time it was, but she at least knew it was daytime. She guessed morning, but she had no way of knowing. Her sense of time had been deprived as part of her captivity.

Her shoulder burned as the men pulled her down the sidewalk. She tried to keep pace to alleviate the pressure, but after hours of sitting, her muscles were stiff and her legs barely moved. She was also dehydrated and hungry, further weakening her ability to keep pace.

"Hello, Agent Decker," a male voice said as the men stopped her. Through her hood, she barely made out the silhouette of the man she almost instantly recognized to be Xin. His sinister voice was unmistakable.

"If you let me go, I won't kill you," Decker said unconvincingly.

Xin let out a hearty laugh. "You Americans are all alike," he replied. "In any case, your time here is now done."

"Where are you taking me?" Decker demanded as the two men started pulling her down the sidewalk again. Decker felt the sun against her skin as they dragged her around the corner of the building. She could hear seagulls in the distance and what sounded like waves gently crashing against the sea wall.

The two men continued pulling on her arms as they walked her across what seemed like hundreds of feet of parking lot. She could see more shipping containers and giant cranes through her hood. She realized she was at a harbor and she guessed they were taking her toward the bay.

They took her up a series of stairs. Her legs felt better after walking. She still felt weak, but the exercise restored some of the circulation and worked out the cramps. She knew she would need every ounce of energy.

As they reached the top of the stairs, the men stopped. They said something in Chinese to another man who grabbed her by the collar and pulled her forward. She felt unsteady as she walked forward. Looking down through the hood, she could see that she was on a narrow bridge way from the dock to a medium sized boat. *Now or never.*

Reaching the midway point on the narrow bridge, Decker abruptly stopped, causing the guard behind her to attempt to push her forward. Decker kicked her leg straight back and up, striking him in the groin as he stopped behind her. The man in front turned and closed the distance. Decker stepped forward and when she thought he was close enough, head butted him as hard as she could. The loud crack of his nose and a yelp told her that she had been successful. With her immediate attackers stunned, Decker took a deep breath and rolled over the metal chain serving as a guardrail for the narrow plank.

The fall was longer than Decker expected. She tried to straighten her body, but was unsuccessful as she hit the water at an awkward angle. The impact of the water jarred her body, but the adrenaline kept her moving. Ignoring the pain from her shoulder, she pulled her hands under her feet to get her handcuffed hands out in front of her. *The years of swimming in high school would be worth something.*

Decker started swimming toward the surface as she pulled the thick hood off her head. She gasped for air as she reached the calm surface, continuing to swim as best she could. She heard yelling as she continued to swim toward what she thought was land, away from the boat and the sea wall.

As Decker struggled to stay afloat and swim away, rounds started peppering the water around her, causing her to dive back down beneath the surface. She felt like she was going nowhere as she continued kicking and flailing beneath the water. As she came up for air at the surface, she heard more gunfire and the sound of boat engines nearing her position.

Her lungs burned and every muscle wanted to give up, but Decker continued kicking, hoping to reach land before they reached her. She felt her body losing strength as she kept going. She realized her muscles would fail before she made it to safety, and found herself wondering if she had been swimming in circles.

Willing herself to continue, Decker suddenly felt a massive wake push her back beneath the surface. She struggled to get back up above the surface as the water filled her lungs. Suddenly, she felt something grab her hair and pull her up above the surface as she choked and gasped for air.

After what seemed like an eternity, she found herself on the deck of a boat, staring at the clear blue sky as a man in dark blue hovered over her.

"Ma'am, ma'am," the man said, shaking her. "Are you ok?"

Decker rolled over to her side and coughed up water before losing consciousness.

CHAPTER TWENTY SEVEN

Tampa International Airport
Tampa, FL
1005 Local Time

Special Agent Simms checked his phone messages as he waited for his bag at Baggage Carousel Three in the Tampa International Airport. Due to a higher priority tasking, the FBI had been unable to send a jet to Baton Rouge to pick him up. Instead, he was forced to ride with Agent Venable to New Orleans at the crack of dawn to catch the one-way flight from New Orleans International to Tampa.

After dropping Simms off at the airport, Venable would continue his investigation into what Cal Martin had been doing in New Orleans when he responded to Mr. Jennings's message. Simms knew it would probably be a dead end, but the young agent needed some experience in field work anyway.

As the carousel whirred to life, Simms put his black sport coat on and waited for his bag to show up. He found the number in his smartphone for the field agent in Tampa he had been assigned and sent him a text letting him know he had made it to baggage claim. The agent responded that he would be waiting out front in a dark blue SUV.

Finding his black hardened suitcase on the conveyer, Simms grabbed it and headed for the exit. The dark blue SUV was parked in the airport's passenger loading and unloading zone. Simms confirmed it was his contact and threw his suitcase and laptop bag into the back seat and entered the front passenger seat.

"I'm Special Agent Simms," he said, introducing himself to the agent wearing a black polo shirt and tactical pants in the driver's seat.

"Agent Cooper," the agent replied. "Welcome to Tampa." Cooper put the SUV in gear and pulled out into the line of taxis toward the airport exit.

"Thank you for picking me up, Agent Cooper," Simms responded. "I trust you've read the case briefing I sent you?" Upon learning that Cooper would be his liaison, Simms had wasted no time in sending the notes and briefings he'd prepared via secure e-mail to Cooper. He didn't have time to explain every detail to a new agent.

"Oh, I'm very familiar with the case, Agent Simms," Cooper replied. "Thank you for sending such thorough notes."

"Good," Simms said. He smiled smugly as he put on his Ray Ban Aviator sunglasses and went back to checking messages on his phone.

"I do have one question though," Cooper said as he pulled onto the freeway.

Simms's phone buzzed as he started to answer. "One sec," he said, holding his long, slender finger up in the air to silence Cooper as he answered the phone.

"What do you have, Venable?" Simms said.

"Hey boss, I'm over here with NOPD, and I think I figured out where Martin went last night," Venable responded.

"I'm listening," Simms said impatiently.

"Yesterday evening around six o'clock, there was a break in on the sixteenth floor of One Shell Square on Poydras Street. That's just a few blocks from the Internet café we traced Martin's computer to," Venable continued. "He took down a security guard and escaped before police arrived."

"What kind of business was it?" Simms asked.

"Hua Xia Holdings," Venable replied slowly as he struggled to pronounce the name. "The report said he broke into their safe and destroyed most of the offices."

"Hua Xia Holdings? Do we know what they do?" Simms repeated. Cooper turned and looked Simms as he heard the name.

"Unknown so far," Venable replied. "A quick Google Search shows that they're a Chinese investment and holding company, but I'll have to do more research."

"Wait, that name sounds familiar," Simms said as he reached into the back seat to pull out the file from his laptop bag. "Hold on," he said as he thumbed through the massive file he had on the case.

"Hua Xia Holdings, here it is," Simms said. "The hotel room where Svetlana Mitchell was arrested was rented to a David Hernandez and paid for using a corporate account through Hua Xia Holdings."

"I'm going to go with the Detectives here in a few minutes to the scene. I'll see what I can dig up on that connection," Venable offered.

"Keep me updated," Simms ordered. He hung up the phone without waiting for a response as he turned his attention back to Cooper. "Now, what was your question, Agent Cooper?"

"Oh, umm," Cooper said, caught off guard after eavesdropping on Simms's conversation. "Cal Martin…"

"Yes? What about him?" Simms snapped impatiently.

"Do you really think he's in Tampa?" Cooper asked as they pulled into the parking lot of the large FBI building.

"Do you think I would be here if I didn't?" Simms asked with a disgusted look on his face. *Cal Martin is a dangerous fugitive from justice and this is the quality of help I get?* Simms thought.

"I didn't mean to question your methods, Agent Simms," Cooper responded. "I just didn't quite pick up the connection from your report."

"Call it a hunch after talking to Mr. Jennings," Simms replied coolly. "If he isn't already here, I think he's on his way for Agent Decker."

"You're right, I'm sorry," Cooper finally said. "Speaking of which, I'm going to drop you off here now. I'll be back in an hour or so. You can use my desk if you need a workspace."

"Where are you going?" Simms asked.

"To assist Agent Kemp with a lead on the Decker case," Cooper said.

"Why are you just telling me about this now?" Simms snapped. "I'm going with you."

"I'm sorry," Cooper replied. "I know she works with you in Miami, but I wasn't sure how relevant it was to this case. Besides, we're not sure it's even related to her case. I know you're busy and I didn't want to interrupt you with it."

"What is the lead?" Simms asked.

"The Coast Guard just picked up an unidentified woman in the East Bay near the Industrial Area," Cooper responded.

"Dead or alive?" Simms demanded.

"Last I talked to Kemp, she was barely hanging on. That was before I picked you up," Cooper said, shaking his head.

"Let's go," Simms ordered.

"Like I said, it could be completed unrelated to either case, I—"

"I said, let's go," Simms said, cutting him off.

"Ok, but I warned you," Cooper said forebodingly as he put the SUV in reverse.

CHAPTER TWENTY EIGHT

Project Archangel Detention Facility
MacDill AFB, FL
1022 Local Time

Spectre closed his eyes as he tried to minimize the pain of his throbbing headache in the hot room. After knocking him out cold, they had stripped him of his armor and weapons, leaving him only with a t-shirt and khaki tactical pants. His hands and feet were handcuffed and chained to a metal chair in the room that was surrounded by a steel cage.

Spectre was furious with himself for getting caught. The fighter pilot in him forced a debrief of every failure. How he had missed the team of operatives escaped him, but he suspected if he had been better rested, he might have done a better job of seeing them and modifying his plan.

He had come to as the panel van transporting him had made it through the gate. Although a sack had been placed over his head, he recognized the voices of the men in the van and heard the gate guard welcome them onto MacDill Air Force Base. He had been taken by Project Archangel.

It was ironic to Spectre to find himself once again sitting in the steel cage. They had used the very facility he was sitting in as part of his enhanced interrogation training. Kruger had conducted most of the training, building upon what he learned as part of his training at Survival, Evasion, Resistance, and Escape school in the Air Force. It was some of the most challenging training he had ever been subjected to. At many times, he found himself thinking he wouldn't make the cut, but when it was over, he was thankful he wouldn't have to do it again.

That had been different. That was training. They had rules and guidelines to follow. Spectre knew that the training was a walk in the park comparatively speaking. Kruger, if that's who they assigned to talk to him, wouldn't be so reserved this time. Permanent injuries would no longer be a concern. *This was real life.*

Spectre's mind drifted back to Victor's statement in the barn. "*You're a marked man. They want you and your friends dead. And they won't stop until you are. You can't fight them. You can only hide and hope they never find you. But they will. They're in every level of your government. They're watching and listening to everything that you do.*" Victor's words echoed in Spectre's head. *Was Project Archangel part of it all? Had they taken Michelle?*

Someone had set him up in Syria, that much was clear to Spectre. Radios just didn't deregister themselves from secure rescue satellites. Nor did messages telling him to rendezvous with indigenous forces randomly show up on those radios. Someone had caused that to happen. *Someone had set him up.*

Deep down, Spectre had always suspected Ironman was involved at the very least. His comments about flying drones shortly before Spectre and his friends were attacked in a drone strike couldn't be a coincidence. And Michelle Decker being captive in Tampa wasn't a coincidence either. *Were they trying to lure him there? Had they intercepted his messaging with Bear?* The more Spectre thought about it, the more paranoid he became.

Spectre tried to keep his mind in check. Solving the mystery of his predicament would get him no closer to escaping and rescuing Michelle. *If she's even still alive,* he thought. The people he faced were cold, calculating, and ruthless. He didn't put it past them to kill her once they had achieved their objective. He only wondered what information they hoped to obtain before killing him as well.

Spectre heard the magnetic lock click open as the far door opened. A bearded man in an Under Armor Shirt and black tactical pants emerged into the light. He entered a six digit PIN on the keypad and opened the metal cage. It was Kruger.

"Hello, Spectre," Kruger said as he took his seat across from him. "I'll be honest. I didn't expect you here today."

"Somehow, I don't believe that," Spectre said, closing his eyes and tilting his head back. "But fuck you anyway."

Kruger shook his head as he crossed his leg and draped his arm over the back of the chair. "Look, bub, it doesn't have to be like that."

"Is that right?" Spectre asked as he opened his eyes and stared at Kruger. "You think I don't know what's about to happen? You don't remember training me yourself?"

"Well, you could at least humor me and pretend like you remember what I taught you," Kruger said with a crooked smile.

Spectre stared angrily at Kruger.

"Would you like some water?" Kruger asked, pulling out a water bottle from his right cargo pants pocket.

"No, I'm sure I'll be getting plenty water soon enough," Spectre shot back as he remembered Kruger waterboarding him as part of his training.

"Look, dude, you need to get it together," Kruger warned. "This will not go well for you if you keep this up."

"Fuck it, I'm dead anyway," Spectre replied. "Where is Michelle? Is she safe? You can let her go now that you have me. I'll tell you whatever you want to know if you let her go." Spectre jerked against his restraints, causing the chains to rattle.

"Easy there, cowboy," Kruger said, holding his hands up. "I think we need to reestablish the roles here."

"I told you, I'll do whatever you want," Spectre reiterated. "As long as you prove to me that you're letting her go."

"Ok, I'll tell you what," Kruger said as he leaned forward with both elbows on the small table between them. "I'll be totally honest and upfront with you if you do the same with me. Deal?"

Spectre was exhausted, but he recognized Kruger's tactic. It was a technique he had seen Kruger try hundreds of times over the nearly month long training. The problem was that Spectre didn't care. He didn't feel the need to resist. He wasn't guarding state secrets or critical troop movements. He just wanted to guarantee Michelle's safety.

"I told you that I would tell you anything you want to know," Spectre said calmly, "as long as you let Michelle Decker go. You won't even have to play these games."

"You're not getting it, Cal," Kruger replied. "It's not a game. I don't have Michelle Decker."

"Then I guess we're at an impasse," Spectre snapped. "Because I think you're a fucking liar and you and Ironman are working with Xin. You can argue semantics all day about who actually has her, but you won't get anything out of me until you let her go."

Kruger swiftly and violently shot across the table, grabbing Spectre by the throat and squeezing his windpipe. Spectre attempted to jerk back out of the choke, but Kruger's grip was too strong. "Listen to me very carefully," Kruger growled.

"Brian Tanning and James Redman are dead because of whatever the fuck is going on here. They were two of the best men I've ever known, and I will not rest until I find out who's behind this. If you call me a liar again, I will assume you are part of the problem and rip your fucking throat out, do you understand me?"

Spectre nodded as he struggled to stay conscious. Kruger jerked his hand back, causing Spectre to choke and wheeze as he tried to regain his breath.

"Now, let's start over," Kruger said as Spectre continued coughing. "What were you doing in the shipping yard?"

"Trying… to… save… Michelle," Spectre said, still coughing.

Kruger waited for him to finish coughing before offering him water again. Spectre nodded and Kruger poured the water into Spectre's mouth. He choked and coughed a few more times before he finally regained his composure.

"What do you know about Xin?" Kruger asked.

"He's a Lieutenant for a Chinese intelligence operative named Zhang," Spectre replied. His voice was hoarse from being choked and coughing. "He's been trying to kill me. What happened to Tanning and Redman?"

"Your girlfriend was here asking questions, so Ironman had Redman follow her to make sure she didn't dig into our programs," Kruger replied as he sat back in his chair. "She was attacked in broad daylight and Redman brought her back to the safe house. A team of Chinese mercenaries overran them and took Decker."

"And then you tried to play John Rambo," Kruger said with a chuckle as he shook his head. "I would ask if you learned anything from us, but if this interrogation and you attacking a shipping yard in alone broad daylight are any indication, I think I already know that answer."

"They were taking her somewhere, I had to act," Spectre replied defensively. "She's in there because of me."

"In any case, she didn't need you," Kruger said.

Spectre gave Kruger a confused look.

"While you were tying up our guys, Agent Decker escaped as they were loading her into a transport boat," Kruger said. "Coast Guard plucked her out of the water shortly after."

"Is she ok?" Spectre asked nervously.

Kruger frowned. "She nearly drowned, but the Coasties were able to get her to Tampa General Hospital pretty quickly. Last I heard, she's in ICU."

"You have to let me go see her!" Spectre yelled.

As Kruger started to answer, he was interrupted by the metal lock. Behind him, Ironman walked in, opened the steel cage, and put his hand on Spectre's shoulder. "I'll take it from here," Ironman said.

"Do you mind if I stay?" Kruger asked as he stood to face Ironman.

"I would rather that you didn't," Ironman said with a frown as he shook his head. Kruger nodded and started for the cage door.

"We'll talk more later, Cal," Kruger said as he locked the steel cage and walked out the main door.

As he cleared, Ironman walked to the corner of the room and unplugged the cable from the observation camera. Spectre hadn't even noticed it before. He then walked back to the table and turned it on its side away from Spectre. He disconnected the hidden microphone and stuffed it in his pocket before flipping the table back upright.

"You're quite the sticky booger, Cal," Ironman said as he paced around the room. "Do you have any idea what you've gotten yourself into?"

"So you're involved?" Spectre asked.

"I wasn't," Ironman said as he paced around the room. "You weren't even a blip on my radar until you decided to get yourself shot down in Syria."

"I didn't decide anything," Spectre argued. "The intel was wrong. You know there were no alert MiGs in that area. Someone had to task them directly!"

Ironman waved his hand up dismissively. "It doesn't matter anymore. The bottom line is that you got yourself into trouble with some very bad people, and now we're all taking a bite of this shit sandwich."

"Who took my radio off the net in Iraq? Who sent the messages telling me to link up with the ISF troops? Do you think I just willy-nilly got myself captured?" Spectre asked.

"I told you it doesn't matter anymore," Ironman said as he grimaced.

"The hell it doesn't!" Spectre shouted. "Are you working with Xin? Is that it? Are you in on it with the Chinese?"

"Jiang Xin," Ironman said with a forced laugh. "Of all the people in this world you had to piss off, you just *had* to pick him. How did you make his list, anyway?"

"It sounds like he's your buddy, why don't you tell me?" Spectre asked as he gritted his teeth and clenched his fists. "I should have known!"

"Oh, he's not my buddy," Ironman replied. "But I'll tell you what I do know."

"What's that?" Spectre asked.

Ironman paced behind Spectre as he answered the question, "You're a dead man."

"I've been hearing that a lot lately," Spectre quipped. "And yet here I am."

Ironman continued making his way around the table and sat in the chair across from Spectre. He rubbed his bald head as he seemed to study Spectre for a minute.

"Cute," Ironman replied. "But I was hoping you would be smarter than that."

"What difference does it make?" Spectre asked. "You kill me. He kills me. In the end, we're all dead men anyway."

"Do you care about the girl?" Ironman asked. His voice had become lower and more serious.

"I wouldn't be here right now if I didn't," Spectre replied.

"Do you know where she is right now?" Ironman asked.

"Kruger just told me she's in the hospital," Spectre asked. "And if you're done, I'd like to go see her now."

"She's on a ventilator in ICU," Ironman said, ignoring Spectre's request. "She has some of the best doctors in Tampa working on her, but how safe do you think she really is there?"

The question hung in the air as Spectre's eyes widened. He knew what the people he faced were capable of. They had killed Marcus in the hospital and made an attempt on Spectre's life as well.

"I'll kill you if you so much as look at her wrong," Spectre growled.

"No, you won't," Ironman said after a prolonged sigh. "You have to lose this illusion of control. I know it's hard as a fighter pilot. It took me a while to come to grips with it as well, but the sooner you figure out the reality, the better off you'll be."

"And that is?" Spectre asked.

"As I said before, you're a dead man," Ironman said solemnly. "One way or another, you will die. The question is how you choose to meet that end and how many people you choose to take with you."

"What are you suggesting?" Spectre asked softly.

"Decker doesn't have to die," Ironman said with a pained expression. "You are very correct in your assertion that she's only in this because of you. The only way to save her is to give yourself up."

Spectre stared intensely at Ironman. "I don't know if you noticed, *boss*, but I'm not exactly on the run right now," Spectre said facetiously as he rattled his arm and leg chains.

"I won't let you compromise this operation any more than you already have," Ironman replied. "You will be released as soon as you and I are finished talking. I will not lose another man because of you."

"And then?" Spectre asked.

"And then you will have a choice to make," Ironman replied as he stood.

Spectre watched as Ironman walked back up to the camera in the corner of the room.

"Die alone, or take the girl with you," Ironman said as he plugged it back in.

Ironman then walked to the table and reinstalled the microphone. "Maybe it's time you start thinking about more than just yourself, Cal," Ironman said before walking out.

CHAPTER TWENTY NINE

Intensive Care Unit
Tampa General Hospital
Tampa, FL
1115 Local Time

Simms walked into the small waiting area of the Intensive Care unit with Agent Cooper following closely in trail. Agent Kemp was sitting with a young Coast Guard Petty Officer wearing a dark blue working uniform. The two stood as Simms and Cooper entered.

"You must be Special Agent Simms," Kemp said as he extended his hand. Simms accepted the handshake with his slender hand and looked out through the observation window into the Intensive Care Unit.

"Is she in there?" Simms asked, ignoring the Petty Officer still waiting to introduce himself.

"She had no identification on her, sir," the Petty Officer said.

"Who is this?" Simms asked.

"Sir, I'm Petty Officer Waskowski with Port Security," Waskowski replied. "My team picked her up at out the water a little over an hour ago."

"How do you know that's Decker?" Simms asked Kemp as he looked out into the ICU. He could barely see a blonde haired woman with a ventilator surrounded by IVs and machines.

"She's still technically Jane Doe," Kemp responded. "That's why I told Agent Cooper not to bother you with it yet." There was something about the way Kemp said it that caught Simms's attention. It was almost as if he were avoiding the question.

"What are you not telling me, Agent Kemp?" Simms asked.

"Beg your pardon?" Kemp asked with a look of shock.

"You haven't been showing up to every hospital for every Jane Doe in the area, have you?" Simms asked.

Kemp laughed. "Of course not, Agent Simms," he replied.

"So why this one?"

"We put out a BOLO on Decker as soon as we found her car," Cooper interjected. "Hospitals were notified to call us if they found anyone matching Decker's description."

"And when the nurse said that she had been brought in by the Coast Guard, I decided to check it out," Kemp added.

"How did you find her?" Simms asked, turning to the Petty Officer.

"Well, sir, we were transitioning on our patrol from McKay Bay to the East Bay Channel when we saw what looked to be a woman in the water," Waskowski said. "At that time, we were able to locate her and pull her out of the water. Her hands were bound by zip ties and she had nearly drowned."

"Do you know where she might have been coming from?" Simms asked.

"No, sir," Waskowski replied. "She was on the south end of the East Bay Channel across from Black Point, so she could've been on either side or dropped off by a boat."

"Were there any other boats in the area?" Simms asked.

"At the time, there were none transiting the channel," Waskowski replied. "But there were boats docked on the western side."

As Simms started to ask another series of questions, he was interrupted by a nurse opening the door from the ICU.

"Agent Kemp, she can have visitors now," the short brunette nurse said.

"How is she?" Simms asked.

The nurse frowned and shook her head slightly. "Her lungs were full of fluid. She's stable, but she has a long road ahead of her," the nurse responded.

"Agent Kemp, I'll follow up with you once I finish my report," Waskowski said as he excused himself.

The trio of agents followed the petite nurse into the room with the blonde woman.

"That's Decker," Simms said amidst the beeps and whirrs of the various life support machines in the room. Her face looked pale and swollen as the tube protruded from her mouth.

"No doubt about it, that's her," Simms repeated.

"I'll stay with her until we can get a protective detail with shifts set up," Kemp said in a low voice.

"Good idea," Simms said as he stared at Decker. "Cooper, let's go to the harbor where she was found."

Cooper and Kemp exchanged a look. Kemp gave Cooper a knowing nod as Simms continued looking on at Decker struggling to survive.

"Whatever you want," Cooper replied.

* * *

South Harbor Industrial Complex
Tampa, FL
1202 Local Time

Cooper's SUV crept slowly along the seawall on South Harbor Boulevard as they passed the quiet warehouses along the East Bay Channel. They had been unable to come into contact with anyone – it seemed most of the operations had closed or were never opened on Saturday. So far there had been nothing noteworthy.

Simms studied their position on his tablet's moving map as they continued south. Based on what the Coast Guard Petty Officer had told him, they were still at least a third of a mile from where they had picked up Decker.

"Looks like we're as far as we can go," Cooper said as he stopped in front of a twelve foot chain linked fence blocking the road.

"Turn right and follow the fence line," Simms said, pointing toward the access road they were intersecting. "Maybe we can find a way in."

"I don't know how you do things in Miami, but we're going to need a warrant to go in there," Cooper responded sharply.

"Donovan v. Dewey, Agent Cooper, didn't you pay attention at the Academy?" Simms responded smugly.

"It is commercial property. Now turn right," Simms said in response to the virtual question mark hovering over Cooper's head.

Cooper hesitated and then reluctantly complied, traveling west along the fence line of the shipping complex. Simms leaned forward, looking past Cooper as they neared two gates separated by a guard shack.

"Looks like no one is home," Cooper said with a shrug.

"Keep going," Simms ordered.

They continued down the narrow access road, following it north as it curved back toward the exit of the industrial area. Simms pointed left as they reached a stop sign for the road that intersected South Harbor Boulevard to their right.

"That goes to the plant," Cooper said. His patience had grown thin with the demanding agent from Miami.

"Take a left, and then take your first left on the white gravel road," Simms replied, holding up the moving map on his tablet. "I think we might be able to get in that way."

Cooper rolled his eyes and punched the gas, causing the tires to chirp as he accelerated down the two lane road. Frustrated by Simms's demands, he slammed on the brakes and turned down the gravel road, flooring it once again as rocks peppered the wheel wells.

"Is that a car?" Simms asked as they sped down the gravel road. He could see the glimmer of a windshield in the distance.

Cooper slowed as they approached the parked car. It appeared to be an older Camaro. It was red with racing stripes.

"Now why do you think a car would be out here?" Simms said with a look of smug satisfaction. "A little bit of patience goes a long way."

Cooper pulled up to the Camaro and put the SUV in park. Simms didn't wait as he exited and headed for the car. As he exited, he took his jacket off after pulling a pair of blue Nitrile gloves from the pocket and putting them on.

"Let's have a look," Simms said. Cooper followed as Simms inspected the seemingly abandoned vehicle. It was parked with the right side tires partially in the grass, facing north. Simms walked up to the driver's side door and tried the handle. The door opened to his surprise.

"Call the Crime Lab and get a team out here," Simms ordered. Cooper turned and walked back toward the SUV as he dialed his cell phone in response. Simms looked inside the car, careful not to disturb any evidence. He noticed a stack of papers on the passenger seat, reached over and picked them up as he stepped back from the car.

Simms studied the papers. He recognized them as a ledger, but there was no indication of what company it belonged to. He shuffled through the pages and then flipped them over, finding scribbled handwritten directions to their current location.

"Are they on their way?" Simms asked as Cooper returned.

"Everything is taken care of," Cooper responded. Simms handed him the papers and walked around to the passenger side door. He opened it and leaned in. Simms opened the glove compartment to find a registration to a woman in New Roads, Louisiana. If he had to guess, Simms figured that the address would map to a location close to the house that Jennings had been hiding Martin. Simms pressed the yellow hatch release as the hatchback thumped open.

Cooper was still reading through the papers as Simms walked to the back of the Camaro and raised the hatch. "What are these?" Cooper asked, holding up the papers.

"A ledger of some sort," Simms responded. He did a cursory search of the bags in the trunk. Most were empty, but there were a few bags full of loaded magazines. Simms picked up a full looking duffel bag and unzipped it, revealing stacks of neatly wrapped hundred dollar bills.

"Drug dealer?" Cooper asked.

"A man on the run," Simms said as he put the bag down. He noticed a crumpled up piece of paper in the corner of the trunk area and opened it. It appeared to be another page of the ledger, except one entry in particular showing Warehouse 118 and an address in Tampa was highlighted.

"Bingo," Simms said, holding it up for Cooper to see. "Martin was here for something."

"Do you think she was running from him?" Cooper asked.

Simms shook his head. "No, the timing doesn't match up. It might have to do with Hua Xia Holdings though."

"Who?" Cooper asked as he watched Simms pacing around the car looking for more clues.

"Hua Xia Holdings. Martin ransacked their office in New Orleans last night before coming here. I'll bet there's a connection," Simms said as he studied the ground around the car. "Ah ha! Boot marks!"

Simms carefully tracked the boot marks into the nearby tree line. He could see where the brush had been moved and laid down. He carefully stepped through the thick brush as he followed the track through the tree line to the other side.

"I found it!" Simms yelled as Cooper held his position. "Cooper, get over here!"

Cooper grumbled several choice words as he navigated through the brush in pursuit of Simms. As he emerged into the open, he saw Simms standing on the other side of the fence, having crawled through a small cutout in the chain link.

"This is how he got in," Simms yelled as he waved for Cooper to follow.

"I think we need a warrant," Cooper said as he approached the cutout in the fence.

"Exigent circumstances," Simms said as he drew his holstered Glock 17." He may still be on the premises."

Cooper reluctantly followed once again, crawling through the small opening in the fence as he took up position behind Simms. The two continued through the rows of shipping containers toward the warehouse in the distance. There were no signs that anyone had been there. It was completely quiet.

Simms stopped as he reached the last row of shipping containers. He cleared left and right, looking for any signs of

Martin. Satisfied he had found none, he headed toward the main warehouse, keeping his weapon up and ready as he neared the raised sidewalk.

"Someone was dragged here," Simms said as he stopped short of the sidewalk.

"How the hell can you tell that?" Cooper asked as he joined Simms.

"Scuff marks, and they look pretty fresh," Simms said." They appear to have come from that door." Simms pointed to a nearby entryway to his right.

"You're going to clear this entire warehouse with just the two of us?" Cooper asked.

"If you're nervous, you can go back and wait in the SUV for backup," Simms said dismissively. "If Cal Martin is in there, I'm going to get him."

Cooper rolled his eyes as Simms headed for the door. He lowered his weapon as he tried the doorknob. *Unlocked.* Simms signaled to Cooper that he would open the door and follow in behind Cooper. Cooper nodded, and after a silent countdown, Simms opened the door.

The lights of the spacious warehouse were still on as the two entered and j-hooked to their respective sides as they cleared the room.

"Clear left," Cooper said.

"Clear right," Simms responded.

Simms noticed a shipping container immediately in front of them with the door open. He walked toward it as Cooper stayed back.

"I'll bet this was where they were keeping her," he said as he neared the back wall.

"Really?" Cooper asked.

Simms holstered his weapon and squatted down. He picked up a strand of blonde hair that contrasted well against his light blue gloves. "Absolutely," he said.

Simms froze as he turned to show Cooper the proof. Cooper's gun was still drawn, but it was now pointing right at Simms's slender face.

"What are you doing?" Simms demanded.

"Turn around and face the wall. Put your hands on the wall, do it now," Cooper ordered. Simms slowly complied. As soon as Simms turned, Cooper rushed in and took the Glock from its holster and stuffed it in his belt at the small of his back. Cooper then took Simms's handcuffs from their pouch and used them to handcuff him.

"What are you doing?" Simms shrieked as Cooper patted him down and emptied his pockets. "This isn't funny, Agent Cooper."

"I warned you," Cooper said as he shoved Simms's keys, wallet, and cell phone into his own pockets. "You just had to John Wayne it."

Cooper kicked Simms's leg out from underneath him, causing him to drop to the floor. "I guess you're the one who should've paid better attention," Cooper added as Simms rolled over to face him.

"So you're going to kill me?" Simms said. His voice was quivering as his brown eyes became glassy.

"Don't be so dramatic!" Cooper laughed. "You're going to be given a choice."

"A choice?" Simms asked cautiously.

"Yes, and I suggest you pay attention this time," Cooper said as he laughed and turned to walk out.

"Wait!" Simms squealed.

Cooper ignored him as he exited the shipping container and closed the door behind him, leaving the handcuffed Simms alone in the dark shipping container. As the *clunk* of the latch engaging echoed throughout the hollow container, Simms collapsed in the corner and began to shake as the feeling of panic set in.

CHAPTER THIRTY

Taylor's Steakhouse
Tampa, FL
1950 Local Time

"I'll have a fourteen-ounce rib eye, medium well," Spectre said as he handed the menu to the waitress.

"I'll have the same, but make mine rare," Ironman said as the waitress turned to take his order. The woman repeated their orders and scurried off with their orders.

Spectre rubbed his freshly shaven face. After Ironman had left the interrogation room, he had been given food, a hot shower, and a fresh change of clothes before taking a six-hour nap in the crew rest area. After living out of his car and being on the run, he finally felt rested and recharged.

"So I have to ask, does Kruger know?" Spectre asked, breaking the silence after taking a sip of his water. The two had said very little to each other since leaving the Project Archangel Operations Building.

Ironman shook his head. "No, I've kept everyone from the team out of it. It's better that way," Ironman replied.

"Good," Spectre said. "He's a good man. Joe always liked him."

"Carpenter was a good man too," Ironman said solemnly. "I'm really sorry about what happened."

Spectre's eyes narrowed. "Were you part of that too?" Spectre asked as his anger built.

"No!" Ironman replied, vigorously shaking his head. "I told you at the funeral, I wanted to help. I had no idea what happened."

"This Xin person, did he do it?" Spectre asked. The more he thought about the death of his best friend, the more his anger grew.

"I don't know," Ironman replied with a shrug. "Look, Cal, I know you think I'm some terrible monster, but I'm really not."

Spectre was interrupted by the server bringing their steaks as he started to answer. After making sure they didn't need anything else, she walked away. Spectre waited until she was out of sight from their corner booth.

"No, you're just a saint," Spectre said with a forced smile. "You were even kind enough to buy me this last supper."

"I truly wish there were another way, Cal," Ironman replied as he attempted to hold eye contact with Spectre. "But you have no idea how dangerous these people are."

"How are your daughters?" Spectre asked, changing the subject as he cut into his steak and took a bite. "They're both teenagers now, right?"

"Sixteen and thirteen," Ironman said. Spectre could see his somber demeanor change at the mention of his two girls. They had always been a source of great pride and Ironman loved talking about them. "Sarah just started driving last week."

"Boyfriends?" Spectre asked.

"Luckily, Sarah has been too shy to date so far, but Meg already has boys calling every night," Ironman replied.

"I would hate to have daughters," Spectre laughed. "Too much stress."

Ironman's eyes lit up. "No way," Ironman said with a warm smile. "There's nothing better in the world than coming home to my girls. *Nothing.*"

"You're a good father," Spectre replied. "I still wish I could talk to my dad."

"He was an AC-130 pilot wasn't he?"

Spectre nodded.

"Is that how you got the callsign?" Ironman asked as he finished off the last of his steak.

"Sort of," Spectre said. "People always said I was a ghost when it came to hanging out in the squadron bar. No one could ever find me. And since we already had a 'Casper,' they gave me 'Spectre'. It also helped that I bought them a case of Jack Daniels to buy some of the terrible names off the board."

"Like what?"

"Monkey Vulva," Spectre said with a chuckle.

"You Air Force guys are weird," Ironman laughed.

Spectre shrugged. The bus boy arrived and took their plates as they made idle chit chat, avoiding what lay ahead. Ironman settled up the tab with a healthy tip and the two headed for the parking lot.

"Oh, I almost forgot," Ironman said as he reached the car. He pulled out a small white box and handed it to Spectre. "Parting gift."

"A watch?" Spectre asked as he opened it and pulled out a digital watch with a black wristband. "Seriously?"

The two entered Ironman's white sedan. "You know they're just going to kill me, right?" Spectre asked as he stared at the watch.

"Maybe," Ironman replied as they pulled out of the parking lot and headed toward the highway. "Or they're going to question you first."

"Thanks, I guess," Spectre said as he reluctantly put the watch on.

"You're welcome," said Ironman.

The two drove in relative silence as they made the hour and a half long journey from the restaurant to the meeting area. They pulled off the highway and down narrow two lane roads until they arrived in an industrial area with several pieces of heavy equipment. They past a gated area with a sign labeling it as FLORIDA ROCK QUARRY OF PENDOLA POINT.

Ironman drove to the center of the dusty quarry and killed the engine. "Are you ready?" he asked as he looked over at Spectre.

"Promise me you'll keep Michelle safe," Spectre said as Ironman waited for a response.

"As one fighter pilot to another, I promise that I will do everything in my power to ensure nothing happens to her," Ironman replied. "It ends tonight."

"Thank you," Spectre replied, extending his hand. Ironman looked Spectre in the eyes and shook his hand. "Make sure you hug your daughters tonight."

Ironman smiled. "I will."

The two men exited the sedan and met at the trunk. Ironman pulled out a pair of nickel handcuffs as Spectre turned away. Ironman cuffed Spectre's hands behind his back and guided him forward.

They walked out to the center of the dark quarry into the halogen spotlights, finding Xin and two men with AK-74s waiting for them.

Ironman stopped twenty feet away from Xin and his entourage, holding Spectre's left arm. "I've done what you've asked," Ironman said.

"Yes, you have," Xin said with a sinister grin. "Hello, Mr. Martin, it's nice to finally meet you."

"I've given myself up freely because I'm told that you will agree not to hurt Michelle Decker," Spectre said. "Is that true?"

"Agent Decker is safe in the hospital for now, Mr. Martin," Xin replied as he took a step toward Spectre and Ironman. "I have no use for her. You and I must chat, however."

"I will tell you whatever you want to know if you leave her alone," Spectre shouted.

"This is not a negotiation," Xin said as he took several more steps forward. He was now less than fifteen feet from Spectre and Ironman. Spectre could see his right arm was held behind his back.

"We have a deal, Xin," Ironman said tersely. "You have what you wanted."

"You are correct," Xin said. He raised his right arm, revealing a silenced handgun as he pointed it at Spectre. "We do have a deal."

Ironman dropped his grip from Spectre's arm as Xin trained the weapon on Spectre's forehead. Spectre swallowed hard as he faced his last moments. He had expected Xin to take him in for interrogation – not kill him on the spot.

"Did you talk to Victor Alvarez?" he asked. He stepped forward once more. Spectre estimated he was now ten feet from them as Xin's men stayed watchful from their original position.

"Yes," Spectre replied.

"And did he tell you about our operation?" Xin asked. As the distance decreased, Spectre could make out the weapon. It was a Sig Sauer P226.

"Yes," Spectre said.

Without warning, Xin turned and the suppressed Sig spat a round. Spectre saw Ironman drop to the ground out of the corner of his eye.

"Ironman!" Spectre yelled as he turned and dropped to his knees. He could do little to render first aid with his hands cuffed behind his back. "Goddammit! No!"

As Ironman lay on the ground, Spectre saw Xin approaching. The round had hit Ironman in the chest. Ironman groaned as blood oozed from his mouth.

"My daughters," Ironman gasped as Spectre frantically looked on at his dying former boss.

"Relax," Xin said casually. "I was never going to do anything to them." He walked up to Ironman and squeezed the trigger once more, sending a round through Ironman's forehead and ending his gasps.

"You Americans are so easy," Xin said as he holstered his weapon and motioned for the guards to approach.

"You piece of shit!" Spectre yelled as the guards each grabbed Spectre's arms and lifted him back to his feet.

"Take him to the holding area," Xin ordered.

"I will kill you!" Spectre yelled as he wrestled away from the men. The guard to his right took his rifle butt and struck Spectre in the stomach, knocking the wind out of him as he doubled over in pain.

"You're going to beg me to let you die," Xin said.

The guards put a burlap sack over Spectre's head and walked him to the dock. Spectre heard the sound of an outboard engine firing up as they threw him onto the deck of the boat. Moments later, he felt the wind against his skin and heard waves crashing as the boat took off at high speed.

The boat ride was short. As they reached another shore, more men grabbed Spectre and dragged him to his feet, forcing him to walk quickly. He could tell that he was easily a head taller than the men that were escorting him. They made him walk what felt like another two hundred yards before he saw bright lighting through his hood. He was in a large, open building of some sort.

He heard another lock open and a metal door creak open. The men escorting him violently pushed him in and slammed the door behind him. Spectre lost his balance and tripped forward, falling on what he thought was a dead body.

As he fell on the body, Spectre rolled over and pushed himself away with his feet until his back was against the wall.

"Hello?" a weak male voice groaned. "Who is there?"

"Who are you?" Spectre asked cautiously.

"I'm… I'm… Ca… Ca…" the man said, struggling to form the words.

"Who?" Spectre asked again.

"Carl… Carl Simms… Special Agent."

CHAPTER THIRTY ONE

As Spectre leaned against the wall, he was still stunned by what he had just witnessed. Ironman was dead. Of all the outcomes he had played over and over in his mind, there was no way he could have guessed that Xin would kill Ironman in cold blood.

Spectre's feelings were mixed about Ironman. It was clear that Ironman had gotten in too far over his head with Xin, but when he confessed that Xin had threatened his family, Spectre believed him. Everything Spectre knew about the way the Chinese intelligence services operated validated the threat. They would achieve their objectives at all costs.

He couldn't blame Ironman for wanting to do whatever it took to save his family. Spectre had basically made the same choice in agreeing to hand himself over in exchange for Decker's safety. At least, that's what he hoped. After watching Xin terminate his agreement with Ironman with a well-placed bullet, he wasn't so sure anymore.

"Who are you?" Simms asked again. After giving Spectre his name, he had started another sobbing fit. Spectre ignored him. He had never heard of Simms and didn't really care who he worked for. It was too late in life to start making new friends.

"I said, who are you?" Simms asked again. This time his voice was louder and more confident.

"Look, buddy, I don't know who you are and what you're doing here, but I really don't care," Spectre snapped.

"I'm just an accountant," Simms said as his voice cracked and wavered. "I shouldn't be here."

Is this dude going to start crying? Spectre thought.

Spectre let out an exhausted sigh. "I don't care."

"Do you think they're going to kill us?" Simms asked.

"Probably," Spectre replied flatly.

"Oh God, no!" Simms wailed.

"Jesus, dude, what kind of Special Agent are you, anyway?" Spectre asked, disgusted by the man's pitiful state. "IRS? EPA?"

"Federal Bureau of Investigation," Simms said between sobs.

"FBI? No kidding? How did you get yourself in here?" Spectre asked.

Simms rolled over onto his side and sat up. He was also wearing a hood that they had put on him a few hours before.

"I was investigating the disappearance of another agent, and my partner locked me in here," Simms said. "Are you FBI too?"

"Me?" Spectre said with a laugh. "Not so much."

"Why won't you tell me your name?" Simms asked.

"Because it doesn't matter," Spectre replied. "Do you know where we are?"

"Warehouse 118, I think," Simms replied. "At least that's what the address said."

Warehouse 118. Spectre's mind went full throttle as he put the pieces together. Simms had been investigating a missing agent at the same warehouse where he had been grabbed by Project Archangel. *Decker!* This guy was investigating Decker and got caught up with Xin.

"Michelle Decker?" Spectre asked. "That's who you were looking for?"

"Yes!" Simms said enthusiastically. "Although she's in the hospital. Do you know her?"

"She's a friend of mine," Spectre replied coolly.

"I think she was in this container in captivity. I was trying to find a man I think might have been involved. His name is Cal Martin, have you heard of him too?" Simms asked. His voice was suddenly more upbeat.

"I have," Spectre replied.

"He's very dangerous," Simms said. "He killed a lot of good agents down in Homestead. I think he might be working with whoever is running this operation."

"Really?" Spectre asked. He was grinning beneath his hood. *This guy!*

"Yes, I've been tracking him for several days now," Simms replied. "I think he's working with the Cubans and Chinese."

"Is that who put you in here?" Spectre asked.

"Well, no," Simms replied. "Agent Cooper did that. I haven't figured out how he fits into all of this."

"Wait, Kellen Cooper?" Spectre asked. The name rang a bell, but he wanted to be sure.

"I actually don't know his first name," Simms admitted, "but he works in the Tampa Field Office. Are you law enforcement too? You sound like one of us."

Special Agent Cooper. It has to be him, Spectre thought. Cooper was Project Archangel's assigned agent. Spectre had met him briefly during his new hire orientation. Spectre's stomach turned as he realized that Cooper was involved. Ironman had assured him that Cooper would see to Decker's safety. *Did Ironman know that Cooper was dirty?* Spectre's jaw tightened.

"How many men did you see when you were outside?" Spectre asked as he began formulating a plan.

"None," Simms replied. "It was just Cooper and me when we showed up here. I got in through a hole in the fence after I found a car on a nearby gravel road that Martin had been driving."

"Is that car still there?" Spectre asked.

"I think so," Simms replied. "But that was a long time ago."

"Did Cooper say anything after he locked you in here?" Spectre asked. "Did he say where he was going?"

"No," Simms replied slowly. "Just that I would have to make a choice soon, but when they came in and put the hood on me, it was two men. Chinese I think."

As Spectre began to ask his next questions, the door flung open. Two men moved quickly into the narrow container and grabbed Simms. They jerked him up to his feet and started him toward the door.

"Wait! Where are you taking me? Please don't hurt me!" Simms pleaded as he started to sob.

"Bye, Carl," Spectre said as they stopped and patted him down.

"You never told me your name!" Simms yelled.

"Oh, right," Spectre replied. "It's Cal Martin, but most people call me Spectre."

"Huh?" Simms said.

Before Spectre could answer, the men pulled Simms out of the container as he tried to process what he had just heard. *Cal Martin?* Simms thought. *Had he really just been having a conversation with the man he had been chasing for days straight?* Simms shrugged it off. *That guy is just messing with me.*

The two men dragged him out into the open warehouse. Simms tripped over his own feet as he struggled to keep pace with them, still distracted by the name he had just heard. It had put the fear of death out of his head as he tried to process the reality of the situation.

The men took him up a set of stairs and into an office. They pushed him down into a plush chair and removed his hood. A Chinese man with a goatee was sitting in the executive chair across from him.

"Hello, Agent Simms," the man said. His eyes were dark and empty. He smiled, but it was not reassuring to Simms. It only served to frighten him more.

"Hello," Simms replied in an unsure tone.

"Do you know why you are here?" the man asked.

"Please don't kill me! I'll do anything you want!" Simms pleaded.

The man held up his hand. "Have some dignity, Agent Simms."

"I'm sorry," Simms replied.

"My name is Xin," the man said. "I am here to offer you a very easy choice."

Simms said nothing as he stared at the man. He had managed to stop the sobbing, but his body was starting to tremble. *Accountants are not made for this!*

"It is simple, Agent Simms. You can work for us," Xin said. "It just so happens that we have an opening in your home office that we need to be filled down in Miami. Your timing is excellent. And your current assignment will be complete after tonight."

"Work for you?"

"In a manner of speaking, yes," Xin replied. "You will be compensated, of course, but you will also be part of something much bigger."

"I'm not a traitor," Simms said as he tried to muster up the last of his courage.

"No one is asking you to betray your country, Agent Simms," Xin replied.

"That's exactly what you're asking me to do," Simms said defiantly. "What if I say no?"

Xin considered the question for a moment and frowned. "Perhaps you need more time to think about it," he said as he gestured to the guard in the corner of the room.

"It is a decision that could change your life, after all," Xin said as the guard grabbed Simms and forced him to his feet. Xin said something to the guard in Chinese as he dragged Simms out of the room.

"Please! Please don't kill me," Simms yelled as he started sobbing again.

CHAPTER THIRTY TWO

"Welcome back, Carl," Spectre said as Simms stumbled into the container and the two guards escorting him started for Spectre. "Watch your step."

Simms stumbled and fell into the corner of the room. The two men grabbed Spectre and walked him out into the warehouse. Spectre counted the number of paces as they walked, trying to maintain situational awareness of his surroundings. They walked him into a small room and sat him down before removing his hood. He was in a small office that was empty except for two folding chairs, a metal folding table, and a bucket of water in the corner of the room. Spectre had a pretty good idea of what that meant. His experiences in training had been sufficient to steady his resolve — he hated waterboarding.

Moments after the two guards left, the door open. A man entered and casually took his seat across from Spectre. It was

Xin. He was wearing a shoulder holster carrying his P226. Spectre eyed the weapon as Xin sat down.

"Hello again, Mr. Martin," Xin said.

"I've been looking forward to this chat," Spectre said. "Although I'm sad that you picked me last."

Xin's brow furrowed. "You are quite arrogant for a man in your position, Mr. Martin."

"Hey, if you're going to die anyway, might as well go out smiling, right?" Spectre replied with a grin.

Xin pulled out his smart phone and turned it to face Spectre. Spectre saw a black and white video feed of a woman in a hospital bed. She had a tube in her mouth and appeared to be in serious condition. Spectre's face reddened.

"You recognize Agent Decker, no?" Xin said as he stood and moved the phone to within a few inches of Spectre's face.

"You don't have to threaten me, Xin," Spectre said as he tried to slow his rapid heart rate and budding anger. "You don't even need the bucket of water in the corner. I will tell you whatever you want to know. She has already been through enough."

"That she has, Mr. Martin," Xin said as he put the phone back in his pocket. "I've been made to understand that she is very fond of you."

"What can I say? Chicks dig fighter pilots," Spectre replied as he reached back into his comfort zone. Spectre knew he was staring death himself in the face and laughing. It was invigorating.

Xin let out a mocking laugh as he sat back down. "You are a well-trained man, Mr. Martin. I'm sure you know what comes next, no?"

"Well, we could continue this little verbal judo match, or you could tell me what you know and save us both the trouble," Spectre said with a sly smile. "I've never been a fan of false pretenses."

"You are nothing if not unique, Mr. Martin," Xin replied. "But I will be the one asking the questions this evening."

"Ask away," Spectre said, shifting in his chair.

"What did Victor Alvarez tell you?" Xin said, wasting no time.

"Everything," Spectre said with a smile and nodded as he shifted in his chair again. "Now you tell me something, were you the one that set me up? Are you the reason that guy pissing his pants in there with me has been chasing my ass for the last few days?"

"I think it's time for more advanced methods," Xin said menacingly. "You are not being very cooperative."

"Did you know Marcus was like a father to me?" Spectre asked, ignoring Xin's threats.

Xin leaned forward over the table separating him and Spectre." Do you know how easy it is to kill someone in ICU, Mr. Martin?"

"No," Spectre mumbled.

Xin smiled. "You may not be afraid of me, Mr. Martin, but if you don't start cooperating, I will show you."

Spectre surged toward Xin. His left hand reached for the back of Xin's head as his right hand attacked holding the open handcuff. He drove the pointy end of the open handcuff into the space between Xin's clavicle and neck as he smashed Xin's head into the table and stood. Xin's nose cracked as blood splattered the table from Xin's face and chest.

Spectre pounced on Xin, ripping the handcuff out as it tore through his neck. As Xin fell to the floor, Spectre stood, stomping Xin's face with the heel of his boot before pulling the Sig Sauer P226 out of the dying man's shoulder holster and pocketing the spare magazines. Spectre searched Xin, finding the suppressor Xin had used with Ironman in his back pocket.

As Xin lay motionless, Spectre removed the handcuff key from the open cuff and used it to release the handcuff on his right hand. Ironman had saved his life with the watch. As he sat in the shipping container, he had realized it was one of Project Archangel's survival watch bands that contained an embedded handcuff key, Kevlar friction saw, and ceramic razor blade.

Spectre screwed the suppressor onto the P226 and pointed it at Xin's head. The gun effortlessly spat a 9MM bullet, striking Xin in the face. He may have already been dead before the shot, but Spectre had to be sure.

"That's for my friends," Spectre said as he moved to the area behind the inward opening door. Spectre used his fist to bang on the door three times as he lay in wait. Spectre hid behind the door as a guard carrying an AK-74 walked in and then rushed to Xin's body. Spectre fired two shots, dropping the guard. He pulled the AK-74 out of his lifeless hands.

He checked the man for spare magazines and found none. He slung the AK-74 over his shoulder and readied the Sig. It was better to stay quiet until all hell broke loose.

Spectre exited the office into the open floor warehouse with his weapon high and ready. He sprinted the short distance to the lone shipping container as he scanned left and right for threats. As he rounded the corner toward the door, he found a guard standing idle. Spectre fired two rounds, striking the man in the chest and throat as he dropped to the floor. Spectre ran over to the man and grabbed the AK-74 before pulling out its magazine and recovering two spare magazines off the guard.

Satisfied that there were no other immediate threats, Spectre opened the shipping container's heavy door.

"I'll do whatever you want!" Simms yelled from the back.

"Carl, get your ass over here!" Spectre yelled back. Simms stood and headed for the door. They hadn't put the hood back on him since his last trip out of the container. He carefully walked toward Spectre.

"Turn around," Spectre ordered as he looked back out to check for threats.

"What are you doing?" Simms demanded.

Spectre grabbed his arm and spun him around. He held the Sig in his right hand as he used his free hand to release Simms's right handcuff.

"Here," Spectre said, handing the key to Simms so he could continue uncuffing himself.

"What are you doing?" Simms repeated as he tossed the handcuffs to the side. "You're going to get us both killed."

Spectre grabbed Simms by the collar and pushed him forward toward the nearby access door. "Die now or die later. Let's go."

"This is stupid!" Simms said as they exited into the warm night air. Spectre pushed Simms forward toward the rows of shipping containers. He cleared right with his weapon as he found a slowly approaching guard. He sent two rounds toward the man, striking him in the chest with one and missing with the second. The slide on the Sig locked back. Spectre discharged the magazine and stuffed in a fresh magazine from his pocket as they sprinted toward the containers.

As they reached the first row, rounds peppered the hollow containers. Spectre turned to see several armed guards running toward them, firing their rifles.

"Take this and keep running," Spectre said as he handed Simms the handgun and unslung his rifle.

Simms took the gun and started running away from Spectre toward the fence line. Spectre fired at the approaching men, hoping to pin them down as he ducked away from the ricocheting rounds zipping by him.

Spectre fired another three round burst, hitting one of the men. He took off running to catch up with Simms, who had just fallen again. Spectre grabbed him by the collar and pulled him up as he continued running. The two reached the hole in the fence. Simms dropped to his knees to crawl through as Spectre turned to cover. A guard approached from a corner. Spectre pinned him down with a short burst as Simms crawled stood up on the other side of the fence.

Spectre waited briefly as the guard leaned around the corner. Using the red dot scope on his AK-74, Spectre fired and hit the guard, dropping him to the ground. Spectre ran toward the fence and quickly crawled through the opening before sprinting to the tree line and catching up.

"Keep running!" Spectre yelled as Simms stopped to wait for him.

As the two emerged from the trees, Simms found the Camaro still sitting with both doors open. "The keys aren't in it!" Simms cried in a panic.

"I'm driving. Get in!" Spectre ordered. Spectre opened the fuel filler lid and pulled out the spare key, then hopped in and fired up the Camaro's V8 engine.

Spectre put the six-speed transmission in gear, revved up the engine, and dropped the clutch, shooting rocks and dirt everywhere as the Camaro struggled to find a grip on the gravel road. The Camaro took off as the dim headlights barely lit the narrow road.

"Holy shit, that was insane!" Simms shouted. "I think I peed a little."

"We're not safe yet," Spectre said as he turned left onto the main road with squealing tires. Two sets of headlights approached from behind in hot pursuit as Spectre rowed through the gears. The back end kicked out slightly as Spectre maneuvered the ninety-degree right hand turned marked for thirty-five at nearly seventy miles per hour. He could see the headlights receding in his rear view mirror as he pressed the gas pedal to the floor and grabbed another gear.

"Did we lose them?" Simms asked nervously.

Spectre slowed slightly from one hundred twenty miles per hour as he negotiated a sweeping right and turn and then accelerated through one hundred forty as he reached the straightaway. The pursuit vehicles were nowhere in sight as he slammed the brakes and downshifted before turning left onto the onramp of Highway 41.

"I think we can slow down now," Simms said as Spectre weaved in an out of the light traffic at speeds averaging over one hundred miles per hour. "Seriously."

Spectre let the car idle down to highway speeds as he watched for approaching headlights in the rear view mirror. Satisfied he had lost them, Spectre slowed and merged onto the Selmon Expressway.

"Where are we going now?" Simms asked, visibly shaken from the escape.

"The hospital," Spectre said stoically.

"For me or you?" Simms asked.

"Michelle," Spectre replied as he shifted gears and accelerated past one hundred miles per hour on the expressway.

CHAPTER THIRTY THREE

Tampa General Hospital
Tampa, FL
2335 Local Time

Spectre backed the Camaro into a spot at the far end of the mostly empty parking lot at the top of the parking garage and killed the engine. Without wasting any time, he popped the hatchback and immediately went to the back of the car to inventory the equipment he had left.

"What are you going to do?" Simms asked nervously as he met Spectre at the back of the car. "You should be turning yourself into the police!"

Spectre glared at Simms. "Who's going to arrest me?" Spectre asked as he turned and stepped toward Simms. "You? The crooked cops holding Michelle hostage right now?"

"You're still a wanted man," Simms mumbled as he retreated from Spectre. "This is a police matter. There are laws that should be followed."

"I'll tell you what, Carl," Spectre replied as he closed the range Simms had just gained between them. "As soon as I know she's safe, we can talk about following rules. Until then, you're either helping me or you're the enemy. So which is it?"

"I want to see Agent Decker safe too," Simms said weakly.

"Good," Spectre said as he turned his attention back to the contents of the back hatch. Project Archangel had stripped him of most of his gear when they apprehended him. It was mostly empty bags except for his small tool bag. Spectre also noticed his bag of cash had been taken.

"What's this doing in here?" Simms asked as he pulled a black sport coat from the hatch. "This is mine!"

"Were you wearing it when you found the car?" Spectre asked.

"I took it off before we started," Simms replied as he studied his coat.

"They were trying to pin your disappearance on me," Spectre replied. "Just like everything else."

"But what if I had said yes?" Simms wondered aloud.

"Yes to what?" Spectre asked.

"Nothing," Simms replied quickly.

"I won't ask you again," Spectre warned. Although Spectre was an inch shorter than the lanky Simms, he was easily twenty pounds more muscular. Simms held up his hands as he stumbled backwards.

"Xin wanted me to work for him," Simms said reluctantly. "But I told him no! I'm not a traitor!" Simms added as Spectre stared him down.

Spectre considered their options as he sized up the potential defector in front of him. He wasn't particularly fond of Simms, but he had very few options left. He had to get to whoever was watching Decker before they found out that he had killed Xin.

"No, you are a traitor, Carl," Spectre replied casually.

"Huh?"

"You actually told him yes," Spectre said, nodding his head. "And you're here to warn whoever's in there that I've escaped."

"I am?" Simms asked nervously.

* * *

Visiting hours had long been over when Simms tapped on the glass door near the Nurses Station of the intensive care unit. A nurse that had been typing patient notes was startled by his sudden presence and shook her head while pointing at her watch as Simms pleaded for her to open the door.

"Sir, it is almost midnight, can I help you?" the elder nurse snapped. She looked over Simms's tattered appearance. His pants were covered in dirt and his silk white shirt had been ripped.

"Yes, ma'am, sorry," Simms replied softly. "I'm Special Agent Simms with the FBI and I need to speak to the Agent in Michelle Decker's room. It's quite urgent."

"Let me see some ID," the nurse said impatiently.

Simms froze as he realized Cooper had taken his wallet and credentials before locking him in the shipping container. He had nothing to identify himself as anything but a lunatic trying to get into the ICU after hours.

"I'm calling security," the nurse said as she watched Simms freeze like a deer in headlights.

"Ma'am, this is an urgent matter," Simms said as he struggled to find his confidence. "Please ask the agent to come out to speak to me. I don't have my credentials on me, but I assure you, the agent in there will want to speak to me. You do not want to interfere in this matter."

"If you turn out to be another lost drunk, I'm going to press charges," the woman said as she turned and closed the door behind her.

Simms watched her until she disappeared out of view. Moments later, the woman reappeared with Agent Kemp in tow.

"Do you know this man?" the woman asked bluntly, as she opened the door.

"Jesus, Simms, what the hell happened to you?" Kemp said. "Yes, I know him."

Satisfied that Simms would no longer be her problem, the woman retreated back to her nurses' station in a huff and closed the door behind her. Kemp grabbed Simms's arm and ushered him into the nearby waiting room.

"What the hell are you doing here, Simms?" Kemp asked in a hushed tone after confirming the nurse was out of view.

"We don't have much time," Simms replied. "Martin killed Xin and kidnapped me."

"Kidnapped you?" Kemp asked as he stepped back with his hand on his service weapon.

"No! No!" Simms said, holding up his hands. "I took the deal. That's why I'm here. I wanted to warn you."

Kemp relaxed slightly at the mention of Xin's deal. "Go on," Kemp said cautiously.

"Martin kidnapped me and forced me here against my will," Simms whispered. "He wanted me to get you outside so he could kill you and get the girl."

Kemp pulled his phone out of his pocket with his left hand and dialed as he kept his right hand on his holstered weapon. He held the phone up to his ear as it rang.

"Wait! Who are you calling?" Simms asked frantically.

"We'll see if your story holds up," Kemp replied as he waited for an answer. When there was none, Kemp dialed another number and put the phone back up to his ear.

"Cooper, it's Kemp," he said as the other end picked up. "Yeah, have you heard from the harbor lately? You either? Yeah, you might want to get over here."

Kemp hung up the phone and frowned at Simms as he slid the phone back into his pocket. "So, you said he's dead? You saw it?"

Simms shook his head. "No, I didn't see it, but I did see him shoot most of Xin's men before he grabbed me at gunpoint. He's here for the girl."

"Why didn't you arrest him?" Kemp asked.

"Because he blindsided me and then took my gun," Simms replied. "He's a murderous psychopath, and I will watch him burn. He's outside right now and he thinks I'm just going to walk you out to him."

"You do know that if Xin is really dead, whatever deal you made is off, right?" Kemp asked.

Simms shrugged. "It's personal with Martin. I don't care what happens after that."

Kemp smiled. "Fair enough."

"Should we go out and get him?" Simms asked. "I don't want him to suspect anything and run again."

"Cooper is on his way. Where is he expecting us?" Kemp asked as he pulled his phone out to text Cooper.

"He wanted me to get you to the boardwalk by the parking garage," Simms said. "He said if I could get you out by the water, he'd take care of the rest."

"Where is he hiding?" Kemp pressed.

"He said he would be waiting by the northeast elevator," Simms replied. "He told me to make sure I'm on your left side and not stand too close."

Kemp laughed as he relayed the message to Cooper via text message. "And how did he expect you to get me out there?"

"He thinks he's smart," Simms replied. "He told me that if I told you that Xin had sent his boat from the shipping yard, you'd believe it."

"Wow," Kemp replied, shaking his head in disbelief as he texted the amplifying data to Cooper. "Well, that won't be happening tonight. Cooper will be here in a few minutes. Let's not keep Martin waiting any longer."

CHAPTER THIRTY FOUR

Spectre watched from the parking garage as Simms emerged from the hospital complex with another man close by his side. The two crossed the short crosswalk and stepped onto the boardwalk toward the parking garage. For the moment, everything was going according to plan.

Spectre had been worried that Simms would lose his nerve. It had taken quite a bit of coaching to talk him down from his visibly shaken state and convince him that Spectre's plan was the only way to save Michelle's life. After what seemed like an eternity of waiting, Spectre almost believed Simms had run off to hide in the bathroom, but seeing the two men slowly approaching his position eased his concerns.

Confident that the plan was safely in motion, Spectre relocated to the place of concealment he had picked out on the first floor between two large SUVs. As he reached the location, he heard voices and footsteps. *Too soon.* Spectre had just seen Simms and the agent on the boardwalk. They couldn't have covered the distance that quickly.

Spectre watched as the two men approached from his left. One was wearing what appeared to be a suit and the other had on cargo pants. Spectre crouched lower as the men passed him toward the northeast corner of the parking garage, clearing left and right. They seemed to be searching between nearby cars as they cleared the corner.

Taking aim with Xin's suppressed P226 at the man in the suit, Spectre sprang into action. As he was the nearest threat, Spectre aimed at the man's center of mass and squeezed off two rounds, hitting him squarely in the chest as the other man turned toward Spectre. The man managed to fire before Spectre followed up with two more shots, hitting him in the throat and chest. The register of the man's handgun was deafening as it echoed in the parking garage.

Spectre covered the two men with his weapon as he rushed over to them and kicked their handguns out of reach. He immediately recognized the man in the suit as Agent Cooper. The other appeared to be a guard from the shipping harbor.

Spectre looked out onto the boardwalk to see Simms awkwardly swinging his lanky arm at the huskier agent. The agent ducked the errant swing and followed up with an uppercut that nearly lifted Simms up off his feet as he was sent stumbling backward.

Distracted by the spectacle of Simms flailing his way through the fight, Spectre didn't notice Cooper stirring behind him. Cooper charged Spectre from behind, knocking the P226 out of his hand as the two slammed into a concrete wall next to the elevator door. Spectre picked up his right leg and pushed off the wall, separating himself from Cooper in the process.

Spectre sized up his opponent as the two faced off. He could see the navy blue exposed vest through the bullet hole tears in Cooper's shirt. He had made a critical mistake in assuming the threat had been neutralized.

Cooper lunged forward, swinging with his right hand as Spectre blocked and struck Cooper's face with an open palm, sending his fingers into Cooper's eyes. As Cooper raised his hands to protect his eyes, Spectre followed up with an elbow strike that went crashing into Cooper's nose with a solid crack. He then continued thrashing Cooper with two more elbow strikes before grabbing Cooper's head with both hands and driving his knee into Cooper's midsection.

As Cooper went tumbling to the ground, Spectre picked up the Glock Cooper had been carrying and aimed it at Cooper's bloodied face. He hesitated for a moment, but then squeezed the trigger as he realized that Cooper had likely been on his way to kill Decker. *No one is innocent.*

As the shot rang out, Spectre looked over to see Simms still fighting with the other agent. Spectre took off in a sprint toward the two men as he watched Simms fall to the ground and the other agent continue to land blow after blow on Simms's battered face. As the man pulled back to drive another punishing blow into Simms, Spectre fired while running toward them. The round hit the agent under his arm and caused him to double over onto Simms.

As Spectre arrived, he kicked the agent off of Simms and confirmed that the agent was dead. Spectre leaned over to render aid to Simms as he heard approaching sirens wailing in the distance.

"Did you get them?" Simms slurred. His eyes were swollen shut and his face looked even more disfigured to Spectre than it did naturally.

"Just hang tight, Carl," Spectre said as he checked Simms for any life threatening injuries. "Everything's going to be ok."

CHAPTER THIRTY FIVE

Project Archangel Operations Center
MacDill AFB, FL
2330 Local Time

"Ok, Coolio, where is he?" Kruger asked as he handed Analyst Julio Meeks a thirty-two ounce can of his favorite energy drink. He had tasked Meeks with finding Ironman after he had attempted to call Ironman only to find that both his work and personal cell phones had been turned off and were going straight to voice mail. After a quick call to Ironman's wife to confirm he hadn't gone home, Kruger decided to take action.

"Ok, this is really weird," Meeks replied as he stared at the computer screen through his hipster glasses. "Neither phone can be pinged off the towers in the area – like battery and SIM card removed."

"What about the GPS locator in his work phone?" Kruger asked.

"Last location was off Pendola Point Road before it stopped responding," Meeks said, shaking his head.

"What's there?" Kruger asked.

"Looks like a rock quarry," Meeks replied as he zoomed in on the satellite image.

Kruger picked up the phone next to Meeks and dialed four numbers. "Tell Tuna to get with Shorty and get a Blackhawk ready to launch. And bring a medic," Kruger said before hanging up the phone. The hair on the back of his neck was standing up. Ironman had left with Spectre four hours prior saying that they were going to dinner and he would be back by 2130 to discuss how to proceed with tracking down Redman and Tanning's killers. Spectre was a loose cannon with a rocky history. Kruger feared the worst.

"Here's something interesting, though," Meeks said excitedly. "Remember those watches we ordered a while back that you guys refused to wear?"

"The MacGyver that couldn't even change time zones?" Kruger asked, remembering the short lived nature of the watch that Ironman had purchased for them to wear.

"Yeah, Ironman is the only one that didn't give his back," Meeks said. "And it's responding to satellite pings."

"Where is he?" Kruger pushed.

Meeks pulled up another map with a jagged blue line showing the path of travel. "According to these pings every fifteen minutes, he somehow crossed the channel, spent some time at that warehouse we had under surveillance, and then ended up at Tampa General Hospital."

"Tampa General?" Kruger asked as he looked at the map over Meeks's shoulder. *Decker? Was he going to see about Decker? Why wouldn't he have his phone on?* "Where is he now?"

"Hold on, it's updating," Meeks said as the screen refreshed. Meeks zoomed in on the blue dot on top of the satellite image. The dot sat at the southern edge of a parking garage next to the hospital. "Looks like he's still there as of one minute ago."

"Do we have any real time imagery?" Kruger asked as he picked up the phone again.

"No satellites," Meeks replied, shaking his head. "But I can try to see what I can find with surveillance cameras. It may take a few minutes to get into their network."

"Hey, it's Kruger again," Kruger said into the phone after dialing the same four numbers. "Tampa General Hospital, I'll brief you in the air. Stay low. Green light."

* * *

"Tuna" Turner checked his MP7 one last time as the blacked out helicopter sped just a few feet above the calm bay waters at ninety knots. Although he had spent most of his career flying in blacked out helicopters doing high-risk nighttime insertions, he always felt more comfortable when Jake "Shorty" Roberts was at the controls. The six foot four inch former Warrant Officer with the Army's 160th Special Operations Aviation Regiment was the most experienced helicopter pilot in Project Archangel, and his copilot, the younger former Air Force Pavehawk pilot "Zombie" Jacobs, was equally respected. The two effortlessly piloted the Blackhawk through the darkness using their panoramic Night Vision Goggles to navigate in the moonless night.

"We identified Martin on one of the security cameras," Kruger said over the secure radio as Tuna and the rest of his team listened to the briefing. "Shots have been fired and police are inbound, so you'll need to snatch and grab before the police arrive on the scene."

"What's the objective?" Tuna asked.

"Grab Martin and whoever is with him," Kruger replied. "We do not have eyes on Ironman at this time, so Martin may be our only link."

"Level of risk?" Tuna asked.

"High," Kruger replied. "Get in and grab Martin. If you have time, find out where Ironman is from him. Shoot only in self-defense, but we need him alive. Do not engage the locals, copy?"

"Punisher Zero One copies," Tuna replied. He looked around the cabin, waiting for acknowledgement from the other three members of his team. Mike Roland, "Axe" Axelrod, and John Wilson all acknowledged with thumbs up. Wilson checked his medical kit one last time; the former Air Force PJ was the team's medic for the mission.

"One minute," Shorty announced over the intercom as the Blackhawk sped along the channel past the Peter K. Knight Airport. The team flipped down their Night Vision Goggles and disconnected their harnesses as they prepared to exit.

"Left door!" the crew chief manning the side fifty-caliber machine gun called out.

Tuna could see a man standing over two bodies as the Blackhawk rounded the last corner. He grabbed a hand hold as Shorty aggressively pitched up the nose before slowing and entering a hover over the boardwalk. The distance between the building and trees lining the boardwalk was barely one hundred feet, but Shorty expertly wedged the helicopter between the two and set it down on the access road while the crew chief counted down the distance to touchdown.

With the main wheels on deck, Tuna and his team exited the chopper jogging toward the man holding his gun over the two bodies. Roland and Axe fanned out into a V formation as Wilson covered behind them.

"Drop your weapon!" Tuna yelled over the sound of the helicopter and approaching sirens as he pointed his gun at the man. Through his Night Vision Goggles, Tuna saw his green IR marker and the dots of Axe and Roland's weapons trained on the man's chest as well.

"Friendly!" the man yelled, placing the gun down and putting his hands behind his head as he dropped to his knees next to the body. As Tuna and his team advanced closer, he recognized the man to be Martin.

"Where is Ironman?" Tuna asked as he covered Spectre while Axe and Roland grabbed him and Flexi cuffed his hands behind his back. Wilson checked the larger body and then moved to the man next to Spectre.

"This one is still alive," Wilson said, checking the man over.

"Is he critical?" Tuna asked. The approaching sirens grew louder.

"He's pretty badly beaten," Wilson replied. "But he has a steady pulse."

"Leave him here," Tuna ordered as he turned back to Spectre. "Where's Ironman?"

"He's dead!" Spectre yelled. "Xin killed him."

Tuna paused momentarily as he looked for signs of deception in Spectre's face. The locals would be arriving any minute. They didn't have any more time to waste.

"Let's get out of here," Tuna ordered as he motioned for Axe and Roland to head toward the waiting helicopter with Spectre.

CHAPTER THIRTY SIX

MacDill AFB
Tampa, FL
0035 Local Time

It had just started to rain as the Blackhawk's spotlight illuminated in the distance. Kruger could barely make out the helicopter's silhouette against the bright flashes of lightning as it sped toward the Project Archangel ramp. He was standing at the Operations Desk next to the windows overlooking the flight line. He rested his right hand on the butt of his holstered Glock 17 as he impatiently waited for the helicopter to land in the worsening rain shower.

Tuna had called in just minutes prior on their base radio. Martin was in custody, another individual was down and had been left for the authorities, and four KIA on the scene. No sign of Ironman; however, Spectre reported that he had been killed.

Kruger hadn't figured Spectre out. He had never had any issues with the guy when Spectre flew for Project Archangel. He seemed like a good enough pilot. He was a hard worker and always showed up prepared for every training event. There was nothing obvious about him that made Kruger think he was capable of turning on the team.

But Ironman had fired Spectre, and after all he had been through, Spectre outright told Kruger that he thought Ironman was working with the Chinese and the source of all of his troubles. *Had he acted on it when they left?* Kruger clenched his teeth.

Ironman had been cryptic when he and Spectre left the Operations Building. He had told Kruger that he and Spectre were going to share a last meal together and go their separate ways. They had come to an understanding in the interrogation room, and Spectre would no longer be interfering with their operations. Kruger felt like he was missing a secret decoder ring to translate what Ironman was saying, but he never expected Ironman to go missing. He couldn't shake the feeling that he had missed something.

As the Blackhawk hover-taxied to its parking spot, Kruger took off at a jog in the rain to meet it. The side door opened as the crew chief hopped out and chocked the wheels. Tuna was behind him as Axe and Wilson unstrapped Spectre from his seat and prepared to transport him.

"Kruger, he said-" Tuna began before Kruger pushed past him to the door. Roland was attempting to exit behind Tuna as Kruger maneuvered past him and went straight for Spectre. He grabbed Spectre's shirt and yanked him back, pulling him out of the helicopter and causing him to fall to the wet asphalt. Kruger immediately pounced, landing on top of him as he drew his holstered Glock and shoved it in Spectre's surprised face.

The swiftness and violence of the action surprised everyone, including Spectre who said, "Kruger, what the-"

"What did I tell you about being part of the problem?" Kruger yelled, cutting Spectre off. "What happened to Ironman?"

"Xin killed him. I'm sorry," Spectre said as he squirmed under Kruger's weight. Spectre's hands were still zip tied behind his back. Kruger was kneeling over Spectre with his left forearm pressed against Spectre's chest and the barrel of his weapon applying pressure into Spectre's forehead.

"You're lying!" Kruger growled. "Last chance."

"Kruger, easy man," Tuna said, patting Kruger on the shoulder with the back of his hand. "He's been cooperative."

"Go inside," Kruger ordered over the sound of the Blackhawk's turbines spooling down.

Tuna started to protest, but Kruger stared him down, causing him to back down as he motioned for his team to follow him back to the Operations Building.

"I will ask again," Kruger said as the Tuna and his men cleared the area. "Where is Ironman?"

"We met Xin at a rock quarry," Spectre replied. "Xin shot Ironman."

"What were you doing there?"

Spectre hesitated. Kruger moved his forearm from Spectre's chest to his throat and applied pressure.

"Now, Spectre!" Kruger shouted.

"Turning myself into Xin," Spectre said as he started to choke. "Ironman saved my life."

"Bullshit! Why didn't he tell anyone where you were going?"

"Because Xin was going to kill his family," Spectre replied.

Kruger relaxed pressure and shifted his weight back to his heels while still keeping the gun pointed at Spectre. His face and clothes were drenched and dripping as the rain continued to pour on them.

"What?" Kruger asked as he tried to process what Spectre had just told him.'" That doesn't make sense."

"Xin wanted me and was going to kill Ironman's family and Michelle Decker if Ironman didn't bring me to him. He didn't have a choice," Spectre replied. "I know you don't trust me, but I've got no reason to lie. I was ready to die tonight and Ironman saved my life."

"How?" Kruger asked skeptically.

"He gave me a watch with a survival band and handcuff key," Spectre replied. "He wanted me to escape and have a chance to at least die fighting."

"Where is Xin, now?" Kruger said, not moving his aim from Spectre's forehead.

"Dead," Spectre replied angrily. "Fuck him."

Kruger holstered his weapon. He had no doubt anymore that Spectre was telling the truth or believed every word he was saying. His blind rage had passed, and as he began to think more clearly, he realized that Spectre wasn't the threat Kruger initially thought he was. The rain turned to a light drizzle as Kruger grabbed Spectre under his arm and helped him to his feet.

"Let's get inside and get you debriefed," Kruger said as he guided Spectre toward the Operations Building. "There are a lot of unanswered questions here."

"Wait," Spectre said as he stopped to face Kruger.

"What is it?" Kruger asked.

"If you won't let me go, at least send some guys to go watch Michelle in the hospital," Spectre said. "I don't know how many others are involved in this, but before Tuna showed up, I had just finished dealing with two FBI agents that were in with Xin."

"I'll see what I can do," Kruger replied as they resumed their walk inside.

CHAPTER THIRTY SEVEN

Project Archangel Operations Building
MacDill AFB
Tampa, FL
1730 Local Time

Tucked away inside its fifteen thousand square foot secure facility, Project Archangel's auditorium was completely crowded with a mix of people wearing civilian clothes, flight suits, and tactical clothing. Every seat was filled while the walls were lined with operators and pilots standing as they waited for the briefing to begin.

The idle chatter fell to a hush as Kruger entered through a side door at the front of the room. Spectre followed behind him and took his place standing against the wall as Kruger stopped at the center of the room and looked out into the sea of covert operators. He had called every member of Project Archangel to attend. Despite not giving a single reason or explanation, not a single person of the nearly two hundred men and women gave an excuse as to why they wouldn't be able to make it. Whether they were on leave or just out with family, they all said "Copy that" and vowed to be there.

The team had learned to expect short notice phone calls involving rapid deployments to anywhere in the world. They all knew not to speculate or fuel the rumor mill. Everyone in the room had enough experience to know how deployments were announced, and although they usually involved mass briefings in that same auditorium, the tension in the air was palpable. Those that hadn't been included in the missions of the last few days could sense that something was very wrong amongst the tight-lipped operators sitting next to them that had been.

"Thank you all for coming on such short notice," Kruger began. Although Ironman was the Director of Project Archangel, Kruger was the de facto second in command of the organization. He was on a first name or callsign basis with everyone in the room and required no introduction.

"For those of you that have not been around for the last two days, I wanted to tell you in person. This is not easy news," Kruger said as he paused and swallowed hard. "But over the weekend we lost Brian Tanning, James Redman, and Charles Steele in the course of DAs."

There was a collective gasp in the room as the men and women of the team processed what they had just heard. DA was the term the team used for Direct Action events involving the enemy. Kruger expected the room to erupt in chatter, but was surprised when he found stunned silence instead. No one said a word as they waited for Kruger to explain.

"Tanning and Redman were killed while defending an FBI agent in our safe house," Kruger continued. "The house was attacked by a group of Chinese intelligence operatives. That same FBI agent was taken as a hostage as a result, and on Friday we began a small scale local operation to recover that agent and find the people responsible for that action."

"During the operation, Ironman was executed by Chinese Intelligence Agent Jiang Xin. We recovered his body last night and I notified his family late last night," Kruger said with a pained expression. "Xin was killed as well as Special Agent Cooper, who we later learned was working for the Chinese."

Kruger could see the anger on the faces of the operators in the front row as he mentioned Cooper's name. In a brotherhood that relied on trust, they didn't take kindly to traitors at any level.

"Xin was a Lieutenant for a man named Jun Zhang of the Chinese Ministry of State Security," Kruger said. "He was working under Zhang's orders and is currently still somewhere uninvited in our country. It is my intention to give him a permanent eviction notice

Kruger paused as he watched the sea of heads nodding in the audience. "With 7.62," Kruger added as the room erupted with cheering.

"Anything going forward is unsanctioned," Kruger warned as the applause died down. "I cannot ask any of you to risk your lives for this. I have not briefed the SECDEF on anything that has happened this weekend, and I don't intend to until Zhang is getting ass raped in hell with Xin by Saddam and Bin Laden. So, if anyone is uncomfortable with this mission or wants to sit on the sidelines, you are free to do so. I won't think any less of you for sitting this one out. I don't think anyone else will either. It's a decision you have to make for yourself and only you can make it."

"Those of you who are not in are free to leave at this time," Kruger said. He waited as the room was silent. Everyone looked around the room at each other, but no one moved from their seats or places against the wall. It was an overwhelming show of support and loyalty – for both Ironman and the team he had put together.

"Ok then," Kruger said as he nodded to Meeks to lower the projector screens behind him and turn on the projectors. "While we wait for the brief to come up, you may have noticed 'Spectre' Martin follow me in. He will be part of this mission, so for now he's read back in. Treat him as you would any other team member."

"Does anyone have any questions before we begin?" Kruger asked as the presentation finished loading.

"Yeah, I have one," a voice in the back of the auditorium said. A tall blonde man with a close-cropped haircut stood up. It was John "Ivan" Winston, the former Army Ranger nicknamed for his uncanny resemblance to Ivan Drago from *Rocky IV*.

"Whatcha got, Ivan?" Kruger asked.

Ivan stood. "Why was an FBI agent in our safe house?"

"Well, *she* was recovered by Redman and Tanning after Ironman asked them to look out for her," Kruger replied. "She was investigating an unrelated case and the Chinese attacked her."

"What did they want with her?" Ivan asked. "I feel like we're not getting the whole story here."

"I'll answer," Spectre said, walking up to Kruger from the side of the room. Kruger stepped to the side as Spectre turned to address Ivan.

"They wanted to use her to get to me," Spectre replied. "You see, a year ago I was just a guy working in a gun store in Florida. But at the urging of a Cuban intelligence agent, my fiancée at the time flew an F-16 into Cuba. Now, I can go to jail for telling you all this, but frankly, I don't give a shit about jail anymore. At the time, I thought she had been forced, and my friends and I went in to go get her."

Ivan sat down as the audience intently listened to Spectre's story. "At the time, I had no idea the Chinese were behind the entire operation and were trying to steal the jet for its avionics. They killed my fiancée as we tried to get to her and I flew the jet out to Homestead. Shortly after, Ironman hired me to fly with you guys."

Spectre paused to see Kruger also engrossed by the story. Other than the people involved, Spectre had never told the story to anyone.

"Y'all might remember an incident in Syria, where I had to jettison the aircraft crossing back into Iraq. And Julio, you might remember my radio being deregistered from the network," Spectre said as he turned to look at Julio at the computer podium. Julio nodded enthusiastically in response.

"Well, after I was fired, I found out that my little incident with the Syrian MiGs and the deregistered radio was the first in a long series of attempts of the Chinese trying to kill me – namely Jun Zhang, who was the operative behind the Cuban operation. In the process, he managed to kill most of the people involved in that mission, including my two best friends – Joe Carpenter and Marcus Anderson."

Spectre saw the look of recognition in the jaded operators' faces. Joe Carpenter was a guy that everyone on the team liked and respected, but few even knew he had been killed after leaving Project Archangel.

"I will take the blame for everything that has happened," Spectre said solemnly. "After Joe was killed, I broke down. I tried to quit, and after it was all said in done, I ran away. I tried to hide." Spectre shook his head in disgust at himself.

"Her name is Michelle Decker, and I am pretty sure she was here trying to figure out what happened, and I let her down," Spectre said. "When I got here, Xin had already gotten to her. And Ironman."

Kruger shook his head slowly at Spectre as he recognized what Spectre was about to say next. Spectre held up his hand and pressed on. "Ironman was a good man, but he got caught up in this too. Xin threatened his family. And we all know how much he loved his girls."

"So that's how we got to this place. Ironman came with me as I turned myself in to Xin to try to save Michelle and Ironman's family. Xin shot him in cold blood. Xin is dead now. Zhang is next," Spectre said with a focused look.

"I am not going to stand here and claim that I deserve to be standing amongst true warriors like all of you," Spectre said humbly. "But I will see justice done. And if I have to go it alone, so be it. I'll do whatever it takes because it's the right thing to do. For Joe. For Marcus. For Baxter. And for Ironman."

"Once an Angel!" one of the pilots shouted from the front row.

"Always an Angel!" the entire room shouted back in unison.

Spectre nodded modestly at the gesture of support he had just been given as he walked back to his place against the wall. Kruger stood silently for a moment as he tried to gather his thoughts.

"Ironman was a mentor and a friend to me," Kruger said softly. "Don't ever judge a man until you've walked a mile in his boots."

Kruger turned to face Spectre. "You won't be alone, brother."

"Alright, down to business," Kruger said, turning back to the crowd. "Our objective is Zhang, but as it stands right now, we do not have any definite Intel on where he might be other than the Southeast United States. During an operation Friday night, we were able to capture a pilot and a spook from the Chinese Ministry of State Security operating here locally. Apparently Xin was operating independently."

"During our interrogation, the pilot told us that the Chief of Operations for Chinese MSS here in Tampa is Kato Ling, who was flown in on Friday," Kruger said as Meeks advanced the presentation and a CIA file photo of Kato Ling projected on the two screens.

"The pilot had no further information for us, but after an advanced interrogation session this morning with the spook known as Quan Chi, we were able to ascertain Ling's approximate location and patterns of movement," Kruger continued. Meeks advanced the slide again and pulled up a map of Tampa.

"Ling is staying at this compound here in East Tampa," Kruger said as a red circle appeared on the map. "Based on aerial surveillance launched earlier this afternoon, the compound is heavily guarded and conveniently located next to a police substation."

"According to Chi, however, Ling is set to meet tonight with a mid-level Venezuelan drug cartel boss named Emilio Leon at Leon's luxury estate on Harbour Island. That meeting is set for 2100 hours local time, which means Chi should be leaving his estate somewhere between 2015 and 2040.

"After a bit of gentle convincing," Kruger continued with a wicked grin, "Chi told us that Ling travels in a two SUV convoy with four trained operatives per vehicle."

"Ladies and gentlemen, our primary objective tonight is to grab Ling before he and his men reach Leon's estate," Kruger said. "Are there any questions?"

Kruger paused for a moment, waiting for hands to go up. When there were no questions, Kruger looked at his watch and continued, "Alright then, the pre-mission brief for the individual fire teams and aviation support assets is in thirty minutes. Let's get these fuckers in honor of our fallen heroes."

CHAPTER THIRTY EIGHT

East Tampa, FL
2035 Local Time

"Toadstool is leaving the castle," JAX announced from the U-28 orbiting high above. "He's in the trail vehicle. Lead vehicle is occupied four times and trail is occupied times two."

"Nightmare Zero One copies," Kruger responded. He was sitting in the back of the Blackhawk as it headed toward the objective in close formation with two MH-6 Little Bird helicopters at just over a thousand feet.

Kruger was sitting next to former Marine Sniper Tim "Thumper" Carter in the back of the blacked out helicopter. The two Little Birds each had four operators with body armor and four-tube Panoramic NVGs attached to their lightweight helmets. It was a relatively light force for the mission ahead.

"One minute," Shorty called over the intercom. He was piloting the Blackhawk and leading the three-ship into the objective area.

Kruger smiled as the familiar adrenaline surge sent his blood pumping. He loved being on the pointy end of the spear and riding into battle. It was far better to have the humid night air flowing across his beard than sitting in his office trying to figure out a better way to hide expenditures from nosy Senators.

Kruger and Thumper checked their weapons one more time. They were both carrying M107A1 Rifles with high-powered thermal scopes chambered in .50BMG Armor Piercing rounds. Both side doors of the helicopter were open, allowing the two men to shoot from opposite sides using specially made door slings to support the barrel of the rifle and increase accuracy.

"Toadstool is headed west on Hartford Street," JAX announced as he followed the convoy movement with the U-28s sensors. "Twenty-five miles per hour."

"Green light," Kruger said as he shifted his weight to his back leg from his crouched position.

The two Little Birds detached from the formation diving low to just a few feet off the water as they sped along the canal in the East Bay. The Blackhawk started a climb as it headed east toward the objective area where the two SUVs would be approaching.

"Vehicles in sight, coming to you Kruger," Shorty said over the intercom. The helicopter made a slight pedal turn to the right and shifted to a crabbing flight path as it continued toward the approaching vehicles. Kruger adjusted his scope and found the two approaching SUVs, zeroing in on the hot engine compartment of the trail vehicle where the armor would be most susceptible. In his interrogation, Chi had told Kruger that both SUVs were heavily armored Escalades, but had been reinforced mostly in the passenger compartment and windows.

Kruger steadied his aim as the Blackhawk slowed. He steadied his breathing and squeezed the trigger, sending the massive fifty-caliber bullet toward the trail vehicle. As Kruger recovered from the recoil, he readjusted and fired a second time, hitting the SUV again in the hood.

The lead vehicle sped forward while the trail vehicle started to slow under the catastrophic engine failure. The two Little Birds bracketed the convoy. The lead Little Bird slowed to a hover in front of the disabled SUV, causing the driver to slam on his brakes as the trail Little Bird landed behind it.

With the trail vehicle successfully stopped, the four men from the trail Little Bird dismounted with weapons drawn and surrounded the SUV. Shorty piloted the Blackhawk into a cover position just in front of the disabled vehicle as the men below went to work.

"Lead vehicle is stopping," JAX announced. The lead vehicle had gained several hundred feet before realizing that the trail vehicle had stopped. "Attempting to turn around now."

Thumper took aim at the SUV attempting to stop and turn. As the vehicle stopped, Thumper shot, hitting the vehicle in the left front tire. With no shoulder, the SUV tried backing up before Thumper fired again and struck the left rear tire.

The lead Little Bird repositioned to the west side of the lead vehicle, landing in front of it as the four men dismounted. As the men in the SUV exited and fired toward them, they were easily picked off by the four operators.

"Toadstool is ready," Tuna called from the team at the rear vehicle.

"Hold on," Shorty said over the intercom. The Blackhawk aggressively descended and turned toward the SUV. Tuna was standing on top, holding up a three-foot loop as the other three men covered the SUV.

The Blackhawk hovered to within a few feet of Tuna as he attached the loop to the hook on the bottom of the helicopter and jumped off and out of the way.

"All clear," Tuna announced over the tactical frequency.

The four men moved out of the way and headed back toward the waiting Little Bird as the sling-loaded SUV was lifted into the sky by the Blackhawk.

With all men accounted for, the two Little Birds rejoined to each side of the loaded down Blackhawk. The three helicopters headed out toward the bay and back to MacDill Air Force Base, where they could take their time in disabling the SUV's security features and extracting its occupants without causing too much of a scene with the locals.

Kruger checked his watch as they cleared back into the bay. The entire mission had taken seven minutes from the time he had given the green light to the time they were feet wet again.

CHAPTER THIRTY NINE

Project Archangel Operations Building
MacDill AFB, FL
2155 Local Time

After watching the video data link feed of the mission from the U-28 real time in the Operations Center, Spectre had met the helicopters on the ramp. For the last hour, Spectre had been watching from the observation window of the large Project Archangel Maintenance Facility hangar. The extraction team worked quickly and efficiently to remove Kato Ling and his bodyguard from the armored Cadillac Escalade.

The team used high voltage electrical cables to disable the vehicle's electrical system and its electrified door handles before pumping tear gas through the vehicle's ventilation system. Wearing masks, the team then proceeded to cut the armored doors off the vehicle and extract its coughing and crying occupants with little struggle.

"Spectre, we're having a ceremony in the bar if you want to attend," Kruger said as he entered the room. "Starts in five minutes."

Spectre watched the technicians secure the two men's hands and put hoods over their heads. He looked at his watch as he turned toward Kruger. "What's the plan with these guys?"

"We'll soften them up with a little mood music before I have a chat with Mr. Ling," Kruger said with a wry smile.

"Yoko Ono?" Spectre said, thinking back to his training with the team and the hours upon hours of her music that they played to expose him to psychological warfare.

Kruger laughed as he led Spectre out of the observation room. "This guy would probably like that kind of music. No, it's much worse."

Spectre tilted his head at Kruger as he waited for an answer.

"Justin Bieber," Kruger finally said. "And Nickleback."

"Sooo… Twenty minutes until they talk?" Spectre joked.

The two laughed as they exited the hangar and crossed the ramp to the Operations Building. Spectre followed Kruger through the myriad of vault doors requiring badge swipes and access vaults as they entered the heart almost twenty thousand square foot secure facility.

Officially, the squadron bar was called the "break room." It had two high tables where most people could eat their lunch and still discuss classified information while a twenty-four hour cable news channel played on a multitude of flat screen TVs lining the walls. Unofficially, it was the squadron bar – the place where the team could get together after hours and have drinks, shoot their watches, tell tales, and not worry about having to censor themselves for fear of divulging classified information or offending virgin ears. The walls were lined with memorabilia of warriors of days past, as well as a wall mural of a hovering hooded and armored warrior with angel wings who held a sword low and ready as he prepared to face off against a hoard of approaching demon warriors.

Spectre stood back in the back of the crowded bar as Kruger pushed his way forward through the multitude of pilots and operators standing around socializing with drinks in their hands. Kruger stopped at a wooden bar lined with bar stools and turned as the crowd spread out to give him room to talk.

"Can I have everyone's attention, please?" Kruger yelled as the dull roar of the fifty or so conversations subsided and everyone turned their attention to the center of the bar.

"First off, good work to everyone involved on tonight's mission," Kruger said. "We executed with zero friendly losses. The objective is in custody and we will start the interrogation soon."

Kruger paused as the crowd acknowledged the successful mission. As the celebratory applause died down, Kruger held up his hand. "Now, let's get to why we're here."

"Tonight, we honor our three fallen comrades: Ironman, Tanning, and Redman," Kruger said as his tone changed. "This is not a funeral. There's no crying here. We're going to give them a warrior's send off and get back to business. I wish this was our first, but it's not. Does anyone have any questions on the ROE?"

Kruger waited as everyone in the bar stood silently. The Rules of Engagement for a Project Archangel wake were simple. As long as the floor was open, anyone could come up, tell a joke, story, or sing a song as long as it honored the dead. At the end of each speaker, they would toast the fallen.

"Good, I'll start," Kruger said with a pause as he gained his composure. "James Redman was never known for having a strong stomach. My first experience with him was six years ago on an OP in the Kunar Province. We had to sneak into a village to grab a mid-level Taliban fucktard and then link up with the helo to extract.

"Well, the village was completely asleep, and we were able to get to this guy's hut without so much as a barking dog. As soon as Redman grabbed the guy, it scared our Taliban buddy so bad that he literally shit himself. I don't know what he had been eating, but the smell was so bad that Redman threw up right on the guy, which made the smell even worse. It was the funniest and most disgusting thing I've ever seen. I think he threw up at least three more times on that hike to meet the helo," Kruger said as the crowd laughed with him.

"To James Redman," Kruger said as he stopped and picked up the red Solo cup one of the pilots had prepared for him.

"Once an Angel," Kruger challenged with his cup held high.

"Always an Angel!" the crowd responded in unison.

"Ok, I've got one," Jenny said as she pushed her way to the front of the bar next to Kruger. Kruger, in turn, yielded the floor to the petite brunette wearing desert tan flight suit. "This actually happened recently."

"So as some of you may know, I bought a 2012 Corvette ZR1 with the tax-free money from our deployment time last year. And as many of you might also know, I also have a bit of a lead foot," Jenny said as the crowd chuckled.

"I may have been arrested for allegedly turning the lights out and cruising down a deserted highway at slightly above the posted speed limit while wearing Night Vision Goggles. *Allegedly*. Anyway, Ironman knew about it before I made it to County lockup and had the charges dropped before I even had a chance to work on my prison shank.

"I seriously thought Ironman would send me packing from the team, but he had only one question as he drove me to pick up my car from the impound lot," Jenny paused for effect.

"He said, 'The guy said you were doing 170.' So, of course, I held my head low and said, 'Yeah, boss, I did.' I thought for sure my career was over, until he looked over at me, smiled with that goofy grin of his, and said, 'But I thought you said that was a two hundred mile per hour car?' And then he laughed at me!"

Jenny waited for the laughter to subside and then held up her beer mug. "To Ironman. Once an Angel," she called.

"Always an Angel!" the crowd replied.

As Jenny disappeared back into the crowd, the burly former Navy SEAL Mike Roland emerged in the center next to Kruger and held up his mug as he closed his eyes.

"I'm a lover, a fighter. An American naval UDT SEAL diver. That's a rootin' tootin' shootin' paratroopin' SCUBA diving demolition double cap crippin' Frogman - last of the bare-knuckle fighters. No muff too tough, I dive for five. Tuck suck fuck nibble 'n chew. Dine and interwine, masturbate. Ejaculate and copulate. Drive Navy trucks 2bys, 4bys, 6bys and those big mother fuckers that go Shhh Shhh and bend in the middle. Been around the world twice. Been there and done that twice. Talked to everyone once, seen two white whales fuckin. Been to two pig picking picnics, and I met a man with a marble head and a wooden cock," Roland paused as he took a sip of his beer from his mug. "And ladies, if ya don't like my face, you can sit on it! To Tanning and Redman, Frogmen until the end! Once an Angel!"

"Always an Angel!" the crowd fired back as the room erupted in laughter.

As the laughter subsided, Spectre stepped forward.

"Joe Carpenter wasn't an Angel when he died, but he was killed by the same people, and he will always be an Angel. I met him in college, and I'll never forget the night we were at a party with these two cheerleaders. Apparently the one I was with failed to mention she had a boyfriend while we were going out. *Allegedly.* Anyway, this guy shows up at the party and he's 6'5 and almost three hundred pounds. I can't really blame him for being pissed, but Joe went right up to him and said, 'If you ever want to make your ugly kids, I suggest you forget about this girl and find someone else.' Of course, the guy was furious and went after Joe. That was until Joe kicked him squarely in the nuts and said, 'I warned you.' It was the biggest fight I think I had ever been in, and I wouldn't have had it any other way. To my best friend, rest in peace, brother. Once an Angel!"

"Always an Angel!" the crowd chanted.

They continued telling jokes, quoting poems, and singing songs for another hour until Kruger closed the floor and instructed everyone to proceed to the bar in an orderly line. It was lined with a hundred shot glasses filled with Jeremiah Weed whiskey.

Kruger picked up the first glass and led the procession of warriors to the far end of the room where the warrior angel was. He stopped a few feet from the covered painting and said, "To the fallen Angels," before downing the shot and throwing the shot glass against the mural. The glass shattered as it fell to the ground.

The men and women behind him followed suit as glass after glass shattered against the wall. Spectre found Kruger standing in the hallway after the proceedings were over.

"That was good shit, man. Ironman would be proud," Spectre said.

Kruger nodded. Spectre could see the pain of losing his brothers in arms in Kruger's glassy eyes. It was easily recognizable to Spectre. "What's next?" Spectre asked, changing the subject.

"Vengeance," Kruger replied.

CHAPTER FORTY

WHODAT Airspace
95 Miles East of New Orleans, LA
1012 Local Time

Looking out on her right wing, the F-15 looked like a giant tennis court compared to the F/A-18s Mary was used to flying against. She checked her parameters one last time to make sure her Hornet was at the appropriate airspeed, altitude, and distance from Foxworthy's F-15.

"Hammer One One, Speed and Angels on the left," she said after confirming she was at eighteen thousand feet and four hundred and fifty knots per their permission coordination. The air to air TACAN distance on her center display showed that their two aircraft were a mile and a half apart.

"Bayou Three One ready," Foxworthy replied.

Mary sighed behind her mask. No matter how many times she had flown against him, Foxworthy always refused to mimic her wording. Instead, he always called it "dumb boat people speak" and laughed it off.

"Turn in, left to left," she said as she pushed her throttle forward and entered a hard right turn to point at the massive F-15. She took a radar lock as she watched the twin-tailed aircraft rapidly approaching.

"Fight's on!" she called as she lit the afterburner and started a left turn across the F-15's tail. She squeezed her abdominal and leg muscles as her G-suit inflated under the G-forces. Her HUD G-meter showed seven Gs as she looked back to find the F-15 across the turn circle also in a left hand turn. *Last one to turn sets the fight.*

Foxworthy had opted to use his Eagle's superior turn rate around the turn circle to attempt to gain an advantage. Using the Hornet's superior nose authority, Mary overbanked and cut to the inside, attempting to cut across the imaginary turn circle and point at Foxworthy's aircraft first.

As her nose tracked low toward Foxworthy's aircraft, she saw him overbank to meet her down low. Her nose tracked more quickly, allowing her to get a radar lock and call a simulated air to air missile shot. She watched as flares popped out of his aircraft as they met at a second merge.

As the two aircraft crossed, Mary rolled the Hornet onto its back and pulled, transitioning the fight to an in-close knife fight. Foxworthy reacted and made a slicing turn back toward her as well. As she craned her neck back over her shoulder and pulled to the Hornet's angle of attack tone, she saw Foxworthy's aircraft moving forward toward her canopy bow. *She was winning.*

Foxworthy attempted to reverse again as their aircraft merged a third time. As they raced toward the training floor, the two aircraft had entered a slow speed fight. Mary maneuvered behind Foxworthy as his F-15 struggled to stay flying at slow speed. Rocking the ACM mode selector back on the stick with her thumb, she selected GUN and racked the gun pipper across the massive target in front of her.

"Bayou Three One is Bingo," Foxworthy called over the radio, indicating he was at the preplanned fuel state to return to base.

"Hammer One One guns track kill Eagle left hand turn," Mary said proudly over their fight frequency.

"Hammer One One knock it off," she called to end the fight.

"Bayou Three One knock it off," Foxworthy replied. She smiled as she dropped her mask. She could hear the frustration in Foxworthy's voice. *Beat by a girl. And a Navy girl at that. Ha!*

"Do you want me to lead you home?" Mary asked over the radio.

"Sure," Foxworthy said grudgingly.

Foxworthy rejoined on Mary's left wing as she pointed west to go home. As she looked over and flipped him off, she saw the oil rigs scattered about the Gulf and realized they were near the location of the source of Foxworthy's recent obsession. *Ever since the alert scramble, and even more so since talking to the engineer with supposed first-hand knowledge, he just wouldn't shut up about it.*

"Do you have any extra gas?" Mary asked over the radio.

"Bayou is Bingo," Foxworthy said.

"Ok," Mary replied. "But that oil rig you like so much is right below us. I thought you might want to see it in the daylight."

After a pregnant pause on the radio, Foxworthy finally responded. "I have enough gas for that," he said.

Mary laughed. She knew he had only been calling Bingo because it was their third fight and would be the third time she gunned him. He was just using the fuel as an excuse to say he had quit fighting and that's how she won.

"Copy that," Mary said, still laughing as she keyed the radio. "Follow me."

Mary started a shallow, descending right-hand turn. She checked her Radar Warning Receiver to see if she had any indications of a missile targeting her. It was silent. She turned the aircraft back east as she descended through five thousand feet.

"You take the right, I'll take the left," Mary directed over the radio.

"Two," Foxworthy replied sharply.

They descended to five hundred feet over the water and leveled off. Mary could hear the characteristic buzz of the high-speed air flow crossing the leading edge extensions of the wing as they hit four hundred and fifty knots.

"Hammer One One naked," Mary said, letting Foxworthy know that she wasn't receiving any indications.

"Bayou Three One naked," Foxworthy replied.

The two aircraft bracketed the oil platform as they flew by at high speed. Mary pitched her jet's nose up to climb back up to cruising altitude for their flight back home.

"See anything interesting?" Mary asked over the radio.

"Negative," Foxworthy replied. He was never one to chit chat over the radio.

"Copy, let's RTB," Mary replied.

She pointed their formation toward NAS JRB New Orleans and contacted Houston Center. The skies were completely clear, giving her excellent visibility. She could make out the city in the distance.

"City tour?" she asked.

"Sure," Foxworthy replied.

The controller switched her to New Orleans Approach where she asked to maintain VFR over the city. Foxworthy tucked his aircraft in close as Mary flew over the Crescent City Connection Bridge and over the French Quarter before making a left turn to cross over the Mercedes-Benz Superdome to head back to base.

Foxworthy maintained his position off Mary's right wing as she lined up for the initial for Runway 4 at NAS JRB New Orleans. As they reached the numbers of the runway, Mary gave Foxworthy the kiss off signal and entered a hard left turn to bleed off speed and enter downwind.

Once below two hundred and fifty knots, Mary lowered the gear and flaps and called her position to the tower. The controller cleared the flight to land and the two aircraft landed.

"Talk to you in a few, cleared off," Mary said on the interflight frequency as she cleared the runway.

Mary called for taxi clearance and made the right hand turn toward her line as Foxworthy made a left toward his ramp.

* * *

As he stepped out of the U-28, Spectre stopped to watch the F/A-18 leading the F-15 enter the left-hand break overhead. He thought it was cool to see the size difference of the two aircraft as the jet engines roared overhead. As they entered the downwind, Spectre grabbed his bag and turned his attention back to unloading their gear from the U-28.

Kruger had broken Ling relatively easily that morning. Although he never heard the details of Kruger's methods, Spectre assumed that a more advanced approach was needed for such a senior operative, although they hadn't learned much.

Ling claimed to be in the dark on Zhang's operations. The only thing he was able to tell Kruger was that Zhang was operating out of New Orleans and doing something related to drilling oil in the Gulf of Mexico. The only genuinely new information that he could offer beyond that was that they often flew a resupply flight to one of the platforms using a floatplane flying from an airport in Yucatan, Mexico.

It wasn't what Spectre had been hoping for, but it was a good start. Spectre remembered seeing information about an oil company on Chang's ledger. Spectre and Kruger decided that he would be the best person to start with.

Kruger was followed by Meeks, Tuna, Axe, and Greene exiting the U-28. They were all wearing 5.11 Tactical Pants and Polo shirts and carrying backpacks as they descended the stairway.

Spectre turned as the F-15 taxied by. He waved back awkwardly as he saw the pilot waving enthusiastically at him. He wondered if that were Foxworthy. He hadn't seen him since Carpenter's funeral. *It seems like so long ago,* Spectre thought. *But it has only been a couple of weeks.*

Spectre and the team continued unloading the bags and rifle cases from the baggage area of the PC-12. Minutes later, a young Navy enlisted sailor with a blue van showed up at the aircraft. They loaded all of their equipment into the back and got in. It took them to the nearby transient hangar used for detachments. Meeks started setting up his computer equipment and the rest of the team secured their gear before walking back out onto the ramp to help Jenny and JAX secure the aircraft and get it towed into the hangar.

"Spectre!" a voice behind him yelled. Spectre turned to see Foxworthy approaching from the gate wearing his green flight suit.

"Foxworthy?" Spectre asked. "What are you doing here?"

"I was going to ask you the same thing!" Foxworthy said as he reached Spectre and shoved his hand out. "You flying these things now?"

"Just a passenger for now," Spectre replied.

"I know, these airplanes are secret squirrel shit," Foxworthy said, holding up his hands. "I hope the money is good."

"I'm just a contractor. But what about you, man? Are you flying with the Guard full time?" Spectre asked, changing the subject.

Foxworthy laughed and shook his head, "Me? Oh hell no! No way could I do that grind. I like being a part timer. I'm mostly doing work with my company now. Things are great."

"Company? Did you tell me about it last time we talked? I can't remember," Spectre said, doing his best to be polite despite wanting Foxworthy to get out of his hair.

"I'm not sure," Foxworthy replied. "But it's called Mach Two Consulting. We do consulting work in the oil and gas industry. Lots of cool stuff on oil rigs out in the Gulf. They love fighter pilots."

"Oh really?" Spectre asked.

"Yeah man, if you ever want to take me up on flying Eagles down here, I could probably use you for some of the stuff we do. Right now, it's just me and two other pilots doing the seminars. There aren't enough Louisiana boys in the squadrons down here, ya know?" Foxworthy asked with a wink and a nudge.

"Is business that good?" Spectre asked.

"We just got back from a three-day trip. In fact, I've got two more trips later this week. The girl I just flew with does a great job lining up contracts for us. Do you know "Mary" Jane? She flies Hornets down the street," replied Foxworthy.

"Can't say I do," Spectre said.

"I'm actually on my way to debrief with her. You should meet her sometime. Her dad is the President of an Oil and Gas exploration company, so that helps," Foxworthy said with a grin.

Spectre paused for a moment. "Wait, what's her name?"

"Her real name is Meghan Jane, but her callsign is Mary," Foxworthy replied.

"And her dad is Tom Jane. As in Cajun Oil and Gas?" Spectre asked. His interest was suddenly piqued.

"Same guy! Why? Do you know him? He's a really nice guy," Foxworthy said.

"Never met him, but I have heard of him. Anyway, do you have a card or something?" Spectre asked.

"Sure do!" Foxworthy replied, pulling his wallet out of his lower left leg flight suit pocket and pulling out a stack of cards. "Here, take a couple."

"Thanks," Spectre replied as he stuffed the cards in his cargo pants pocket.

"Say, whatever happened to that hot little blonde that was with you at the funeral?" Foxworthy asked with a perverted smile. "Please tell me you're hitting that."

Spectre rolled his eyes. "Nope," he replied.

"Well, if you're not interested, give her one of those cards," Foxworthy said, pointing to Spectre's cargo pants pocket.

"Sure thing," Spectre replied facetiously. "Anyway, I've got a lot of work to do here. I'll be in touch."

"Ok man, let me know if you want to meet up for drinks while you're in town," Foxworthy replied. "Your buddies can come too."

CHAPTER FORTY ONE

Poydras St
New Orleans, LA
1204 Local Time

Spectre entered the downtown apartment building with Kruger and Tuna right behind him. Axe and Greene each took a corner on the street level to keep watch as the team went to find Chang. They had all changed into civilian clothes and were wearing covert in-ear communication pieces with concealed Glock 19s.

Spectre led them up the stairs toward Chang's apartment, careful to avoid the surveillance cameras in the lobby. Although it was a Monday, Chang had mentioned that he always went home for lunch during the week during his lunch hour. Spectre was hoping to catch him away from the office that was likely still a crime scene after his staged break in.

Finding the door, Axe and Kruger each took a side of the doorway. As Spectre started to knock, Kruger stopped him and pointed at the frame. It was damaged and splintered as if someone had kicked it in and then attempted to close it back.

"You smell that?" Kruger whispered. Axe and Spectre both took deep sniffs. Spectre scrunched his face as he recognized the smell.

"You don't think?" Spectre asked, dreading what might be on the other side of the door.

Kruger frowned and nodded. All three drew their concealed Glocks and prepared for entry. After confirming that Axe and Kruger were ready through hand signals, Spectre took a step back with his gun ready.

Kruger initiated a silent countdown with his hands. At the expiration, Spectre stepped forward and kicked the door in with his boot. He used his momentum to continue forward and cleared left as both men filed in behind him and cleared right. The room appeared to be empty, but the smell grew stronger.

Spectre checked the small kitchenette to his left as Kruger and Axe entered the living area and headed toward the bedroom. The apartment was spotless and appeared to have been unused for several days.

Satisfied the kitchen was clear, Spectre joined Kruger and Axe at the bedroom door. This time Axe opened the door and Spectre filed in behind Kruger to clear. Axe immediately turned left with the door as Kruger and Spectre cleared their sections to the right.

The queen-sized bed was still perfectly made and the room appeared to be spotless. Despite the smell growing stronger, there was still no sign of Chang. Kruger turned toward the closed bathroom door and pointed.

"Kruger," Greene said over the radio. "Heads up, two marked units and a Tahoe with suits just pulled up in front. Looks like they might be heading inside."

"Copy," Kruger responded.

"You want me to stop them?" Greene asked.

"Negative. Just keep an eye out on them," Kruger responded. Kruger pointed to Axe, who nodded and left the bedroom to keep watch at the apartment entrance.

"Roger that," Green said.

Kruger and Spectre entered with guns raised. As they stepped into the small master bath, the smell of rotting flesh was like hitting a brick wall. Both men stopped as they saw Chang's decomposing body lying in the bathtub.

"Goddammit!" Spectre yelled as his fears were realized.

"Looks like he was tortured," Kruger said, pointing out the burn marks on his arm and bruises on his face and chest.

Spectre looked at the body. Chang was naked, lying in a bloodstained empty bathtub with his eyes closed. It appeared to be more than just a murder. *Whoever had done this was trying to send a message.*

"Alright, this is a dead end," Kruger said, shaking his head in disgust. He pulled out his digital camera and took several pictures before shoving the small camera back in his pocket. "Let's get out of here. Don't touch anything."

Spectre nodded as he followed Kruger out of the bathroom and into the bedroom.

"Elevator is on its way up," Axe announced over their earpieces.

Kruger and Spectre sprinted toward the door. Spectre made a quick scan as he followed Kruger out, looking for anything of use that might help them pin down the location of Zhang.

"Looks like they're stopping on this floor," Axe warned.

Spectre hesitated as they reached the doorway, still frantically searching for something that might give them a clue.

"Let's go Spectre!" Kruger yelled.

"Elevator is opening," Axe said.

Frustrated that he couldn't find anything, Spectre reluctantly followed as they linked up with Kruger and raced out of the apartment. Spectre looked over his shoulder to see one of the uniformed officers stop to give chase.

"You! Stop! Stop right now!" the officer yelled.

Holstering their weapons, the three took off toward the nearby stairs as they ran from the officers.

"Get the vehicle and meet us at Lafayette Street," Kruger ordered. They had studied possible routes of escape. They had parked their rental Suburban in a lot south of Chang's apartment.

"Copy that," Tuna responded.

They made it to the exit and emerged onto the sidewalk, still running at full speed. As they looked back, two uniformed officers and a man in a suit were still chasing them on foot. Spectre could hear sirens in the distance. He assumed they had called for backup during their chase.

"Stop right there!" they yelled.

The three continued running on Poydras and then turned south on O'Keefe Avenue. Spectre hoped the Suburban with Axe and Greene would be waiting as they sprinted south toward their rendezvous point. He didn't want to get into a daylight shootout with a trigger-happy police department if he could help it.

As they reached the end of the block, they saw the black Suburban speeding toward them from their left. They took off running down Lafayette Street to intercept and Axe skidded the Suburban to a stop in front of them. They piled into the rear passenger door and Axe floored it, darting in and out of traffic to avoid the approaching marked units.

Spectre pulled out his wallet and dug for the card Foxworthy had given him as Axe weaved in and out of traffic trying to lose the marked police cars in the distance.

"Let me see your phone," Spectre said, gesturing to Kruger as they were jostled around the back seat of the Suburban.

"Seriously? Right now?" Kruger asked as he held on while Axe made a hard left turn toward the interstate.

"Yes, right now," Spectre replied. "I think the guy I talked to earlier might be able to help. I don't want to waste any more time."

"I like your attitude," Kruger said with a laugh as he handed Spectre his phone.

CHAPTER FORTY TWO

Hangar 4
NAS JRB New Orleans, LA
1325 Local Time

"I gotta tell ya, I didn't expect to hear back from you so soon," Foxworthy said as he met Spectre at the access gate to the secure hangar. "Is the beer light on already?"

"I thought it would be best to talk in person," Spectre replied as he led Foxworthy into the vast hangar. Their U-28 sat in the middle of the spacious hangar that once was home to A-10s and P-3s. "Glad I caught you before you went home."

"What's this about, Cal?" Foxworthy asked. His jovial tone had turned serious as he noticed the intensity in Spectre's expression.

"We can talk upstairs," Spectre replied. Spectre led him up the stairs to the second floor that once served as the operations area for a P-3 squadron. Its briefing rooms and offices had been remodeled before the squadron closed its doors due to funding and fleet modernization priorities. The hangar now served as a temporary operating area for visiting Air Force and Navy squadrons training with the F/A-18 and F-15 squadrons on base.

They walked past the individual and main briefing rooms and into the offices where Kruger was seated at the desk. He hung up the phone as Spectre and Foxworthy entered.

"Have a seat," Spectre directed and pointed to an open chair across from Kruger. Foxworthy sat nervously as Spectre leaned against the bookcase next to the desk.

"What is this about?" Foxworthy asked.

"Tell me about your company," Spectre said, initiating the conversation.

Foxworthy gave Spectre a confused look. "Like I told you earlier, I do consultation with oil and gas companies. What the fuck is this? Are you interrogating me? Who is he?"

"No, Mr. Vaughan, we're not," Kruger said as he smiled through his beard. "My name is Freddie Mack, and I work for a company called Dynamic Aviation Consulting. We're just here doing a site survey and Cal thought you might be able to help."

"Consulting, huh?" Foxworthy asked. "I've never heard of you."

"Don't worry, we don't do the same kind of consulting you do," Kruger said with a chuckle. "But we are interested in getting your help."

"With what?" Foxworthy asked.

"You said Tom Jane's daughter works for you, right?" Spectre asked.

"She's engaged to a murse, dude," Foxworthy said dismissively. "I don't think she'd be interested in you."

ARCHANGEL FALLEN

Spectre groaned at Foxworthy's insistence that everything involved women or the pursuit of women. "What do you know about Tom Jane?" Spectre asked. He didn't have time to deal with Foxworthy's sophomoric sense of humor.

"He started out as a roughneck in New Iberia in the late seventies. He worked his way to the top until he founded Cajun Oil and Gas. Now he's a multimillionaire," Foxworthy replied.

"You've done business with his company, correct?" Kruger asked.

Foxworthy nodded. "All the time. In fact, I was telling Spectre that we just finished a three-day seminar on an oil rig for them a couple of days ago."

"Have you ever heard of Hua Xia Holdings?" Spectre asked.

"Hua who?" Foxworthy asked. "What the hell language is that?"

"Hua Xia Holdings," Spectre repeated.

Foxworthy was silent as he tried to place the name. It sounded familiar, but he wasn't sure he had ever heard of it before.

"It's a Chinese holding company. They are investors with Cajun Oil and Gas," Spectre added.

Suddenly Foxworthy's eyes widened as he made the connection. "Chinese!"

"Yes, Chinese," Spectre said, surprised by Foxworthy's sudden outburst. "You know them?"

"Chinati?" Foxworthy asked as he thought back to the engineer he had spoken to a few days prior.

"Chinati?" Spectre asked as he shared a confused look with Kruger. "Wait, do you mean Chinese National Oil?"

"Holy shit," Foxworthy muttered, still trying to piece together everything he had learned since the scramble a week ago. "That's it!"

"Mind filling us in?" Kruger asked.

"Ok, but this can't leave this room," Foxworthy said as he slid to the edge of his seat and lowered his voice.

"You never talked to us," Kruger said reassuringly.

"Last Monday, I was sitting alert down the street when we were scrambled on an aircraft penetrating the Air Defense Identification Zone without talking or squawking. Usually, those are standard and boring, but on this one, we came across a seaplane landing at an oil rig," Foxworthy said as Kruger and Spectre listened intently.

Spectre thought back to the interrogation of Ling. It sounded like Foxworthy had been scrambled to intercept the resupply flight out of Mexico. He gestured for Foxworthy to continue.

"Well, as we orbited and watched it land, my wingman and I were both lit up by SAM tracking radar indications!" Foxworthy continued. "Everyone said we were full of shit, but I know what I saw, and Mary said she's had the same thing happen to her from the carrier."

"I believe it," Spectre offered. "Then what happened?"

"I asked Mary to ask her dad about it, and she said he was acting weird and avoiding the question," Foxworthy said excitedly. He finally felt vindicated despite his doubters. He couldn't wait to tell Crash how wrong he had been for insisting that he just drop it. "And when we were on the Freedom Star, I met an engineer who worked for Cajun Oil, who said that he had been on that rig. That's where I got Chinati. That's the name he said was on his paycheck."

"Do you know where the rig is, exactly?" Spectre asked as he began formulating a plan of attack.

Foxworthy nodded enthusiastically. "It's called the Jupiter Rising, and I can get you its coordinates if you like. But tell me, what is all this about?"

"Ever heard of Jun Zhang?" Spectre pushed.

"Who?" Foxworthy asked.

"He works for the Chinese Ministry of State Security — their version of the CIA. We think he might be doing something with these oil rigs," Kruger answered.

"Are you guys spooks or something?" Foxworthy asked.

"Zhang killed Joe," Spectre said abruptly. "That's why we're looking for him."

Foxworthy fell silent. He and Joe Carpenter had also been friends in college, although not quite as close as Spectre and Carpenter were.

"So what do you need from me?" Foxworthy said finally.

"Mr. Vaughan, I think you've been more than helpful—" Kruger said.

"Can you get us on the Jupiter Rising?" Spectre interrupted.

CHAPTER FORTY THREE

Spectre met Kruger and company in the mission planning room after escorting Foxworthy back to the gate. Meeks had taken over the room once used by P-3 pilots to plan missions. He set up his mobile network of computers on the tables lining the walls.

"Do you think he'll come through for us?" Kruger asked. He had just finished backfilling the team on what they had learned from Foxworthy and the tentative plan going forward.

Spectre shrugged. "He liked Joe in college and his alert scramble really bothered him. I think he's motivated to want to help. Not sure if he can get Jane's daughter on board, but if not, there are other options," Spectre said as he took his place next to the other operators surrounding the mission-planning table in the center of the room.

"We need to have a Plan B if this thing doesn't get off the ground in the next twelve hours," Kruger said. "I was on the phone with Becky back home before you guys came in." Kruger frowned and shook his head.

"Uh oh," Spectre said.

"Uh oh is right," Kruger replied. "Somehow the SECDEF found out about Ironman between yesterday and today."

"How?" Axe asked.

"I don't know, but he's sending his little pencil neck Deputy Secretary down to Tampa to do an investigation," Kruger replied.

"Chaz or whatever that little dweeb's name is?" Greene asked with a snicker.

"Chaz Hunt IV," Kruger said mockingly.

"How long do we have?" Spectre asked.

"She said he was making it a priority, so I'd guess anywhere from twenty four to forty eight hours before he graces us with his presence and tells us how badass he used to be in his Paintball League," Kruger replied.

"No shit? He said that?" Spectre asked incredulously.

"Yup!" Kruger said as they all laughed. "During one of their little visits, he watched us grab a Somali warlord on the video uplink. When we got back, he no kidding tried to debrief me on my technique by giving me a few pointers from his league as team captain. Am I lying, Tuna?"

Tuna laughed and said, "Nope! I thought you were going to choke him out when he said that."

"So why even worry about him?" Spectre asked.

"Because he's the man now that SECDEF is off trying to be VP. He can shut us down in a heartbeat, especially if he finds out we're here," Kruger said. "We need to get this wrapped up before he starts asking too many questions."

* * *

"You have got to be shitting me!" Mary yelled at Foxworthy. They were sitting alone in her squadron's legacy room where pilots would go to hang out after flying. Much like Project Archangel's bar, it was filled with memorabilia and included its own bar top with beers on tap. Mary sat in one of their leather chairs across from Foxworthy on the couch near the flat screen TV.

"Calm down," Foxworthy said. The squadron's Ready Room was right next door. He didn't want other pilots from her squadron hearing them.

"You're accusing me dad of working with the fucking *Chinese* and I'm supposed to calm down?" the fiery redhead shot back. "What kind of bullshit is that?"

"Maybe he doesn't know what they're up to," Foxworthy offered. "After all, there are lots of international investors in this industry. He wouldn't be the first."

Mary glared at Foxworthy. "Papa Bear is not an idiot, Jeff," she said. "He doesn't do business with anyone unless he knows everything about them. If what you say is true, then *he knows.*"

"I'm sorry, Mary, but you know it all adds up. You said yourself that your dad was acting weird when you asked him about it. And remember what that guy Zweeben said on the Freedom Star? About the Jupiter Rising and the weird shit he had seen?" Foxworthy asked cautiously.

"I know," Mary said, hanging her head as she realized the implications of it all. "I just can't believe he would do something like that. Papa Bear is the most patriotic man I know."

"The only thing we can do is talk to him, Mary. You know that," Foxworthy said softly. "Your dad is a good man that has treated me well. I respect him. He's like a mentor to me. I don't want to believe it either."

"Who are these people anyway?" Mary asked as she leaned forward and held her head in her hands. "What do they want?"

"I think they're working for a three letter agency," Foxworthy said in a hushed tone. "They're chasing a Chinese spy that killed one of my friends. Remember that funeral I went to a couple of weeks ago?"

"Yeah, but how did you get wrapped up in this?" Mary asked.

"Remember that old college buddy I told you about during our debrief? The one that was in the U-28 parked at Hangar 4?" Foxworthy asked.

Mary nodded.

"Well, he called me back and asked me to meet with him. And when I went over there, they told me what they were working on with the Chinese guy. It all makes sense now, Mary," Foxworthy reiterated.

"Ok," Mary replied, resigning herself to the idea that her dad might be part of a greater conspiracy. "What do they want from me?"

"Just arrange the meeting," Foxworthy replied.

"When?" Mary asked as she lifted her head up. Foxworthy could see that her green eyes were watery as she fought back tears.

"Tonight," Foxworthy replied.

"Tonight?" Mary squealed. "Dude, no way! His calendar is booked weeks in advance. There's no way he'll agree to that. Jack would have a fit."

Foxworthy cringed at the thought of Jack Robertson meeting Spectre and his bearded associate. Robertson was Tom Jane's head of security. Nothing happened on Jane's schedule without being vetted through Robertson, especially not meeting new people.

"You're his baby girl," Foxworthy pleaded. "Do your magic."

"So you want me to lie to my father and introduce him to people that may want to hurt him all the while playing the 'baby girl' card? Are you hypoxic?"

"I have a feeling these guys will get to him one way or another, Mary," Foxworthy replied. "Wouldn't you rather be there to make sure he's ok?"

"I guess," Mary said reluctantly.

"Besides, I'd still like to believe he's innocent in all of this. Wouldn't you feel better to know for sure?" Foxworthy added.

Mary let out a long sigh. "Fine."

"But I want to go meet these people before I make any phone calls," Mary said.

"Valid," Foxworthy replied with a smile.

CHAPTER FORTY FOUR

N'Tini's Steak and Martinis
Mandeville, LA
1930 Local Time

"You know, Wednesday night is when all the swingers show up here," Foxworthy said, breaking the tension at the table as the four sat waiting for Tom Jane to arrive.

"Of course, you would know that," Mary said as she rolled her eyes and groaned at Foxworthy's refusal to take anything seriously.

A waitress took their drink order as they continued waiting. Spectre and Kruger had purchased button down shirts, slacks, and ties at the Navy Exchange for the night's event, having only brought casual and tactical clothes for the trip. The four sat around the white-clothed table with an open chair for Jane.

"He said he'd be here at 7:30, right?" Foxworthy asked, checking his watch.

"Relax, he'll be here," Mary replied. "I'm sure he just ran into Baton Rouge traffic on his way out of the office."

Spectre looked across the table to see Kruger checking his watch as well. Although Jane was late, Spectre knew it was more likely to do with the urgency of their mission. Kruger was still very concerned about Chaz Hunt's visit. He had been talking about it all afternoon, even after they had spoken to Mary in person and steadied her resolve to help.

For the moment, Mary's willingness to help seemed like the only sure thing to Spectre. Whatever Foxworthy had told her had been effective, and by the time she met with the team in the transient hangar, she seemed eager and willing to hear them make their case.

Spectre had done all of the talking. He anchored the conversation on what he had learned from Chang and how dangerous a threat Zhang was. The pictures Kruger had taken had been most convincing. Spectre used them to show Mary how dangerous the man they were chasing was, and that even if her dad were part of it, Zhang had to be stopped before the same thing happened to Mr. Jane.

Mary had pulled her phone out on the spot and set up the meeting with her father. She picked his favorite restaurant just a few blocks from Mach Two's office in Mandeville. She told him that she had a consulting team that she wanted him to meet for future work, and used her "daddy's girl" charm to win him over in agreeing to meet that night. Spectre hoped he would hold true to his word. The "Plan B" he and Kruger had come up with was a much more difficult proposition without the benefit of their usual contingent of air support.

"Hi Daddy," Mary said as she popped up from the table and rushed to embrace her approaching father. Spectre and Kruger turned back to see the large businessman stop and hug the smaller redhead, lifting her up as he held her embrace. He was a large man – Spectre guessed he was easily 6'2" and close to 300 lbs. He had a full head of completely white hair and leathery skin tanned by years of working in the sun.

Spectre, Kruger, and Foxworthy stood as the father and daughter ended their embrace and approached the table.

"Jeff, how the hell are you?" Jane said jovially as he shook Foxworthy's hand with his beefy paw.

"Mr. Jane, I'd like you to meet Cal Martin and Fred Mack," Foxworthy said, turning to introduce the two.

Jane paused momentarily as he sized them up before introducing himself to each of them and shaking their hands. After all of the introductions were over, they took their seats back at the table. The young waitress returned and took Jane's wine order.

"So what kind of consulting do you guys do?" Jane asked as he unfolded his napkin and placed it in his lap. "You look like a roughneck," he added, pointing at the bearded Kruger.

"No, Daddy, these guys are consultants like us," Mary interjected. "Cal was a fighter pilot."

"Oh really?" Jane asked. "I am a huge aviation enthusiast. What do you fly?"

"I used to fly F-16s," Spectre responded flatly.

"That's one of my favorites, next to the F/A-18 of course," he said, winking at Mary. "What about you?" he asked, nodding at Kruger.

"I was just a grunt in the Army," Kruger said with a grin. "You wouldn't want me flying planes, bub."

The waitress returned with Jane's bottle of wine and took their dinner orders.

"So, Mr. Jane, we have a request for you," Foxworthy said as the waitress left.

"You know I don't talk business until after dinner," Jane said with a frown. "Now, what do you guys think about the

Saints Friday night? The defense is looking pretty bad this year, huh?"

They made idle dinner conversation as their food was prepared and delivered. Neither Spectre nor Kruger had a problem with waiting for Jane to finish his bottle of wine and meal before talking to him. The wine was an excellent way to lower his resistance for them.

"Ok, so let's get down to business," Jane said as he finished his prime rib and wiped off his face with his napkin. "What's your proposal?"

"The Jupiter Rising," Spectre said, taking the lead. "We'd like you to get us on it."

Jane's face reddened as his eyes widened. "I'm sorry; son, but I don't know what that is."

"Sure you do," Spectre said casually. "You helped staff it. Paid for by Hua Xia Holdings."

Spectre watched as Jane folded his arms. He could see him try to subtly press a button on the bracelet on his right hand as he looked around nervously.

"Don't bother," Kruger said, also seeing Jane hit the panic bracelet. "He's a little preoccupied at the moment."

"How is Mr. Robertson's knee, by the way?" Spectre asked with a wry smile. "I hope his limp isn't too bad."

"It was you!" Jane bellowed as he recognized Spectre. "You're a criminal! The police and FBI are looking for you, son."

"If you recognize me, then you know that I know everything," Spectre said. "And you know what I'm capable of."

Jane shot Mary a look of betrayal as the burly man fidgeted nervously in his chair. "Meghan what are you doing? What is the meaning of this?" he demanded.

"Is it true, Daddy? Are you really working with the Chinese?" Mary responded in a hushed tone.

"Sweetheart, I do business with lots of investors," Jane said.

"Liu Chang, right?" Spectre asked. He watched Jane try the panic button on his bracelet again. This time, he made no effort to hide his attempts.

"Your Chief of Security won't be coming in to help you, Mr. Jane," Kruger warned. "He is otherwise occupied in the parking lot at the moment."

"Who are you people?" Jane asked nervously. "I haven't done anything wrong!"

Kruger pulled out the digital camera from his pocket, turned it on, and scrolled to the pictures of Chang in the bathtub. He pushed it across the table to Jane. Jane nervously picked it up, grimacing as he saw Chang's body.

"You did this?" Jane said as his face went pale.

"No," Spectre said, shaking his head. "But the people you are in bed with did. And if they did that to him, what do you think they'll do to you?"

"I'm just a businessman," Jane said softly. "I did what I had to do to make this company survive. Do you know how bad it got after the BP Oil Spill?"

"We don't care," Spectre replied.

"Well, don't judge me until you've been in my shoes," Jane replied. "I'm responsible for hundreds of families. I did what I had to do to keep us in business."

"Daddy, you knew about these people?" Mary asked with a look of disappointment.

"Sweetheart, they were just contracts," Jane explained. "I didn't know they were mobsters or mafia or whatever you're calling them."

"Chinese Intelligence, Mr. Jane," Kruger said. "You've been aiding a high-level Chinese operative that was responsible for the deaths of many American servicemen."

"I swear I had no idea!" Jane pleaded.

"Then make it right, Daddy!" Mary demanded. "Do the right thing."

"What do you want me to do? Turn myself in to the FBI?" Jane asked as he looked over at Spectre. "Ok, Mr. Martin, let's both go and do that."

"As long as you help us, you are not our concern," Kruger said. "You can do whatever you want when this is over."

"So what do you want from me?" Jane asked.

"Get us on that oil rig," Spectre replied.

Jane laughed. "You think it's just that easy? How do you propose I do that?"

"I'm sure you can figure something out," Spectre replied.

"And if I don't?"

Kruger reached across the table, grabbed the camera, and held it up. "Good luck when he comes for you next," Kruger said.

* * *

"Clampett is on his way to you," Tuna said over their tactical frequency as they watched the white Cadillac Escalade pull in front of the restaurant. The large businessman exited the vehicle, adjusted a bracelet on his wrist, and headed in while the Escalade pulled around to the back of the parking spot and backed into its spot.

Tuna was sitting with Axe in the Black Suburban a few rows over, while Greene was seated at a café in the adjacent strip mall covering the door of the restaurant.

"Should we say hi?" Tuna asked as he looked over at Axe.

Axe smiled and nodded with a thumbs up.

"Greene how many did you see in the Escalade?" Tuna asked over the radio.

"Looked like a driver and passenger in the front seat," Greene replied. Everyone was wearing in-ear communicators, including Spectre and Kruger inside.

Tuna checked his Glock 19 tucked in his in-the-waistband holster and stepped out of the Suburban. He pulled his t-shirt out, making sure to conceal his weapon as Axe joined him. The two turned left and approached the running Escalade from the front.

As the two men noticed Tuna and Axe approaching, they killed the engine and stepped out. The passenger was a middle-aged man wearing a sport coat with a high and tight haircut. He walked with a distinct limp as he eyeballed Tuna. The driver was a younger, more athletic looking man wearing a tight black t-shirt and a gold chain.

"Can I help you?" the passenger asked smugly as he pulled back his sport coat to reveal his holstered handgun. He put his left hand on his hip and rested his right on the butt of the weapon.

"Hello, friend," Axe said as he hunched his shoulders forward to create a less threatening posture. "We were just wondering if you had heard the good news."

"You two hippies need to move along," the passenger replied.

"But sir, you've obviously done well for yourself," Tuna replied as they continued advancing toward the two men. Tuna approached the passenger as Axe took the much larger driver.

"I'm not going to tell you again," the passenger replied. "Leave before you get yourselves hurt."

"But sir, you haven't even asked about the good news," Axe said as they stopped just a few feet from the two men from the Escalade.

"Maybe you're not hearing me," the passenger said. He and the driver both stepped forward toward Axe and Tuna. Tuna grabbed the passenger's outstretched arm at the wrist and rolled it away from his body as he struck and dislocated the man's elbow. He used the man's momentum to drive his face into the fender of the Escalade before taking him to the ground.

Axe's attacker was much more aggressive. Axe sidestepped the man's punch and struck him with an open palm in the chin. The man dropped as Axe's strike hit the nerve clusters in the chin. It was as if he had pressed the man's reset button.

With both men on the ground, Tuna and Axe each pulled out their Flexi-cuffs from their back pockets and secured the men's hands before dragging them to the curb behind the Escalade.

"Parking lot is secure," Tuna announced over the tactical frequency. He walked over to the passenger who was still groaning from the hits to his head and elbow.

"Now do you want to hear the good news?" he asked as he squatted over the man.

"Who are you?" the man groaned.

"I'm just kidding," Tuna said with a laugh. "There is no good news. You're both probably going to get fired."

CHAPTER FORTY FIVE

Narby and Sons Marine Operators, LLC
Venice, LA
0545 Local Time

"You boys must be pretty important," Ben Narby said as he led them to the forty-six foot blue and white crew boat. The tall, muscular boat captain appeared to be in his late fifties, weathered by years of working out on the water. He spoke with a slight southern drawl as he smiled warmly at his guests. "Mr. Jane has never called me himself. Hell, I wasn't sure he really even existed."

"We appreciate you taking us out on such short notice," Spectre replied graciously.

"No, sir, don't thank me," Narby said, shaking his head. "Mr. Jane has more than tripled our daily rate. Whatever you boys are doing for him, it must be awfully important."

"What exactly did Mr. Jane tell you?" Kruger asked from behind Spectre. JAX had dropped them off promptly at five AM. The team consisting of Axe, Greene, Tuna, Kruger and Spectre had been given a quick safety brief before being led out to the boat by Captain Narby.

Narby smiled knowingly. "To take you boys where you need to go and stay until you're ready to come home," he replied.

"Have you ever been to the Jupiter Rising?" Spectre asked as they walked down the narrow wooden dock.

"I've made a few runs out that way," Narby said without stopping. "But I've never stayed and we always come back empty."

"Is that normal?" Spectre asked.

Narby stopped and looked at Spectre as they reached the crew boat. "I don't ask questions anymore, Mr. Martin. Nothing about *that* rig is normal."

They stopped at the catwalk as two younger men stood on the boat waiting. The boat's twin diesel engines were idling as the deck hands waited to help the team with their bags.

"Gentlemen, these are my two sons, Doug and Morgan," he said as the two shyly waved. "If y'all need anything at all, please let any of us know."

Doug appeared to Spectre to be the older brother, although significantly shorter than both Morgan and his father. His head was shaved and he wore a goatee. Spectre guessed Morgan was the youngest. Although he was as tall as his father six foot four inch father, he had a baby face that seemed incapable of growing facial hair.

Spectre and the team declined their offer to help with their equipment and carried their bags and hardened Pelican cases up the ramp and into the boat. As the group settled into the passenger area behind the wheelhouse, the Narby sons cast off the moorings and Captain Narby took his position at the helm of the *Miss Barb*.

The diesel engines droned as the small crew boat pulled out of the harbor and out into the channel, heading east toward the Gulf. It was still dark out, but the orange glow of the approaching sunrise could be seen off in the distance. Narby had briefed the team that their estimated time en route would be approximately four hours.

Kruger pulled out a pair of Toughbook laptops and satellite antennas from one of the black Pelican cases. He ran the antenna to the back cargo deck of the boat and connected it to a router between the two laptops. The system had a relay for their in-ear communication pieces to allow them to communicate with Meeks back at the base via satellite as well as each other on a line of sight basis.

"Comm check," Kruger said as he tested the earpiece and the laptop powered on.

"Got you five by five," Meeks replied. His communication sounded a bit choppy at first, but it seemed to clear up as the reception bar indicator on the computer finally stabilized. "The documents Mr. Jane just gave me should be in your inbox."

"Copy that," Kruger responded. Tom Jane had insisted that he be allowed to watch the mission from the control room with Meeks. He had offered to be there to answer any questions on the layout and setup of the rig as well as to answer any questions that might arise during their mission.

"Got'em," Kruger said a few minutes later as the document files populated his inbox. Meeks had sent him schematics, crew manifests, and the paperwork Jane had come up with to get them on the rig. They were to pose as contractors there to do preventative service on the rig's Annular Blowout Preventer (BOP) that was found to be faulty on another rig maintained by the same group. Jane had also given them documentation and schematics of the Annular BOP at the top of the BOP stack and its location on the oil rig. It wasn't enough to become experts in four hours, but it would at least get their foot in the door.

"I'm also sending over SongBird Four satellite imagery," Meeks said. Kruger pulled up the satellite link on his display. The SongBird Four was a brand new spy satellite capable of up to twelve inch resolution. Although it wasn't as useful as having the U-28 on station with a sensor operator, they didn't want to chance a possible Surface to Air Missile launch if Foxworthy's claims were correct. The satellite imagery would give them the best chance of finding and targeting threats on the southern platform of the two-platform rig.

"We're going to finish planning the mission now," Kruger said. "I'll get back with you in two hours for the actual brief."

"Copy that," Meeks replied.

Kruger pulled out his communicator and plugged it into the charger. After studying the schematics, he walked up to the wheelhouse where Tuna and Axe were admiring the boat's brand new radar and GPS.

"You guys ready to do this?" Kruger asked.

Tuna glanced at Kruger and then looked over at Spectre. He was sitting in the passenger area bent over and staring at the floor with his head in his hands. He appeared to be in deep thought. "You know it, but is he?"

Kruger turned to look at Spectre. "He'll be fine," Kruger said. "After all, this is his plan."

"What about you?" Axe asked.

"A good plan, violently executed now, is better than a perfect plan next week," Kruger replied, doing his best Patton impression.

"Yeah, but if you're going to quote Patton, he also said that nobody ever won a war by dying for his country," Axe said. "I don't really feel like throwing any more shot glasses."

Kruger grinned through his thick red beard. "Don't be such a pussy. Who said anything about dying?" he asked. "I'm going to make that other son of a bitch die for his country."

* * *

"Well, they're on their way," Meeks said as he rolled his chair back from the computers. "We should be hearing back from them in an hour or so."

Foxworthy and Mary were sitting in chairs next to Meeks. They were both wearing jeans and t-shirts, having slept very little before meeting Spectre and company at the base to send them off. Tom Jane stood leaning against the center mission planning table with a permanent frown affixed to his tan and weathered face.

"What's wrong, Daddy?" Mary asked, standing to comfort him.

Jane didn't move as she touched his arm. His gaze was fixed into a thousand yard stare. "It wasn't supposed to be like this," he said. "This was never the plan."

"What happened?" Mary asked. "How could you get in bed with the Chinese?"

The disappointment in Mary's voice caused Jane to withdraw from her touch. He started pacing around the mission-planning table, rubbing his temples.

"Tell me, Daddy," Mary pressed as she intercepted him in front of the table. Everyone in the room watched as she pushed him harder for answers.

"You were off in the Navy," Jane responded softly. "You have no idea what I went through to save this company."

"Just tell me!" Mary insisted.

Jane let out a pained sigh. "When the Deepwater Horizon had its oil spill in 2010, the government shut down thirty three oil rigs. We had ten of them. *Ten*," Jane said, pausing as he held up ten fingers.

"They were down for over six months, and even when it came back, the inspectors were so far up our asses that we could only bring one back up per month. We were way in the red. Kerry was nominated by the President to become the next Secretary of Defense and he wanted to cash out," Jane said, shaking his head.

"Wait, so Kerry Johnson was your business partner?" Meeks asked excitedly.

Jane nodded. "He owned forty percent and helped get us off the ground, but he wanted to get into politics and had been to Vietnam. The President wanted a fresh face not involved with Washington politics to come in and be the face of a new anti-war military. So he cashed out and went to Washington. Hua Xia Holdings came in and bought him out and then some," Jane said.

"They started pumping cash into Cajun and gave us contracts off the Cuban coast," Jane continued. "We just supplied the expertise and equipment here and there and let them do the rest."

"So you had no idea what they were really doing?" Mary asked.

"Sweetie, I'm not a perfect man," he replied. "I did what I had to do to keep this company afloat. And yes, I sent Robertson out to get his hands dirty a few times, but I had no idea they were anything but Chinese capitalists. They were secretive on so many things. I thought it was just better if I didn't know."

There was a long silence as Jane held his head low in shame. "But you know I love this country," he added. "That's why I want those boys out there to succeed."

"I know, Daddy," Mary replied softly.

Jane put his beefy hands on her shoulders and looked her in the eyes. "I am so very sorry, sweetheart. I really am."

"I know," she said as he pulled her in to hug her.

CHAPTER FORTY SIX

Jupiter Rising
Gulf of Mexico
0956 Local Time

Spectre took a deep breath and exhaled slowly as he stepped onto the orange platform and grabbed onto the netting of the personal basket transfer system that had been lowered onto the cargo deck of the *Miss Barb*. Kruger stepped onto it across from him as Doug Narby gave the crane operator a thumbs up.

Spectre and Kruger were wearing orange life jackets over the red crew jumpsuits Jane had given them before they left. Spectre held onto his hard hat with one hand and wrapped his arm through the rope webbing with the other as the basket gently lifted off the cargo deck toward the massive twin-platform oil rig.

Spectre looked south toward the second platform. A single catwalk connected the two platforms. They both looked somewhat similar, but the southern platform had a helipad and an array of antennas and round structures that the northern platform lacked. From their briefing, Spectre knew that those were likely the tracking and guiding radars that Foxworthy had encountered on the scramble, and the reason they were unable to get air support from the U-28.

Although it was Spectre's plan, the briefing had been led by Kruger. They had gone over the schematics and assignments in depth nearly an hour prior to making contact with the Jupiter Rising. The risk level of the mission was high. Each team member knew that it was all or nothing and that even the slightest deviation from the plan could lead to failure, capture, and eventually death. But at the end of the brief, it was a risk each person acknowledged and was more than willing to take.

Spectre thought of the fighter pilot's prayer as the basket gently lowered to the deck of the northern platform where a dozen or so men in hard hats and working uniforms stood waiting for them. *God, I don't care if I die, just please don't let me fuck up.* It was a prayer he had said to himself before every combat mission in Iraq. A fighter pilot's greatest fear wasn't dying, but failing and letting his team down.

As they neared the deck, the ground crew grabbed onto two guide ropes and helped stabilize the basket. The crane operator slowly lowered it until the circular platform softly touched down on the deck and Spectre and Kruger stepped off.

"Right this way, gentleman," a man wearing an orange hard hat said. Most of the crew appeared to be Chinese, but this man looked like one of the few Americans scattered about. He was burly with a barrel chest and full beard. He was wearing Oakley sunglasses and spoke with a thick Southern accent.

They followed the man down a set of stairs to the second deck of the platform. There was a mix of Chinese and American

ARCHANGEL FALLEN

roughnecks busily working as they ignored Kruger and Spectre. The man led them into a small classroom and stopped at the door.

"Wait here," he said abruptly.

Spectre and Kruger walked in as the door slammed behind them. They took off their red jumpsuits and checked their concealed Glock 19s and spare magazines.

"Comm check," Kruger said over his in-ear radio.

"Loud and clear," Meeks said. There was a considerable amount of static, but Meeks was readable. Spectre nodded at Kruger to indicate he could hear Meeks as well.

"Good comms. We're in," Kruger said.

"Tracking," Meeks replied, indicating their personal locators were also active.

Spectre took an inventory of the room. They were in a small classroom with two side by side tables with four chairs. It appeared to be a room used for briefing inbound crews. Posters with warnings about wearing protective equipment and hazards on the vessel lined the wall in both English and Chinese. There was a projector on the ceiling and a pull down screen over a whiteboard that was smeared with poorly erased markers.

"You ready to put an end to this?" Kruger asked as he turned to Spectre.

"Fuck'em if they can't take a joke," Spectre said as the two exchanged a fist bump.

They heard the approaching footsteps and took seats at the nearest table. Moments later, the door flung open. An older Chinese man appeared with two younger operatives dressed in fatigues on either side. They both had AK-74s slung over their chests. The older man was unarmed and wearing a dark suit. They walked in and closed the door behind them.

The older man walked to the center of the room while his two associates circled back behind Spectre and Kruger. Spectre looked back to see weapons raised and pointed at their heads.

"Keep your hands on the table, please," the man said with a heavy Chinese accent. Spectre and Kruger complied, keeping their hands on the table in plain view. One of the operatives lifted Spectre's shirt and removed the Glock from his holster as the other operative covered. He dropped the magazine and cleared the gun before placing it on the table next to them, and then he moved on to Kruger and repeated the process. Once both Kruger and Spectre were disarmed, the operative secured the weapons at the rear of the room and took up his previous position with his weapon trained on Spectre.

"Arrogant Americans," the man said. "You thought you could just walk in and I would not notice?"

"You're Zhang, right?" Kruger asked.

"Yes, my name is Jun Zhang," Zhang responded. "*You* are Fred Mack."

Zhang looked right at Spectre and stepped toward him. "And you are Cal Martin. You have been a thorn in my side for quite some time now. But it is no bother. That will be corrected today."

"That's right. You wanted me," Spectre said coolly. "Here I am. Now what?"

Zhang laughed. "You think you have a plan?" Zhang asked mockingly. "That I'm not going to torture you and kill you?"

Spectre shrugged and looked at Kruger, who shrugged back in return.

"Your plan has failed," Zhang said. "My men have already boarded your boat. Your backup will not be coming. You sit here smugly because you think someone will rescue you, but I assure you that is not the case. You have failed."

Zhang noticed Kruger momentarily check his watch. He turned his attention to Kruger and stepped toward him. "It is a shame that you bring all of these extra people into this, Mr. Martin," Zhang said.

"Think of all of the innocent people that had to die because you constantly interfere where you shouldn't. Why do you insist on killing all of your friends?" Zhang asked as he pointed to Kruger.

"You killed them," Spectre said with clenched jaw.

"Nonsense, Mr. Martin. I had no business with your friends until you stuck your arrogant nose into my operation. They would all be alive today were it not for your hubris," Zhang said. "Including this man right here."

"Don't worry about me, bub," Kruger said.

"Oh, I liked you, Mr. Mack," Zhang said. "You *and* Project Archangel. I even liked Mr. Steele."

Kruger's eyes widened at the mention of Project Archangel. *There was no way a Chinese Intelligence operative should know anything about a program so highly classified.* His blood boiled.

"Don't be naïve," Zhang said, latching on to Kruger's surprise. "I am very good at my job. It is a pity that you weren't better at yours. Or else you could've seen how toxic Cal Martin truly is."

"It's still early," Kruger growled.

Zhang laughed. "You have followed this man to your death, but not just your death. The death of those men on the boat and the death of your organization, Mr. Mack."

"Say again?" Kruger said.

"Project Archangel is going to be disbanded, haven't you heard?" Zhang asked with a smile.

"Fuck you," Kruger said as his face reddened. He looked over at Spectre who seemed to be staring off in the distance, apparently deep in thought.

"No, it's true," Zhang said confidently. "The death of Mr. Steele was unfortunate indeed. Since you defected with the criminal Cal Martin, there was no one left to take over. The group will be disbanded and Project Archangel will never have existed."

As Kruger stared angrily at Zhang, Spectre started laughing hysterically.

Confused by Spectre's sudden outburst, Zhang walked over to Spectre and stood just a foot from him. "What is so funny, Mr. Martin?"

"You built a fake oil rig just to steal radar emissions from fighters?" Spectre asked, still chuckling at what Meeks had just told him over their tactical radio.

Zhang gave Spectre a confused look.

"You weren't trying to shoot airplanes down," Spectre said as he stopped laughing. "You have emitters and sniffers on that south rig. You're trying to gather intelligence to see what tactics our fighters use and what frequencies our radars are using. *Now* it all makes sense!"

"How could you possibly know that?" Zhang asked, still dumbfounded by Spectre's outburst.

Spectre looked at his watch and slowly looked back up before nodding at Kruger. "Because in ten seconds, it will cease to exist. And then I'm going to kill you."

CHAPTER FORTY SEVEN

Jupiter Rising
Gulf of Mexico
0930 Local Time

"You know I hate water," Greene complained as Axe finished checking his equipment for him one last time. He was wearing a LAR V Draeger Rebreather designed to eliminate bubbles common to scuba gear. It was a system particularly useful for clandestine operations. "That's why I joined the Marines, so I wouldn't have to swim."

"Don't be such a pussy," Axe replied as he turned to check Tuna's gear. "It's not like this is your first time."

"It's not his first time crying about it either," Tuna added. The three men were all wearing rebreathers, black tactical dry suits, body armor, and MP-7s. The silenced MP-7s were covered with resealing dry bags capable of being shot through in water and still keep the weapons dry.

"Suck it!" Greene shot back as he pulled down his goggles.

The *Miss Barb* was floating a half mile from the Jupiter Rising and was bobbing in the calm Gulf of Mexico as the team prepared its ingress. Kruger walked up to Tuna as the three man team finished making its last preparations for the mission.

"The Raven is airborne and on its way. Meeks has a good handshake with it," Kruger said. He had unpacked and launched the four and a half foot wide RQ-11 Raven B unmanned aerial vehicle. Meeks and JAX would be controlling it via satellite from New Orleans as it orbited the Jupiter Rising at five hundred feet – just far enough that its small size and quiet electric motor would make it impossible for anyone to see or hear while offering real time infrared imagery of the oil platforms.

"You guys ready?" Kruger asked as the three divers stood near the back of the cargo deck of the *Miss Barb*.

"I live for this shit," Tuna said as he pulled down his mask and bit down on his rebreather. The other two gave a thumbs up before they all jumped into the calm waters. With the help of the oldest Narby brother, Spectre and Kruger pushed the Diver Propulsion Device in after them. The four-man DPD-XT was a dual motor diver propulsion device capable of towing up to four divers underwater. It would allow them to traverse the half mile to the south platform covertly with speed while keeping the team from getting tired.

As the divers cleared the *Miss Barb*, Tuna climbed into the DPD-XT and took up the pilot position while Greene and Axe took up prone positions on the fully extended eight foot propulsion device. Once Tuna had the system's Recon Navigation system ready, he looked back to get thumbs up from both Greene and Axe as they held on to the handholds.

They dove down to fifty feet below the water as the *Miss Barb* throttled up again toward the smaller southern platform of the Jupiter Rising. The DPD-XT effortlessly propelled them through the water toward their target.

"The *Miss Barb* has reached the main platform," Meeks said over their tactical radio.

Tuna checked the navigation and confirmed that they were still on course. The timing would be tight, but assuming they maintained the element of surprise, they were still on track.

As they reached the buoyant support structures of the semisubmersible, Axe and Greene dismounted and started swimming out in opposite directions. Tuna dismounted and ditched the DPD as he headed toward the nearest support pillar and reached back into his waterproof bag. He pulled out a large C4 charge and attached it to the pillar.

With the C4 attached at their respective support structures, the three rejoined and swam toward the "Plus Ten" platform. Named for its position ten feet above sea level, the Plus Ten was used as an alternative for crew boat loading and unloading.

"Tango on the south side of the plus ten," JAX announced on the tactical frequency. "Armed singleton. Another on the second level, unknown if armed."

Tuna pointed toward the south side of the plus ten and directed Axe and Greene to spread out. He swam to the southernmost part of the platform, finding the man staring out into the horizon. With his MP-7 slung over his back, he waited for the man to drop.

Greene and Axe swam to the opposite end of the platform. As Axe climbed up, Greene readied his MP-7. The man turned as he heard Axe emerge from the calm waters. Greene shot two rounds into the man's chest, causing him to fall forward as Tuna caught him and stabbed him in the chest with his boot knife.

"First level clear," JAX said, watching it unfold on the video feed. "Still one remaining on the second level."

The three men climbed onto the plus ten and discarded their rebreathers, goggles, and flippers as they removed the dry bags from their MP-7s. Axe and Greene fell into a single line behind Tuna as the three men ascended the stairs.

"Contact right," Tuna said. With a single shot to the head, he dropped the man standing on the second level as they turned left and sped up the next level of stairs. After verifying the man was dead, they continued past him. "We're aboard."

"Roger, be advised two tangos have boarded the *Miss Barb*," JAX said.

"*Shit!*" Tuna hissed. "Where are they?"

"Still holding next to the northern platform," JAX replied.

"We'll deal with them when we get across," Tuna said.

"Copy that," JAX replied. "Heads up, Nightmare One and Two are in place. I've got three hostiles on the catwalk heading to their location. Suspected Kingpin."

"Roger," Tuna replied. Spectre and Kruger were using the callsigns Nightmare Zero One and Nightmare Zero Two on a different discrete frequency from Tuna and his team. Sitting right next to Meeks, JAX was relaying mission updates as they happened for timing purposes. Kingpin was the code word for Zhang. *Need to speed up,* Tuna thought.

They moved quickly and efficiently to the main level of the southern platform. Unlike the multi-deck oil rig to the north, the southern platform appeared to only have one main deck. Above it was the helipad and the antenna arrays that they suspected to be the SAM site in their pre-mission briefing. Tuna and his team had planned to quickly clear the southern platform before crossing over to the north.

The three men fanned out into a tactical V formation with their weapons high and ready as they entered the main deck.

"Contact right," Axe said as his MP-7 spat two rounds, dropping the unaware mercenary.

They moved forward toward the main building as JAX called out targets approaching their position.

"Contact left," said Greene. He and Tuna took down two more hostiles walking casually toward their position. As they reached the entryway to the main facility, JAX gave them an "all clear" as they prepared to breach.

Greene placed the explosive charge against the door as Tuna and Axe stacked up on the right side of the door. Once it was set, Greene gave a silent countdown with his fingers before initiating the detonator and blowing the door.

Tuna was the first through the door, j-hooking left as Axe and Greene entered behind him entering to the right. The room appeared to be a control room of some sort with radar screens, computer terminals, and large displays spread out in the room. Surprised by the blast, the lone-armed guard was unable to ready his rifle before Greene sent two rounds into his chest.

One of the technicians at the control station attempted to pull a handgun but was dropped immediately by Axe. The other technician dove for the man's fallen weapon. Axe readjusted his aim and fired two more rounds at the diving technician.

"Control room is clear," Tuna announced. "What's the status of Nightmare One?"

"Standby," JAX said.

As they waited for JAX to confer with Meeks, the team started pulling hard drives and searched for other Intel in the room. They stuffed what they could in their backpacks and started toward the exit.

"Offline at the moment," JAX said finally. "They are on the second deck of the northern platform with Kingpin and two tangos."

"Copy that," Tuna replied. "Relay to Nightmare that we're headed that direction. It doesn't appear that this was a SAM site. They have a whole bunch of F-15 and F/A-18 data laying around and some gibberish about frequencies. We're going to finish up here and be inbound to their location."

"Will relay," JAX replied. "You're green all the way to the catwalk."

They rallied back up at the door and proceeded back out onto the platform as they looked for any pop-up threats. They cleared high and low, as they moved quickly toward the catwalk. As they reached the storage container for the jet fuel used by the helicopter, they stopped. Axe and Tuna maintained cover as Greene placed more C4 charges next to it.

Once he was set, they headed toward the fifty-foot catwalk connected the southern platform to the main oil rig. Tuna watched for threats as they ran across the catwalk single file. He strained to see the *Miss Barb*, but with its position on the northern end of the Jupiter Rising, he could only make out the blue back end.

"Nightmare is on the second level, I'll talk you on," JAX said. "Recommend we execute Zulu."

Tuna slowed for a minute, nearly causing Axe to run into him. Zulu was their backup plan. Spectre and Kruger were supposed to meet them at the catwalk to egress via the crew boat that was supposed to be holding away from the Jupiter Rising. But with the *Miss Barb* under duress and Spectre and Kruger presumably in trouble, they were running out of options.

"Confirm Zulu?" Tuna asked as Axe pushed him forward.

"Affirm," JAX said. "Roll to Zulu."

They cleared the catwalk and stopped, taking a knee as they watched for threats.

"Copy that," Tuna replied reluctantly. "Relay to Nightmare – twenty seconds."

CHAPTER FORTY EIGHT

"You are a fool," Zhang said as he watched Spectre countdown while looking at his watch. "I will enjoy-"

"Three... two... one," Spectre interrupted. There was a pause as they waited for the explosion. When none came, Zhang and his men laughed.

As Zhang began to speak, there was a loud explosion outside. The walls rattled and the floor shook as multiple explosions rocked the small briefing room. As the walls continued to shake, a loud siren sounded with a prerecorded voice instructing crew members to proceed to muster stations and abandon the oil rig. The alarm began in English and then repeated in Chinese.

Taking advantage of the confusion, Kruger and Spectre leapt into action. Kruger turned and grabbed the rifle of the man pointing the AK-74 at his head. He pushed the muzzle down and then grabbed the butt of the rifle, ripping it away before striking the man in the nose with it.

Spectre flipped the table over and lunged toward Zhang. In one fluid movement, he drew his Benchmade Infidel auto-opening knife from his cargo pants, flicked open the blade using his thumb on the thumb slide button, and thrust it toward Zhang's throat. The double-edged steel blade sliced cleanly through Zhang's jugular notch as Spectre quickly stabbed him and withdrew the blade. He spun Zhang around and rotated the knife in his hand as he stepped behind Zhang and grabbed him in a chokehold with his left hand.

The remaining guard fired off a shot toward Spectre, but struck Zhang in the shoulder. Spectre drove the blade into Zhang's chest as he held the man up as a shield. Kruger flipped his newly acquired AK-74 around and fired a round into the guard's chest before shooting the guard he had just disarmed as well.

Spectre pushed the knife in harder as Zhang's body fell limp. He withdrew the bloody blade and shoved it into Zhang's chest a second time as he held up Zhang's body. All of the anger and loss he had felt over the last year surfaced as he continued stabbing Zhang's body. He stabbed for Marcus and Joe. For Baxter and Ironman. For ruining the life he was starting with Chloe. For making him a criminal. For destroying his life.

"Spectre!" Kruger yelled over the blaring "Abandon Platform" alarm.

Spectre continued stabbing with blind rage as Zhang's body fell to the ground.

"Dude, get it together!" Kruger yelled again as he walked up to Spectre standing over Zhang's bloodied corpse and tried to pull Spectre off with his free hand.

"Spectre!" Kruger said again.

Spectre was breathing heavily as Kruger finally pulled him away from Zhang's mangled and bloodied body. The four-inch blade dripped with blood. Spectre stood staring at Zhang, ignoring Kruger's attempts to snap him out of his blind rage.

"Grab a weapon and let's go," Kruger said. He went back to the second guard's body and grabbed his AK-74. Kruger walked back to Spectre and handed him the rifle. "Are you going to make it?"

Spectre finally shook off the haze and accepted the AK-74 Kruger was holding for him. His heart was racing and he was out of breath. The blind rage that he felt for the man beneath him had overtaken him. He had heard nothing and seen only red as he exacted bloody vengeance on the man that had destroyed his life and killed his only friends.

"Spectre, goddammit," Kruger said, grabbing Spectre by the collar. "Fuck that guy, but we need to move, bub."

"I'm good," Spectre said. He pulled the AK-74 sling over his shoulder and checked the weapon, holding it up and ready. "On you."

"Coolio, switch us up to Punisher's freq," Kruger said over his in-ear radio.

"You're up on a common frequency now," Meeks responded.

Kruger motioned for Spectre to follow as he raised his weapon and exited the small room. He turned left and headed toward the outer walkway.

"Punisher, this is Nightmare Zero One, what's your location?" Kruger asked.

"We're currently engaged, moving to your position," Tuna responded. Spectre could hear gunshots in the background.

"Copy that, we're mobile, rally on the second deck breezeway and we'll move to extract," Kruger directed.

"Punisher Two One copies," Tuna responded.

Spectre followed Kruger down the narrow passageway lined with offices. They cleared left and right as they held their weapons up and ready. The offices were empty as most of the workers had begun trying to evacuate the platform.

"Nightmare, heads up, tangos at the breezeway near your location," JAX advised over the common frequency. "Will be approaching from your right."

"Copy," Kruger replied.

The two continued toward the exit. As they reached the doorway, Kruger gestured to Spectre to open the door. Spectre opened the door and Kruger exited to the right. He fired two rounds hitting the lead man. Spectre followed and cleared left before following up with another shot into the lead man and two more shots into the trail man. Both men dropped their handguns and fell nearly instantly.

Spectre and Kruger continued toward the stairs. Spectre could see the dozens of men and women in red, blue, and orange jump suits heading toward the escape capsules on the west side of the platform.

"Friendlies coming down," JAX announced. Kruger and Spectre held their position as the three man team led by Tuna descended the stairs toward them.

"On you," Kruger said to Tuna. Spectre and Kruger filed in between Tuna and Axe, as Greene picked up rear cover. They continued down the stairs, searching for threats as they descended down toward the north platform's "plus ten."

"What's the status of our ride?" Kruger asked over the radio.

"In position," JAX replied.

Tuna picked off an armed guard with his MP-7 as they continued down the metal stairwell. Spectre could see the *Miss Barb* backed up against the "Plus Ten" platform as they waited for the approaching team.

The team reached the platform without engaging any more hostiles. Tuna stopped and turned, setting up a defensive position as Kruger and Spectre jumped from the platform into the waiting boat.

Spectre stumbled as he made the five-foot drop onto the cargo deck and nearly tripped over two bodies. The older Narby son stood holding a shotgun at the aft end a few feet from the bodies.

"Unexpected guests?" Spectre asked, pointing at the bodies as the rest of the team made it aboard.

"Nothing a little buckshot couldn't handle," Narby replied, tapping the Mossberg 500 Special Purpose Mariner shotgun in his hands.

The older son gave Captain Narby a thumbs up as the rest of the team was secured on the cargo deck. Captain Narby firewalled the twin diesel engines, causing the boat to speed away from the platform as escape pods continued to drop from the rig.

"Did you set the secondary charges?" Kruger asked Tuna.

"That's affirm, sir," Tuna said, holding up the detonator. After blowing the southern platform, they had set charges on the oil and diesel storage tanks they had run into en route to a rendezvous with Spectre and Kruger.

"Light'em up," Kruger replied. "And don't call me sir. I work for a living."

CHAPTER FORTY NINE

Tampa General Hospital
Tampa, FL
0932 Local Time

Kruger pulled the white Chevy Tahoe into the space next to Spectre's recently purchased Camaro SS and put the SUV in park. The car was still exactly as Spectre had left it three days earlier.

"You're good people, Spectre," Kruger said as he looked over at Spectre. "I know you said you just want to go fly bug smashers somewhere, but if you ever change your mind, you're more than welcome to fly with us again."

"Thanks, man," Spectre replied. "But I think I've had enough excitement for one lifetime."

"Pussy," Kruger replied with a laugh.

"Probably so," Spectre laughed. "So what's next for you? Are you going to take over for Ironman?"

Kruger shrugged and pushed his sunglasses to the top of his head. "I really don't know. If they let me, I'll do it. But Captain Paintball will be here this afternoon and there's no telling what he'll try to do. Hell, he might try to run it himself."

Spectre rolled his eyes at the thought of a bureaucrat running a secret group of highly trained pilots and operators. "And you want me to go back to *that*?" Spectre asked.

"Fair point," Kruger replied. "Well, if you need anything, you've got my number."

"Thanks, buddy," Spectre replied. "Stay safe out there."

"Say hi to Roland and Wilson for me," Kruger said before Spectre stepped out of the Tahoe. The former Green Beret and Air Force PJ had been acting as Decker's protective detail while she was in the hospital.

"Wilco," Spectre replied.

Spectre grabbed his bag and exited the Tahoe. He opened the hatchback of the Camaro and threw his bag in before closing it and locking the door. Kruger pulled his sunglasses back down and drove toward the exit of the multi-level parking garage.

Spectre took a deep breath and exhaled slowly as he headed toward the stairs of the parking garage. He didn't know what to expect inside. Roland had reported that Decker had been moved to a room as she recovered from her near drowning. She had a constant stream of visitors from the FBI, but so far none had actually questioned their presence as they took turns keeping watch.

He didn't know exactly what his status was with law enforcement. Spectre could only assume that he was still a wanted man – he had killed two FBI agents before being grabbed by Project Archangel. Spectre knew how guilty that made him look.

But Spectre didn't care. He had faced his demons and dispatched them appropriately. Zhang was dead. He didn't want to run anymore. Part of settling down and rejoining the quiet life would involve facing the consequences for his actions. *Spectre was finally ok with that.*

Spectre made his way through the parking garage and into the hospital. He found the reception desk and asked for the information on Michelle Decker's room. A young girl wearing a pink jacket directed him to a room on the third floor.

Spectre took the elevator and made a left toward Decker's room. He stopped as he saw three men in suits leaving Decker's room. *This is it*, he thought. His heart raced. Despite his relative peace with the idea of facing the consequences, the sight of the three agents still sent adrenaline pumping through his veins. *Fight or flight.*

As the three agents approached, he saw the look of recognition in the older agent's face. He said something that caused the two agents to reach for their holstered weapons. Spectre immediately dropped to his knees and put his hands behind his head.

Spectre recognized the older agent as the three drew closer. It was Special Agent in Charge Fields from Miami – the man that had put him in protective custody. He saw Fields say something to the two agents. They kept their hands on their weapons, but did not draw.

"Cal Martin!" Fields yelled as he drew closer. The roar of his thunderous voice caused all of the nurses and orderlies at the nearby nurses' station to stop and stare at the unfolding scene.

"I will not resist," Spectre announced calmly. "I'm not running anymore."

Fields stopped short of Spectre as the other two agents moved to either side. Spectre waited for them to grab him and drive him face down into the floor to handcuff him.

"Get up," Fields said. "You're not under arrest."

Spectre looked up at Fields with a confused look. The two agents to either side appeared to be studying Spectre's every movement, but neither seemed to be taking an aggressive posture.

"Stand up," Fields repeated. "Let's talk."

Spectre slowly put his hands down and stood. He kept his hands out just to show that he was non-threatening.

"In here," Fields said, pointing to an empty room nearby. Spectre reluctantly followed Fields into the room as the two agents followed close behind. Spectre's mind was racing. *Was Fields part of this?* He instinctively started assessing his self-defense options, building a plan to fight his way out if necessary.

They walked into the empty two-bed room and the trail agent closed the door behind them. Spectre crossed his arms as he watched their every move.

"You killed two agents," Fields said in a low voice.

Spectre looked back at the two agents behind him. He calculated that he could begin his attack on Fields with a front push kick before following up with a back kick on the agent to his left and a back fist to the attacker to his right.

"And they were both working for Chinese intelligence," Fields continued. "We had double agents in our own organization and no one had any idea. Do you know what kind of black eye this gives the agency after what happened in Miami?"

"Excuse me?" Spectre asked, still confused by the abruptness of the senior agent's query.

"You were under our protection and were taken by a Cuban intelligence agent," Fields replied. "And instead of looking for you, we made you a criminal. All the while we had bad agents under our noses. This looks really bad for the agency."

"I'm still not following you," Spectre said.

"Maybe you should go talk to Simms instead," Fields offered. "Maybe that will clear it up for you."

"Ok," Spectre replied cautiously. "But who are these two?"

"Sorry," Fields replied. "Cal Martin, this is Special Agent Venable from Baton Rouge and Special Agent Daniels from Tampa. They have been working your case here and in Louisiana."

Spectre followed Fields out of the room and down the hallway with the other two agents. They continued to the opposite wing of the floor to a room with SIMMS written on the dry erase board outside. After lightly knocking on the door, Fields entered as a nurses' aid finished taking Simms's blood pressure.

"I have a visitor for you, Agent Simms," Fields announced as they walked in.

Simms was sitting up in the bed as Spectre entered behind Fields. His face was still swollen and bruised. His arm was in a cast. He looked badly beaten, but smiled anyway, as Spectre walked in.

"Cal Martin," Simms said. "You finally made it."

"Hello, Carl," Spectre replied.

"I was just trying to explain the situation to Mr. Martin," Fields interjected. "But I figured it would be best coming from you."

"You saved my life," Simms said. "And I owe you an apology."

Spectre smiled humbly. "I did what needed to be done."

"No, I owe you an apology," Simms pressed. "I had you pegged as the bad guy from the beginning. I never even saw the ATM footage from the Motel before I was convinced that you were a criminal. I was in that shipping container because I was looking to put you away for a long time. Did you know that?"

"Yes," Spectre said.

"And yet you still helped me!" Simms replied. "We've been talking about you a lot lately, but after putting everything together with what Agent Decker found and what I went through, we realized that I really screwed up here. Have you seen her? She's been asking about you."

"Not yet," Spectre replied.

"You should go talk to her," Simms said. "She's had relatives hanging out with her for the last couple of days."

"Relatives, huh?" Spectre laughed. "So back to this case. Are you saying there are no charges?"

"Well, that's what I wanted to talk to you about," Fields said. "Yes, there are pending charges with the Florida Highway Patrol for disarming the trooper and evading, but…"

"But what?" Spectre pushed.

"But I'm willing to make those go away," Fields said.

"In exchange for what?" Spectre asked skeptically.

"A nondisclosure agreement and hold harmless," Fields replied.

Spectre laughed. "Are you serious? You're seriously worried about me suing you? And you're holding charges over my head to make me do it?"

"I'm not holding anything over your head, Mr. Martin," Fields replied. "But I think we can help each other out here."

Spectre thought about it for a moment as Fields watched him intently.

"You know what? Fine," Spectre said. "I just want to move on with my life."

Fields smiled. "That's the best way to do it," he said as he put his hand on Spectre's shoulder.

"Can I go see Michelle now?" Spectre asked, shrugging Fields's hand off.

"Absolutely," Fields said. "She's right down the hall in room 354."

"Cal," Simms said as Spectre turned to walk out.

"Yeah?" Spectre asked.

"Seriously, thank you," Simms said. "You really have no idea how much I owe you for what you've done."

"Don't sweat it," Spectre said. "When will you get back to work?"

"I'm not," Simms replied. "I'm done with wearing a badge."

"Really?" Spectre asked.

"Yeah. I'm going back to Ohio to open up my own accounting firm. I think the quiet life is much better for me," Simms replied.

"You and me both, buddy," Spectre said as he walked out. "Take care."

Spectre left the four agents in the room and headed toward Decker's room. The nurses all stared at him as he walked by, having just watched the spectacle of him on his knees with his hands behind his head in the middle of the hallway. He walked up to the room marked 354 and knocked on the door.

A man appeared at the door. He opened the door partially and then opened it wider when he recognized Spectre.

"Spectre!" Roland said. "You're back!"

"Yeah, how's Michelle?" Spectre asked, trying to peek inside.

Roland opened the door and gestured for Spectre to enter. "I'm sure she'd be happy to see you, come on in," he said as he stepped aside.

Spectre slowly walked in as Decker peered around the corner with anticipation. His heart flipped as he saw her sparkling blue eyes and beautiful smile looking back at him.

"We have to stop meeting like this," Decker quipped as he cautiously walked in.

"I'll be outside if you need me," Roland said as he walked out and closed the door behind him.

"How are you feeling?" Spectre asked as he walked up to the side of Decker's bed. Her face was bruised and she had a nasal cannula for breathing oxygen with IVs protruding from her arms. Spectre barely noticed any of it. He was still taken by how beautiful she was.

"I'll live," Decker said shyly. "But what about you? I thought you were dead! I was so worried about you!"

"It's been a rough week," Spectre said, shaking his head.

Decker sat up and patted the side of the bed as she moved her blanket to the side. "Sit," she said. "Tell me about it."

Spectre sat on the edge of the bed, careful not to disturb any of the nearby equipment.

"I don't know," Spectre replied with a shrug. "Stuff happened, I guess."

"Stuff happened?" Decker said mockingly. "You were kidnapped and almost killed. And God only knows what you've been up to since then. That's more than just stuff."

"You've been through a lot yourself," Spectre said, nodding at Decker's bruises. "I hope they give you a raise for doing all of this."

Decker rolled her eyes. "A raise? Ha! I'll be lucky to keep my job when I get out of here," Decker said.

"What are you talking about?" Spectre asked. "You found a pretty significant espionage operation here!"

"I wasn't even supposed to be here," Decker replied. "Fields took me off the case last week. I'm on a forced vacation!"

Spectre laughed. "Hell of a vacation," he joked.

"I'll say," Decker replied. "The food here sucks."

"Well, thanks for not giving up on me," Spectre said. "You really saved my life."

"I saved your life?" Decker asked skeptically. "I ended up getting kidnapped!"

"You did," Spectre repeated softly.

"How?" Decker asked.

"You gave me a reason to fight again," Spectre said as he looked into her eyes. "You gave me purpose."

Decker put her hand on Spectre's. "That's sweet, Cal," she said.

Spectre leaned in, closing his eyes as he went in for a kiss. As he tilted his head to the side, expecting her to meet him, he was met instead with a finger pressed against his lips. He withdrew as he realized he had just been rejected.

"No way!" she said.

Spectre stood and stepped back, embarrassed that he had somehow misinterpreted the signs pointing to a romantic interest between the two of them.

"I'm so sorry," Spectre said. "I just—"

"I will not have our first kiss happen with me being in a hospital bed and wearing this gown," she said, grinning as she pulled up on the collar of her white floral hospital gown.

"Huh?"

"You're going to take me to dinner," Decker said with a smile. "On a real date."

"Yes, ma'am," Spectre said as he started laughing with her.

CHAPTER FIFTY

Project Archangel Operations Building
MacDill AFB, FL
1300 Local Time

Kruger didn't bother going out to greet the Deputy Secretary of Defense as the unmarked white Gulfstream IV taxied onto the ramp next to the Project Archangel fleet of King Airs, U-28s, Super Tucanos, and helicopters. He stood looking out the window as the maintenance personnel chocked the wheels and the door opened and the stairway extended.

"Are you going to go out there?" Axe asked, standing next to Kruger.

"Nope," Kruger replied. "Let that little bastard come to me."

Axe laughed and shook his head. "You're just making friends and influencing people left and right aren't you?"

"I don't trust this guy," Kruger said. "Something is just not right."

"Well, he's the boss now," Axe warned. "So my advice is to shut up and color so he doesn't have a reason to stick around and micromanage your operation."

Your operation. The words hung in the air for Kruger. He had always been the de facto second in command for Project Archangel, but the realization that he would be taking over hadn't sunk in yet. He no longer had the luxury of focusing on operations and getting things done. Being at the top involved babysitting and managing personal programs, appeasing political appointees, and playing nicely with others. *Kruger hated it already.*

As the engines of the Gulfstream spooled down, a small man in a black suit emerged from the doorway and descended down the stairs, followed by two much larger men also in suits. The trio approached the door of the Operations Building. Kruger and Axe walked to greet them as Kruger pressed the red lock release button on the side of the door.

"Good afternoon, Mr. Mack," the smaller man said as Kruger held the door open for them.

"Chaz," Kruger replied. Chaz Hunt was a small statured man in his early fifties. He wore thick glasses and sported an extreme comb over to mask his rapidly receding hairline. He was easily a six inches shorter than the six foot tall Kruger, adding to the Napoleon complex Kruger had always thought him to have.

"Deputy Secretary of Defense," Hunt corrected him. "Or Mr. Secretary if you prefer."

"Got it," Kruger said as he exchanged a look with Axe. He already wanted to choke the little man who arrogantly walked into their building.

"Take me to your office so we can talk," Hunt ordered. "And I will have a Diet Coke when you get a chance as well."

Axe nudged Kruger as he saw Kruger's fists ball up and his freckled knuckles turn white. "I'll get it, boss. You want ice, Mr. Secretary?"

"That will be fine, thanks," Hunt replied.

"My office is in the vault," Kruger replied. He paused and pointed at Hunt's two bodyguards. "But they're not cleared."

"You don't need to worry about that, Mr. Mack," Hunt said dismissively.

"Sorry, bub, they're not coming in the vault without clearance," Kruger said, blocking the steel vault door. "No exceptions."

"You don't want to have this battle here, Mr. Mack," Hunt said. "Either you let them in or we can discuss it here in front of everyone. But they come with me."

Kruger looked over at Axe, who was standing behind Hunt and his men shaking his head, trying to get Kruger to calm down.

"We can just turn the blue light on," Axe offered as he returned with a red plastic cup with ice and a Diet Coke and handed it to Hunt. The blue light was a switch that allowed visitors without clearance to enter the vault. It was a series of blue lights spread throughout the vault letting people know that visitors were present and to cease classified discussions until they left.

"Fine," Kruger relented. He swiped his identification badge and entered his access code. The large vault door clicked and Kruger opened it. He reached in and flipped up a switch, illuminating a blue rotating light in the "man trap" between the main vault door and the secondary vault door.

"They will at least sign in," Kruger said as he handed them a clipboard. The men each took turns writing down their name and signing next to it. When they were finished, Kruger motioned for them to follow and led them through the second vault door and into the secure facility. He made a right, passing Ironman's office and headed for his office across the hall.

"He should stay out there," Hall said as Axe attempted to follow them into Kruger's office. Axe made no objection and quickly turned around, closing the door behind him. Hall took a seat across from Kruger's desk as his two bodyguards stood near the rear of the room.

"What can I do for you, *Mr. Secretary*," Kruger said as he sat down in his executive chair.

Hall took a long sip of his Diet Coke and paused, looking at the various military pictures lining the walls. "You've been all over the world, haven't you?"

"I've gone where I've needed to go," Kruger replied.

"Does that include New Orleans?" Hunt asked with a raised eyebrow.

"If that's where you need me to go," Kruger deflected.

"Clever," Hunt replied. "But you shouldn't play me for a fool."

"Excuse me?" Kruger asked.

"I know all about your little side missions in the last few days, Mr. Mack," Hunt said smugly.

"Then you also know that the FBI Agent *your* office gave us as a liaison was working for the Chinese and that we lost three damned good men as a result," Kruger shot back.

Hunt held his hand up. "That does not excuse you taking it upon yourself to execute missions on American soil in complete violation of the Posse Comitatus Act."

"Last I checked, we're not military, so that doesn't apply to us," Kruger replied.

"It doesn't matter," Hunt said. "That's not why I'm here."

"Why are you here?" Kruger asked impatiently.

"To shut this program down," Hunt replied. "All of it. As of midnight tonight, this organization no longer exists and you will receive no further funding."

ARCHANGEL FALLEN

"For what reason?" Kruger asked angrily as he stood from his chair. The two bodyguards took a step forward in unison, ready to intercept Kruger if he tried to attack their boss.

Hunt smiled arrogantly at Kruger's reaction. "You have no director and your services are no longer needed," Hunt answered.

"Bullshit!" Kruger barked. "The Middle East is on fire right now and there are plenty of people in this organization capable of stepping up to lead. That is horseshit!"

"Your director was working for the Chinese. You took government assets on an unauthorized mission on U.S. soil. This entire organization has been compromised. The Secretary of Defense won't have this and neither will I," Hunt replied calmly.

"Where are you getting this information?" Kruger asked as he leaned forward and put both hands on the desk. How the man in front of him knew anything of the past four days bothered Kruger.

"You don't think we have contacts in the intelligence community? Where do you think I found out?" Hunt asked.

Kruger stared at Hunt without saying anything.

"The fact that I know anything is a testament to the lack of viability of this organization!" Hunt shouted as he stood up to Kruger. "Your operational cover has been blown. *You* fucked up!"

Kruger stood upright and stepped back as he tried to process Hunt's claims. Zhang knew about Project Archangel. There had been a breach somewhere. *Had it been Ironman? How did the intelligence community already know?*

"Now, I'm willing to work with everyone in this group to keep them employed. Severance packages and reassignments are approved across the board. It was not an easy decision, but let's face it, this group cannot function if I'm getting calls from the CIA asking me why I'm running a DOD operation on U.S. soil," Hunt said.

The normally sharp-tongued Kruger was speechless. Hunt was right. It didn't matter how he'd found out. The fact that *he knew* was enough in itself.

"It's an election year and neither the President nor Secretary Johnson can afford to have this blow up in their faces. Believe me, I was looking forward to taking over and working with this group, but my hands are tied," Hunt said. "I wish you had talked to me first."

"If you call everyone together, I can break the news to them while I'm down here," Hunt offered.

"No," Kruger said softly. "It would be better coming from me. I'll tell them."

"Then I'll leave it to you," Hunt said as he looked back and nodded at his guards. "I will get back with you next week on reassignments for everyone. Let me know what everyone's preferences are, including your own."

"Ok," Kruger said, still trying to shake off the shock of what had just happened.

"I know it's a bit of a shock and you've sacrificed a lot for this organization. Thank you for your service to our country, and please relay my thanks to everyone for their service as well when you break the news," Hunt said as he turned to walk out.

CHAPTER FIFTY ONE

Bayshore Steak and Seafood
Tampa, FL
2010 Local Time

Spectre held the door open as Decker smiled and walked through. She was wearing jeans and a red top. Having been discharged from the hospital earlier in the day, she only had the clothes Fields had brought her from her impounded car. The FBI had set her up in a local hotel to stay while they debriefed her and completed their investigation.

Spectre didn't really care what she chose to wear on their date. He had realized that she was beautiful no matter what she wore. Whether her hair was up or down, jeans or a pantsuit, hospital gown or yoga pants. It didn't seem to matter. She managed to grab his attention and that of every other man in the room as she walked by. Spectre felt overchicked.

Spectre's choice of attire for the evening wasn't much more formal. He only had an assortment of polo shirts and cargo pants from Project Archangel and what he had in his go-bag. For the evening, he had chosen a simple black polo shirt with khaki cargo pants. As they were seated by the hostess, Spectre realized it didn't really matter. No one was looking at him anyway.

They were seated at a table in the corner by the window. Located on Bayshore Drive, the restaurant had an excellent view of the bay and Tampa skyline in the distance. They could barely hear the restaurant's live band warming up in an area partitioned from the dining area.

"Nice place," Decker said as she unfolded her napkin and placed it in her lap.

"Yeah, Ironman used to always rave about how great the food and music were," Spectre said.

"That's Steele, right?" Decker asked.

Spectre nodded as he took a sip of water. "He was a good man."

"Well, that's a change from the last time I saw you," Decker said with a furrowed brow. "Tell me, Cal, what have you been up to this last week?"

Spectre recounted everything that happened since Decker tried to pull him out of his drunken stupor in the motel in Miami under FBI protective custody, stopping only for them to order their steaks with the waitress. He told her about Alvarez and how he had escaped only to learn that Alvarez was a small part of a much larger conspiracy with the Chinese.

"You thought you were protecting me?" Decker asked.

"I couldn't risk it," Spectre said stoically. "Alvarez said that every level of government was infiltrated and that they were after me and anyone I cared about."

Decker reached across the table and put her hand on Spectre's. Her touch was both soothing and invigorating.

"So that's why you disarmed the Trooper?" Decker asked.

"I didn't know who I could trust," Spectre said as he used his free hand to take a sip of wine. "At least not in the government. So that's when I went to Bear."

"Bear?" Decker asked.

Spectre explained his relationship with "Bear" Jennings as a childhood mentor and father figure. He told her about Bear's Sheriff friend who helped them get Spectre out before Simms and his team could find him as he tracked down the leads from Alvarez's laptop in Baton Rouge.

"And then I found out you were missing here in Tampa, so I headed this way," Spectre said. They reluctantly let go of their hold as the servers brought out their entrees.

As the servers cleared, Spectre said, "By the way, how did you end up here?"

Decker smiled sheepishly. "Well, let's just say it's been a long week for both of us," she said as she cut into her steak.

As the conversation continued, Decker told Spectre of her pursuit of the Russian assassin Svetlana Mitchell on the rooftop of the Biltmore Hotel in Miami. She told Spectre about Simms and his determination after the explosion at the farmhouse that killed Agent Baxter.

"I liked Baxter," Spectre said solemnly. Although he hadn't known Baxter long before he was killed, Spectre thought highly of Baxter and appreciated his help in the mission to Cuba. Spectre respected him and thought he was a good agent.

"Did you know about Marcus?" Decker asked with a look of concern.

"Yes," Spectre mumbled. "It still hasn't all really set in yet."

"I'm sorry, sweetie," Decker said. "I really am."

"But how did you get to Tampa?" Spectre asked, changing the subject from the pain of the death of his friends.

"Well," Decker continued, "after the barn explosion, Fields gave Simms the lead on the case. I decided to pay your old boss a visit to see what I could find out about the people behind it, since you were so sure Steele had killed Joe."

"I was way off on that," Spectre said, shaking his head. "I was wrong about Ironman."

Decker frowned. "I'm not sure I believe he was innocent. He wasn't exactly cooperative when I talked to him," she said.

"He had a lot at stake," Spectre replied. "I think they were threatening his family."

"Well, in any event, he gave me your personnel file and a key to your storage building," Decker said. "I was on my way to that when the Chinese made their first attempt at taking me."

Spectre stopped cutting into his steak and looked up at Decker. "Wait, where were you going?" Spectre asked.

"To your storage unit," Decker repeated.

"What storage unit?" Spectre asked with a confused look.

"The storage unit in your personnel jacket," Decker said. "It was a key in an envelope with a gate code and an address. I assumed it's where you stored stuff while you were deployed."

"I never had a storage unit here," Spectre said. "I sold everything when I moved out of the house in Homestead. Are you sure that's what it was?"

"That's what the address said," Decker replied.

"That's weird," Spectre said as his mind tried to think of a valid reason for a storage unit key to be in his file folder. "And you're sure the file was mine?"

Decker laughed. "Oh yeah, your psychiatric evaluation was quite interesting," she said with a wink.

"Junk science," Spectre laughed. "I think they just pulled my horoscope and used that anyway."

"Right," Decker replied. "I bet."

"That's interesting," Spectre said, still fixating on the mysterious storage unit. "So then what happened?"

Decker wrapped up her story, telling Spectre how the two strangers entered a shootout to save her and how the crooked

FBI agents picked her up at the scene. Then she told him about her captivity and eventual escape before being rescued by a Coast Guard patrol boat.

"Your turn," Decker said enthusiastically as she finished her story.

"Maybe another night," Spectre replied, not wanting to get into his attempt at storming the warehouse on his own and being intercepted by Project Archangel.

Decker gave Spectre a look of disappointment. "Well, that's not fair," she said. "I told you my story."

"Let's talk about something less serious," Spectre offered. "Besides, we have to save something for the second date."

Decker gave Spectre an impish grin. "What makes you think there's going to be a second date?"

"You read my psych profile," Spectre replied with a chuckle. "You tell me."

As the band started to play a slow country song, Decker rolled her eyes and stood, grabbing Spectre's hand. "This is my favorite song. Let's go," she said as she pulled Spectre up.

"I don't dance," Spectre said as he reluctantly followed.

"You do now," she said, leading him out of the dining area and onto the dance floor.

As the band played on, Decker drew Spectre close and placed his hands on her hips as she wrapped her arms around his neck. They moved slowly, like two nervous teenagers at a junior high dance. But as they danced alone on the empty dance floor, the awkwardness went away. Spectre didn't feel nervous. *It felt right.* Decker rested her head against his shoulder as they swayed with the music.

For the first time in years, Spectre felt at peace. All of the turmoil and anguish he had built up inside over years of rejection and battling uphill seemed to melt away. As the band reached the final verse, Spectre silently prayed that the song would never end.

But as quickly as the moment had started, it was over. The singer held out the last note as the song ended. As they transitioned to the next song, Decker stopped and looked up into Spectre's eyes. He wasn't worried about being rejected again. He leaned in as she tiptoed up to him. As their lips touched, Spectre moved his hands to her face. The kiss was passionate, yet tender. It was intense, yet soothing. Spectre had never known anything like it, not even with Chloe. *It was all so surreal.*

As the moment ended, Decker hugged Spectre and they walked back to their table.

"Thank you," she said softly as they walked hand in hand.

"For what?" Spectre said hoarsely, still in awe of what had just happened.

"A lovely evening," Decker replied as they reached their table. "You're a real gentleman, Cal."

Spectre's mind raced for something smooth and romantic to say. He was trained in flying fighters, Krav Maga, firearms, and hundreds of ways to escape really bad people, but the moment he found himself trying to say something romantic with a pretty girl that he really liked, his mind went blank. *Escaping Syria was easier than this,* Spectre thought.

"You're a good girl," Spectre replied, stumbling over his words.

"Uhhh…Thanks?" Decker replied, laughing at Spectre's awkwardness.

Spectre blushed and looked away. "Sorry," Spectre said. "I'm going to go jump in the bay now."

"Oh, don't worry about it," Decker replied, hugging Spectre's arm. "I think it's cute."

CHAPTER FIFTY TWO

FBI Tampa Field Office
Tampa, FL
1516 Local Time

Spectre pulled the commemorative Camaro into the parking lot of the FBI field office and killed the engine. He had taken the T-Tops off at the hotel and had been enjoying the mild, crystal clear day.

The last twenty-four hours had been the most relaxed Spectre had been in years. After dinner the night prior, Spectre and Decker had taken a romantic stroll by the bay, taking in the Tampa skyline as they shared in conversation and laughter. Spectre drove them back to the hotel right around midnight, kissed Decker goodnight, and headed to his own room a few doors down. It was a relationship he just didn't want to rush.

The next morning, Spectre drove Decker to the FBI field office for debriefing and an interview with the investigating agents. He spent the day doing something he hadn't been able to do in a long time — relaxing. After getting back to the hotel room, Spectre completed a quick workout consisting of weights and running on the treadmill before heading to the hotel's pool to hang out and enjoy the lovely weather. He swam and took in the sun before heading back to the room to hang out and watch TV as he waited for 3 PM to roll around.

He arrived early and waited. He had nowhere else to be and it was a welcome relief. The adrenaline-fueled, sleepless nights had taken a toll on his mind and body. Hanging out and doing nothing was a much-needed break. Spectre wasn't complaining. The only thing still lingering on his mind was the storage building. He had tried to forget about it so he could finally move on with his life, but every so often it would pop back up in his mind. *Why was it there?*

Just after 3:30, Decker emerged from the FBI building, carrying her backpack and wearing her aviator sunglasses. Spectre got out and met her, taking her bag as she kissed him. He threw the bag in the back seat of the Camaro and opened the door for Decker as she slid into the leather seat.

"How was your day?" Spectre asked as he fired up the Camaro's LS1 V8 engine.

"Exhausting," Decker said with a sigh. "But it looks like I'll be on administrative leave for the foreseeable future, so there's that."

"You need a break," Spectre said as he took her hand. "We both do."

"Probably so. But hey, you'll be happy to know that your friend was released yesterday," Decker said as she pulled out her notes from her bag.

"Bear?" Spectre asked.

"Jennings," Decker said, looking at her notes. "They cleared him and sent him home."

Spectre laughed. "I don't know if that's a good thing or not. His buddy is the Sheriff. I think they were treating him pretty well."

Decker covered her mouth and looked away as she started coughing. Although she was cleared medically, she still felt the effects of the near drowning.

"You ok?" Spectre asked.

"I'm fine," Decker said between coughs. "Tell me about your day. Did you do anything fun?"

"Just did a little swim—" Spectre said, catching himself as he realized it might be a sore subject given Decker's escape. "I mean, I lounged around and had an awesome day."

Decker laughed as she punched Spectre gently in the arm. "Must be nice," she said. "Next time, *you* can sit in meetings all day."

"No, thanks," Spectre replied. "So where to now?"

"Back to the hotel," Decker directed. "I need a hot shower."

Spectre raised an eyebrow and gave Decker a cheesy grin.

"Hey, you're the one who decided to get his own room," Decker said with a wink.

"Yeah, but—" Spectre replied.

"I'm just kidding!" Decker said, laughing at Spectre's struggle to find the right words. "I appreciate the fact that you're a gentleman."

"As long as I don't end up in the friend zone," Spectre joked as he put the Camaro in gear and headed toward the parking lot exit.

"Nah, I like the fact that you're a big dork," Decker said with a smile.

Spectre pulled onto the main highway toward their hotel. Spectre pointed as they passed a self-storage lot. "Did y'all talk about what the key was for?" he asked.

"That's still bothering you, huh?" Decker asked.

"It just doesn't make sense," Spectre confessed. "At no point did I ever have a storage building, and it was never discussed as part of my employment there."

Using her free hand, Decker pulled out Spectre's personnel jacket and flipped it to the envelope with the key. "This was still in my bag when they gave it back to me," Decker said. "If it will make you feel better, we can go look."

Spectre nodded. "Do you mind?" Spectre asked.

"If it will finally give you closure, I'm all for it," Decker replied. She gave Spectre directions from memory. They were just a few miles away from where Decker had been intercepted by the Chinese operatives.

Spectre pulled into the gated storage units and typed in the access code as Decker read the PIN to him. The gate opened and Spectre drove through, searching for the unit listed on the piece of paper. They stopped in front of the five by five-storage unit.

"This is it," Spectre said, confirming the number.

Decker held up the key. They exited the Camaro as Decker used it to unlock the padlock. Spectre rolled the door up, revealing a seemingly empty storage unit.

"There's nothing here," Spectre said as he ducked and walked in.

"It was more than likely just something they assigned to you for safe keeping of items while you were deployed," Decker said as she stood at the entrance. "Do you feel better now?"

Spectre looked around the small storage unit. The concrete floor was completely clean. There were no scuff marks or traces of anything. The unit was empty and appeared to have never been used.

Spectre walked to the back of the unit, looking for anything that might explain its purpose. He ran his left hand behind the wooden support beams to his left. When he found nothing, he shrugged and turned back to Decker.

"I guess you're right," Spectre said with a shrug. Decker walked in and passed him. She checked behind the support beams on the right as Spectre had just done.

"What's this?" Decker asked as she maneuvered her hand behind the far wooden beam. She angled her hands to get behind it, emerging with a small brown cardboard box that had been wedged between the beam and the wall.

"Holy shit," Spectre said as Decker held the box up.

"Always check both sides," Decker said as she handed the box to Spectre. Spectre accepted it and pulled his knife out. He flicked open the blade with his thumb and cut around the tape to open it. Inside, he found a small black thumb drive.

"What do you think is on here?" Spectre asked as he held the drive up.

"Something Steele wanted one of us to find," Decker said as she examined the thumb drive in Spectre's hand.

CHAPTER FIFTY THREE

After leaving the storage unit, Spectre and Decker stopped by an electronics store and bought a laptop on their way back to the hotel. Decker's laptop had been destroyed in the crash, and Spectre wanted to see what was on the thumb drive as soon as possible.

Reaching Decker's room, Spectre cleared off the small desk next to the TV and went to work as Decker sat on the bed behind him. He wasted no time in unpacking the newly purchased laptop and powering it up. He spent several minutes clicking through loading and setup screens before the laptop was finally ready. Once the computer was up and running, Spectre inserted the thumb drive into the computer and waited for it to be recognized.

"Here we go," Spectre said as the computer scanned the thumb drive for viruses.

As the computer finished its scan, a file menu popped up, showing a tiled list of several audio files arranged by date. Spectre double clicked on the oldest one and let it play.

"Charles Steele, unsecured line, how may I help you?"

"Chuck, it's Kerry."

"Good morning, Mr. Secretary."

"Yeah, good morning. Listen, Chuck, can you go secure for me?"

Spectre turned and looked at Decker as the file ended. Ironman had been called by the SECDEF and immediately asked to cut the recorded line. Other than the timestamp and the fact that Ironman had talked to his boss, the audio had given very little information. Spectre clicked on the second audio clip and hit play.

"This is Secretary Johnson."

"Hey sir, it's Steele."

"Good afternoon, Chuck, what's up?"

"Per your orders, Martin has been released."

"Good job. Do you know where he's going?"

"He told one of my guys he was going to meet a friend on a houseboat in Key Largo."

"Thanks."

"Is there a reason you wanted that info, sir?"

"As I told you last time we spoke, the VP nomination is coming soon. I want to keep tabs on him so he doesn't go to the media."

"Roger that, sir."

"Anything else?"

"Actually, yes sir, there is."

"Go on."

"It's about Martin's survival radio."

"And?"

"When he was captured, it was deregistered from the network, which delayed our rescue attempts."

"So?"

"My computer guy was able to trace the messages he received. They were coming from the Chinese Embassy in Tripoli."

"Martin is gone, Chuck. Let it go."

"But sir, we have a pretty big security vulnerability here."

"Let it go."

"Roger that, sir."

As the audio finished playing, Spectre turned and looked at Decker. "That son of a bitch!" he said.

"What's wrong?" Decker asked.

"He was working with the Chinese!" Spectre shouted. "Goddammit."

"I don't disagree with you, but that's pretty circumstantial," Decker said.

Spectre angrily clicked on the next file and hit play.

"Charles Steele, unsecured line, how may I help you?"

"Chuck, go secure."

There was a brief pause in the audio, but unlike the first clip, it suddenly continued.

"So I want you to meet with him tomorrow night after the funeral."

"What's his name again, sir?"

"Jiang Xin. He works for a holding company out of New Orleans. He'll meet you before your flight back."

"And what's this about, sir?"

"He has information about your security breach in Syria."

"Roger that, sir."

"This must have been right before Joe's funeral. Ironman must have met Xin after we saw him at the graveyard," Spectre said. He moved on to the next file and hit play again.

"Secretary Johnson."

"Sir, we need to talk."

"Just do what the man asks you to do and you'll be fine."

"But sir, I think he might be Chinese Intelligence."

"Cal Martin is a traitor, Chuck. This guy is doing us a favor."

"Martin called me today. He wants to meet tonight."

"Then meet him so we can all move on. Listen, I'm really busy and have a campaign to run. Chaz will be taking over for me pretty soon. Don't mention any of this to him, do you understand?"

"Yes, sir."

Spectre clicked on the next audio file. Unlike the previous files, this one had much more background and wind noise, as if he were outside.

"I want out."

"It's nice to see you again, Mr. Steele."

"Martin didn't show up. You saw it. What else do you want me to do?"

"Do as I say and you will be fine."

"Look, Xin, I don't know who you think you are but—"

"Before you continue, you might want to look at these."

"What is this?"

"Just a reminder of why your cooperation is most appreciated."

"You son of a bitch! This is my family! Where did you get these?"

"I took them."

"If you touch the first hair on any of my girls' heads, I will—"

"You will do nothing, Mr. Steele. Just as you did not protest the million dollars in your account."

"What account?"

"The one that will be used to prove that you are a traitor and frozen along with your other assets, should you continue to test me."

"I don't—"

"Do as you are told and your family will not be harmed."

"What do you want from me?"

"Martin and anyone who asks of him."

The clip ended. Without saying anything, Spectre clicked on the final audio file in the folder and hit play.

"My name is Charles Steele. If you are listening to this, I am likely already dead. The man I work for, Secretary of Defense Kerry Johnson, is working for the Chinese. I discovered this after one of my aircrew was shot down in Syria.

Through my own research, I later found that Johnson or his staff had given the Chinese Embassy in Tripoli our flight schedule, including detailed mission times and mission package details. The Chinese used that information to alert the Syrians to launch a flight to intercept and shoot down our aircraft.

During the rescue, the aircrew was given false rendezvous instructions in an attempt to capture our downed pilot. My analysts were able to track the signals to the same Embassy that had received the flight schedules.

Upon returning to the states, Cal Martin was summarily dismissed. I was later contacted by Secretary of Defense Johnson to retrieve his personnel file and send a copy to Johnson's office. Secretary Johnson said that it was due to a public relations concern with his upcoming campaign.

After learning of the death of one of my former employees, I made plans to fly to Louisiana for the funeral. Secretary Johnson instructed me to meet with a man named Jiang Xin. I was told that Xin was a possible contact with the information regarding the security breach in Syria.

I met Xin after the funeral. At that time, he told me that Martin had been working with Chinese Intelligence and had since gone rogue. The Chinese were looking for him, and in exchange for cooperation, he would give me the information on the breach. At the time, I did not know that Johnson's staff had given the Chinese Embassy our flight schedule and mission information.

During a later meeting, Xin threatened me directly. He had pictures of my wife and two daughters, taken at close range at their school and my wife's job. He told me that they had set me up with wire transfers and that if I did not comply, my family would be in jeopardy and I would be exposed as a traitor.

I love my family very much. I am making this recording because I want to see justice done. Xin is a very dangerous man. Please protect my family. I am sorry for what I have done.

As the recording stopped, Spectre felt Decker's hand on his shoulder. He could not believe what he had just heard.

"This is nuclear," Spectre mumbled.

"We need to get this to the Attorney General," Decker said as she rubbed Spectre's tense shoulders.

Spectre swiveled around in the chair to face Decker.

"No way," Spectre said, shaking his head. "This goes well beyond the AG."

"What do you mean? Johnson needs to be investigated," Decker said.

"This is way bigger than I ever imagined," Spectre said. "Think about what he said. 'Loose ends.' That was his plan all along."

"I'm not following," Decker said as she sat back down on the bed facing Spectre.

"Remember that conference room in Homestead? When SECDEF wouldn't approve the rescue mission?"

"Yeah?"

"This is why! Xin worked for Zhang. Zhang ran the operation in Cuba. I'll bet you anything SECDEF was working with Zhang and didn't want to commit assets to expose the operation," Spectre said excitedly as the pieces fell into place. "The loose ends were everyone involved in that mission. He's running for VP now."

"So?"

"So, other than that crooked FBI agent when did people involved start dying?"

"Six months ago, roughly," Decker said.

"Bingo!" Spectre said. "He may have only recently been nominated as a running mate, but the primaries have been going on for about six months. He needed to clean this up before someone attached him to it."

"So how does a successful businessman like Johnson get involved with Chinese spies?" Decker asked.

"That's the part of the story I didn't get to last night," Spectre explained. "We found Zhang on an oil rig in the Gulf of Mexico. He was using it to gather emitter intelligence on the planes flying overhead. That oil rig was owned by Hua Xia Holdings."

"Wait, isn't that the company that paid for Victor's room at the Biltmore?"

"Yup!" Spectre responded. "And I found out after the mission from my buddy that Hua Xia bought out Johnson's interest in Cajun Oil and Gas right before he was appointed as SECDEF."

"So Johnson was giving top cover for Zhang for his Cuban mission?" Decker asked, circling back to their first encounter with Johnson.

Spectre nodded. "That's why they were trying to find me. Victor told me all about Zhang when I questioned him in the barn. They were afraid I'd talk to the media and ruin Johnson's chances."

"Then we definitely need to take this to the AG," Decker said.

Spectre shook his head vigorously.

"Why not?" Decker asked. "Johnson needs to go to jail!"

"I had to kill two FBI agents," Spectre said. "The same two that got you in the ambulance."

"Yeah, but—"

"No, listen to me," Spectre said, holding his hand up. "I don't believe for a second that Zhang and Xin were the only two involved here. This goes well beyond anything I ever imagined. Victor was right. They are in every level of government. The only person that could even remotely do anything about this would be the President."

"And he's coasting through the end of his second term. He won't risk a scandal that keeps his party out of office," Decker said as she considered Spectre's point.

"Exactly," Spectre said. "This is a no win."

"So what do you want to do? Just let it go and let someone who's in bed with the Chinese become the Vice President of the United States?" Decker asked. "Really, Cal?"

Spectre leaned forward and grabbed both of Decker's hands. "I don't care anymore," Spectre said as he looked into her eyes. "One crook or another, does it even matter? What I do care about is you. I am not willing to risk it anymore."

Decker squeezed Spectre's hands. "I care about you too, but I can't just sit idly by and let this happen."

"Then don't," Spectre replied. "Wait and see what happens with the election and then we'll go from there. Let them forget about us for a little while."

"What are you suggesting?"

"Let's get the hell out of here," Spectre said. "I've got a bag of cash, a dog that misses me, and nowhere to be. We can lay low for a while and let the storm pass."

"I have a job, Cal," Decker said. "I can't just leave."

"Well, not with that attitude you can't," Spectre said with a boyish grin.

Decker leaned forward and kissed Spectre. "What the hell," she said. "It wouldn't be the craziest thing I've done this month."

EPILOGUE

Gulf of Mexico
1254 Local Time
One Month Later

"Bayou Zero One, Watchdog, snap BRAA 100/25, 28,000 track west," the female controller said. Foxworthy adjusted his mask as he maneuvered his F-15 toward the target aircraft twenty-five miles away at twenty-eight thousand feet.

It was Foxworthy's second Alert period for the week, and other than a practice scramble on his first twenty-four hour shift, it was his first scramble. The Southeastern Air Defense Sector had been alerted by Jacksonville Center that a light civilian jet aircraft had stopped responding somewhere midway over the Gulf of Mexico.

Foxworthy focused on running a good intercept as his wingman, "Echo" Jase set up in a comfortable cover position two miles off his right wing. With the elections just a month away, the terrorist group known as the Islamic State of Iraq and the Levant (ISIL) had stepped up its rhetoric on attacking Americans in response to coalition intervention in Iraq and Syria. The latest intelligence reports suggested that the ISIL fighters were using captured Syrians to help train pilots to be used in 9/11-style terror attacks flying civilian aircraft from private fields. Although the chances of them flying across the Gulf of Mexico to execute such an attack were low, Foxworthy knew he needed to have his guard up.

Offsetting to the south, Foxworthy intended to maneuver his formation to arrive in trail of the unresponsive aircraft. Although combat intercepts typically called for higher aspect merges, being able to observe from a position behind the aircraft would give them a tactical advantage without being seen.

Looking through his helmet-mounted display, Foxworthy saw a black dot in the clear blue sky surrounded by a green container. They were now ten miles away from the target aircraft, and he could just barely make out a small business jet.

"Tally one, ten miles," Foxworthy called out to his wingman on their auxiliary frequency.

"Two's tally one," Echo responded.

"Watchdog, Bayou Zero One, do you have a tail number for the aircraft we're going to be working with?" Foxworthy asked the controller.

"Jacksonville Center reports that it's November One Four Eight Whiskey Tango," the controller responded.

"Bayou," Foxworthy responded. *Where have I heard that tail number?* Foxworthy thought. Shaking it off, Foxworthy continued the intercept.

As they rolled in behind the droning business jet, Echo took up a high cover position behind Foxworthy's aircraft. The two jets slowly overtook the twin-engine jet. As they came within a thousand feet, Foxworthy recognized the white aircraft as a Cessna Citation CJ1.

"Watchdog, Bayou is holding hands with the Citation; can you confirm it's November One Four Eight Whiskey Tango?" Foxworthy asked.

"And Bayou, that's affirm, November One Four Eight Whiskey Tango," the controller replied.

Foxworthy pulled his aircraft alongside the Citation. He confirmed the tail number, as he got closer. *It looks familiar, but from where?*

"Watchdog, do you have the registration information on the aircraft?" Foxworthy asked.

A few moments later, Watchdog responded, "Corporate aircraft registered to Cajun Oil and Gas. IFR flight plan from Opa Locka to New Orleans Lakefront. Two souls on board, three plus zero zero fuel."

Foxworthy froze. As the controller read the information to him, it immediately hit him. *Tom Jane!* Foxworthy knew Jane was in a partnership on a corporate jet with someone else, but he had never flown with him. As an avid aviation enthusiast, Jane was also a pilot. Foxworthy's stomach turned.

Foxworthy eased his aircraft alongside the Citation. It appeared to be holding a stable altitude and airspeed on autopilot. As he got closer, he saw a large man slumped over the controls in the left seat of the aircraft.

"Jesus Christ," Foxworthy mumbled to himself.

"What are you seeing?" Echo asked, still holding the position of high cover behind him.

"One pilot, appears to be unconscious," Foxworthy replied, shaken by the realization that Jane was in the aircraft and there was nothing he could do to save him.

"Watchdog, Bayou Zero One, the pilot appears to be slumped over at the controls," Foxworthy said. His voice was shaking as he said it.

"Watchdog copies, monitor," the controller directed.

"Watchdog, what was the last frequency that this aircraft made contact on?" Foxworthy asked.

"Miami Center on 128.45," the controller responded.

"One will be off Aux," Foxworthy advised his wingman as he switched his backup radio to 128.45.

"November One Four Eight Whiskey Tango, this is Bayou Zero One," Foxworthy said on the new frequency, as he looked over, hoping to see movement from Jane in the cockpit.

"Tom, it's Jeff, if you can hear me, I need you to put your mask on," Foxworthy said. "Mr. Jane, please, if you can hear me, put on your oxygen."

Foxworthy watched intently, hoping for movement in the cockpit. When there was none, he tried again. "Tom Jane, put on your mask."

No response.

Foxworthy switched back to his interflight frequency on the backup radio. "You're cleared in to chase, I'm going to see if I can't get his attention," Foxworthy said.

"Two," Echo responded.

Foxworthy lit the afterburners of his F-15 and banked slightly left before coming back hard right across the Citation's nose. As he crossed, he let out a string of flares, hoping to get Jane's attention. He knew it was unlikely, but with no other options, he was willing to try anything.

As Foxworthy crossed the Citation's nose, he cancelled the afterburner and opened the massive speed brake on the spine of the Eagle, slowing back down to rejoin on the right wing. Echo took up position on the aircraft's left wing.

"One pilot, completely unresponsive," Foxworthy informed Echo. "I tried the last frequency they had him on. No joy."

"Didn't they say the flight plan showed two on board?" Echo asked.

"Affirm," Foxworthy responded as he tucked in close trying to look into the cockpit. The windscreen was slightly fogged over. It was clear that there had been some malfunction with the cockpit pressurization system.

"I'm only seeing the pilot," Echo said.

"One same," Foxworthy replied. "But the windows are fogged up in the back, there's no telling."

"Watchdog, the pilot is unresponsive and it appears that the cockpit has had a decompression," Foxworthy told the controller.

"Watchdog copies, monitor," the controller responded.

The aircraft appeared to make a shallow right-hand turn and level off. The autopilot was coupled with a preplanned route. It would likely fly that way until the route ended and it ran out of fuel.

Foxworthy and his wingman took up observation positions a few thousand feet off each wing and followed it. Foxworthy felt sick to his stomach as he helplessly watched the ghost aircraft. There was nothing he could do to save his friend's father. At this point, he would only be a witness for the crash investigators.

As they neared the marsh and swamps of Louisiana, the aircraft suddenly and violently pitched up. Foxworthy and Echo maneuvered their aircraft away to avoid hitting the Citation as it started climbing and slowing down.

"Watchdog, Bayou, the aircraft has pitched up, let Center know in case they need to reroute traffic above us," Foxworthy said as he turned to keep sight of the climbing jet.

"Watchdog," the female controller responded.

Foxworthy turned back to chase the climbing aircraft. Reaching the top of its sudden climb, the aircraft stalled. It seemed to fall for a moment before it pitched back down and started accelerating. The aircraft entered a steep dive as it accelerated toward the marsh.

"Aircraft is in a dive now," Foxworthy advised.

Foxworthy rolled his F-15 around the Citation's flight path and followed it. He watched as his speed accelerated, following the plummeting aircraft. The airspeed indicator in his helmet showed Mach 1 as they descended through twenty thousand feet.

"Spread it out," Foxworthy directed his wingman. They took up positions out of the debris path of the aircraft. Foxworthy knew that as the aircraft accelerated, it would eventually exceed its structural limitations.

The aircraft began a slow roll as it continued to increase its dive angle. Foxworthy deployed his speed brake and slowed down, building distance between himself and the aircraft hurtling toward the swamp below.

As the right wing of the Citation separated, the aircraft's roll rate increased. It sped toward the swamp until it impacted the mud and water below. Foxworthy leveled off and started an orbit with his wingman.

"Launch the SAR aircraft," he told WatchDog meekly. He could barely get the words out. He felt like he was going to throw up and his breathing had gone shallow. He had just watched his friend die in a fiery crash.

Tom Jane was dead.

Thanks for reading!

Turn the page for a sneak preview of C.W. Lemoine's fourth book in the ***SPECTRE SERIES***:

EXECUTIVE REACTION
SPECTRE SERIES: BOOK FOUR

AVAILABLE IN EBOOK AND PAPERBACK FALL 2015.

VISIT WWW.CWLEMOINE.COM FOR MORE INFORMATION ON RELEASE DATES, BOOK SIGNINGS, AND EXCLUSIVE SPECIAL OFFERS.

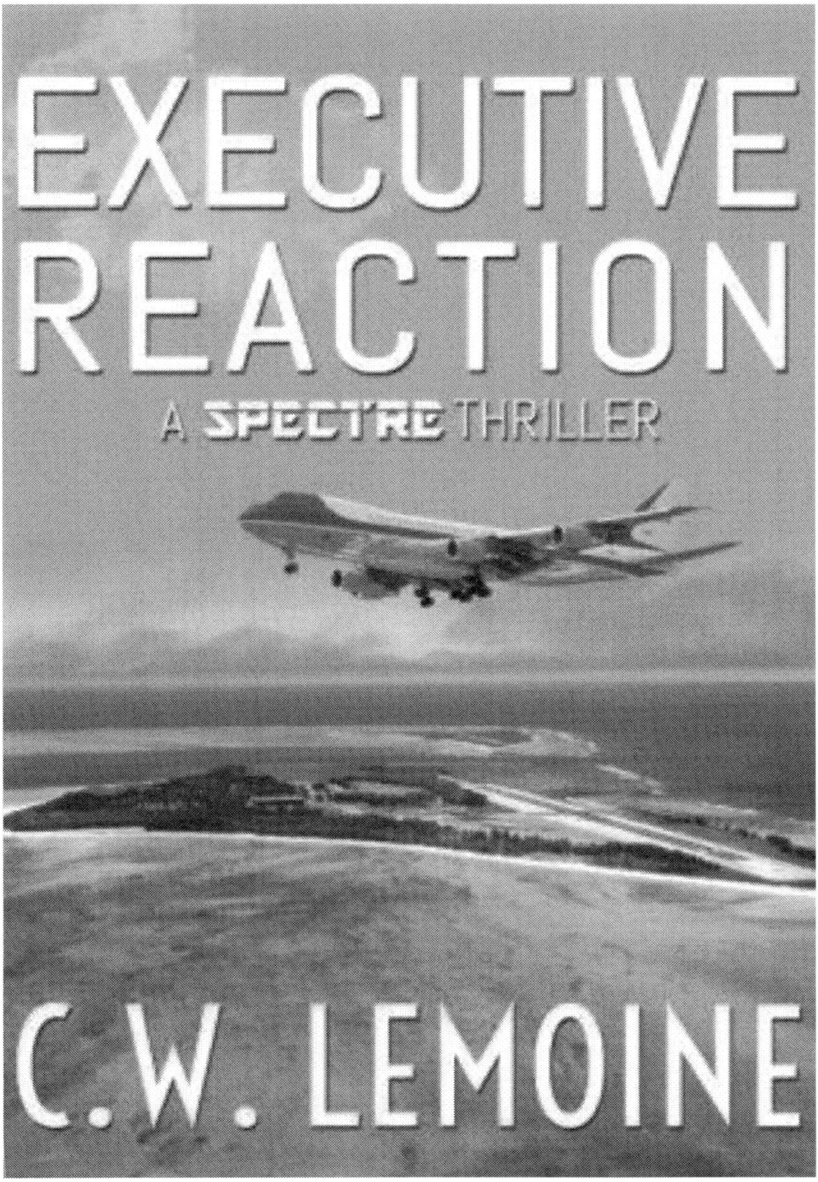
EXECUTIVE
REACTION
A SPECTRE THRILLER
C.W. LEMOINE

PROLOGUE

Springfield, Virginia
12 February
2028 Local Time

As Lt Colonel Jason Waxburn pulled his BMW 5-series into the narrow driveway of his two-story suburban home, the hair on the back of his neck instantly stood. The porch light that his wife always turned on as soon as she got home was off, despite her minivan still parked in the garage.

With Jason's twenty-year career as an Air Force pilot, Jason's wife Clara had grown used to his constantly changing schedule and the late hours he often put in at work. Putting on the light to welcome him home had become a tradition in their family. Whenever he came back from a long trip or worked late, she would always leave the light on for him, and most of the time she and their ten-year-old son would be outside sitting in their porch rocking chairs as he drove up.

But tonight was very different. He had tried both the house phone and her cell phone on his commute home and had been unable to make contact. He had only been gone for three days – a short trip in his line of work – and when he had last spoken to her the night prior, they had planned for a late dinner after his estimated arrival at 8:30 PM.

Jason pulled into the garage until the hanging tennis ball touched the windshield and he killed the engine. He grabbed his garment bag from the back seat as the garage door closed behind him. He had changed out of his Air Force blues before leaving base and was wearing a blue polo shirt and jeans for the commute home.

The house alarm chirped as he walked through the doorway into the laundry room that attached to the kitchen. It was not armed – something he and his wife religiously ensured when they left the house. As Jason walked into the kitchen, it was completely dark. *The house seemed completely empty.*

"Hello? Clare?" he said as he flipped on the light switch. "John? Where are you guys?"

There was nothing but silence as he looked around the kitchen. Dishes were in the sink and a couple of bills had been opened on the granite countertop. An orange juice carton sat unopened on the cooking island in the center of the room next to two unused glasses. After setting his garment bag down on a nearby chair, Jason grabbed the carton to put it back in the refrigerator, noticing that it was room temperature.

"Clare?" he called out again. "This isn't funny. I know y'all are here."

Jason's heart started racing as he considered the possibilities. He walked into the living room as he searched for clues. He turned on the light, revealing the leather couches and plasma TV near the fireplace. There were no signs of foul play. The house was just as neat and orderly as he had left it three days ago.

As Jason turned toward his office, his cell phone rang. He desperately pulled it out of his pocket and answered the call, barely noticing the caller ID reading "BLOCKED" as he pressed the phone against his ear. "Clare?" he asked.

"Turn on your television and press play," a male voice said. It was deep and robotic, sounding like a protected witness on the crime drama shows Jason and his wife often enjoyed watching,

"What? Who is this?" Jason demanded.

"Just do it," the voice said before abruptly hanging up.

Jason looked at his phone as the "Call Ended" notification flashed on the screen. He found the remote on the coffee table and powered the TV and Blu-Ray player on. As the blue screen came on, Jason hit play and the disc in the player spun to life.

A man wearing a black balaclava and black tactical clothing appeared on screen. He was standing in front of what appeared to be a black flag.

"Colonel Waxburn," the man said in the same deep, metallic voice as the one on the phone. "You must cooperate."

Jason's heart sank as the man stepped back to reveal his wife and son gagged, their limbs bound to chairs. Their faces were bruised and their eyes darted back and forth frantically. He could see the fear and panic in his wife's eyes while his son tried to remain stoic. He was immediately overcome with mixed feelings of rage, panic, and desperation.

"We have your wife and son," the man continued as he walked back and stood between them. "If you do as we say, they will be released upon completion of your tasking. You will also be rewarded handsomely for your efforts."

"But if you do not. If you attempt to alert the authorities, or fail to comply with our instructions exactly as they are given to you, you will get them back piece by piece," the man warned as he pulled out a knife from his pocket.

"I am sorry, but I must now show you that this is not a game," the man said as he reached for Clare's left hand that was tied to the arm of the chair.

Jason ran his hands through his silver and gray hair as the muffled, but still blood-curdling screams from his wife echoed throughout the living room. The man stood in front of her, blocking out the camera as she twisted and writhed in the background. Moments later, the man turned back toward the camera, holding up her detached ring finger in front of the cameraman as another masked man tended to her wound.

"Your first instructions are in your mailbox. Go now," the man said, holding up the finger. "This is your only warning."

Jason felt nauseous as the video ended and the blue screen reappeared on the TV. He shoved his phone back in his pocket and raced toward the front door and out into the street. He reached the mailbox and opened it, revealing a sixteen-inch bubble mailer that had been stuffed in the box.

He ripped open the mailer. Inside there was a piece of paper and something wrapped in bubble wrap. As he unwrapped the object, it suddenly became clear. It was Clare's ring finger with her titanium wedding ring still attached. Jason dropped it as the nausea grew worse. He steadied himself against the mailbox.

As he picked up the piece of paper that had fallen, his phone rang. He studied the caller ID this time as he pulled the phone out of his pocket. Again, the screen showed "BLOCKED." He answered it.

"Do you understand your instructions?" the same voice from the video said.

Jason bent over, picked up the paper, and read it. He had flown combat missions into Afghanistan in C-17s with Night Vision Goggles and no runway lighting, but he had never felt more scared in his life. They were asking him to choose between his country and his family.

"I can't... What you're asking is just..." Jason said with a trembling voice.

"Your next warning will be from your son," the voice replied menacingly.

"No! Please!" Jason shouted. "This is suicide though. It will never work."

"Do exactly as we say, and your family will survive and you will be fine. Do not test us. Do you understand?"

"Yes," Jason replied meekly.

"Good. Pick up your wife's ring and go back inside. Study the instructions you have been given and then burn them. Do not be late for the first check-in," the voice said before hanging up.

Jason stood in shocked silence as the phone went dead. He looked around the small suburban neighborhood to find the source of the call. The man on the other end was presumably watching him, but the neighborhood was quiet. There was nothing suspicious anywhere around.

He picked up the finger and shoved it back into the mailer along with the letter. He made it halfway down the walkway to his house before throwing up on his freshly manicured lawn. After twenty years of blissful marriage and twenty-three years of serving his country, he had been forced to choose between the two things he loved the most in the world. *Family or country.*

CHAPTER ONE

Yigo, Guam
14 February
0545 Local Time

Roke Quitugua sat quietly eating his breakfast in the modest two-bedroom house. His wife and two-year-old son were still sleeping in their master bedroom. As he finished the last spoonful of his cereal, he wondered if he would ever see them again.

Roke stood from the small table and dumped the remaining milk from his cereal bowl into the sink. When he finished washing the bowl, he set it aside to dry and started toward the bedroom.

His wife, Ana, lay cuddling with their son in their small master bedroom. The two were still peacefully asleep. Roke paused for a moment and stood in the doorway admiring them. He felt lucky to have such a beautiful family.

He turned away and sighed softly, hoping it wouldn't be the last time he saw them. After years of diligently working, his day had finally come. If all went well, he would return home to see their beautiful faces. If he were discovered early or he somehow failed his mission, he would likely end up dead.

Roke pushed away the negative thoughts and headed out toward the tool shed in his small backyard. There he found the large black backpack he had been given a few days earlier. He simply had to ensure it was at the right place at the right time and with the timer successfully activated. After that, he was home free.

He checked its contents one more time and ensured the timer powered on and off before zipping the main zipper and strapping it to his back. The pack was heavy – at least thirty pounds, but despite Roke's small frame, he managed it easily.

He walked through the hurricane fence gate and into the front yard where his scooter was parked. He steadied himself with the weight of the backpack as he sat on the scooter and put on the red helmet.

Roke made the four-mile drive through light traffic toward Andersen Air Force base. It was chilly, despite his nylon jacket and long pants. As he made the turn off the main two-lane road, he joined the long procession of cars waiting to show their identification to the Air Force Security Forces guards.

Established December 3, 1944, Andersen Air Force Base served as one of four Pacific Region forward operating locations for the United States Air Force. Although not home to any tenant units, Andersen routinely housed strategic bombers for deployed operations and fighters for military exercises. Roke had even seen B-2 stealth bombers parked outside many times before.

At age twenty-nine, Roke had worked as a civilian contractor on base for the majority of his adult life. He started at age nineteen, cleaning the numerous squadron buildings and bathrooms until moving into grounds keeping and facility maintenance. He much preferred working outside with his hands to cleaning toilets, but he did often miss interacting with the pilots and officers.

Roke had been recruited just a few months after his twentieth birthday to spy on the Americans. He never thought of it as spying, though. His job was simply to observe and report. For doing so, he was rewarded with a generous stipend every month. At first, it was just good spending money, but as he settled down with his wife, Ana, it became a supplement to support his budding family. He depended on that money.

As Roke waited behind the long line of cars, the adrenaline started coursing through his veins. Usually, the guards would just wave him through after showing his ID indicating that he was a Department of Defense employee, but sometimes they would perform random vehicle and bag inspections.

His handler had been clear in his instructions. If Roke suspected that he had been selected for additional screening, he was to pull the tab from the bottom of the backpack. They hadn't told him what pulling the tab would do, but Roke guessed that it was a detonator of some sort. His family, he had been assured, would be well taken care of, and his son would grow up never wanting for money.

Roke was hesitant to accept the job, but the people he had dealt with were very dangerous. He had heard of bad things happening to the families of those who refused. The thought of dying was scary, but the thought of something happening to his beautiful wife and son was absolutely terrifying.

Roke pulled out his ID from his shirt pocket as the car in front of him was directed to pull off to the side for additional screening. Roke's heart rate nearly doubled. *They're doing additional screening!* He tried to calm himself as he rolled forward toward the guard who was still watching to ensure the car pulled over to the side.

"Good morning," the guard said as he turned to Roke.

Roke nodded and smiled nervously as the guard took Roke's ID and scanned it with the handheld ID scanner. He slowly reached back with his right hand toward the tab on his backpack in anticipation of the guard's next move.

"Have a good day, Mr. Quitugua," the guard said before motioning with his right arm across his body.

Relieved, Roke started to drive off through the staggered barricades before the guard that was screening the car in front of him stepped out to stop him. He appeared to be talking to the other guard on his radio.

Roke started to panic. In his rear view mirror, he could see the gate guard running toward him as the other guard stood in front of him holding his hand out to tell him to stop. Roke's hand went to the backpack, this time he found the tab and gripped it as his eyes darted between the two guards.

The approaching guard stopped short of Roke. Roke turned toward him with his hand still firmly holding the tab.

"Sir! You forgot your ID!" the guard shouted as he came within a few feet of Roke's scooter.

Roke pulled the tab in a panic, never hearing the guard's reason for stopping him. After a brief click and an audible beep, the suitcase electromagnetic pulse bomb detonated. The initial explosive charge killed Roke and destroyed everything within a fifty-foot radius before the high power microwave bomb sent a short, high energy pulse that reached up to ten gigawatts extending out for a five-mile radius, disabling all unshielded electronics and power grids within its path.

ACKNOWLEDGMENTS

As always, first and foremost, I would like to thank you, the reader. Publishing this series has been a rewarding experience, made possible only by the wonderful readers. I have enjoyed the feedback, excitement, and interest in Cal "Spectre" Martin's continuing story. Thank you all for the positive reviews and messages. As an independent author, that's the only way word gets out about my work, and I appreciate it very much! Please feel free to continue and leave a positive review if you enjoyed this book.

To **Douglas "Damntheman" Narby**, thank you for being the sounding board that I have come to lean on for this writing adventure. Thank you for the feedback, mentoring, and friendship as I bug you to no end to "read the next chapter." You rock.

To my friends, family, and beta readers, thank you. Especially, **Pat Byrnes,** I have enjoyed reading your comments and reactions, as this series has been written.

I'm very fortunate to have such an amazing support network. It hasn't always been easy, but the show will go on. I'm looking forward to continue to share in Spectre's adventures.

Thanks for reading!

C.W. Lemoine is the author of *SPECTRE RISING*, *AVOID. NEGOTIATE. KILL.*, *ARCHANGEL FALLEN*, *EXECUTIVE REACTION*, and *BRICK BY BRICK.* He graduated from the A.B. Freeman School of Business at Tulane University in 2005 and Air Force Officer Training School in 2006. He is a military pilot that has flown the F-16 and F/A-18. He is also a certified Survival Krav Maga Instructor and sheriff's deputy.

www.cwlemoine.com

Facebook
http://www.facebook.com/cwlemoine/
Twitter:
@CWLemoine